PRAISE FOR AMALIE HOWARD'S
ALPHA GODDESS:

A Spring 2014 Indie Next Pick

"I was absolutely immersed in Sera's world! *Alpha Goddess* is a fiery, gripping twist on a timeless love story. The rich mythology and exotic themes were beautifully imagined and unlike anything I've ever read before. Brilliantly dark and powerful. A must-read!"
—Colleen Houck, *New York Times* bestselling author of the Tiger's Curse series

"*Alpha Goddess* is a touching depiction of the strength of family and the importance of love and loyalty. Fans of books blending the modern with the mythical will enjoy Sera's story and the love triangle involving her best friend and her immortal love."
—*VOYA* Magazine, starred review

"Howard's *Alpha Goddess* is a breath of fresh air for any young adult fantasy fan. Sera's adventures in discovering her parentage and her existence as the reincarnation of Lakshmi, one of the most powerful beings in the created universe, are exciting and interesting. Sera finds herself caught amid the battle between good and evil and must choose to take her place as the savior of the known world. Howard's writing is excellent and her concept stands out among the flood of angel and demon fiction already populating the genre."
—Demi Marshall for the Spring 2014 Kids' Indie Next List

"Complete with non-stop action and deft writing, *Alpha Goddess* is mesmerizing and inventive. Overall, this is an intriguing read full of surprises!"
—*RT Book Reviews*

"This isn't a typical love triangle, and this isn't a typical good versus evil story. Nothing is quite that straightforward. The twists were brilliantly crafted, and the plot moved along smoothly and at a good pace. I cared for the characters (mainly Sera, Dev, and Nate) and was fully invested in their journey. *Alpha Goddess* is a rich Hindu mythology novel with powerful gods, deadly realms, and fierce battles."
—*YA Books Central*

"Amalie Howard has done it again! With *Alpha Goddess*, she brings us an amazing, gorgeous story with vivid, detailed mythology, amazing characters and wonderful prose."
—*Pandora's Books*

PRAISE FOR AMALIE HOWARD'S
THE ALMOST GIRL:

"*The Almost Girl* is a feminist tour de force. This sexy, fast-paced story is impossible to put down. A must read! Fans of *Divergent* will love it!"
— Kim Purcell, author of *Trafficked*

"A riveting union of science fiction thriller, romance, family drama, and conspiracy theory, *The Almost Girl* had me wishing I could crawl inside the pages and join Riven on her epic journey between parallel worlds. Amalie Howard's writing is sharp and smart."
— Page Morgan, author of *The Beautiful and the Cursed*

"Amalie Howard writes a fast paced and thrilling story with a kick butt, authentic heroine and a brilliantly crafted world."
— Eve Silver, author of *Rush*

"A high-octane thriller. [Sci-fi] and dystopia fans will be right at home with this book and its fierce, capable heroine."
— *Publishers Weekly*

PRAISE FOR AMALIE HOWARD'S
THE FALLEN PRINCE:

"An engaging combination of soap opera and space cowboys, this sequel to *The Almost Girl* charges along from action scene to action scene, with a few tender moments thrown in."
— *Booklist*

"Hand this . . . to fans of *The Hunger Games* and *Divergent* who are still looking for new dystopian battles to get invested in."
— *School Library Journal*

"[P]acked with action . . . Imagery is the highlight of this book."
— *VOYA* Magazine

DARK GODDESS

Also by Amalie Howard

Alpha Goddess
Bloodspell
Bloodcraft
Waterfell (The Aquarathi)
Oceanborn (The Aquarathi)
The Almost Girl (The Riven Chronicles)
The Fallen Prince (The Riven Chronicles)

DARK GODDESS

AMALIE HOWARD

Sky Pony Press
New York

www.skyponypress.com
www.amaliehoward.com

10 9 8 7 6 5 4 3 2 1

Library of Congress Cataloging-in-Publication Data is available on file.

Cover design by Brian Peterson
Cover photo credit: iStockphoto

Print ISBN: 978-1-5107-0989-8
E-book ISBN: 978-1-5107-0998-0

Printed in the United States of America

For anyone who has ever felt invisible—I see you.

"You must not lose faith in humanity. Humanity is like an ocean; if a few drops of the ocean are dirty, the ocean does not become dirty."

—Mahatma Gandhi

CONTENTS

Prologue...xiii

Goddess Warfare...1

Secrets...16

Roll of the Dice...33

The Sisters Divine...47

The Goddess You Know.......................................61

Love Is a Slippery Slope.....................................73

Like Father, Like Son..86

What Are Friends For?.......................................100

Demon Tracking..116

The Belly of the Beast.......................................128

Keep Your Friends Close....................................141

Xibalba Claims Its Own.....................................154

Beneath the Bowels...163

The Devil You Know..178

The Light and the Darkness...............................191

An Eye for an Eye...201

Keep Your Enemies Closer.................................214

Revenge Is Best Served Cold.............................227

The Cost of a Soul..240

Power Play...254

Goddess Immortal..266

The Champion of Xibalba 278

The Gateway to Hell 291

To the Death 305

The End of the World 319

The Glade 332

Epilogue 346

Pavamana Mantra 353

Author's Note 355

Acknowledgments 359

DARK GODDESS

PROLOGUE

❧

Demons were festering in the Mortal Realm.

No matter how hard they attempted to hide their disguises—human, animal, or otherwise—the Goddess of Destruction could see the rakshasas plain as day, scattered like black poisonous dust, tainting the very air around them. They lurked in any dark hole they could find.

Waiting.

The goddess frowned. Size was immaterial. Small demons were as clever and insidious as their larger counterparts. At times, even more so. Even now, she could foresee the black dust multiplying, paving the path for something monstrous . . . a plague that would only spread if left unimpeded.

Lord Devendra had been wise to forestall the end of the world by banishing the Kali rakshasa months before, with the help of his consort Lady Serjana and their mutual ally Kalias. But the truth was, the fate of man had been sealed the minute the binding wards of the Mortal Realm had been breached by Ra'al, the Demon Lord of the seventh level of hell. The gates of Xibalba had been opened, its very stench seeping through its seams and into the human world.

The goddess's third eye slid shut; she contemplated what she'd seen.

It was too late.

The Mortal Realm had to be cleansed. It had to be destroyed.

GODDESS WARFARE

❦

K yle Knox inhaled deeply as the tingling sensation he'd felt in his arms and legs disappeared for the moment. It had been a shiver of something that caused a dull ache in his bones—that cold, numbing feeling of a storm brewing. He must be tired. After everything that had happened in the last few months—namely, the near extinction of everything human—it would be strange *not* to be out of sorts. And, of course, there had been his miraculous transformation from human boy to immortal guardian of the Mortal Realm. Miraculous because it was granted by the Trimurtas, the gods of Illysia, and mostly because he hadn't been sentenced to eternal damnation.

He gave himself a stern shake and shrugged off the strange feeling. "I am an Azura Lord."

The words felt strange in his mouth. What they meant felt even stranger. *An Azura Lord*, responsible for keeping the demons where they belonged: in the seven domains of Xibalba, what humans called hell. For so long, he'd been confused about his humanity, nearly losing himself to the Dark Realms. But he'd fought the pull, letting his love for his best friend, Sera Caelum, become his moral compass. And even though Sera wasn't into him—she was in love with someone else—that didn't mean what he felt just went away. He'd fallen, hard and fast, from the moment he'd met her. Love like that didn't disappear overnight. It stuck around and tortured you with what you couldn't have.

Kyle sighed.

Being immortal had its perks, but it didn't earn him any bonus points with Sera. It was kind of hard to compete when the girl of his dreams was dating a powerful god who happened to be the protector of the entire world. Not to mention that the two of them had been destined to be together from the dawn of stinking time. It was freaking unfair, that's what it was. Even so, Sera had chosen to stay in the Mortal Realm with him, instead of taking her rightful place in Illysia—the Light Realm—with Dev.

That had to mean something, didn't it?

"Hey! Get out of the way!" someone screamed behind him just as a black Ducati motorcycle squealed past and into the high school parking lot. Kyle twisted out of the way, barely clearing the hissing rear wheel. The bike skidded to a stop, acrid smoke billowing in its wake.

"What the heck are you—" Kyle's voice stuck like sand in his throat as a tall, slender girl got off the bike and pulled a black helmet from her head, releasing waves of glossy dark hair, which tumbled down her back. The girl was dressed all in black—black T-shirt, black leather pants, black boots— except the black and white skull belt hanging low on her hips. Her hair was a shimmery ebony, so sleek it looked liquid, moving with her every step as if it had a life of its own. She glanced at him over her shoulder, tossing a lock of hair to the side as she hoisted her backpack on her arm.

"Sorry." The girl's voice was smoky and rich . . . the kind of voice that suggested it guarded dark, decadent secrets. One word, and Kyle's chest felt two sizes too small, his stomach like it was suspended in midair. He gaped as she passed him, but the girl barely slowed as she surveyed him from head to toe. From the look in her jet-black, kohl-lined eyes, he wasn't worth much more than her cursory glance. Kyle could smell a hint of her musky, cinnamon perfume lingering in the air as she disappeared from view.

"Who was that?" Sera's voice startled him so much that he nearly dropped his books. She had a knowing look in her clear, light eyes, a smirk on her lips.

"Who?" Kyle's tongue tripped over the word.

"Miss I-Hate-The-World new girl who nearly ran you over without blinking," Sera said. "You should wipe the drool off your chin, by the way. Very unbecoming of an Azura Lord."

Kyle smirked, though his heart was still hammering. Clearing his head of dark eyes and cinnamon musk, he forced his breathing to slow and calm. "Looks like I still have some of my human traits. Pretty girls will always get me hot and bothered."

"I can't even with you," Sera said, eyeing him. "Plus, it's not like you need any more distractions at school. Especially not some girl who looks like more trouble than you can handle. You should be focusing on keeping all of the demon riffraff out of the Mortal Realm."

"Sure, *Mom*. Though that doesn't mean I can't have a little fun playing the field, right?" Kyle winked as they walked toward the school entrance. "After all, I did come back to finish senior year, even though high school's pretty pointless when you're fighting hordes of acid-spewing demons."

"High school's a must," Sera tossed back.

"Overrated. Who needs trigonometry when you're an all-powerful, portal-defending Azura Lord?"

"You wouldn't say that if you were caught between a rock, a hard place, and a bunch of demons and needed to figure out escape routes. Trig is useful, and learning, in general, keeps your mind sharp."

"Woodshop is useful for designing weapons," he grumbled. "But I guess you have a point." He shook his head and smiled. Only Sera could come up with a reason to use trig or statistics mid-battle. Though she was right, he supposed. Demon fighting was in a class all its own, requiring dexterity and finesse unlike other fighting styles. One wrong move could cost you more than your life—and pretty much guaranteed an eternity of pain. He sobered at the thought. "On a more serious note, any more news on what's happening with the rest of the demons?"

Sera's face drew tight. "My parents are still battling, along with the rest of the Daevas, to get rid of the ones that are in hiding here. It's tough, though—they know how to conceal themselves. Some are even taking human form."

He blinked his surprise. "Like possession?"

"Similar, though not what you'd expect from the movies. No veined faces and clotted blood patches, or anything like that. Possessed humans look completely normal. Like you and me." Sera laughed at herself. "Well, not *exactly* you and me. These days, you can hardly tell what a possessed human host looks like." She tapped her head. "My dad says you need to use your senses to feel them. The stronger demons are nearly undetectable."

"Great." Kyle sighed. Sera's dad would know—he was an ex-Azura Lord turned human. So he knew more about human souls than just about anyone. "How are we supposed to send them back to hell if we can't even see them? Does Samsar have a cheat sheet or something? Cliffs Notes? Post-its?"

Sera rolled her eyes at him. "Practice. Plus, you'll learn to sense them after a while. With your abilities, it should be a piece of cake." She shivered, shadows gathering in her pale eyes. "They feel . . . oily. Like scum coating your skin."

"Thanks for the tip."

Inside, the school hallways were bustling with students back from summer break. Kyle watched Sera say a shy hello to some girls she knew and then head over to her locker. Things had changed for her since she'd come into her own as a goddess—not that the other kids knew that's what had happened. But discovering her true identity, and dropping the shade her mother had placed on her to hide her other-worldly looks, had transformed Sera's appearance. Her natural auburn suited her more than the goth-black hair color she'd worn most of the previous year. It was eye-opening how shallow most teens were—some of them acted as if they hadn't known who she was anymore. Then again, in high school, something as superficial as a makeover could change your entire social life. And Sera was immortal. Without her shade, she tended to attract people without trying.

Occupational hazard, Kyle figured.

No one waved to him—he'd always been a loner. And that wasn't going to change just because he'd moved up the cosmic food chain and gotten a new, indestructible body. Unlike Sera, he wasn't a god and his looks remained the same—his black, curly Mohawk and tattoos told people to stay the heck away if they knew what was good for them. And they did.

He studied his human peers moving like animals, survival instincts primed. A trio of football players slammed into a skinny, freckle-faced boy at his locker, making him drop his belongings. An apple rolled out of a brown paper bag and one of the boys kicked it across the linoleum floor. They snickered and high-fived one another like a bunch of hyenas determined to play with their food before eating it.

It wasn't his business, he told himself. And then he sighed. That kid's entire semester could be ruined because of this one moment. Didn't Sera's mother always say that life was determined by a series of moments and choices?

"It's only the first day. Why don't you guys knock it off?" Kyle snapped, drawing surprised looks his way. As if sensing danger on the wind, the football players' gazes flickered with uncertainty before they banded together, seeming to decide that strength in numbers would give them a sort of edge.

The tallest of the three sneered at him. "What's it to you, loser? You want to be next?"

Kyle raised an eyebrow and folded his arms across his chest. "Sure. Come and get it."

The wide receiver who'd tossed the taunt threw the first punch. Kyle saw the fist coming toward his jaw and stopped it mid-strike with the heel of his palm. He closed his hand around the other boy's and squeezed, watching his face contort, then leaned in, his voice low: "Pick on someone your own size next time, or you won't be using this arm anytime soon, got it?" He released his hold.

Thin-lipped, the wide receiver nodded and clutched his injured hand, scuttling back to his friends. Once he was out of reach, safe among his packmates, he glared daggers at Kyle. "Watch your back, man."

"I'll keep that in mind."

As they took off down the hallway, Kyle shook his head. Sometimes, high school was worse than the lowest level of hell. He considered helping the other boy gather his things, but decided against it. He didn't have to go *all* out to be a good guy.

"So, I'll catch you later for chem?" Sera said, walking back toward him with her books in hand. She narrowed her eyes at the retreating football players as one turned around to give Kyle the finger. "What's with them?"

"They're just having a bad first day," Kyle replied. "Wait, you're not going to English?"

"I have a note. I need to see the guidance counselor about some AP courses I'm taking."

"AP? What for?" Kyle asked. "You're a deity. Why do you need advanced placement classes?"

She tucked her books under one arm with an earnest look. "If I'm planning to stay in this realm, I can't exactly be a bum on my parents' couch. My mom still wants me to get into a good college. You'd be smart to think about that, too."

"Hell, no. I promised Carla I'd graduate high school, and that's it. I'll get a job working at Sal's rather than voluntarily signing up for another four years of eternal death."

Sera put one hand on her hip. She leaned in, her voice

a low whisper. "You knock school, but seriously, where do you think all the demons hide out?" Kyle felt his stomach curl. "High school. *College*. My dad says teenagers and young adults are more susceptible to possession. They're not as innocent as children and not as jaded as grownups. The middle ground is the easiest to penetrate and, in some really messed-up cases, the teens even like it. Demonic possession makes them popular, believe it or not."

Kyle grimaced. How could any kid enjoy having a demon inside of them? "What do you mean they *like* it? That makes no sense."

"Demons have huge egos. They love themselves more than anything. You don't think that translates into a bonus to some insecure teenager who's been bullied half his life? When a kid's possessed, he becomes insanely confident, dresses differently, talks differently, and basically stops being afraid of anyone. It's like a creepy symbiotic relationship. The demon depends on the host to exist in the Mortal Realm, and the host depends on the demon for social survival."

He'd never thought of it that way, but the theory made sense. "That's messed up."

"Tell me about it," she agreed. "See, you may want to rethink your strategy about college. Anyway, keep your eyes open and your Azura demon-banishing skills primed. Catch you later." As they arrived at his classroom, Sera gestured at someone behind him and grinned before heading in the opposite direction. "And try not to hurt yourself."

He turned, his gaze colliding with a scorchingly dark stare that made patches of actual sweat break out on his skin. The girl from the parking lot was in his class? Sweet baby Jesus on a skateboard. Closing his eyes, he seriously considered ditching for a moment. He'd been joking earlier about playing the field; the act was mostly all bravado. Girls weren't into him. They never had been.

He took a deep breath and entered the classroom, unable to take his eyes off the girl. She was lounging in one of the seats in the second to last row, her boot propped on the chair beside her. Kyle tried to keep his eyes down, despite the immediate response somewhere deep in the pit of his belly, but he couldn't stop glancing in her direction.

"See something you like?" Her voice was light, amused.

He shook his head quickly. "Just looking for a seat," he muttered, almost crashing into another kid as he backed away, only to find himself wedged in by someone else on her way into the classroom. Kyle sighed, looking around the room— all the good seats were already taken, with the exception of the one beside the new girl, or the front row. His eyes slid to hers, and he swallowed hard. Her lips twitched as if she was enjoying his predicament.

A boy behind the girl tapped her on the shoulder, then passed her a flyer, and Kyle dragged his eyes away. Her teeth flashed white at something the boy said; something silver glinted in her mouth. She had a tongue-ring.

Kyle's knees felt boneless. *God*, she was hot.

But hot girls were high maintenance. And way more trouble than he needed this year. He was an Azura Lord now, and he had a mission. Glancing around the room, he spotted an open seat in the far corner that he hadn't seen earlier and edged his way to the back of the classroom. He took a deep, clarifying breath, and focused on Sera's earlier words in the hallway. Of course she was right. Even during school, they all had a job to do.

Sera's was to guide humanity; his was to defend it from the bad guys trying to take up residence in the Mortal Realm. Demons loved to prey on human flesh, he'd learned. As a Portal Guardian, he could send trespassing demons back instantly. It was also his job to keep an eye on any human souls being lured into the Dark Realms.

Kyle, of course, could travel to Xibalba if he needed to, but it wasn't something he enjoyed, exactly. The seven hells that made up the Dark Realms appealed far too deeply to his darker nature, drawing his more wicked instincts to the fore. Lust, pride, ego, power. The temptation to sin was always there, thanks to the tainted blood of his father, the Demon Lord of the seventh and lowest dimension of hell. Kyle couldn't trust himself when he was in Xibalba. And the Trimurtas didn't trust him, either. They were only allowing him to remain in the Mortal Realm because of his relationship with Sera.

Sera was a goddess, and one of the strongest. Though she had chosen to remain in the Mortal Realm with her family, she was the consort of one of the Trimurtas Lords, Lord Devendra. Some thought she had chosen him over Dev, but deep down, Kyle knew better. Sera cared about him—loved him to a fault, even—but she'd made her choice. And it wasn't him. That was the way of things, and because *he* was in love with her, Kyle knew he would accept whatever she was willing to offer him, even if it was only friendship. And the truth was, he liked Dev, too.

Love triangles freaking sucked.

Lost in concentration, he didn't notice that someone had slid into the empty seat in the back row. Crap. That meant he would be stuck up front. As he walked past her for the second time, he took another look at the new girl and froze. She was staring right at him, her inky eyes dark and intense. He couldn't help but notice her dewy skin—the color of deeply brown polished stone.

"You're back," she said with a smirk, eyebrow raised. Once more, Kyle realized he'd been caught gawking. "I'm Kira. We met in the parking lot, right?"

"Kyle," he choked out, almost butchering his own name. He collected himself with a strangled breath, searching for something clever to say. "And we didn't officially meet. You tried to run me over with your motorcycle. Great way to make friends, by the way."

Wonderful. He sounded like a wounded Goody Two-Shoes.

But Kira chuckled, throwing her head back and exposing a long bronze throat. All eyes in the room went to her—the girls, with envy, the boys with poorly masked longing. Kira didn't flinch, keeping her own gaze focused on Kyle as if he were the only one there. She toyed with the silver stud on her tongue between her teeth. "Yeah, sorry about that. I kind of have speeding issues—and road rage. Not a good combo."

Despite Sera's warning looping in his head, he nodded to the seat beside Kira, the one she'd propped her leg on. "That taken?"

"It is now," she said, removing her foot slowly and smiling as she pushed it toward him so that the edge of the metal nudged his calf. He flinched. For some reason, it felt as though she'd touched him herself.

"Thanks." The warm scent of cinnamon wafted toward him as he settled in the seat. Trying not to breathe, he opened his English textbook, determined to avoid making an idiot of himself.

Kira leaned toward him. "So, who was the redhead you were talking to before? In the hallway. Girlfriend?"

"No, Sera's . . . my friend," he said quickly. Kira's eyes widened with a strange look, but it was gone as fast as it had appeared.

Kyle shifted uncomfortably as a surge of guilt flooded through him. It wasn't like he and Sera were together. They *were* just friends. He could flirt with a girl if he wanted to, especially if said girl was flirting back . . . which, however inconceivably, Kira seemed to be doing. "Are you a transfer student?" he asked her.

Kira nodded. "I moved from the city."

"City girl," Kyle said. "It's a big change from Manhattan up here in the boonies." He pointed at the window with an overly bright grin. "Out here, we have these really cool things—called grass and trees."

"I know, right?" she joked back with an elegant shrug of her shoulder. "Though I'm not a huge fan of the outdoors. I miss the buildings and the streets in the city. It was structured. Ordered."

New York City? *Order?* Kyle frowned at her strange choice of words, but quickly smiled to try to hide it. He found the city too overwhelming, but different strokes for different folks. "Well, let me be the first person to officially welcome you to Silver Lake. It's a small town, but everyone's pretty friendly."

Except for the demons, he thought just as Mr. Moss walked in and rapped on his desk. "I can show you around after school if you'd like," he added quickly.

"I'd like that."

For the rest of the class, Kyle was acutely aware of the girl beside him . . . the way she smelled, the dark gleam of her skin, the soft movements of her body, her overall magnetism. Not only was she striking to look at, she practically oozed self-confidence. He wasn't the only one staring. Everyone else seemed to be peeking over at her whenever they got the chance. Normally, kids at Silver Lake High School would give the new kid the once-over, and then life went back to normal. But this girl held them all in thrall.

Suddenly, Sera's words popped into his head again—*the stronger demons are nearly undetectable*. Could Kira be possessed by one of them? For a second, Kyle wished that Sera was in this class. She would have known in an instant. Then again, Sera hadn't said anything about the girl earlier in the parking lot or in the hallway—and she would have. He was being paranoid.

His breath caught in his throat as he felt a gentle tug on the sleeve of his T-shirt. Kira's breath was warm on his neck as she leaned toward him. "Hey, do you have a pen I can borrow?"

"Sure." Handing over his only pen—and mentally cursing his idiocy—his fingers grazed hers, direct skin to skin contact this time. Red-hot spirals shot through his hand and sank deep into his chest. He snatched his arm away.

One of Kira's elegant eyebrows rose, a frown puckering her smooth brown forehead. Had she sensed something, too? Unlikely, though it wasn't outside of the realm of possibility. Some humans had extrasensory perception—a real ability, as he'd learned. Most of the Ne'feri, human fighters who defended the Mortal Realm from evil forces, possessed some form of it. They worked with the Daevas, guardian spirits on earth, to protect the Mortal Realm and were trained to dispatch demons just as effectively as their immortal companions.

His skin tingled, and his paranoia surged back in full force. No human girl could make someone feel like this, could she?

Or maybe he was overreacting. After all, he hadn't exactly had a lot of contact with the opposite sex over the last few months while he'd been mooning over Sera.

Kyle took a deep breath, trying to focus. Kira's confidence made him pause. Despite being oblivious to everyone else, she seemed to be all too aware of the effect she was having on him . . . as if she was enjoying making him squirm. *Could* she be a demon?

He had to be sure.

Leaning back in his chair, he cleared his mind and let his senses reach outward, just as Sera had said to do. Demons had to be felt, not seen. And she said it would feel oily and scummy. Drawing on his newly enhanced Azura abilities, he let his consciousness push toward Kira. After a minute, it encountered hers.

Mortal.

And definitely not scummy. Kyle could see flashes of her in an instant—pieces of her childhood in Manhattan, her last school, her recent birthdays—and he couldn't help feeling intense relief as he pulled away. If she had been a demon, or possessed by one, he would have had to banish her, no matter how hot she was. Shaking his head and glancing to the left, his eyes connected with hers.

"What?" he asked Kira.

"You were staring at me like you were in some kind of weird trance," she said in a low voice. "It was borderline creepy."

"Oh, sorry," he blurted out, going red. "I was thinking about homework and zoning out."

"Homework on the first day?" she asked.

"I like to study." Immediately regretting the lie, he studied his open textbook. With Sera, his feelings had grown over time, but with this girl, the attraction made him stupidly tongue-tied. Though, apparently, a convincing liar. Kyle frowned.

Lust was one of the seven deadly sins. And a definite path to Xibalba.

So was pride. Yes, he was a powerful Azura Lord, but he was also just a teenage boy. Without a girlfriend. He had nothing to lose, and if Sera could make the effort to befriend new people, so could he.

He felt Kira's eyes settle on him again. "That makes one of us," she whispered. "Maybe you could give me a few pointers sometime?"

Kyle wasn't dumb enough not to realize that she was interested. She was practically asking him out. He smiled at her as he forced his fears to subside. "You bet."

Senior year seemed to be off to a promising start.

SECRETS

❧᷇

S era bent over a table tucked between the library stacks, staring at the tiny lotus-flower flames that danced in the middle of her palm. Being a reincarnated deity—not to mention the conduit between heaven and hell—wasn't everything it was cracked up to be.

It made her important. Responsible for the survival of the realms.

And Sera wasn't entirely sure she was up to the challenge.

She flipped her palm over, watching the flame flicker between her knuckles like a dancing coin. It returned to her palm and she curled her fingers into a fist, snuffing the fire flower out.

Whether she wanted it or not, Sera couldn't change who she was. Not only was she Lakshmi reincarnated—consort to Lord Devendra and one of the three female rulers of Illysia known as the Tridevi—she was also born of a Sanrak deity and an Azura Lord. As a result, she was the only goddess who could walk all three planes of existence. It was a power that many had coveted—none more so than her own uncle, Lord Azrath. Several months ago, he'd released the Kali rakshasa demon in an attempt to usher in the KaliYuga, and tried to use Sera's powers to create a portal he could use to enter Illysia. And he'd almost succeeded.

But then, Kyle and Dev had saved them all.

Her stomach fluttered as she thought of Dev. He was her other half, and he always would be, even though she had chosen to remain in the Mortal Realm, where she couldn't be near him. It had been months since she'd seen him last. He had offered to return her to Illysia, but she hadn't been able to leave her family—her father, her mother, her brother Nate.

And Kyle.

He needed her more than ever now. Just because they had narrowly escaped death in Xibalba didn't mean either of them were free. The latest rakshasa infestation was only the tip of a very monstrous iceberg. After they'd halted the KaliYuga in its tracks, they'd hoped to strengthen the wards between the realms and keep the rakshasas in Xibalba where they belonged. But somehow, demons were once again appearing in the Mortal Realm—a quiet, consistent, and noticeable number of them.

Which made the Trimurtas, and everyone else who'd nearly died to save the realms, very uneasy.

"Hey, Sera." A quiet voice interrupted her thoughts. Beth Davenport. Like her parents and her recently initiated brother, Beth was a part of the Ne'feri Order, but she had graduated from Silver Lake High the year before.

Sera blinked. "What are you doing here?"

Beth smiled at her confusion. "I'm taking a year off between high school and college. I'm helping out in the library. How was your summer?"

Sera recalled her parents mentioning that the Davenports had gone to Europe . . . something to do with the other Ne'feri Orders and coordinating a global effort against the new demon influx. They wanted to neutralize any threat before it became an infestation. Sera couldn't help thinking that she wouldn't have minded visiting Paris or London for a couple months. Instead, she'd been here. Killing monsters.

So Sera almost laughed at Beth's question about her summer. "Not bad," she whispered, though their corner of the library was deserted. "You know, banishing rakshasas and starting my last year of high school. All in a day's work, right?"

"Glad to see you haven't lost your sense of humor."

Sera grinned. "Sometimes I think it's the only thing keeping me sane. How was Europe?"

"Eye-opening. Mind if I sit for a minute?"

Sera nodded at the seat on the other side of the narrow table. "Go ahead. Can't beat a free period right before lunch. It's just too bad Kyle isn't in many of my classes this year. It kind of sucks, actually."

"How is he doing?" Beth asked tersely, running her fingers through her short hair. "With the changes and everything?"

Sera knew that Beth trusted her, but she'd never been a big fan of Kyle.

"He's doing okay, I think," Sera said, then frowned as a thought suddenly occurred to her. "Wait, did you take the year off because you really need a break between high school and college? Or because you wanted to keep an eye on him?"

Beth shrugged as if she'd been anticipating the question. "It's complicated."

"How?" Sera asked. "The Trimurtas made him an Azura Lord—they trust him. That should be enough for the Ne'feri."

"He's still Ra'al's son."

Sera leaned forward, an edge to her tone. "He *died* to save the entire Mortal Realm from an apocalypse demon—and any part of him that was tied to Ra'al is gone. You know that. He's proven himself a hundred times over."

"Maybe. I know you trust him, Sera, but—"

She cut Beth off, her voice shaking. "I do. Completely. He sacrificed himself for me, for all of us. And you're treating him as if he's some kind of demon-spawn leper."

Beth extended her arms in a conciliatory gesture. "Look, calm down. I'm just doing what I've been told, that's all. I hope to the gods that you're right about him. But there's been a lot of talk . . ." she trailed off, looking around uneasily, as if she expected someone to be listening in. "You missed the last Ne'feri meeting."

Sera exhaled slowly, guilty heat rising in her cheeks. She *had* missed the last meeting—for no reason other than that she hadn't felt like going. She hadn't wanted to sit through hours of tedious details about the statuses of the various portals between the realms. Though her parents hadn't made a big deal of her refusal to go, Sera knew that she had disappointed them.

The truth was, some days she was fine with being a goddess, and all the responsibilities that entailed: keeping demons and humans where they belonged, and making sure mortals were safe. Other days . . . well, it wasn't always easy to be responsible for the fate of everyone. She was only seventeen, for heaven's sake—as she'd reminded her mother just the week before.

"What teenager behaves like a full-grown adult all the time?" Sera had cried in frustration.

"One who understands the significance of the lives she has lived. And you're not exactly a teenager, are you?"

Sera had rolled her eyes. "That doesn't mean I'm a thousand years old in *this* life. I just want to be normal this year. I want to think about senior prom and dresses, getting into college and having fun." The words had felt stupid and immature to her, even at the time, but something perverse had driven her to say them. Maybe it was part of the darkness that crept within her—her shadowy side that allowed her to survive in Xibalba.

Her mother had smiled sadly. "That's not your karma."

Karma. According to Sera's mother, her entire future existence was set. In freaking stone.

"I didn't ask for any of this," she had said.

"I know it's hard, but we don't choose who we are. We choose who we become. If you decide to be a teen who wants to do all those things and live a normal life, then I cannot stop you."

Of course not. But the consequences of her decision would fall squarely on her shoulders. She had shaken her head miserably. "But if I do that, the Mortal Realm will be defenseless."

"Perhaps. Perhaps not. Humans are stronger than we give them credit for."

"I can't just abandon them." Sera had sighed. "I can't escape who I am, can I? I'm sorry for being such a brat. It's too much sometimes. I feel like I'm going to break apart from the pressure."

"I know it's hard, my love, but it will get easier, I promise."

"How?"

"Same as everything else, one day at a time," her mother had replied. "It's the action, not the fruit of the action, that's important. Mahatma Gandhi said that. You only need to try."

Trying aside, everything had happened so quickly after Sera learned her true identity that she hadn't had enough time to process it all. Whenever she thought about any of it—her exposure to Xibalba, Jude and the Preta, her uncle's betrayal, the final battle with Ra'al and the Kali rakshasa—it seemed too fantastical to be real. Like a terrible dream. But none of it was a dream. It was the harsh reality. They lived in a world of monsters and gods. And she was its cornerstone.

Her mother was right. She couldn't *not* try. Not even when she felt like burying her head in the proverbial sand.

Sera swallowed hard at the memory of their fight and focused on Beth. "What happened at the meeting? What did the Ne'feri say?"

"That when the portal was open during the demon apocalypse, more demons might have made it through than we thought. It's getting harder and harder to find the ones that escaped." She paused, taking a deep breath and dropping her voice to a whisper. "Ever since that portal was created, there've been dozens more rakshasas appearing."

"But the portal was closed," Sera said. "We destroyed it. How are more of them getting through?"

"We don't know."

Sera shook her head. "That doesn't make sense. Rakshasas can't just appear out of nowhere—it goes against the laws of the realms. Are we talking about lower level demons, or something bigger?"

The thought of any of the Demon Lords, the powerful

Azura who controlled the seven hells in Xibalba, making an appearance was a sickening one.

"No, just the smaller ones."

"There has to be a fissure somewhere, something we're not seeing. What are the other Ne'feri Orders saying?"

"The ones on the west coast are seeing the same thing," Beth said. "Lots of demons. All lower for now, but it feels like something big is on the verge of happening. As if they're . . . waiting for something."

"Waiting for *what*?"

Beth shrugged, but her eyes were troubled. "I don't know. Here's the thing: more of them seem to appear when—"

But Beth's words lodged in her throat as time literally came to a halt. The gilded dust shimmering in the bands of sunlight from the windows froze, and only Beth and Sera were left moving. Beth's eyelashes swept closed in slow motion as she blinked, her lips parting on a silent exhale.

And then came a heavy rustling of deifyre wings.

Along with the materialization of other immortals.

An eerie quiet descended when two Yoddha appeared. One Sera didn't recognize, but the other was Mara, who Sera had learned was the sister of Maeve, a seasoned Yoddha who had died at Sera's uncle's hands months before. Mara was all bronze-colored limbs and luminescent gold deifyre—the bright goddess aura they wore like a veil. Mara's resemblance to Maeve always made something in Sera's chest ache—a reminder of the loss, perhaps.

Mara floated to the ground and bowed to Sera before turning to Beth and saying, in a voice like wind chimes, "Enough. It is not the time."

Sera flushed. She was still not used to the deference the powerful warrior deities showed her, or the fact that they served her. But then Mara's words registered. Sera's eyes narrowed and she forgot her discomfort. "What's not the time?"

"The Lord Protector will discuss it further with you, Eminence."

Cringing at the address, Sera sucked air through her teeth in frustration. That would be all well and good if the *Lord Protector* were here, but Dev was far away, on another plane of existence. And he had been for some time. "Explain it now."

"I cannot." Mara bowed again, the deference at odds with her refusal. "I am sorry, my lady. This is the Lord Protector's command."

Humiliation heated Sera's cheeks. What was the point of being some unique, all-powerful immortal if everyone treated her like a child? And by Dev's order, no less! The Lord Protector knew best, did he? Well, she wanted to punch him right in his arrogant, know-it-all nose.

Her eyes slid to the deity at Mara's side. "Who's this?" Sera asked brusquely to cover her embarrassment. Unlike Mara, the stranger was pale-skinned and slight in stature.

"Ilani. She's in training."

"Lucky for her she got you for babysitting duty." Sera couldn't stop the sour words from slipping from her mouth, but she only felt worse when she saw the slight tremor of Mara's lips. None of this was Mara's fault—she was only doing what Dev and the Trimurtas felt were best. How could the Yoddha trust her when it appeared that even Dev himself didn't?

"That is not it," Mara said, as if reading her mind.

Sera frowned, unable to recall whether the Yoddha could read the minds of other immortals. "Not what?" she asked carefully.

"That they don't trust you."

"I wasn't—"

"It is written all over your face." She cleared her throat. "They want you to be safe, and since you are not where you belong, at the Protector's side in Illysia, they worry for you. Your mother and Lord Devendra especially."

Sera drummed her fingers on the table, fighting frustration and shame in equal measure. She knew exactly what everyone was so worried about, and it had nothing to do with her safety. It had to do with *theirs*. Dev may have asked her to return with him to Illysia, but Sera was sure that the Trimurtas wanted her right where she was. They feared her—feared what she was capable of because of the power that lived within her.

Power both light and dark.

Of Illysia *and* Xibalba.

Her eyes drifted to the sigils on each of her palms—the one on her left hand that marked her as a goddess of light, and its twin on her right that marked her as its opposite. As the only known goddess who could travel to and survive in the Dark Realms, she was an anomaly. And therefore a risk. Though she had chosen to remain in the Mortal Realm for her own reasons, a part of her had understood that she would never be truly welcomed to Illysia . . . not while she was tethered to Xibalba.

She glanced at Beth, who seemed stunned by the sudden appearance of the warrior deities, and Mara's curt command. Sera frowned. "Is that all?" she said coolly to Mara. "You wanted to stop Beth from sharing a secret that only the great and powerful Wizard of Oz can tell me?"

Mara frowned. "Wizard of who?"

"It's a movie about an evil overlord magician. Forget it." Sera rolled her eyes as Mara and Ilani prepared to take their leave. "Wait, were you guys here the whole time?"

"We are always here."

"Oh, *wonderful*."

The corner of Mara's lips curled upward at Sera's sarcastic tone, and she leaned down to whisper something to Beth before shimmering out of sight. Time resumed its normal passage.

"What did she say to you just then?" Sera asked.

The dazed look slipped from Beth's face, and she shook her head as if to clear it. "That the bell was about to ring."

Sera's jaw dropped open in disbelief. "*That's* what she told you?"

"Yes."

Sure enough, seconds later a tone sounded from the speakers at the far end of the library, signaling the end of the period. Sera gathered her things, her eyes on Beth, who still seemed somewhat disoriented. She'd bet anything that that wasn't the only thing Mara had whispered to her. Beth had been about to explain something she suspected about the appearance of the lower level demons. But why would the Yoddha keep something like that from her, of all people?

And why would *Dev* command them to?

She made one last-ditch effort before leaving the library. "Beth, what were you about to tell me before, about the demons?"

"What demons?"

"The ones who—Never mind," Sera said, breaking off mid-sentence as a group of sophomores entered the stacks in a noisy line. She sighed in frustration and stared up at the vaulted glass ceiling. Perhaps it was a blessing in disguise. No doubt Mara and her protégée were both hiding somewhere above, watching, reporting every word back to Dev. "I'll catch up with you later, okay?"

"See you," Beth said, as if they'd been discussing nothing but the weather.

Shaking her head, Sera made a mental note to take it up with her mother. Unless Dev had told *her* not to say anything either. Her aggravation doubled.

She was so caught up in her irritation that as she stopped by her locker to grab her books for advanced calc after lunch, she didn't see the Frisbee flying in her direction until it clocked her in the back. "What the *heck*?" she cried, rubbing her sore shoulder.

"Sorry, my bad," a boy said as she turned to face him. His teeth glowed against the tan skin of his face and the lock of dark hair curling into his eyes. He collected the Frisbee from the floor beneath her, tucking it under his arm with another of those incandescently bright smiles. "Sera, is that you?"

She blinked. "Do I know you?"

"You don't recognize me?" The boy clutched a dramatic hand to his chest. "I'm heartbroken."

Now that she thought of it, he did seem vaguely familiar. It was in the eyes. They were a sparkling, vibrant shade of blue. She stared at him, trying to place his face. "Do we know each other?"

He smirked, blue eyes dancing with mischief. "Seriously?

You don't remember me? Think swimming in a bathtub together. I'm probably the first boy you ever saw naked."

The puzzle fell into place. Those distinct blue eyes had once belonged to a much younger face.

"Jemitra?" Sera said in disbelief as childhood memories rushed to mind. Jemitra Kumar was the son of one of her father's law colleagues. When the Kumars used to live in Silver Lake, their two families had been close. The Kumars had left when Jemitra's dad was transferred for some big case in England, and that'd been nearly seven years ago. Sera had been devastated. The two of them had stayed in touch through letters and phone calls for a little while, but eventually they'd grown apart. Distance, and all that. "What are you doing here?"

His eyes were the same electric shade of blue, but he'd grown up a lot since elementary school. Jemitra was no longer a shy ten-year-old with braces and a weird haircut who loved hot sauce more than life. Maybe he still did; Sera had no idea.

"It's just Jem now," he said. "And we're back in town. I see your mom let you go to high school instead of keeping you home schooled. I remember you really hating that."

Sera smiled. "Took a lot of convincing. Back then, I was lucky she let me do Girl Scouts."

"You're a senior this year, right?" he asked, and Sera nodded. "Me too. I was hoping I'd run into you, but Dad said he wasn't sure you'd be here at Silver Lake High. He's at a different law firm now, but I'm sure he'll be seeing your parents soon." He shook his head in amazement, staring at her. "This is so unreal—I can't believe you're all grown up and standing right in front of me," he said, pulling her into a hug.

"Me, either," Sera replied.

"Whoa, beanpole, you got big," he said, grinning as he released her. "Good thing I was able to catch up a little."

Sera couldn't help smiling at her old nickname. She'd towered over him by nearly a foot when they were both ten. Now they were both close to six feet tall. "I kept hoping I'd stop growing, but my prayers never got answered."

"You look great," he said and squinted at her. "I remember you having darker hair. I like the red, though," he added quickly. "Suits you."

"Thanks," she said. She could hardly tell him that the deep auburn color was actually the natural one. Her nondescript, dark hair had been a shade concocted by her parents to make her less noticeable. She changed the subject. "So, is your dad back for good?"

"Hope so." Jem turned to a boy at the other end of the hallway and tossed him the Frisbee. "I'll catch up with you later, Keith. Don't think this game is finished—I'm still two under par."

Sera watched the other boy shoot them a thumbs-up, toss the Frisbee back to Jem, and saunter away. She eyed the disc, but Jem caught it easily this time. "You do know that's not allowed inside, right?"

Jem faked an innocent look. "Hey, I can't control where Frisbee Golf leads me. Though in this case, it led me to you, so I'm glad I risked the consequences. It's so great to see you, Sera."

"You, too." She meant it. Seeing Jem made her think of simpler times, when she'd been unencumbered by the knowledge of who she was. For a moment, she let herself bask in a forgotten sense of normalcy.

"Hey, Sera, thought we were meeting in the cafeteria," Kyle yelled from down the hallway. "I waited there for twenty minutes."

"Sorry," she said as Kyle strode toward them. "I was at the library, and then got to talking with an old friend. This is Jem. Jem, Kyle."

Sera made the introductions, noticing Kyle's suddenly intense expression. Of course, he would be trying to decide if Jem was a threat—human, deity, or demon. He relaxed quickly, though, apparently having determined that Jem was exactly what he seemed to be—a boy. Sera knew they couldn't be too careful these days, not even for old friends.

"Jem and I grew up together, but he moved away when we were ten."

"That's cool," Kyle said. "So, you're back in town?"

"Yeah, my father's working on some big case in the city, so we figured we'd come back to Silver Lake instead of staying down there. Nicer up here, you know."

"Yeah."

They fell into an uncomfortable silence until Sera cleared her throat and glanced at Jem. "You want to come to lunch with us?"

But Jem shook his head. "I have to go see the guidance counselor and finish doing some transfer paperwork. Can I stop by later?"

"That would be great," she said with a delighted smile. Maybe a dose of nostalgia was exactly what she needed. "You know where I live."

"Nice to meet you, man," Jem said with a nod to Kyle.

"You, too," Kyle replied. Jem took off in the opposite

direction as Sera and Kyle walked toward the cafeteria. He shot her a look. "So, when did you see him naked?"

Sera flushed. "You heard that from the cafeteria? And we were five, so get your head out of the gutter."

"I was already on my way to find you," he said.

She scowled. "And you have super immortal hearing that you choose to use to spy on me."

Kyle shrugged. "Part of my job is still to look out for you. I promised your dad, remember?"

"How could I forget?"

So not only were Mara and Ilani spying on her, but her dad seemed to have Kyle on permanent watch, too. It hadn't bothered her before, but now the attention felt oppressive. Like everyone was expecting her to go off the goddess deep end. Even her own best friend.

They didn't speak again until they sat down with their lunch trays. Kyle promptly started hoovering his food while Sera relayed what Beth had told her. After his spying stunt, she wasn't sure she wanted to tell him much, but Kyle was technically on her side. Still, she left out the part about Mara and Ilani appearing mid-conversation.

"Any idea why there're so many rakshasas?" she asked. "Or where they're coming from?"

"They're not coming through the portals I control," he said around a mouthful of nachos. "I'll have a dig around and see what I can find out. What did Dev say?"

"He hasn't *said* anything," she grumbled.

"Still no word?"

She shook her head. It was no secret that Dev had been busy convening the Trimurtas and convincing the other gods not to go into full lockdown mode after the nearly successful attempt to invade Illysia. She would have appreciated anything—a heads-up, a hello, a hey-just-checking-in. But other than the secondhand message from Mara, his communication had been sparse. She'd said she needed space, so maybe he was trying to respect her wishes. However, his prolonged absence stung.

Sera finished her sandwich and sat back in her chair. Some of the cafeteria windows were opened, letting in fresh air. Though it was still slightly cool, it looked like the overcast morning had given way to a beautiful day. Her gaze wandered to the slim, black-clad figure sitting alone on a bench in the adjacent quad.

Sera gestured toward her. "What's with new girl? She was with you first period, right? Still angry at the world?"

"She's okay," Kyle mumbled, suddenly more interested in his nachos than talking.

Sera grinned, unable to resist teasing him. "Just okay?" Kyle looked up at her, his eyes sliding to Kira and then back to Sera. He looked so confused that she felt sorry for him. "Spit it out. I'm desperate to resume my best friend duties."

His shoulders tensed for a second, but then he sighed. "She's cool, but I don't know how to act around her. It was really weird in class this morning. It's like I can't think when I'm near her. And it's not as if she isn't mortal or anything. I mean, she is, but she's just so . . . *there*. Sorry, it's TMI, I know."

Sera couldn't help laughing at his expression. "Maybe you should pace yourself, okay, lover boy? Don't want to hurt yourself on the first day."

"I'm trying. But I feel like a total loser."

"You're not." Sera gave him a reassuring smile. "Is she into you?"

"I think so, unless I'm reading the signals wrong. Which is totally possible." He paused, looking embarrassed. "I haven't been into anyone since . . . um . . ." Going red, he trailed off and stuffed a handful of nachos into his mouth.

But Sera knew what he meant—since *her*.

Honestly, she was happy that Kyle was trying to move on. She adored him, but there was no doubt of her deep-rooted feelings for Dev. Those feelings surpassed anything she'd ever felt for *anyone*. Their bond, born of an eternal and immortal love, had transcended time, death, and rebirth. She belonged with him, much as he belonged with her. That was another thing she was still getting used to.

Sera's gaze returned to the girl sitting outside as she thought about what Kyle had said. The emotions he'd described sounded like what she felt around Dev—tingling, hopeful, and weightless. She wanted Kyle to feel all those things and more—and if he was interested in this girl, who was she to stand in the way?

It was time for him to find his own happiness.

ROLL OF THE DICE

For the rest of the afternoon, Kyle heeded Sera's advice and kept his eyes to himself. In chem, one of their few classes together, he sat next to Sera and stayed silent for the entire class—so much so that she kept shooting him worried looks. Kira sat in the front of the class, where he couldn't see her face, but he could feel her presence as strongly as if she were sitting right next to him. He could hardly focus. Her magnetic pull was so unsettling that for the second time that day, he had to verify that she was human.

Once they got to their lockers, Sera was on him like a concerned mother hen. "Are you okay? What's wrong? You were on edge for the whole class. Did you sense something?"

Kyle felt heat rise in his cheeks and wanted to kick himself. "No, it's nothing."

"Why are you all shaky? Demon stuff?"

"No, nothing like that. I was trying to . . . I'm just . . . never mind." His voice trailed off as Kira approached them. "Hey."

He cleared his throat and looked from one girl to the other. Sera had a few inches on Kira in height, but the other girl made up for it in sheer presence. They were both equally striking, but Kira's beauty had an edge to it, something dangerous. She reminded him of a jungle cat—stunning and predatory.

"Sera, Kira," he mumbled.

Sera smiled. "Nice to meet you."

"So you're Serjana," Kira drawled, her eyes narrowing slightly as she looked Sera over.

"What?" Sera asked. Kyle was surprised, too, by the use of her full name. "How did you know that?"

"It's on the class list," Kira replied easily. "Nice to meet you, too. I'll catch you both later," she said with a wink, turning to saunter down the hallway. Kyle watched as several students stopped what they were doing to stare.

"What was that about?" Sera muttered.

"No idea," Kyle said. He cleared his throat again, stuffing his hands in his pockets and studying Sera's schedule taped inside her locker. "So, the only other class we have together today is study hall. Want to head over to the senior lounge?"

"Yeah. Let me just run to the bathroom."

While he waited, Kyle nodded to a sandy-haired boy who gave him a respectful look but a wide berth as he walked past. Ryan Davenport was Beth's brother, recently inducted into the ranks of the Ne'feri. Like his sister, Ryan didn't much care for Kyle, and the look on his face was far from friendly.

"What's wrong?" Sera asked, returning from the bathroom.

"Nothing. Ne'feri politics."

Sera peered down the hallway, understanding dawning in her eyes as she caught sight of Ryan. "He'll come around. They're just—"

"Afraid of me."

"Cautious," Sera finished. "They don't know you like I do. Give them time."

"Whatever," Kyle said, slinging his backpack over one shoulder. He didn't need to prove himself to anyone—especially not an arrogant kid who'd never had it hard a day in his life. "Coming?"

In the senior lounge, Kyle and Sera found some space at a table off to the side, near one of the big bay windows. "Remind me again why we have to be here," he grumbled, staring resentfully at the pile of textbooks he'd placed in front of him. "I can't believe we have lab homework already. I'd take studying the Trimurtas tomes or Xibalba over this any day."

He'd spent half the summer reading and learning the pages Samsar had given him that outlined the major and minor gods in the pantheon. It'd been like summer deity school from hell, but at least now he knew who was who. Barely.

"We need to be here to protect the innocent." Sera leveled him with a ferocious look. "And no, you wouldn't."

He shook his head. "You're wrong. I'd literally go day camping in the seventh dimension of hell if I had the choice between that and finishing this chem lab."

"Don't even joke about it." Her look turned into a glare. "You're not Ra'al's son anymore, and you don't belong there. You never did."

"Tell that to everyone else," he muttered. Kyle shrugged in a half-hearted apology and opened his chemistry textbook. He sighed. "I'd bet Ryan would give anything to banish me."

"I'll banish you in a second if you don't stop your moping. The Ne'feri don't even like *me* at the moment. So you're not alone."

"You're not the progeny of the worst Demon Lord in Xibalba," he said sourly.

She rolled her eyes. "For the bazillionth time, we are not having this conversation. When your pity party for one is done, let me know."

They fell into an uncomfortable silence, and Kyle turned the pages of his book listlessly, watching Sera out of the corner of his eye and letting the drone of voices around him fill the troubled spaces in his mind. After a while, he turned away from his book and stared out the window at the dark, gloomy sky.

Kyle frowned. It'd been sunny an hour earlier, and the incoming clouds were thunderous and moving swiftly. It looked like a massive storm was brewing. His frown deepened as three shadows darted into the woods near the edge of the football field.

In the same breath, Kyle felt the tiny hairs on the nape of his neck stand at furious attention. The sensation of something otherworldly wound, snakelike, down his spine. He eyed Sera, who had gone rigid, her clear eyes darting to his. Her palms glowed a little and he tensed immediately. She could call forth weapons of fire from each hand at will—and if she was getting ready to do so, she must have sensed something, too. Something bad.

"You felt that?" he whispered.

"Yes." Sera slid her chair back, and Kyle followed suit. "This way."

He followed her out of the lounge, ignoring a penetrating look from Ryan Davenport. As they walked along the outer corridor, the crawling sensation against his spine intensified until it felt like his back was covered in tiny leeches suctioned to his skin. The tug of it was vile.

"I can feel something, whatever it is," he ground out as they pushed through the gym doors and walked onto the football field, resisting the urge to claw at his back. He jerked his head toward the woods, where he'd seen the shadows disappear before. "That way."

His voice sounded strained, even to him, and Sera's head whipped around. "Are you okay? You look really pale."

"Demons everywhere," he hissed through his teeth. "Can't you tell? They're pulling at me, *devouring* me."

Once they'd reached the edge of the woods, Sera grabbed Kyle's shoulders and shook him firmly. "Release your Azura energy. *You* control *them*, not the other way around. I can't do this without you. You're the only one who can separate any bonded rakshasas from their hosts. And I don't want to hurt innocent kids."

Lightning forked across the sky as Kyle sucked in a deep breath, pushing his energy toward the demonic beings he could feel pressing into him with invisible fingers. He closed his eyes until the flames of his dark nature flared to life inside him. As if by magic, a double-edged black sword with razor sharp teeth materialized in his hand. Its hot, red center pulsed with power, and Sera recoiled. Mordas—his father's weapon—had stolen many lives: demon, human, and immortal alike. But the dark, sentient sword served Kyle now.

In an instant, the tingling stopped, and Kyle nodded to Sera. She had transformed, too. But instead of radiating darkness like Kyle knew he was, she glowed with a brilliant light. A blood-red, flaming rapier extended from one of her hands, its silvery-white twin from the other, and scarlet mehndi curled in scripted vines up her arms and across her forehead. Iridescent armor covered her body, and a fierce look burned in her eyes.

"Let's go," she said.

They plunged deeper into the woods, running until they came to a dark, empty clearing. "Where are they?" Kyle whispered, looking over his shoulder, his grip on Mordas tightening.

"Everywhere," Sera said.

Her weapons flared brighter, and Kyle moved to stand back to back with her. That's when the demons slunk from between the trees. Some had human hosts while others showed their true forms. But they all eyed Kyle and Sera with the same lascivious greed.

"How many?" Kyle said, watching as a sickly green demon with half a head of exposed brains slipped closer. A black demon the size of a bull elephant stood behind him, swaying back and forth, its gaze slitted and furious.

"Forty," Sera said. "Maybe more. There are a lot of humans here. We can't hurt them, Kyle."

"I know."

With shrieks of rage, the demons rushed toward them. Kyle and Sera struck together, their weapons flying. They were careful not to kill any of the mortals, but it was getting harder and harder to differentiate between human and rakshasa as fists flew and teeth snapped. Kyle dipped low to jab the hilt of Mordas into a boy's head—he recognized the kid from biology—then jerked upward to slice through the guts of a scaled yellow demon with a mouth full of broken, blood-crusted teeth.

"There are so many of them," he shouted to Sera as black

ichor from a severed arm spurted into his face. Her arms were moving like liquid fire, dispatching and disarming.

"We're nearly there, I think," she said, panting from the exertion. Most of the humans lay unconscious and incapacitated, a result of their careful, non-lethal blows. Dead demons littered the earth in blackened clumps, reduced to bones and ash.

"I hope so, because I can't tell humans from demons anymore," Kyle shouted, slowing a kill strike as a girl's face loomed in front of him, her eyes bulging.

"They're all demons," a terrible voice echoed from behind them. "And the sooner you see that, the better."

As if by some unseen command, all the fighting stopped. The remaining demons fell, their bodies trembling and eyes rolling back in their heads. The possessed humans froze, rooted to the ground by some inexplicable force. Kyle met Sera's shocked eyes and turned in slow motion, a familiar face coming into view.

"Kira," he whispered.

She smiled, but there was no life in it—just cold fury. "One of my many names," she said.

"But I read your aura," Kyle blurted, his mind racing as Sera gasped beside him. "You're *mortal.*"

"Again, one of my many avatars—Parvati, Durga, Kali." She indicated her current body. "Kira."

"Kali," Sera said. "I should have known."

Kyle swayed, the ground seeming to tilt beneath him as the realization struck. He'd made the exact same mistake with Sera. He had been so worried about her being a demon that he hadn't considered that Kira could be something else. "You're a *goddess?*"

Kira laughed, throwing her head back just like she had in their classroom. Kyle could see black tattoos undulating like vines on her skin, curling up her temples into a black crown of thorns across her brow. "I like this name—Kira," she said, rolling the two syllables out on her tongue. "It means beam of light. Hopeful, really."

Kyle's breath caught. Kali, the goddess of freaking destruction, was here, and the last thing he felt was hope. He'd read about her during his brow-beating study of the Trimurtas texts. Neither Durga nor her berserker incarnation, Kali, had bothered with the happenings of the Mortal Realm for centuries—not since she'd killed a monstrous demon thousands of years ago.

According to the texts, every drop of that demon's blood that had fallen to the earth had created another demon replica, making it invincible and deadly. When Durga appeared to fight the beast, she'd needed help from the gods, and Kali had sprouted from her brow to drink the demon's blood. Kali had consumed the demon's clones and saved all of mankind. Then she'd danced on the bones and blood of the dead—including those of her own consort, Lord Shiva.

Kyle shivered at the mental image. On the battlefield, Kali had hardly been a beam of freaking light. Kira was a terrible name for a berserker goddess.

"Why are you here?" Sera asked.

"Serjana," Kira said with a slight nod of her head. "I was surprised by your choice to remain here on this diseased plane instead of returning to Illysia. Then again, darkness calls to darkness, doesn't it?"

"What are you doing here?" Sera repeated.

Kira's face hardened, but she covered it with an arrogant smirk. The air shimmered slightly around her as her body shifted, her skin going from bronzed brown to smoky black as a second pair of arms materialized out of her side. One held a bloodied sword, the other a trident. Her remaining hands were conspicuously empty. She waved them in a relaxed shrug, her eyes blazing from ebony to crimson.

"You already know why I'm here," Kira said. "To restore the balance. Ashes to ashes, and all that."

"But why?" Kyle said.

Kira bared blood-red lips, her teeth like sharp fangs, and she gestured toward the smoldering bodies before her. "Ignorance, decay, death, disease. I destroy only to re-create. The Mortal Realm must be flushed clean."

"It will be," Sera said slowly. "But there are innocent kids here. You don't need to destroy them to restore the balance."

"No one is innocent," Kira countered. "Especially not your companion."

Kyle bristled as those lightless eyes fastened on him. "I am an Azura Lord—a title granted by the gods you serve in Illysia."

"I serve no one."

Sera flashed him a look that said picking a fight with the goddess of destruction wasn't the best idea. He took a deep breath and swallowed the biting retort that had risen to his lips.

"We can save the humans," Sera interjected. "Kyle can release them and banish the demons back to Xibalba."

Kira propped one pair of hands on her hips, studying Kyle with her lower lip between her teeth. Even in goddess form, she made his thoughts fumble. To his dismay, he found his ears burning. A smile twitched at the corner of her mouth, as if she knew exactly what he was thinking. He flushed more deeply, and her smile widened. Was her power over him *that* transparent?

"To what end?" Kira asked after a beat. "Those demons will only return, slinking out of whichever portal they've come from. No, this plane must be purged."

Sera's eyes flashed silvery fire, and her weapons flared. "I can't let you do that."

"You're going to stop me?"

Kyle straightened, hefting Mordas in his palm. "No, she isn't. We are."

"Me, too." Ryan Davenport walked into the clearing, a crossbow in his hands.

Kira rolled her eyes. "Mortals. You always think you're more powerful than you are. What chance do you think you have, facing me? A child goddess who relinquishes her place in Illysia for this festering realm, a Ne'feri toddler still wet behind the ears, and a boy lord who doesn't know whether he wants to defy me or date me," she mocked. Kyle felt himself flushing, but he held his stance, gritting his teeth. Kira's smile widened to a grimace. "So be it."

The dark goddess moved swiftly then, demons scattering left and right as she cut a path through them to Kyle. She swung her sword to clash into Mordas, steel bearing down on steel, with gritted teeth. Kyle could feel her rage in the blow and it took almost all of his strength not to collapse beneath its weight. He swung back up, but Kira deflected his blow with her sword while thrusting her trident toward

Sera's stomach. Sera sidestepped, her red sword tracing a fiery trail down Kira's back. She howled, a red tongue lolling from her mouth in rage, and kicked Ryan in the stomach just as he darted in. He went flying and slammed against a tree, crumpling to the earth and not moving again.

Sera dashed to Ryan's side, mouthing to Kyle that he was alive before hurling herself back into the scuffle, her cries shattering the stillness. Sera was a silver and crimson blur, Kira a dark tornado of movement, and Kyle could barely keep up with either of them. He halted, panting, unwilling to risk striking Sera. Mordas, as he'd learned, would gorge itself on friend or foe.

The battle seemed evenly matched, but Kyle felt afraid for Sera nonetheless. She was a skilled fighter, but this was *Kali*. Rage embodied. The mistress of time and everything beyond. According to what he'd read, she was what remained when the universe ended. Which didn't bode well for this universe—and everyone in it.

The two goddesses moved so fast that it seemed as if the earth was moving instead of their bodies. Demons in their path were ground into dust. Humans, too. Sera's face went white with pain at each human casualty, but every ounce of her strength was caught up in keeping Kira on the defensive.

And then the unthinkable happened. Kira darted forward, her sword arm and trident swinging, cleaver-like, at Sera's neck. Sera dodged the attack, but couldn't quite twist away from the third arm swooping in below to clutch her throat in a death grip. Kyle gasped. As an immortal, Sera couldn't die, but if she lost to Kira, hundreds of people would.

He had to do something.

Without thinking, Kyle summoned his Azura energy, the power filling him to the brim and crackling beneath the surface of his skin like electricity. His teeth chattered with the force of it, and his entire body ached from holding it in. Focusing on the bemused humans—some awake, some not— he thrust the power outward, peeling all the demons from their hosts in one fell swoop. Their screeches cut through the ear like the howls of cats as they relinquished the bodies they'd defiled.

Both Sera and Kira froze to stare at him, their arms and weapons falling to their sides, but Kyle didn't stop. He dragged each of the demons toward him, kneeling and placing his hand on the singed earth. Red embers glowed beneath his fingers as he chanted a guttural language under his breath. A glowing red circle appeared and, one by one, he banished each of the remaining demons through the portal.

"There," he said gruffly. "Are we good now? Demons, banished. Humans, saved. I think we're done here."

Sera was staring at him with shock in her eyes, while Kira's gaze burned with something like grudging respect.

"It's not about a handful of demons," Kira said. "It's the infestation of this entire plane."

"An infestation we can end," he replied coolly. "One *I* can end."

She was silent for a long moment, as if considering. Kyle held his breath and waited for her to speak. Her response would decide the fate of humanity.

Kira's voice, when it came, was soft. "Can you do this on a large scale, as you did just now?"

"Yes."

"Very well." Nodding, she turned and dipped into a short bow in Sera's direction. Sera returned the formality, though her face remained wary. "Then perhaps my mandate can wait for a bit. See if you can restore order," Kira said slowly. "This is the only chance I will grant you, so use it wisely."

Shifting into her human shade, Kira walked to Kyle's side. He stiffened. After a searching look in their direction, Sera turned around to tend to some of the unconscious kids lying around the clearing. Kyle's gaze returned to Kira.

"Your powers are more impressive than I expected," she said with a smile.

"Were you really going to kill everyone?" Kyle asked. "Wipe out the earth?"

Kira smiled wider. "I've done it before. Purging from time to time is healthy."

"But not now?"

"But not now," she agreed, stepping closer so that they were almost nose-to-nose. Kyle could smell cinnamon and sweat. He held his breath. "I could make you forget her, you know," Kira whispered.

"I know you can." Kyle licked dry lips, trying to hold his stupid body in check while his thoughts ran wild. "And I'd like to take you up on that one day. But not now." Then he tapped the ground with his foot so that the portal he'd summoned to Illysia glowed white. "Safe travels, Kira."

Her dark eyes went wide and her laugh as she vanished was as carefree and uninhibited as it had been before. He stared at the portal cinching shut, the sound of Kira's laughter strumming along his nerve endings. He hadn't felt so alive in months, and it was because of a goddess.

Another goddess. Seriously, couldn't he fall for a normal girl—one who couldn't kick his butt without blinking? Was that too much to ask? He had to be cursed or something.

He turned to Sera, who was now crouched at Ryan's side. "How's he doing?"

"A bit banged up, but he'll be fine."

"What about the others?"

"Most of the survivors are confused, but unhurt," Sera said as she looked around, assessing the carnage. Sorrow swam in her eyes. "We've lost so many."

Kyle didn't respond. Though people had died, the truth was, they could have lost so many more. They could have lost all of humanity. Kira—or Kali, or whoever she was—had given them a generous reprieve. Who knew how long it would last?

They needed to figure out how the demons were getting into the Mortal Realm, and fast. Or face the end of the world as they knew it.

Kali wouldn't be so forgiving a third time.

THE SISTERS DIVINE

❧❧

"What do you mean, *Kali* showed up at your school?" Sera's mother shrieked. Her gaze flew between her human husband and her goddess daughter, who was now intently focused on the apple she was eating. "What was she doing there?"

"She called herself Kira, and she said the Mortal Realm needed to be cleansed," Sera said, avoiding her furious eyes. The last thing she wanted was for her mother to see how scared she'd really been. "We took care of it, Mom. Kyle and I."

"She's not something you can *take care of*!" Her mom turned, exasperated, to her dad. "Sam—"

Her father stood up, rubbing his wife's shoulders. "Sera said she's gone now, Sophia. Everything is okay, at least for the moment. We'll figure it out with the Trimurtas."

"It's not okay," Sophia said. "She shouldn't have come at all. I doubt that the Trimurtas would have resorted to this— not now, not after everything we and the Ne'feri have been doing. So perhaps she's doing this of her own volition, which would make her very, *very* dangerous." Her voice shook as her gaze darted back to Sera. "There's a reason she is called the destroyer of the universe. Trust me, she's not interested in making friends." Her brow furrowed. "Was she in goddess form or mortal form?"

"Both," Sera said. "In her human shade, she looked like any other student."

Well, not exactly *like any other student,* she amended in her head, remembering the goddess's drop-dead good looks and superstar charisma.

"Are you sure it was her?" Sophia asked hopefully. "There are thousands of deities, or incarnations of them—maybe you're thinking of someone else. The last thing Kali looks like is anyone else."

Sera stopped chewing. "It was Kali, mom. She morphed into a version of her goddess self when we were fighting the demons, and she looked just like how she's described in the texts. Ebony skin, crazy hair, red eyes, skulls everywhere."

"Demons?" her mother whispered, paling. "You were fighting demons with her—*today*?"

Sera stared at her mother. She lowered the apple. "Mom? Are you okay?" Seriously, the woman looked like she was about to faint.

"There's only one reason she'd come," her mother whispered, almost to herself, shaking her head as if in denial. "Eleanor was right."

Eleanor was Beth's mom, and head of the Ne'feri of the eastern seaboard. Sera perked up. What was Eleanor right about? Was it anything to do with what Beth had been trying to tell her today? Maybe she'd finally get some answers.

"Mom, what happened at the last Ne'feri meeting?" Sera asked. "I saw Beth today, and she said something weird about a demon infestation. Then Mara and some new Yoddha-in-training appeared before she could explain why she thought so many demons were appearing on the Mortal Plane." She took a shallow breath. "And get this—she made Beth drop what she was saying. Like she was trying to keep something from me. Something Mara said *Dev* wanted hidden."

Her parents exchanged a weighted glance before Sophia cleared her throat and shook her head. "Wait a moment, are you sure it was Kali you saw, and not Durga?" she asked.

"What?" Sera said, frowning. "Aren't they versions of the same goddess?"

"Sometimes. It depends. Kali appears in extreme circumstances."

Sera shrugged. Even as a goddess herself, she couldn't keep track of all the gods' different incarnations. Apparently, even she had been several of them in previous lifetimes. "Well, it was Kali this time. She said so. Anyway, she's gone. Kyle sent her back to Illysia. Now will you stop stalling and answer my question about the last meeting?"

Sophia and Sam's meaningful glances were starting to irritate Sera. She opened her mouth to complain, but shut it as her father spoke, with a pained exhale.

"Beth's right," Sam said. "About the rakshasa infestation. It's . . . concerning."

Something in his tone made her eyes snap to his.

"Concerning, as in Kali Yuga proportions?" The Mortal Realm couldn't survive another near apocalypse, not so soon after the last.

Sam shook his head. "We don't know."

"You . . . don't know," Sera repeated slowly, searching her father's face. There was more he wasn't telling her. She knew she could break past the human defenses of his mind if she had to—goddess power and all that—but she held back. He was her *dad*, after all. She might be immortal, but she was still his seventeen-year-old daughter, and Caelum house rules applied. Like "respect your parents" and "no mind reading."

He tugged on his hair, a nervous tell that had Sera's hackles rising. "We have a few theories, but we're working through them."

Sera nodded at his bland response, tempering her frustration. Clearly, she wasn't going to get any more out of him.

Just then, the small blond hurricane that was her brother, Nate, burst into the room.

"Hey, bud," Sam said, rumpling his son's head of curls. "How was your first day of middle school?"

"Awesome, Dad," Nate said, throwing his backpack onto the kitchen counter and grabbing a banana from the fruit bowl. "I made a bunch of friends," he said with his mouth full. "Get this, there's a boy there whose dad is a producer in Hollywood. Like, the *real* Hollywood."

Sera rolled her eyes. Nate's obsession with filmmaking was an epic pain in the butt. Months before, he'd tried to make a documentary profiling Xibalba and the seven levels of hell, nearly getting himself abducted and killed in the process. Unlike Sera, Nate wasn't immortal—while Sam had been Azura when Sera was born, he'd become human before Nate was conceived. But he *was* half Sanrak, and though he'd never shown signs of having divine gifts, Sera knew they could manifest at any time.

"Planning to conquer the film industry?" Sera asked her brother drily.

"That's how I roll." Nate grinned. He spread his palms wide, the dimple in his cheek deepening and his eyes flashing with mischief. "Fake it 'til you make it."

Sera bit her cheek to suppress a giggle and smirked at her parents. "Bet you're regretting letting him go to middle school."

Sophia smiled weakly, her troubled expression not quite fading. "Home school is always an option."

Nate's eyes went wide. "No way."

"Mom's only teasing," Dad said. "Go do your homework. We have some old friends coming over for dinner. My old partner from the law firm and his family—the Kumars? They're back in town."

"I saw Jemitra—I mean Jem—at school today," Sera said, a warm feeling spreading in her stomach. It had been the only bright, *normal* spot in her day.

"Who?" Nate said.

"You wouldn't remember them," Sera said. "But when you were three, you used to follow Jem around everywhere."

"They moved into the Becketts' old house a few streets over." Her father smiled. "Like old times, right?"

Sure—aside from her mother being a goddess, her father being a former Azura Lord, and Sera practically being married to one of the Lords of Illysia, it was *exactly* like old times. Sera sighed. Still, dinner with the Kumars would be nice. No demons, no goddess history, no fate of the world hanging on her shoulders.

Sera headed for her room, grabbing her backpack on the way. It was pathetic how much she was looking forward to doing homework. It was just so *ordinary*. But just as she was closing the door to her bedroom, her phone buzzed with an incoming text from Kyle.

—Hey. You free? Sal's?

Sera thought about it for a minute before her fingers skimmed the phone's screen. Can't. Dinner plans.

—Half hour tops? Need to talk.

Sera sighed, tapping her phone against her palm. Her mother would never allow it. It was a school night, and Sophia was already in a mood about the Kira thing. But Kyle needed her. She'd be back in more than enough time for dinner, and with any luck, her parents wouldn't even know she'd been gone.

—Pick me up? Same spot.

—See you in 10.

She climbed out of her window and edged her way across the slate roofing tiles, chuckling quietly to herself. She was a goddess—she could defy gravity, for heaven's sake—and here she was, creeping around her roof like a human-sized squirrel. Smiling, she inched around to the side of the house that was partially hidden by a large oak tree and jumped— okay, floated—the fifteen feet to the soft grass below.

"You're going to get into trouble doing that, you know," a low voice filtered down to her.

Sera nearly jumped back onto the roof, her heart in her throat, at the sight of the figure propped casually in the limbs of the tree. "Nate! You scared the crap out of me."

"Sneaking out?"

"What are you doing in a tree?" she evaded. "Aren't you supposed to be doing homework?"

Nate eyed his sister pointedly. "Some of us can't just *fly* off the roof."

Sera sucked in a breath. "*You're* sneaking out?"

"Learned from the best."

"You can't. You're too little."

Her brother swung down the last few branches and landed at her feet, wiping his palms on his jeans. "I'll keep your secret if you keep mine." He stuck one hand out toward her. "Shake on it."

"It doesn't work like that. You're eleven. I'm almost eighteen."

"You'll still get into trouble if I tell Mom."

He had her there. She frowned at him. "Where are you going, anyway?"

Nate flushed a violent shade of red, which, with his creamy complexion, made his cheeks look like two shiny red apples. "I promised someone I'd help them with something."

Sera's frown deepened. "Who?"

Nate traced the tip of his sneaker in the dirt, the red from his cheeks seeping down his neck. "Stella."

"Wait, Stella from next door?" she asked. Nate nodded miserably. As understanding dawned on her, Sera nearly giggled, which she knew her brother would not appreciate. "Let me get this straight. You're in public school for one day, and you already have a girlfriend?"

"No," he said quickly. "She needed help with our math assignment, and I did it on the bus."

Sera grinned. "Doing her homework isn't going to win you any brownie points. Trust me."

"How would you know?" Nate shot back. "You didn't go on a single date until last year, and then you found out you were married to a god. I'm pretty sure listening to any of your dating advice would get me ghosted." Sera gaped at Nate's back as he brushed past her. He stopped at the gap in the fence and stared at her over his shoulder. "So, do we have a deal?"

"Yeah," she murmured, dazed. One trip to Xibalba and her sweet, innocent little brother seemed twenty years older. Shaking her head, she checked the front yard and then raced down the sidewalk to two houses down the block, where Kyle was waiting. She collapsed into the front seat of his car, breathing hard.

"You okay?"

"Nate has a girlfriend."

"Whoa. Skills."

Sera shot him a glare. "He's eleven."

"Mad skills?"

She chucked him in the arm. "Is that the only thing boys ever think about? Hooking up with girls?"

Kyle drove off slowly and winked. "We think about other things, too, like eating and sleeping. But yeah, mostly girls. So, who's the babe?"

"Neighbor," she said, ducking as they drove past her house and then the house Dev had lived in the year before, in his human shade, just to be close to her. She wasn't missing the irony of the fact that her little brother was now into their other next-door neighbor.

She sighed, staring at Dev's vacant house, and Kyle glanced over at her. "Seen him at all?"

"Not in a while."

"I'm sure he's busy, ruling Illysia and all," Kyle offered.

"Yeah."

They rode the rest of the way to Sal's diner on the outskirts of town in silence. Sera didn't want to think about why Dev hadn't come to see her, or why he didn't want her to know what was going on with the demons. She wanted to focus on something else—anything else.

She knew she was being stupid. If she wanted to see Dev, she could. Easily.

But she didn't want to. She was too proud to run to him like a kid begging for handouts. If he wanted to keep secrets from her, then fine. She was *fine* with that.

"I'm ordering an entire plate of hash browns," she announced as they entered the diner.

"That bad?" Kyle said with a quirk of his eyebrow.

"Hash browns solve everything."

"So they say."

The diner was jam-packed but they managed to get a booth in the middle. Sera nodded at the owner, who was standing near the kitchen. Big Jim's lips curled into their customary scowl as the waitress came over to take their orders. Kyle ordered his usual bean-and-cheese burrito. After Sera ordered a coffee along with her heaping plate of hash browns, she leaned back in the booth and sighed, studying the faded, peeling, aqua-colored wallpaper in comfortable silence.

Seriously, Sal's was one of the few places where she could just be herself—a girl. No more and no less. No goddesses and demons or secret light and dark dimensions. No pressures and responsibilities. No evil Azuras trying to take over the world. It was Sal's—and that was all she needed. She drummed her fingers on the cracked red vinyl of the booth, tension easing from her body. She felt freer at Sal's than anywhere else—

freer, even, than in the secret world she and Dev had created together.

Sera hadn't been to that world since the day she'd told Dev that she wouldn't be returning with him to Illysia. She was afraid that going back would make her feel that she made the wrong choice. She had chosen the Mortal Realm and her family over the god she was forever linked to. And each day that passed without her seeing Dev felt like a month. Sera would never tell anyone that, though—being so emotionally dependent on someone was all-consuming, in a way she never expected. And now she couldn't even get answers without Dev's permission. Her fingers dug into the vinyl of the seat as she angrily stripped off a thin section. And then felt instantly guilty for defacing private property.

"What's wrong?" Kyle said, squinting at her. "You went all blotchy."

"Nothing."

The waitress poured Sera a steaming cup of coffee and Sera mumbled her thanks. Discarding the strip, she wrapped her marauding fingers around the mug and took a long gulp. "God, this coffee is the best in the world."

"You're deluded," Kyle tossed back, grimacing as he put his cup down. "It tastes like liquid dirt. Dirt with a splash of coffee."

"The best," she said after another sip. "How's Carla?"

"Fine," he said as the waitress delivered a plate of steaming hash browns and Kyle's burrito to the table. "You know Carla. She's just glad I made it to senior year. Now I just have to finish it, and she'll be off my back."

Despite his grouchy tone, Sera knew how much Kyle

loved Carla. His foster mom had always been there for him, and he wanted to make her happy more than anything. If that meant he had to graduate, Sera knew he would do it, despite his constant moaning. "Well, you made it through the first day, so that's a start," she said.

Kyle tucked into his burrito and said, his mouth full, "Barely. Did you forget we almost got creamed by a feral goddess?"

Sera rolled her eyes, spearing some potato with her fork. "As if I could. My mom nearly popped a vein."

"You think she would have done it?" he asked quietly, pausing between bites. "Killed all those kids? Purged the earth?"

Sera shrugged. "My mom seems to think so. From the way she was behaving, you'd think we dodged an atomic bomb. Thanks to you, that is." Her eyes narrowed at him. "How did you do that, anyway? I've never seen you handle so many demons in one go."

"Not sure. I didn't think about it; I just did it."

"You told Kira you could do it again. Can you?"

Kyle's worried gaze met hers. "I honestly don't know." He leaned in, placing his half-eaten burrito down. "What do you think is causing it? All the smaller demons suddenly showing up, possessing human hosts?"

"I was going to ask *you* that. You're the portal master."

"The portals I control are all sealed. The demons have to be coming from somewhere else." His brow scrunched up in concentration. "There's got to be an exit point, somewhere nobody's thought to look—not us and not the Ne'feri. Maybe Ra'al created another gateway to the Dark Realms when he was here, and we missed it."

But Sera shook her head. "Demons can't portal in and out of this realm on their own, unless it's through a portal created by an immortal. Maybe someone's helping them? Like my uncle was."

The thought of Azrath's coup left a sour taste in her mouth—he'd plotted with the worst Demon Lord in Xibalba to murder his own brother and use Sera to get into Illysia.

"Azrath is gone."

"Doesn't mean the Demon Lords couldn't have other allies who want to break into Illysia and to rule the Mortal Realm. Could be anyone."

Kyle shoved the last of his burrito into his mouth, chewing rapidly as he thought. He started to speak and then stopped, looking doubtful. Sera waited. Finally, Kyle took a deep breath. "What if Kira is the one helping them? She wants to purge the earth, right?"

"I don't know," she answered honestly, her brain scanning through what she knew of the goddess. "She's known sometimes as the great protector and the great mother."

"What mother would want to destroy her own children, no matter how awful they are?" His laugh was hollow. "Well, mine would have."

"Yours was a demented Azura."

"True." He fidgeted in his seat, picking at a corner of the peeling tabletop. "I don't trust Kira."

Sera grinned knowingly, reaching for another forkful of potato. "You don't trust yourself, you mean."

"Same difference."

"Not the same at all." She glanced at the clock on the wall and winced. It was nearly five thirty already. It would take a miracle for her to make it home without being discovered. With a contented murmur, she shoved the last of the fried potatoes into her mouth. "I have to go. But admit it—you like her, and that scares you."

The expression on Kyle's face was comical. "She's a goddess. And she's gone."

"Five bucks says she'll be back."

He groaned. "Can we not talk about this right now?"

"You mean about Kira, or your love life in general?"

"Both." He sighed heavily.

"Too late," Sera said, looking past him. "Because you owe me five bucks. Super-crush just walked in."

"What?" Kyle spun around and then turned back to his plate, his expression panicked.

Over his shoulder, Sera studied the girl who had stopped to speak to Big Jim in a low voice. She wore a tan skirt with brown leather boots and a soft ruby-colored sweater. Her glossy, dark hair was fashioned into a neat braid at the base of her neck, and she looked poised and beautiful, a far cry from the leather-clad style of the girl they'd seen at school.

Sera squinted. She was definitely the same person—she had the same bone structure, the same dark eyes, and the same warm brown complexion. Her face was flawless, but the dark rings of kohl around her eyes and the blood-red lipstick she'd flaunted earlier were both conspicuously missing.

Kyle gave her a bewildered look in response to her expression, and Sera shrugged, offering the first explanation she could think of. "She looks . . . different. Maybe she had a job interview, or went to church, or something."

"Why is she here?" Kyle said in a strangled voice. "At Sal's?"

"She could be hungry."

"But why *here*?"

Sera wondered the same thing, but it seemed like all of Illysia knew what she and Kyle were doing at any given moment. No doubt Mara and Ilani were hiding in the rafters. "Maybe she knew you were going to be here?"

Kyle shot her a dirty look as the girl moved to sit at the counter directly across from their booth. Either she hadn't seen them, or she didn't feel like socializing. But after a minute, she turned to look around, her gaze moving past their booth and then returning to them. There was no acknowledgment—or recognition—in the cursory glance.

"Hey, Kira," Sera said.

Confusion flickered across her face for a second, and then smoothed out. She nodded. "Oh, you must mean my sister." Her voice was melodious, the complete opposite to the husky tone they'd both heard her use before.

"Sister?" Kyle blurted out.

The girl smiled, making her eyes sparkle. Her whole face gleamed from the force of that smile. "Yes. I'm Darika. Her twin."

Why would Kira—Kali's mortal avatar—have a twin?

Sera froze, her brain jumping into overdrive. The realization hit her like a cold slap to the face. It wasn't one goddess incarnating as two sisters. It was *two* goddesses.

The blood drained from her body, and her limbs suddenly felt boneless. *Of course.* It all made sense now—if Kali was here, a mortal incarnation of a twin sister could mean only one thing.

Durga was here, too.

THE GODDESS
YOU KNOW

◈◈◈

Twenty minutes later, Kyle was standing in Sera's kitchen—which, strangely, was starting to become as familiar as Sal's—his gaze swinging from Sophia to Sera and back.

Durga. It made sense, and yet it seemed ridiculous. What were the odds that two warrior goddesses, both known for their prowess in battle, would take on human avatars at the same time? Kyle wasn't sure what it meant, but it couldn't be good.

He swallowed hard. "How do you know she's Durga?" he asked Sera's mother. "Aren't they the same?"

"Yes and no," Sophia said, shooting him a wary look. Kyle squirmed. Though she'd come to trust him more in recent months, Sera's mother had always been aloof toward him, especially in the presence of her daughter. Her gaze fell back on Sera. "You remember what I told you? What people believe about the gods of Illysia?"

Sera nodded. "Human beings have different beliefs about heaven and hell, but all religions are versions of one single truth, and all the gods and goddesses are inherently the same, born of one Supreme Being."

"Brahman," Sophia confirmed with a flat smile. "The gods and goddesses we know, and the incarnations of them—like Dev and like you—have all come into being or taken human forms for a specific purpose. They all appear at different times, for different reasons. In your case, it was to defend the Mortal Realm against Ra'al and Azrath." She frowned. "We can only assume that Darika and Kira, too, have been sent here for a reason by the Trimurtas."

"To fight the rakshasa infestation," Sera guessed.

But Kyle shook his head, his stomach clenching into knots. He couldn't ignore his instincts—not when they had served him so well in the past. "No, not fight. Kira said she's here to *purge* the mortal plane. That's a big difference. Those were her words." Their stares converged on him and he stuffed his hands into his pockets. "And if the Trimurtas didn't mean to kill everyone, why send both of them?"

Sophia cleared her throat, her mouth opening and closing a few times. Kyle couldn't recall the last time he'd seen her at a loss for words. She smoothed an ashen brow with shaky fingertips and looked to Sera's dad, who also looked troubled.

"In the scriptures, there are many stories about the reason Kali first came into being," Sam said, almost to himself. "Some say that when Durga fought the fearsome rakshasa Mahishasura millennia ago, Kali burst forth from her forehead in a fit of rage to defeat the demon. Others say that Kali was formed when the goddess Parvati shed part of her skin. But these stories have one thing in common: they describe Kali as the transformer of time, called upon only when the world is at its end."

Sera's gasp was loud. "And you think that's now? But we stopped Ra'al. We stopped the KaliYuga, the apocalypse."

"I agree with Kyle," Sam went on. "It doesn't make sense that Kali and Durga would appear simultaneously. Durga is a warrior goddess in her own right. She is an incarnation of Parvati"—his gaze slid to his daughter—"just as you are an incarnation of Lakshmi."

Kyle frowned, recalling the information Sam had drilled into him. "Isn't Parvati the goddess of love?"

"Yes," Sophia said. "But also of power and divine strength. She's Shiva's consort—and we all know what *he* does."

Sophia didn't have to explain. Kyle knew who Lord Shiva was. The Trimurtas consisted of three main gods—Brahma, who created, Vishnu, who sustained, and Shiva, who dissolved. Shiva was called the Destroyer, just as Dev was known as the Protector.

Kyle felt suddenly queasy. There had to be a reason that the god known as *the Destroyer* had sent his consorts—or wives, or whatever you wanted to call them—to the Mortal Realm, and it wasn't because he was bored.

"This can't be happening," Sophia muttered, leaning heavily on the kitchen counter, her forehead creasing with worry. "If Kali has manifested as Kira, that must mean that the Trimurtas believes the world is on the brink of apocalypse."

Her already ashen countenance had paled considerably. She—an immortal herself—looked haggard, and Kyle sucked in a shaky breath. "But Sera's right," he said. "We prevented the KaliYuga. I killed the rakshasa that Ra'al summoned with my blood."

Sam, who was pacing agitatedly, cleared his throat. "That doesn't mean that Ra'al's forces aren't still at work. Even the Ne'feri have been whispering about something far worse on the horizon. The Demon Lords are persistent. Evil doesn't just stop when we tell it to. Illysia and Xibalba will always be battling for the souls of humankind."

Conversation stalled as a wide-eyed Nate ambled into the kitchen with an innocent look on his face. "Hey, guys."

Kyle stifled a laugh. The guileless expression was pure performance—Nate had probably been eavesdropping on the whole conversation. The kid had a knack for being in the right place at the right time, especially when sensitive information was being discussed. Maybe he'd inherited it. You couldn't be the child of a goddess without being unique in some way.

Kyle went still at the realization.

The boy was special, there was no denying that. He'd never thought to read Nate, to look past the cherubic face and childish humor. There'd never been any need to, but now, Kyle was curious. He opened his power of sight, letting his gift flow through him, and focused on Nate's aura.

At first glance, Nate felt mortal, but there was something indeterminate below the surface that Kyle couldn't quite categorize. It reminded him of when he'd first taken measure of Dev, whose energy had been formless. Kyle withdrew as Nate's green eyes met his, a faintly mocking expression on his face—as if he somehow knew what Kyle had been doing. Kyle shrugged guiltily and looked away.

One thing was certain: if any godlike abilities ever decided to manifest, Nate would be a force to contend with.

"Nate," Sophia warned. "I've told you time and time again that these conversations aren't for your ears."

"I wasn't listening, I swear."

"Save it. Go finish your homework."

"Already did," he chirped. "Aren't we supposed to be having dinner with the Kumars? It's nearly seven."

Sophia shrieked, making everyone flinch. Kyle almost summoned Mordas. "Oh heavens, the casserole!"

Kyle met Sera's eyes across the kitchen counter as Sophia rushed toward the oven and started herding them all out of the room. "Guess I'll catch you later."

"You're not staying?"

"No, thanks," he said with a glance at Sera's mother. He didn't want to outstay his welcome, especially not at a family dinner with old friends. Even if he had nowhere else to be.

Sera walked him to the front door. "You sure?"

"I've got a project proposal for modern world studies that's due tomorrow. I'll see you in school, okay?" He lowered his voice. "Let me know if your parents find out more after they talk with the Ne'feri or the Trimurtas."

He headed back to his car and climbed in. It was still early, and Kyle didn't want to head back to Carla's just yet, despite the homework burning a hole in his backpack. Honestly, who made students nail down their senior research project after the first day of school? Evil teachers, that was who.

Kyle sighed. He had worse things to worry about than some research project—even one investigating the causes of change in the world. He grinned to himself. He could propose a paper on how a bunch of Demon Lords got together and plotted to devour all the souls of the living. That would probably go over *great* with the administration.

He drove aimlessly for several miles before finding himself pulling into the parking lot of Sal's. Even though he'd just left, it was that or Carla's—and he didn't want to talk to his foster mom about school or grades. Kyle got of the car and rolled his neck, groaning at the sharp ache shooting through his shoulders. He leaned against the side of his car and closed his eyes for a moment. It felt like sharp teeth were biting into his muscles. And he still couldn't shake the unsettled feeling that remained in his belly.

The roar of an engine pierced the silence as a familiar sleek black motorcycle pulled into the parking lot next to where he was standing. He sighed outwardly, but inwardly every part of him came alive. It had to be *her*.

He watched as the rider threw one black-clad leg over the side of the bike and pulled her helmet off, glossy hair falling loose. Not Darika this time, but Kira. Kyle couldn't help his immediate response to her. Sure, she was a goddess—a dangerous one, hell-bent on the destruction of the world—but something inside of him responded to that danger with excitement.

"Miss me already?" he drawled. A good offense was the best defense.

"Nice trick earlier," she tossed back, "but I come and go as I please."

"You guys must really like this place," he said, pushing off the side of his car and tucking his hands into his pockets. "Your sister was here, too."

Kira's dark eyes met his, confusion puckering her brow. "She was?"

"Yeah. She looked just like you." His gaze slid from her head to her scuffed leather boots and he smiled. "Not exactly like you," he amended.

As they walked into the diner he nodded to Jim, who glowered back, and headed toward an empty booth in the back. Kira followed, drawing every eye in the place. The minute Kyle sat on the cracked vinyl seat, he felt the tension leave his body.

"Coffee," he told the waitress. Her nametag read NANCY.

"I'll take a shot of the whiskey Big Jim has behind the counter," Kira added with a wink. "The one he keeps for special customers."

Nancy frowned. "Do you have ID?"

"I don't need ID."

Nancy blinked, her eyes glazing over for a moment before she nodded and headed back to the counter. "That's neat," Kyle commented. "Using goddess compulsion on poor mortals. Isn't that frowned upon in Illysia?"

Kira grinned smugly. "I want what I want. And to tell the truth, the whiskey makes it easier to bear being stuck in this human form."

"You mean keeping Kali under wraps."

Her eyes flashed, as did her smile, but she didn't respond. Nancy delivered his coffee along with a shot glass of whiskey. Kyle watched as Kira tossed back the drink, licking her lips, then returned his gaze to his coffee. The blood in his veins thrummed with electricity. He was a good guy at heart—but God, she made him want to do bad things.

Kyle flushed. Being in love with Sera had never made him feel this unhinged. This *combustible*. And Kyle knew just how dangerous this kind of attraction could be. These kinds of romances never turned out well—there was always a casualty, and he'd bet his left arm that it would be him.

He cleared his throat. "So, about your sister. She said her name was Darika."

"Interesting."

"What's interesting?" he asked.

"That she'd be here." She shrugged at his quizzical look. "My sister is . . . eccentric."

"One could say the same thing about you." His laugh was hollow. "You don't get along?"

"No, it's not like that. We just have"—she paused, as if searching for the right words—"different interests. It's strange that she would come to a place like this."

"And you would?"

"Looks like it." An impish smile curved her lips. "Plus, I followed you."

"Not that I don't like being stalked by a cute girl, but you know that's—how did you put it again?—borderline creepy, right," he said, tossing her own words back at her.

"I told you, I want what I want," she replied with a shake of her head. "And I like you. You intrigue me."

"You don't know me."

She smiled again. "Oh, they talk about you plenty in Illysia. How you risked your life to save the Mortal Realm from the designs of your father. How you're gifted with the rare ability to see people for what they truly are." She leaned back, spreading her arms on the back of the booth. "Tell me, Kyle, what do you see when you look at me in my true form?"

"Why?"

"Humor me."

Despite the warning bells pealing in his brain, Kyle let his energy surge forward to meet Kira's. He'd expected to feel something once his aura connected with hers, but the strength of the jolt took him by surprise. Her energy was savage, a powerful void sucking at him, drawing him in.

The waves of her goddess aura, undulating in smoky bands of gray and red, surrounded him. Kyle drew a sharp breath. He could never withstand her strength, he knew, if she chose to overcome him. He took a different approach. Instead of struggling against the push and pull of her turbulent energy, he held himself still, letting its waves break over and around him as if he were a rock.

"You're stronger than I expected," she murmured.

He grunted. "And you're more terrible than I thought."

Kira's burst of laughter drew the attention of most of the diner's patrons. Kyle could feel their energies brighten in response. Even Big Jim, whose sour expression had become a permanent fixture, wore a blissful expression that looked totally nauseating on his face. Kyle shook his head.

"So?" Kira coaxed. "Tell me what you see."

Nodding, he let the murky haze of her aura settle and beheld the goddess Kali in all her terrifying glory. His breath hitched, his heart battering his ribcage—not with fear, though he was more than a little afraid, but with awe. Unlike Sera in her true goddess form—beautiful and timeless, her flickering aura taking the shape of a lotus flower—Kira was fierce. Fearsome.

Her midnight-blue skin gleamed. He knew from his studies that the darkness of it represented the transcendence of all colors because she was the end and the beginning of all things. Her dark hair hung loose and wild, and her eyes blazed with cosmic energy. A long red tongue protruded from her lips. She was nude, but that was not surprising—she was not a goddess who gave in to illusion, including clothing. It was hard to look away from her.

Kyle sucked in a sharp breath at the perfection of her body, unmarred by the garland of skulls hanging from her neck and demon head earrings that swung from her ears. They were both symbolic, but that made them no less gruesome. Two of her four arms were occupied: one with a bloody sword and the other with a freshly severed head. The other two beckoned, offering promises of the comfort of her embrace.

Kyle expelled a shuddering breath and released the connection. His heart was racing. He felt alive, his blood pounding hot and furious in his veins. Kira was pure female energy—shakti. And it was more than intoxicating.

It was deadly.

"I am not as bad as all the stories make me out to be," she said, watching him. "I don't take life without cause. People only fear me because they aren't ready to be liberated."

"Liberated from what?"

"Material attachment. Self-admiration."

Kyle stared at her. "Is that what you intend to do—liberate them?"

One elegant shoulder lifted in a shrug as a smile curled the corner of her lips. "Human beings are bound to their egos, and that is the path to Xibalba. I only offer release and unification with the one Supreme Being. Moksha."

"Moksha?"

"Eternal freedom from samsara, the karmic cycle of death and rebirth. I offer hope for those who are ready to leave the suffering of this world behind."

Playing it cool, Kyle leaned back and rested both arms over the back of the seat. "Sounds complicated."

"Think of moksha like attaining nirvana," Kira said. "It's all about karma. If you do good things, you move forward in your next life. If you do bad things, you go backward. It's pretty straightforward."

"I know what moksha is, Kira. I'm the guy who sends souls on their way. But I like to think of it like a moral bank." He shrugged. "Kind of like those house point hourglasses in *Harry Potter*? You know, where you fill them up with good deeds, not bad ones?"

"*Harry Potter?*"

Kyle grinned at her scathing expression. "Cool stories about a boy wizard. You'd like them."

"Don't be absurd." She paused, her eyes meeting and holding his. Clearly, she wasn't entertained. "My truest followers see me as a benevolent goddess—one who can cleanse away their fears, who can take away sin, decay, and ignorance."

He swallowed, his amusement fading as he tore his gaze away. "I am sure you can be. But you don't want to liberate a few souls. You want to destroy the entire Mortal Realm."

"Bodies are temporary," she said, the intense expression on her face belying her casual shrug. "Creation is born from destruction."

Kyle shivered at her words. Though he and Sera's parents had discussed as much in their kitchen, hearing Kira admit it made his entire body go cold. One thing was clear: if she took it upon herself to demolish the Mortal Realm, there would be little they could do to stop her.

And yet . . . beyond the bands of her aura, Kyle had sensed

something deeply protective. People feared Kali because of her destructive, furious rages, but in truth, she was a fierce guardian. Once provoked, she would stop at nothing to defend the helpless.

But Kira didn't look like an enraged defender now. She looked calm. Purposeful. As if his fate—and everyone else's—had already been decided. A chill sliced through him. "Are you going to do it?" he asked. "Destroy the Mortal Realm?"

"Only if you fail." Kira stood. "And you will, Kalias."

He flinched at the sound of his birth name. "My name is Kyle."

"Your faith in the mortals is misplaced," she said. "They have always welcomed demons with open arms. The path to Xibalba is paved in gold and untold riches, while the path to Illysia is bound in thorns and trials. Human beings will always be seduced by the easier path." Kira tossed a twenty-dollar bill onto the table with a graceful arc of her hand. "And I like the name Kalias. It reminds me of one of my names. I'll see you in school."

"School?" he repeated as she sauntered away.

"I think I'll stay awhile," she said over her shoulder. "Keep an eye on things. See what happens."

"Why?"

"Maybe to prove that I'm not as bad as the stories make me out to be."

LOVE IS A
SLIPPERY SLOPE

❧

The sun was just setting, its last rays scattering across the gilded sand, splashing the landscape in warm, vibrant hues of burnt orange and dusted crimson. In her world between worlds, Sera extended an arm, watching the gold and scarlet flames descend like a waterfall beneath it. Her *wings*. If Xibalba hadn't tainted her, her deifyre would be silvery gold like her mother's. Sera pushed upward, feeling the sunset aura lifting her so that she remained suspended in midair, her body turning in a slow circle. Balmy breezes touched her cheeks and she closed her eyes, letting the wind take her where it wanted.

She hadn't intended to come here, but now that she had, it felt right. It felt like home. And she needed to see Dev. Even though she was angry with him for keeping things from her, she needed answers, and he was the only one who would give them to her.

Eventually, her feet came to rest at the edge of a rocky, desolate canyon. Sera inhaled sharply. This was new. A green river undulated like a serpent in the gorge below. She wondered if the canyon's sudden appearance had anything to do with her agitated state of mind. It was possible. The topology of the realm tended to shift with her moods, and her current state of mind was capricious.

Sera lifted a palm and watched the brilliant light from the setting sun drench it in gold. Her deifyre flared in response, the shimmering hues surrounding her like a star gone supernova. She stared at her glowing palms, her eyes tracing the two sigils on the raised part of each heel. Her two halves. Exhaling softly, she felt the push of her immortal weapons as her two burning swords appeared, one scarlet and the other silver. Both deadly, they stood for different things. But both were intrinsically part of her.

Which was why she was such an anomaly.

A freak.

She smiled at the word. She'd been called a freak her entire life, and while it had been tough to understand why her own mother had shaded her to keep her identity hidden, Sera was now glad she'd grown up odd. Being different had forced her to build a strength she wouldn't have come by otherwise. It'd made her tougher. Harder. And she needed that resilience now more than ever. Being on the outs with a group of teenagers was a cakewalk compared to being a pariah among a group of gods and goddesses.

The gods feared her.

"I know you can hear me, Dev," she called out. "And you can't avoid me forever."

"I'm not avoiding you."

The honeyed voice came from behind her, and Sera turned, her heart thirsty for the first glimpse of him. He was dressed in a yellow shirt with brown pants rolled at the cuffs, and he looked too beautiful for words. His dark hair tumbled in long waves to his shoulders, his brown eyes burning with an inner light. A single gold ring hung at the top of his ear.

Though the last time she'd seen him his skin had been blue—its natural color in his godly form—now he'd reverted to the bronzed, tattooed skin he'd had when they'd first met. Those intricate tattoos in every shade of blue had been one of the first things that intrigued her about him. Even now, their artistry made her breath catch.

Dev looked around as if he, too, had never seen this particular part of her world. "This is different. Stunning, though." He glanced at her. "But then, nothing you create ever fails to astound me."

"I like the complexity of it," Sera said nonchalantly, though she flushed at his praise. "The breadth and depth. We can't always see what's on the surface, can we?"

His fathomless eyes met hers. "No, we cannot."

Suddenly, she remembered what she'd come there for. Sera narrowed her eyes and placed her palms on her hips. But her words left her as he took a few steps toward her closing the distance between them. Her skin prickled, her pulse hiking several notches. It was ridiculous, the effect he had on her.

"I've missed you," he said.

"Stay away," she warned. "I'm pretty mad at you."

The corner of his mouth curled into a half smile that made her heart trip over itself. He ignored her, leaning in to press a kiss to her lips. His hands rose to cradle her face as his lips burned an imprint on hers. The scent of marigolds and cloves filled her nostrils. It took every ounce of her willpower not to grab his shoulders and deepen the kiss. Instead, she pulled away.

You're supposed to be angry, she reminded herself.

"Did you miss me?" he asked, his breath fanning against her cheek as he rested his forehead against hers.

"Hardly."

"Your eyes betray you," he said, his gaze falling to her lips. Dev's thumb grazed her chin and warmth spread through her like wildfire.

With a sharp inhale, she took a step back and cursed her traitorous eyes. "Don't be fooled. They're as pissed off as the rest of me."

"And why are you upset, my love?"

"Why did you tell the Yoddha not to tell me what's going on? I'm not a child, Dev."

"Because I wanted to tell you."

"Why?"

He stared at her for a moment, then sighed. "It's complicated."

"Because of Kali and Durga?" Sera asked, frowning. "Why have they come, Dev?"

Dev paused, as if trying to find the right words. He moved to sit on the edge of the cliff, letting his legs dangle over the side and patting the space beside him. She sat. "There are more demons than ever in the Mortal Realm," he began.

"That seems to be the general consensus." She couldn't quite curb her sarcasm. "Are you going to finally tell me why that is?"

He smiled at her petulant tone, and she scowled in return. "At first we thought they were just trying to escape Xibalba, to feast on human energy. But it's getting harder and harder to find them. They're lying in wait."

"In wait for what?"

Dev exhaled grimly, his fingers reaching out to grasp hers. "Perhaps for someone to help them."

"Like Azrath? But he's dead," Sera said. "We killed him. There's no way the Demon Lords can breach the wards between Xibalba and the Mortal Realm without him." She paused. "And they would need Kyle's blood to even summon an apocalypse demon, which they'll never get. He's on our side."

"Is he?" The words were soft. Silky.

Sera spun to face him, stunned by the tone of accusation. "What do you mean? Of course he's on our side. He's the one who's been banishing demons back to the Dark Realms while the Trimurtas sit in Illysia, resting on their golden laurels."

She snatched her palm out of Dev's. Kyle had done nothing but try to make up for what his father, Ra'al, had tried to do. And now, he was bound by blood oath to protect the human world. He would never betray them.

He would never betray *her*.

"It's a possibility we have to consider," Dev said evenly.

She narrowed her eyes, fuming. "And what possibility is that, exactly?"

"That Kyle is the one letting the demons through."

"You're wrong," she said, her voice rising. "He would never do that."

"You see," he said gently. "This is why I needed to be the one to tell you."

"You've always wanted to believe the worst about him," she said. How could Dev, of all people, suggest such a thing? "Even when he was the one to save you from Xibalba. You *know* that without him everything would have been lost."

"Yes, and we are forever in Kyle's debt for that." Dev hesitated, twisting his body to face her. "I am in his debt, more so than anyone. And I *do* trust him. I trust him with my life, and with you. I was the one who suggested that he take Azrath's place."

Sera moved to the ledge of the overhang, watching the serpentine curve of the river hundreds of feet below. She could still feel Dev's consciousness, like a tether connecting her to him. "If that's true, then why are you saying these things now?"

"I was outvoted."

"Outvoted?"

"There are three of us in the Trimurtas," he explained. "The others did not agree with me that Kyle is not a threat. That's why Shiva wanted to send his consort."

Sera froze mid-step. "Durga I might be able to understand. But Kali? She acts first and thinks later. She's too consumed by blood lust." She drew a worried breath. "And you still haven't explained why they think that Kyle is a threat at all. There wouldn't even *be* a Trimurtas if it weren't for him, and you know it. You'd still be stuck in Xibalba, and demons would be festering in *all* the realms."

"I know, but you need to hear me out, Sera. You're letting your emotions cloud your judgment."

She bristled with indignation. "Of course I am. He's my best friend, and I care about him."

"Sometimes those we trust the most are the ones we should fear."

"You think I should fear *Kyle*?" she asked softly, watching the landscape shift with her mood. Dark gray storm clouds obscured the perfect blue of the sky, and the shimmering green river below transformed into a murky brown. Lightning streaked, brightening the jagged precipice at Sera's toes. She wasn't afraid, but the violent shift in her surroundings startled her.

She drew a few ragged breaths and returned to where Dev sat. He stood, his eyes flicking to the sky. The blue of his tattoos took on an ominous hue, though his eyes remained golden and translucent.

"I didn't say that," he said. "But he is the son of Ra'al, and I do fear that the Demon Lords are plotting. Kyle's blood remains something that they covet—the one thing that can bridge the space between the realms."

"But you made him immortal. He'll never succumb to them."

"The Trimurtas fears that his blood ties are too dangerous, that we—I—have made a mistake in trusting him."

"But you didn't. Kyle is on our side."

"One can only hope that Kyle's will remains strong." Dev paused, stroking a hand across Sera's cheek, his eyes suddenly unreadable. "Power can be corrosive. And his greatest weakness has always been where you are concerned."

She reared back in shock. A roaring gale whipped around them, but Sera didn't care about the gathering storm, all she could think about was the bite of Dev's last sentence. "You think I'm his *weakness*?"

"You chose to stay in the Mortal Realm with him."

"As a friend."

"Unrequited love is the most wounded kind of love. It can transform into bitterness and pain on a whim, breaking the strongest of hearts and conspiring against the strongest of wills."

Sera stilled, Dev's words cutting deep. "Kyle knows that I don't feel that way about him. He's moved on."

"Has he?"

She stared at him, her frown tightening as she struggled to make sense of what Dev was saying. She did love Kyle, but he knew it wasn't *that* kind of love. Though, she *had* led him to believe otherwise once. Sera thought back to the kiss they'd shared months before, after her visit to Xibalba had awakened the dark side of her, and she cringed. Drawn to Kyle's darkness, tangled up in emotions left in the wake of the Dark Realms' influence, she'd kissed him then.

A storm of emotions swept through Sera, the ugliest of all of them guilt. She hadn't meant to lead Kyle on. It'd been instinctual. A one-time thing. And she hadn't yet known about Dev and who he was to her. God, it was such a mess.

Lately, Kyle had made a good show of being interested in other girls. But what if what Dev was saying was true . . . that Kyle still hoped for more?

Kyle understood now that she was bound to Dev. Didn't he?

"Love hopes eternal," Dev said softly, and Sera flushed. "Deep down, he will always put you first, before anyone else." He paused. "And it's not just you. We're not convinced he won't put other people—even himself—before the good of humanity. The pursuit of power led to Azrath's fall from grace."

The sigil on her right wrist burned in response. She clasped it behind her back, feeling the throb spread up her forearm and into her chest. "How is that my fault?"

He stepped toward her. "I didn't say that. But pain and darkness have a unique relationship."

"You sound like Yoda," she said miserably.

"George Lucas is a genius." Dev smiled. "Stop doing this to yourself, Sera. It's not your fault that Kyle loves you. But you asked me to tell you the truth, and I have. Kyle's conflicted feelings for you present a risk." He reached for her right arm, bringing it gently between them and studying the glowing red sigil on the heel of her palm. As always, he was careful not to touch it. "You are marked by Xibalba."

A single tear trickled out of the corner of her eye. "You told me once that that wasn't a bad thing."

"You are the conduit between all the realms, and darkness will always seek to triumph over light." Sera's gaze met his, an odd feeling invading the pit of her stomach as purpose dawned in his eyes. "You have two choices," Dev said. "You can stay here or come back to Illysia with me."

"Illysia?" she stuttered. "I'm marked by the rune of Xibalba. The Trimurtas won't like that."

Dev cleared his throat. "Well . . . yes. You would be a risk to the wards that protect the Light Realms. You would likely be sequestered. For your own safety . . . as well as Illysia's."

"Sequestered." The word felt like a pair of shackles. "You mean locked away. Quarantined, like I'm some kind of disease."

"Not quite," he replied gently. "You would be an honored guest. My guest."

Sera laughed, the sound hollow and devoid of humor. "So, let me get this straight. You want to put me in a cell, far away from Kyle, so I can't cause him to make the wrong choices. Indefinitely."

"Not indefinitely. It's a precaution."

"Until when?"

"Until we can resolve the situation."

Another burst of disbelieving laughter crossed her lips. For sixteen years of her life, she'd been an absolute nobody. And now she'd suddenly become responsible for the future of the entire world. "Don't they teach gods that a person is responsible for their own actions? Locking me up for an eternity is not the answer."

"But it does remove you from the equation."

She eyed him shrewdly. "Are you sure that's all it is? Or is the green-eyed monster rearing its head?"

A muscle leaped in his jaw. "I want you to be safe."

"In Illysia?" she scoffed. "Where I'm not wanted. Where I'm away from my family. Is my mother okay with this?"

"She's the one who suggested it."

Sera's heart sank. Of course Sophia had. She'd always had it out for Kyle. No matter what he did—even though he'd saved the world—he'd never be good enough for them. Rage made warmth from the sigil on her hand flare up her entire arm, until a shower of blood-red flames sprouted around her.

Dev groaned in pain as her hellfyre scorched his immortal skin. But Sera couldn't help it. Her entire body vibrated with the fury consuming her. The earth below cracked as the river water turned to molten lava and rocks crumbled off the cliff face. Her entire world was as angry and vengeful as the one in her head.

"You're jealous of Kyle," she said. "Admit it."

"No."

His calm response made her anger surge. "Well maybe you should be, Dev." Despite his indifference, she watched some emotion interrupt the serenity on his face, and she felt a gloating satisfaction take hold of her. It drew the words from her mouth. "Maybe I *should* be with Kyle. At least he would give a crap if his girlfriend was into someone else."

"Sera, this isn't you talking."

She laughed through a sudden rush of tears. "Of course it's me. It's the part you all fear, isn't it? The part that wants you to lock me away in a prison while someone else decides whether to bring on the end of the world or not. Thanks, but no thanks. I'll take my chances with the demons."

He reached for her. "Sera—"

"I don't want to hurt you."

"You cannot."

This time, she stepped toward him, engulfing him in her flaming aura. Dev grimaced, but he didn't move. She could see the pain flickering in his eyes. Ice-white and gold dei-fyre burst from him to form a protective shroud. They stood there for an eternity, just watching each other while the world erupted in fire and brimstone around them.

"I love you, Serjana," Dev whispered, breaking the spell of silence, "but you must do what you feel is right. And if that means giving your heart to Kyle, then I can only accept that, and wait for you to return to me. That is my karma."

"You'd let me go. To him."

He shook his head somberly. "My heart will never release yours, but I cannot control what you choose to do."

Of course he wouldn't. Hot shame flooded her. No wonder they didn't want her in Illysia. She would probably contaminate them with her stupidity. The flames around her receded, and the skies cleared and parted.

Her voice broke on a sob as she stepped into Dev's waiting arms. "I'm sorry."

"You have nothing to be sorry for."

"I do. I'm a moron."

Dev's smile was crooked. "I forgive you for your temporary lapse in common sense."

Sera laughed, then wept into his shirt as he soothed her by rubbing slow circles on her back and kissing along her hairline. After a while, she felt herself start to calm. She pressed a kiss to his lips. She was ashamed of her behavior, but it didn't change her mind.

She took a fortifying breath. "I love you, too, Dev. But I can't be a prisoner—not here, and not in Illysia. There's no way I'm abandoning my family or my friends."

"I thought you would say as much," he said with a wry expression. "But I had to ask."

She blinked her surprise. "Then what now?"

Dev's eyes were grim. "We do what we were created to do—we protect the mortals as best as we can—from whatever is coming."

"And what do you think that is?" she asked, a pulse of fear making a cold sweat break out on her shoulders. "Please tell me, Dev, I have to know. You can't protect me from this by keeping me in the dark."

"I know." He nodded, blowing out a breath. "The Trimurtas fears that the demon Ra'al summoned was only the beginning," he explained. "That the influx of demons is the start of a plague, heralding the end of the world."

"So that's why Kali thought that wiping out the Mortal Realm was the answer."

Dev's face was solemn. "It might still be. For all we know, it's already too late to save them."

Like Father, Like Son

❧❧

The sky was gray and overcast, lending a frigid bite to the early evening air as Kyle cruised to a stop in front of Ne'feri headquarters. Swearing under his breath, he hunched his shoulders forward, tucked his jacket around himself, and cursed his car's broken heater. You'd think with all the demons plaguing the Mortal Realm, it'd be a few degrees hotter. But he'd learned that demons didn't run hot. Hell did, but demons themselves were great at adapting to their surroundings . . . especially when they wanted to go undetected.

He stared at the ominous building in front of him. It had once been a monastery, but now it was the secret meeting place of the Ne'feri Order. The massive, wooden front doors were closed, and the crumbling structure looked deserted. But looks were deceiving. Kyle swallowed, sighed, and stepped out of his car. His presence would not be welcome here.

"Get used to it," he whispered harshly to himself. "It's not like you're ever going to fit in." He drew himself tall and pushed open the doors.

Conversation in the great hall petered out as every eye fell on him. Kyle blinked, feeling the colossal rush of energies pushing toward him in a wave. There was so much heavenly power in this room that it made him lightheaded. And that wasn't even counting the strength of the hundred or so mortal Ne'feri.

The room was full of immortals. *Powerful* immortals: Sanrak deities, protectors of the Trimurtas; Yoddha deities, warriors of Illysia; Daevas, guardians of the mortals; and the eminent leaders themselves, the Trimurtas. Except . . . there were only two of the three Trimurtas present—Dev and another boy Kyle didn't recognize.

"Hey," Sera said in a low voice, appearing at his side. "You look dazed."

Kyle shook his head to clear it. "There's a lot of power here." He sucked a lungful of air into tight lungs. "I'm not going to be the only one who can sense such a strong shift in the balance. Demons will be drawn to it."

She nodded. "We know. Come on, we're about to start."

The crowd parted as he walked in Sera's wake. Most of those in attendance bowed to her, though they cast wary glances in his direction. Kyle's eyes slid to the commanding figure at the far end of the room. Dev looked much like the boy who had lived next door to Sera for several months— dark-haired and dressed in yellow, with a plethora of blue tattoo art coloring his limbs. As much as Kyle wanted to hate the one who held Sera's heart, he couldn't. He had been given a second chance because of Dev.

Kyle bowed as Sera led him to Dev's end of the room, which pulsed with bright, luminescent energy. "Lord Devendra," he said in greeting.

"Kyle," Dev said, clapping him on the back. "It's good to see you again."

"It's been a while."

A wry smile shaped Dev's lips. "In truth, I'd hoped it would be longer."

"Yeah, me too."

Dev nodded. "Peace, it appears, is elusive." He paused as a tall boy exuding tremendous energy, moved to stand beside them. "This is Lord Taran," Dev added.

Kyle sucked in a breath as he assessed the boy's energy, understanding dawning on him. Taran, he ascertained, was the current mortal avatar of choice for Lord Shiva, the second Trimurtas deity.

He looked the same age as Dev, but Kyle knew that this god, like Dev, was ageless. His human shade was that of a pale boy with matted, dark hair secured into a knot at his crown, a crescent moon comb holding it in place. Black ash smeared his cheeks and bare shoulders, and a tattoo of blue-green cobras, far lighter than Dev's vivid skin art, wound around his neck.

Kyle blinked at the third eye that winked in and out of sight between the boy's slanted, black eyebrows, and realized that he could only see it because of his innate ability to see cosmic energies. None of the other mortals here would be able to see the god's extra eye, unless he intended it to be so.

A shiver climbed up Kyle's spine. As compassionate and benevolent as the god appeared, he knew that Taran was capable of destroying the entire world. Shiva was known as the Destroyer. And he was here. Now. Which meant the world was at its end—or nearing it.

His eyes scanned the crowd. If Shiva was here, then Kira and Darika would be as well. He almost rolled his eyes at the thought. What was it about his luck? He always seemed to have a thing for girls who were spoken for. Then again, Kira hadn't seemed too stressed about it.

"Hey," Taran said in a jovial voice that was at odds with his calm exterior, clapping a hand on Kyle's shoulder. "I have heard a lot about you."

"Thanks . . . I think."

"Dev fought for your return to the mortal realm. Our decision was not unanimous. Though I had other concerns, I agreed to give you a second chance. And yet I fear that I may have been too lenient."

"Well, I hope to prove you wrong," Kyle said, a lump forming in his throat. Did Taran mean to banish him, then? Take away the immortality he had bestowed?

The god's third eye burned for an intense second, stripping past Kyle's walls to his private thoughts. For an unconscionable moment, Kyle had the biggest urge to call forth Mordas, if only in self-defense. But summoning a sword forged in the fires of Xibalba in a room full of Illysia's deities would not be wise. He was already on everyone's hit list as it was. Taran's third eye winked out of sight and he grinned widely, as if reading Kyle's thoughts.

"We shall see, won't we?" Taran said over his shoulder as he stepped past Kyle toward the center of the room. He clapped his hands, drawing the attention of everyone in the hall. "Let's begin."

"Excuse me," Dev said with a short bow. His eyes met Sera's for a long moment before he leaned in to kiss her cheek, squeezing her arm reassuringly. "It will be okay. Trust me."

"What was that about?" Kyle asked with a frown as the meeting began, Taran and Dev addressing the group.

"The meeting could go one of two ways," Sera whispered, "and neither option is good."

"What do you mean?"

Sera stared grimly at him, taking his hand and steering him to a quieter corner of the room, out of hearing of anyone close by. Not that that really mattered—the deities could hear whatever they chose to. Sera's mother's gaze flicked to them, a small smile gracing her lips as her eyes met Kyle's. The compassion in them rocked him. He'd always felt Sophia was against him, but now it felt like she was trying to give him strength . . . like she was on his side.

Oddly, it did not make him feel any better. If she was on his side, then whatever opposed him must be bad. More than bad.

"Either everyone dies," Sera said with a swallow. "Or you . . . go."

A heavy sensation fell across his shoulders. Kyle wasn't sure it was because of what Sera said or something else. He blinked, processing her words. "Go where?"

"The Ne'feri think the demons are waiting for you to help them."

"*Me?* That's a stretch."

"I think so, too," Sera agreed. "But there are many Ne'feri who believe otherwise, and they think that banishing you is the only way to save the Mortal Realm. They were the ones who called this meeting."

"Who, exactly?"

"Beth and her family, for one, but there are others. And there is dissent among the Trimurtas themselves."

Kyle's heart sank. He should have guessed it would be

the Davenports. He had compelled Beth months before when he'd been facing off against a Sanrak—Sera's mother—and one very pissed-off Yoddha. Compulsion was a demon ability; one he hadn't known he'd possessed until he'd coerced Beth into shielding him from a Yoddha's assault with her body. He hadn't meant to do it, of course, but the fact was, he *had*. Because he was part demon. And now it seemed that Beth wanted revenge.

"I'm sorry," Sera said softly, watching his face. "But I thought you would want to know."

"If they want to banish me, why am I even here?" he asked, though he already knew the answer. If the vote went that way, Taran would strip him of his powers then and there. And there would be nothing he could do about it.

"If it makes you feel any better, Dev doesn't agree."

Kyle shrugged. "He's fought on my behalf before. It's not going to work a second time. Not for me, right? Son of the devil?"

"Stop," Sera said, closing the gap between them to put her arms around him. The soft glow of her energy encircled him, too, soothing the violent storm of emotions brewing inside him.

He felt hot. And angry. Hadn't he done enough to prove his worth? To prove that he wasn't the bastard they all assumed he was? Hadn't he *given his life* to defend the Ne'feri? No matter what he did, he would never be good enough. They would never trust him. With each thought, his anger swelled, the force of it buffeting against Sera's strength. Waves of boiling heat radiated off him.

He broke free of Sera's embrace.

"You need to calm down, Kyle," Sera whispered, her eyes worried. "People will notice."

"I *am* calm."

"You're not. You're burning up," she said. "Get a hold of yourself. Or they will believe exactly what you don't want them to."

Flames pulsed beneath his skin. "They already think the worst of me."

"Not all of them do," she said with an anxious glance over her shoulder. "But if you don't control yourself, they will. I can't shade you much longer."

Stunned, he met his best friend's eyes and sighed. She was using her own energy to cloak his. Blinking, he could see the rose-gold flames around her shielding his own pale brown aura, concealing it as it turned more opaque, like a wall of thick smoke. He could feel Dev's gaze settle on him. It wouldn't be long before the warrior deities in the room sensed the shift in his disposition—and considered it a threat.

"I need a minute," he said with a glance at the nearest exit. "Fresh air."

Sera nodded, frowning. "Do what you have to. But get it together. I can't convince them without you there. And right now, we're on the losing end, understand? So get your head together."

He froze at the curt tone of her voice. "I will."

"This isn't a game, Kyle. I didn't stay on earth so you could just give up when things get a little rough. I'm not about to lose my best friend a second time. Take a few minutes to compose yourself, and then get back in here. I mean it, Kyle. Promise me you won't leave, or do anything rash."

Taken aback, he nodded. "I promise."

Huffing a sharp breath, he pushed open the narrow door and cracked the closest window. A welcome rush of crisp air welled into his face. He breathed deeply while his mind raced. It didn't make sense. The demons were bound to the Dark Realms.

No—they are bound to me.

The thought was a blow, forcing the breath from his body. He wasn't a Demon Lord like Ra'al. He *wasn't.* Except . . . a dark, quiet voice rose within him, reminding him that Mordas was loyal only to the ruler of the lowest pit of Xibalba. Kyle shoved the thought away. Mordas was a thing—a blade that bowed to blood, nothing more. And Kyle kept it fed and satisfied. The sword's allegiance did not make him Ra'al's successor. But as strongly as he rejected the notion, a tiny seed of doubt took root in the wake of his insecurity. He felt another wave of heat rise inside him.

Calm down. Calm down. Calm down.

But the more he tried to restrain himself, the more his feelings flamed, reminding him that he could never escape his demonic nature. It was in his blood. Entrenched in his very soul—if he even had a soul.

Kyle shook his head roughly. Of course he had a soul—he'd been born half-human, and the Trimurtas could not have granted him immortality as an Azura Lord if he'd been a demon.

"Hey, hot stuff." A husky voice curled around him. "And I mean that literally. I can see those fumes coming off you from a mile away."

He turned to see Kira watching him, a sardonic grin on her face. She was dressed in a black sweater-dress, one booted foot propped against the far wall, her arms crossed over her chest. Her wild tangle of hair was piled into a bun, tendrils escaping to frame her face, and a pair of carved onyx skulls swung from her earlobes. She looked composed and dangerous all at once.

"Why aren't you in there?" he asked, flushing at the sight of her. The heat in his body amped up a notch. "With Taran? Shiva, I mean. Aren't you his consort, or girlfriend, or whatever?"

She smiled and pushed off the wall. "He and I have an understanding."

"Of what?"

"An open relationship." Kira paused with a grin. "And technically, Parvati is Shiva's consort. I'm just one version of her—so I'm kind of free to do my own thing." She winked. "Sow my wild oats, so to speak."

"And Darika?"

The smile fled from her face, and Kyle flinched at the ugly expression it left behind before she hid it smoothly behind a mask of indifference. "My sister has her own agenda."

"If you're both incarnations of Parvati, then why are you both here?"

The coy smile returned. "I can only answer for myself," she said, taking a step forward and making his breath falter as her fingers grasped his shirtsleeve. "And I was intrigued by a certain Azura Lord."

He ignored the bait. "But why at the same time? I didn't think that was possible."

"That's because you're still limited by your old, mortal ways of thinking." She drew a nail down his arm. "You are immortal now, Kyle, and you should know that the gods are formless. We are all born of the same divine energy, no matter our incarnations and our many avatars. So, of course, I can be present in this form while Darika is in hers. Think of me as the more adventurous version. She maintains the cosmic balance, and—well, we both know what I do."

Kyle's eyes flicked to where her palm pressed against his skin. Strangely, he felt the waves of heat recede at her light touch. He eyed her, grateful for the distraction and feeling his frustration ebb away. "You never answered my question. Why aren't you in there?"

"My presence is not required."

"Because Taran can speak for you?" he asked.

"No." She laughed. "He would never do that. But Darika can. She and I are of similar mindsets, you see. Despite our differences, we both want the same thing. Balance."

"Darika is in there?" he blurted, surprised to feel himself flush again at the thought of Kira's twin. He hadn't thought she'd left much of an impression when he'd met her at Sal's. At the time, he'd thought she seemed tame compared to her sister. "I didn't see her earlier."

"We arrived at the same time." Kira presented him with her elbow. "Let's take a walk. Those gardens behind the building look quiet."

"You don't care about what they're saying in there?" he asked. "Or deciding?" Kira rolled her eyes and started to walk down the corridor.

Of course, Kyle realized. She would know the instant they decided anything, being part of the cosmic fabric and all that. He followed with a glance over his shoulder, remembering his promise to Sera. But it wasn't like he was leaving. He'd be with one of the Tridevi the whole time.

"I thought you said you'd give us a chance to figure out what was happening," he said as he caught up. "Back there at the school." Kira had already started down the stairs leading to the lower level.

"I wanted to, but it's not up to me." She shrugged. "I will do as commanded, whether that's wage war or banish an Azura Lord. Although I admit I will be far more saddened to do the latter."

"Why?"

"I told you," she said, pushing open a door that let a stream of fading evening light into the gloomy interior. "You intrigue me. I see the war you're waging between your two selves. One will win." She paused, squinting back at him as the door swung closed behind them. "Eventually."

The garden was half-dead, but it didn't matter. For the first time since he arrived, he felt as if he could breathe. Kyle hadn't realized how the weight of all the collective energies he could feel from inside the hall had been pushing into him. "And which do you think that is?" he asked Kira. "The side of me that will win?"

"Kalias, the son of Ra'al, or Kyle, the redeemed Azura Lord?"

"Yeah."

She smiled again, but this time it was more like a baring of her perfect white teeth. "That depends on whether you choose to be a king of the demons or a servant to the gods. Most men would choose the former. Power, you see, is the root of all evil."

He jerked his head to the upper hall. "All the Ne'feri think I'm a Demon Lord already. And maybe they're correct. Maybe that's exactly what I should do. Prove them all right."

"You don't believe that. Or you wouldn't be here."

"I don't want to be Ra'al."

"No, of course not," she said. "No one wishes to be a Demon Lord. But sometimes choices are made . . . paths are taken . . . in the face of great provocation."

"What are you saying?"

"You would do anything to save the one you love."

There was only one person Kyle had ever loved. Sure, he loved Carla, and he was fond of Nate, but he knew who Kira was talking about. "You mean Sera."

Kira's smile was gentle. "She is bound to another. And unlike my relationship with Taran, there's no gray area with the two of them," she said softly. "Do you still have feelings for her?"

"No," he said, with a guilty look at her. "Not like that. It's complicated."

Liking Kira wasn't a betrayal of Sera, even though it'd felt that way at first. What he felt for Sera was like an old blanket, comforting and familiar. If she told him right then that she was into him, Kyle didn't know what he would do. She was *Sera*; of course he'd be conflicted. He'd loved her practically forever. And the truth was that if Dev wasn't in the picture, he and Sera might have had half a chance of being together. But Dev *was* the love of her life, and there was nothing any of them could do to change it. Her friendship meant more to him than having nothing at all.

"Love has a way of twisting the most perfect thing into something ugly," Kira said, watching him closely. "It uplifts and destroys in a single breath. Serjana cares for you, but only as a friend—and that will never change, no matter how much you wish it deep down inside."

"I don't wish that. Not anymore." Kyle sucked in a sharp breath, the feeling he'd tried to suffocate rising like a tide. "I was in love with her my whole life. And you're right, it hurt when she chose Dev over me, but I can't fault her for that. And I'm not going to become my father because of it."

"Perhaps. Perhaps not. But you know what they say—the way to hell is paved with the best intentions." Sinking to her knees, she plucked a wilting rose from its stem and held it in her palm, studying its frayed, black-edged petals. Kyle sat cross-legged across from her. It was clear that the bloom she was holding was diseased. "Everything needs to be liberated from decay," Kira mused. "Even this rose. Its time has come. And such is the way of the realms. The Mortal Realm is like this rose. Sooner or later, it will die from the sickness consuming its petals." She closed her fingers, and when she opened them Kyle saw that the rose had crumbled to fine, gilded dust. It swirled in the wind in a tiny golden cyclone and disappeared. "The power of transformation at its best. So, you see, sometimes death is the answer."

Kira seemed almost pensive as she spoke, though her eyes burned with an intense light. Kyle cleared his throat. "Is it true what they say about you—that you drank the blood of a rakshasa demon to protect the Mortal Realm?"

She leaned back on her elbows and grinned. "Mahishasura?"

Kyle nodded. "Yeah."

"Yes, Durga summoned me. The demon could not be killed and every drop of blood from it spawned a new demon." She shrugged, smacking her lips at the memory, and winked. "Worked, didn't it?"

"They said you went crazy, dancing on the dead, and that Shiva was only able to stop you by throwing himself at your feet."

"So they say." She arched an eyebrow. "Would you throw yourself beneath my feet to protect the mortals, if you had the choice?"

He answered her question with one of his own. "Would you stop if you saw it was me?"

This time her burst of laughter was genuine. "Maybe, maybe not. But that's a discussion for another time." Kira rose to her feet and extended her hand. "Now go—you are being summoned."

"You're not coming back in?" he asked as she turned in the opposite direction of the doors.

"I don't do politics." She squeezed his hand and pressed a swift kiss to his lips before vaulting over the low stone wall that separated the garden from the street. "Try not to die, okay? I'm not bored of you just yet."

What Are Friends For?

֍

Sera's gaze swept the room as she looked for Kyle. The discussion was not going well.

She cringed at the swell of fear and the accompanying rise of angry voices. The majority of the Ne'feri were afraid of him, but it felt like an inquisition more than a productive discussion. Despite Dev's staunch support, she could feel the room turning.

Where was Kyle?

She scanned the sea of faces, but could not spot him anywhere. She could feel his presence, but not inside the meeting room. Sera's gaze slid to the slim, dark-haired figure of Darika, standing beside Taran. In her rich red sari, it was hard not to notice her beauty, from the soft sheen of her hair to the classic sculpt of her features. She held herself like the epitome of the divine mother she was. Her expression was neutral, however, betraying no hint of what she was feeling. Taran, on the other hand, seemed responsive. Sera exhaled a breath of relief. It was a good sign. The Trimurtas would be the deciding factor in Kyle's fate, and Dev would need Taran on his side.

"The boy must be banished," Aidan Davenport argued loudly. "It's the only solution."

Beth's father had been the most vocal in his claim that Kyle was responsible for the influx of demons, and Sera knew that he had good reason, given what had happened with Beth.

Dev cleared his throat. "We have no way of knowing that he is the one behind the flood of demons in the Mortal Realm. The portals are all closed."

"Lord Devendra is correct," Taran said. "We cannot accuse the boy without proof."

"By the time we've established proof, it will be too late," Ryan Davenport interjected. "You would condemn us to death."

Sera opened her mouth to respond, but Darika beat her to it.

"Death is always in your future, young one," she said, her voice reverberating through the space like a low-pitched sitar. "Whether that is today or years from now, that outcome is a certainty."

Ryan's response was petulant. "Your job is to protect us."

"Our job is to guide you toward moksha." Darika waved a hand, her pensive face betraying no emotion at Ryan's tone. "The ultimate unification with Brahman. This plane has always been only one of death and rebirth."

Ryan sucked air through his teeth. "Why even protect the mortals if you've accepted that they're all going to die anyway?"

The furious hum in response to his irreverent statement rose to the rafters.

Taran stepped forward, one palm raised to silence the dissent. "Your reasoning is flawed, Ryan. The goal isn't death. It's liberation from samsara, the karmic cycle of death and rebirth. The Daevas guide you onto the path toward Illysia, and the Azura turn you away from it, toward Xibalba. This is the way of the realms. But sometimes, it becomes necessary to wipe the slate clean." He paused meaningfully. "The role of the Ne'feri, which you have been born into, is to defend your brothers and sisters, and guard the portals to this realm."

"I didn't choose this path," Ryan said softly, and Sera's entire body froze. "It was chosen for me. And yet I do it, because I was born into this world. But I can't continue if the Trimurtas blindly supports *him*." As he spoke, his gaze landed on the rear door of the hall, his eyes narrowing. Sera spun to see Kyle reentering.

Kyle's face was a careful mask of indifference, but Sera could sense his indignation. Angry shouts rose again as the rest of the room caught sight of him.

"He is the heir of the seventh," Aidan Davenport shouted. "It's because of him that the demons are here."

The murmur of voices rose to a roar as others took Aidan's side. Several of the Yoddha and Sanrak also nodded. Any dissent between the immortals was a dangerous thing. Dev had said as much, but Sera hadn't fully understood.

They needed to find common ground. Common *sane* ground.

"The heir?" Sera shot back. "Ra'al is still the Demon Lord of the seventh."

Ryan moved to stand beside his father, whose lips were pulled back into an ugly sneer. "According to the laws of succession in Xibalba, since Kyle bested Ra'al in combat, he should have taken Ra'al's place." Aidan Davenport's vitriolic gaze fastened on Kyle. "And since the seventh is now without its *true* successor, the demons are separated from their real master. That's why they're still coming to the Mortal Realm— they're looking for *you*."

Sera blinked, her breath stuttering. Everything inside of her fought against the foul suggestion. There was no way that Kyle was Ra'al's successor. *Right?*

Sera felt, rather than saw, Kyle start to simmer. "You're wrong!" he growled.

"Enough," she said through clenched teeth, squashing the maggot of doubt that had wriggled into her brain. "I have vouched for him. Lord Devendra has vouched for him. He is not the heir of anything. Until you have proof, any attack against Kyle is an attack against me." She took a shaky breath. "We cannot afford to let fear divide us. We must bolster our defenses, defend the humans, and find a solution. Not turn against each other. Kyle is not the enemy."

"He will always be the son of Ra'al," someone shouted. "His blood is tainted."

Sera blinked, focusing on the individual who had spoken. Martin, a Ne'feri veteran. She didn't hesitate, using her goddess power to delve into the man's consciousness and access the threads of his past lives. "Your great-grandfather was a thief and a highwayman. Are you a thief too, since you're related to him?"

Martin paled. "That's not the same."

"But it is," Sera said gently. "What are we all here for, if not to better ourselves? Our belief in karma is the cornerstone of who we are—we all believe that the lives we lead now will determine where we go in the next. Condemning Kyle because you are afraid does not only impact him. It affects you. Think upon that. Do you really want to be responsible for the exile of an innocent person?" Martin flushed and shook his head.

Darika's eyes met Sera's, approval glowing in them. "Lady Serjana is correct. While we do not have the luxury of time, we are here to help the mortals, and to determine the true cause of the infestation. Time is not on our side, and if the demon plague becomes too much to contain, we will have no other choice but to reset the balance. However, I will work with Lady Serjana and Lord Kyle to find the root of the evil. You have my promise that no other action will be taken without just cause."

"How long before there's no other choice but to purge humanity?" asked a Ne'feri Sera didn't know.

"Weeks, if that."

The collective gasp was loud. Sera met her mother's troubled gaze across the room. They had so little time to save the mortals—barely a blink in the history of the universe—but any chance at all was better than the alternative. Darika had given them all a brief reprieve. A chance to save everything and everyone they loved.

"In the meantime, continue to fulfill your oaths," Taran said, his voice booming across the space. "We are all in this together."

As Taran continued, Sera made her way to where Kyle was standing, stiff and defensive. She ushered him out into the hallway.

"Are you okay?"

His cool gaze met hers. "How would you be if everyone hated you that much?"

"They're scared. It's a human response to a terrifying situation."

"Yeah, and I'm the terror."

Sera stared at her best friend. His defeated tone was worrying, and she went for humor to diffuse the situation. "Whiny, much? I seem to recall a boy who laughed in the face of the worst Demon Lord of hell." His gaze fastened to hers as she smirked. "Forget those losers. Come on, let's find Darika. She's the one we have to thank for giving us more time."

By the time they ventured back into the room, most of the crowd had dissipated, including the Davenport family, for which Sera was grateful. She looked for Dev but couldn't see him, though she could feel his presence. A small group had convened near the front of the room, including her parents, Darika, and the two Yoddha from the library, Mara and Ilani. They both bowed to her as she approached, but remained silent and watchful. Sera knew that they were there for her protection.

"So who's got a plan to save the world?" Sera joked. No one smiled, though her father's lip twitched. "Tough crowd tonight."

Kyle scowled at her and propped a booted foot against a nearby wall. "I fail to see the humor in any of this. None of *your* necks are on the line."

"All of our fates are on the line." Darika smiled gently in his direction, and his scowl faded slightly. "And the lives of the human race."

"We don't have many options, short of going to Xibalba ourselves and confronting the Demon Lords," Sam said, frowning. "Though . . . if we could catch a demon here, we could interrogate it."

Darika's eyes drifted to him. "As though a demon would tell us anything."

"It wouldn't have to," Sam replied. "Kyle could delve into its mind, learn how and why they're infiltrating the Mortal Realm. When I was an Azura Lord, it was not difficult to see demons' desires."

"But these demons are different," Darika said, mulling over Sam's proposal. "They're too clever to give anything away."

"It's worth a shot," Sera said, spotting Dev returning from an outer balcony out of the corner of her eye. She could sense that he was agitated.

What's wrong?

She only had to think it for Dev to look up, his golden gaze meeting hers from across the room. Over the past few months, their ability to communicate had grown from sensing each other's feelings to being able to converse through thought. Sera was still getting used to supernatural abilities like this one. Of course, she could close her mind to him, should she so choose. A girl had to have boundaries, after all.

Taran thinks the Ne'feri are going to do something rash to deal with Kyle, he replied mentally, making his way toward her.

Sera bit her lip as Dev reached her side, his hand falling to her lower back. She looked up at him and continued their silent mental exchange. *They're wrong about him.*

Maybe.

A frown drew her brows together. *What do you mean?*

It can't be a coincidence that the demons are appearing in close proximity to him.

Her thoughts were like firecrackers, igniting with frustration. *The demons are here because this is where the KaliYuga nearly happened four months ago. This was where the biggest portal to Xibalba ever recorded was formed. It makes sense that this is where they would gather. And that's not because of Kyle. That's because of Azrath and Ra'al!*

Calm down, my love. You're right, and I promise we will get to the bottom of it.

Dev's hand drew slow, soothing circles along her back, but his reassurances did little to temper the storm brewing inside of her. Sera curled her fingers into a fist, willing her inner tumult to subside.

Kyle pushed off the wall, drawing Sera's attention. "Then the place to catch a demon is Silver Lake High." He shrugged as the stares of the others converged on him. "Don't look at me. I only just found out that demons love teenagers. But high school is pretty much a demon smorgasbord, so what better place to trap one of them?"

"Kyle's brilliant," Sera agreed. "Silver Lake is our best bet. We catch one of the demons, and we use it to figure out what's going on."

Sophia frowned. "I don't think that's a good idea. I can't be there to protect you."

"Mom, I'll have the Yoddha. Mara and Ilani have been spying on me for weeks, anyway." She rolled her eyes in the direction of Dev, whose overprotectiveness knew no bounds.

He only smiled. "Your safety was paramount. And you've proven to be unpredictable. Jump first, think later."

As much as she loved him, sometimes she wanted to punch him in his perfect, patronizing face. She might only be seventeen in this life, but counting the many accruals of her lifetimes, she was as old as he was. And his domineering nature was starting to wear on her.

"I can take care of myself," she said, bristling.

His response was soft. "I know. I'm just not used to having my heart on the outside of my body."

Oh. A lump rose in Sera's throat.

"I'll be there with you," Darika said to her. "And my sister, should she choose to be."

"Choose to be?" Kyle asked.

"Kira does what she wants. She will come if I summon her, or if there's something exciting that draws her. But she is . . . unreliable. She doesn't tend to follow the same rules that we do."

"That's an understatement," Kyle replied under his breath.

To Sera's surprise, Darika grinned at him, nodding emphatically. "We agree on that then."

After saying their goodbyes, Darika, Kyle, and the Yoddha took their leave. Dev pulled Sera to the narrow parapet and tucked her into his side. They stood pressed together for what felt like an eternity, saying nothing.

"I'll be fine, Dev."

"I know. But I don't like leaving you here. I'd rather you be safe in Illysia, where you belong."

She tilted her head to face him. "I belong here."

"You belong with me." He buried his nose in her hair, tightening his embrace, as if he had no intention of letting her go. He took her left hand and brought it to his lips, his mouth skimming over the rune there. *His* rune.

Sera's insides felt like liquid. No boy had ever been able to make her feel the way Dev did. One touch of his lips, even in the midst of so much chaos, and she was lost.

His unique scent curled around her—the smell of spice and marigolds. Sera wound her arms around his neck, sealing her lips to his. When he held her like this, *kissed* her like this, everything fell away. They weren't deities. They weren't immortal. They were two people in love. Dev's kiss was warm and sweet, telling her what no words could—that everything would be okay.

She wanted to believe him. But as they broke apart, a cold numbness settled upon her heart like a layer of frost. "Be careful," she whispered to him. "I love you."

"And I you."

Sera turned to rejoin her parents, but paused when she heard Dev say her name. "What is it?"

Dev cleared his throat, as if afraid of how she might react to what he was about to say. "I know you trust Kyle. And I do, too, but promise me you won't be blinded by your feelings if it turns out that we are wrong about the rules of succession."

"I won't." She exhaled. "And we're not wrong about Kyle. He's with us. With *me*. He always has been—even in the bowels of hell, when he could have been tempted to turn on me. If we give up on him now, he'll have nothing. I'm not about to let that happen."

Her parents were waiting for her, but she stopped to say goodbye to Kyle, who stood leaning against his car. His face was shuttered, but Sera could see past the mask to the worry he was trying to hide.

"It's not you," she told him firmly.

"What if it is?"

"Then we take care of it," she said with a shrug.

His smile was crooked. "That easy, huh?"

"Who said anything about it being easy?" Sera chucked him on the shoulder and signaled to her parents that she'd be there shortly. "But all of this has got to be worth fighting for, right? Evil doesn't just go away after being vanquished once. It's always looking for ways to come back."

"When did you get so smart?"

"I was always smart, but technically those words of wisdom are Nate's," she said. "Kid is some kind of genius prodigy. Wouldn't be surprised if he took over the Ne'feri Order one day."

Kyle shoved his hands into his pockets. "Yeah, me too. He was the one who figured out what Azrath was doing—and I still can't believe he infused himself with deifyre to negate the wards of Illysia. Kid's clever." He grinned and scanned the area, as if searching for Nate's mop of blond curls. "Kind of surprised, actually, that he wasn't here, eavesdropping from the rafters."

"He's at a sleepover. Otherwise I wouldn't put it past him. Honestly, I still don't. He's half human and half Sanrak—he could be here and we wouldn't even know it. Although, Mom's been on the warpath lately with all the demon sightings. Even Nate knows when to cool his heels." The sound of her father's car horn made Sera jump. "Sorry, have to go. I'll see you in school tomorrow, okay?"

"See you."

"And Kyle?"

"Yeah?" he said as he slid into the driver's seat.

She winked at him. "I've always got your back." She reached in to squeeze his shoulder. "You're with me, right?"

"I'm always with you, Sera."

She watched as he drove away, then jogged to her parents' car. The ride to her house was quiet, but Sera could feel her parents' unease. Neither of them spoke, but she knew that they, too, were worried about her safety. And Nate's.

Her father spoke as he pulled the car into their driveway. "Is that Jemitra?"

Sera glanced up to see Jem sitting on the porch, and felt a rush of guilt at the sight of the textbooks in his lap. "Darn, I told him we could study tonight. We have a climate project due in a couple of weeks that I said I'd help him prepare for. He must have been waiting for hours." She hopped out of the car.

"Hey," Jem said, waving to her parents as her father slowed the car on the way into the garage. "Mr. and Mrs. Caelum."

"Jemitra, how you've grown," Sam said with a smile. "We need to reschedule that dinner soon. It was too bad that Vik had to cancel at the last minute."

"Yeah, Dad had an emergency. But I'd like that a lot."

"I'll give him a call," Sam said. "Set something up. I want to know more about what you've been up to. Always thought you had a lot of potential."

Jem went red, and Sera rescued him. "Dad! You're being weird."

Her father laughed and drove past. "Sorry."

"You know how he gets," Sera said to Jem. And he did—when Jem had been a kid, he'd followed her dad around like a shadow. His own father hadn't been the affectionate sort, but Jem had taken to Sam immediately.

Jem shrugged. "He's a good guy."

"So how long have you been here?" Sera asked. "I'm so sorry, I totally forgot I had a thing with my parents tonight."

"Not long at all. And I was studying anyway, hoping I wouldn't embarrass myself once we got started."

"Why didn't you text me?"

"I don't have your cell number. Is it too late for us to cover a couple things?" He shot her a hopeful look.

The last thing she wanted to think about was world geography, but she owed him. "Of course not," she said, heading inside and gesturing for him to follow. "Make yourself comfortable, and I'll go grab my books," she added, indicating the dining room table. She usually studied in her bedroom, but she was sure that wouldn't go over well.

It didn't matter that Sera was several thousand years old; her mother was still overprotective when it came to boys. Sera bit back a smile, remembering the last time she'd caught Kyle in her room. Not that she was remotely interested in Jem. He was cute, sure, but she had more than enough boy trouble on her plate with Dev and Kyle. What she did want was a friend—and she and Jem had been close before.

She raced up the stairs to her bedroom and grabbed her geography books before retracing her steps. "I'm so sorry you had to wait," she apologized again.

"No problem, seriously." He drew a breath and opened the book. "So climate change and world topology. Where do I even start?"

Sera jabbed a finger at the chapter heading. "Have you read this chapter yet? It should give you an idea of what kind of topics you can come up with."

"How did I get stuck with climate change?" he grumbled.

Sera laughed at his expression. "Hey, you could have gotten the effect of modern technology on the environment."

"Good point." Jem stared at her, tapping his pencil on the open pages. He chewed on the end of his pencil, then shot her a surreptitious glance. "You seem so different."

Her pulse tripped, despite the innocence of the question. "How so?"

"Just more composed. The girl I remember was all devil-may-care attitude."

Sera grinned. "Seven years is a long time. I'd be worried if I still behaved like a ten-year-old."

"You hated it when Nate was born," he said and leaned back in his chair. "Remember that? You used to want to put him out with the trash." Jem chuckled and looked around as if expecting to see Nate in the dining room with them. "Where is he? I haven't seen him since we've been back."

"He's at a sleepover. And you won't believe what a little know-it-all he is." She shook her head. "And he kind of grew on me. Little brothers . . . pains in the butt. But I guess I don't want to put him in the recycling bin anymore."

"That's why I'm glad I'm an only child."

They exchanged a grin and Sera relaxed into a comfortable groove. It felt good. Normal. Like how it had been when she'd helped him with fourth-grade math and he'd helped her with messy art projects. She could be herself with Jem. Well, the girl she used to be anyway.

You're not that girl anymore.

Her inner voice was quiet, and Sera ignored it. She might not be the girl she once was, but that didn't mean she didn't crave what she'd lost. An ordinary adolescence. Having a friend over to do homework, laughing about pesky little brothers, and not prepping to defend the world from the apocalypse.

She exhaled. "It's really good to see you, Jem."

"You, too," he said. "You have no idea."

"So how was it? London or wherever you guys were? You moved around a lot, right?"

Jem nodded. "Started out in London, then Zurich, then Frankfurt, and we ended up in Paris for a while. Can't complain though. It's been amazing being able to live in all those different countries. My favorite city was Zurich. I went inside an actual glacier. It was mind-blowing."

"Sounds like fun," Sera said. "Better than here, anyway."

Jem grinned and shot her an amused glance. "What? You mean Silver Lake hasn't gotten any more exciting in all the years I've been gone? Come on. I'd have thought that all these tennis moms would have revolted by now over something—like the lack of decent coffee on Main Street."

"Oh, they have. Only it's over organic produce and appropriately zoned crosswalks." Sera laughed at his comic expression.

"Sounds major."

She wondered what Jem would think of the near apocalypse a few months before he'd moved back, or the demons crawling all over Silver Lake. Most people didn't believe in the supernatural, and before she turned sixteen, she'd been one of them. Now, however, she believed. She'd been to Xibalba—seen its horrors—and nothing could erase the memory of it from her brain.

She smiled at her old friend, determined to keep that part of her life closed off. "Not much more than that happening here, I'm afraid. So, what was school over there like? Did you have a girlfriend?"

"At first I was home schooled because of the language barriers, but I seem to have a knack for foreign languages. Then I enrolled in the local lycée. That's the high school." His lips quirked. "And it was hard to have a boyfriend when we moved around so much."

Sera blinked, and Jem laughed easily.

"What, I thought everyone knew after Ryan Davenport punched me in the nose in fifth grade on the playground."

"He punched you?"

"I did try to kiss him."

She laughed. "God, I wish I'd been there. Unfortunately, not much has changed. His body grew, but his mind stayed the same. Small and stupid."

"Maybe he needs another kiss." They dissolved into laughter as Jem's blue eyes sparkled with humor. "It's great to be back, Sera. I missed hanging out with you. Feels like home."

"I know exactly what you mean."

It was true. Having Jem over brought her back to a simpler time. She'd be lying if she didn't admit how much she liked it.

Demon Tracking

❧

Darika's choice of ride was the opposite of her sister's beast of a motorcycle, though the old Mercedes Roadster was no less flashy. Kira lived like she had a death wish, while Darika was more sedate. But Kyle knew that Darika's calm exterior guarded her strength. Even now, as she exited the car among all the other students in the parking lot, dressed in a simple red sweater and jeans, she had presence.

That's because she's a goddess, you idiot.

If the stories about her were true, she'd wiped out a gazillion demons in her time without breaking a sweat. That taciturn exterior hid a fierce, unflappable core.

She frightened him, though not nearly as much as Kira did.

"Hey," she said, walking up to where he stood at the base of the steps.

"Hi," he said. "No Kira today?"

Darika shrugged, tossing her bag to the ground and reaching up to tuck her glossy, dark hair into a low bun. "We had a difference of opinion regarding capturing a demon for questioning."

"Let me guess—she said that the only demon should be a dead demon?"

116

Darika's teeth were white in her umber-hued face, her eyes twinkling with amusement. "Something like that. Is Sera here already?"

"She texted that she was going to be late, but that she'd get a ride. I usually bring her to school."

"She doesn't drive?"

Kyle shrugged. "Ever heard the term helicopter parent? Her mom is more of a fighter jet parent. Though I guess Sophia has a good reason to be protective. Long story short, she doesn't have her license yet. But I've been teaching her to drive, so hopefully soon."

"I don't have a license."

He stared at her. "You know it's a crime to drive without one, right?" Darika lifted a delicate shoulder, and Kyle grinned sheepishly. "Right . . . cosmic goddess powers."

"You are immortal now, too," she remarked. "You can also do as you wish."

"I don't like to break the law. Force of habit and a misspent youth."

Darika nodded, her brow furrowing for a moment. "Ah yes, I remember. Several stints in juvenile hall."

Kyle squirmed, uncomfortable that she knew his entire past. Apart from spending so much time in juvie and bouncing from foster home to foster home, he'd come way too close to becoming one of the Preta shadow demons whose master had very nearly succeeded in bringing hell on earth.

The tug of Sera's presence jerked him out of his ugly thoughts, but it wasn't her mom's car pulling into the lot. It was a blue truck. He frowned, pushing off the railing. Darika followed his stare.

"What's wrong?" she asked.

"I think that's Sera, but I don't recognize the car."

After a moment, though, he *did* recognize the person hopping out of the driver's seat: Jem. An odd feeling came over Kyle when he saw Sera's old friend at her side. Not jealousy. Something more like unease.

"Sorry about being late," Sera said in a breathless rush as she walked up to them. "Jem came to the rescue. He forgot one of his books at my house last night and swung by to get it this morning. Mom was already on the warpath. She always gets like this, you know, when things with the d—"

"Sera," Kyle warned under his breath.

"Deadlines at work get worse," she said instead, blinking at her near slip as Jem caught up to them. Her eyes fell on the girl at Kyle's side. "Hey, Darika. This is my friend Jem. Jem, this is Darika. And you remember Kyle from the other day, right?"

Jem smiled widely at Darika and bumped his closed fist to Kyle's before turning back to Sera. "I'll catch up with you later, okay? Need to see a man about a horse."

"You're so weird," she said, elbowing him in the side. "Don't forget about dinner tonight."

"Dinner?" Kyle asked as Jem disappeared through the front doors.

"His parents had to cancel the other night, and I felt bad about forgetting, and said I'd help him with his geography debate notes."

"How well do you know him?" Kyle asked.

She narrowed her eyes at him. "I told you, we grew up together. Why?"

"I don't know. It's a feeling, like something about him rubs me the wrong way. He's too . . . controlled."

Sera laughed. "Controlled? Jem's an open book. Always has been. What you see is pretty much what you get." She paused, going quiet for a second, her curious gaze fastening to his. Something flicked through her eyes, but it was gone before he could dwell on it. "I'm not into him, if that's what you're worried about. And he's definitely not into me."

"That's not it," Kyle said quickly, a rush of embarrassed heat flooding his cheeks. "And I'm not worried about you being with anyone. It's just a weird hunch. I could be wrong. I've been too on edge lately, with everything that's going on."

Darika cleared her throat and reached for her bag. "Did you clear him?"

"He's human."

She nodded. "I agree with Kyle that it's smart to be vigilant, but let's focus on the task at hand. Our first priority is the safety of the mortals."

"Agreed," Sera said after an odd look at the two of them.

Kyle followed the two girls into the school in silence. He knew he shouldn't have said anything about Jem. He didn't want to come across as the jealous best friend, and that's exactly what he'd done. The truth was, he didn't trust anyone. Seeing someone's energies didn't tell Kyle what kind of person they were—it just told him *what* they were. But just as a mortal could veer toward good or evil, sometimes there were a few bad apples in the ranks of the immortals.

Jem was simply a new face, and that made Kyle nervous. He'd been Sera's friend for far too long to give up on looking out for her now.

They pushed through the crowds of students congregating in front of the lockers, Darika clearing a path without much effort. He caught up to Sera. "Hey, look, I'm sorry. I didn't mean to make you feel weird about Jem. It's just that, after what happened with Jude, new people get my defenses up."

"I know."

"And we can't be too careful."

She shot him a dry look. "I know, Kyle."

"So, we're good?"

"We're always good," she said, grabbing her binder from her locker. "Tell me the minute you sense anything. The fouler the better."

Kyle knew what she meant. They needed a strong demon. The weaker demons tended to be followers, without access to the kind of knowledge they hoped to get. He nodded and collected his books before following her to their first-period class, one of the few they had together. Darika was in another class, but she'd be able to handle herself. Not that Sera couldn't—but Kyle felt better knowing he was at her side.

It wasn't until geography that he sensed the tug of something otherworldly on his consciousness. The hairs on his body stood stiff. He scanned the auras of the kids in the room as the eerie sensation winked in and out. Kyle knew within seconds that this was the type of rakshasa they were looking for. He blinked as he lost the trace again. Gritting his teeth, he pushed his awareness out to encompass the whole classroom.

Show yourself, he commanded the creature.

But the demon's shade was resilient, and the exercise was more challenging than he'd anticipated. Which could only mean one thing: it had to be an upper level rakshasa.

Methodically, he stripped past his mortal impression of each student. The demon was so close, he could feel it. His heart pounded as his gaze settled on Jem. Tendrils of energy curled around the boy like dirty mist. Kyle squinted, expanding his senses farther as his breath constricted in his chest.

But it wasn't Jem.

It was the sturdily built boy sitting beside him: Steven Peters. Kyle frowned. He should have known. Steven had started senior year with a crowd of shiny new friends—shiny new *popular* friends.

Kyle exhaled and pushed past the rakshasa's disguise. It took effort, but once he recognized the boy's shade for what it was, it wasn't too difficult to see past it. An oily green haze curled around Steven like a shroud.

Without warning, he turned and met Kyle's stare. For a second, the demon flickered into view, its puckered face obscuring Steven's human one. His lips peeled away from his teeth in a rotten grimace of a sneer as the boy stood and excused himself to go to the bathroom.

Jerking out of his seat to follow, Kyle froze at his teacher's reproving hiss. Mrs. Gordon rarely tolerated any kind of disturbance in her class. Kyle should know—she was the homeroom teacher who had sent him to detention on a regular basis junior year.

"You know the rules, Mr. Knox," she said. "Sit down and wait your turn."

"Sorry, Mrs. Gordon. It's an emergency."

Her glare turned acidic. "I'm afraid your emergency will have to wait until Mr. Peters returns."

"No can do."

Amid the stifled giggles from those around him, he tapped Sera on the shoulder on his way to the door. Her eyes snapped to his and he nodded imperceptibly, waiting as she gathered her books and rose.

"Miss Caelum, where do you think you are going?"

"It's an emergency?"

"Neither of you are permitted to leave this classroom. If you do, your next stop will be the principal's office and a week of suspension."

But everything came to a stop as Ilani appeared, her deifyre wings glistening in the morning sunlight streaming through the windows. She carried no weapons, but Kyle knew that she could summon them in the blink of an eye. She bowed to Sera. "Go. I will take care of this."

Kyle blinked, unaccustomed to seeing the Yoddha alone. "How?"

"I shall make her forget the last few minutes."

"You can do that?"

Ilani bowed again. "Only if I am permitted to do so. But Lord Devendra has said that Lady Serjana must be protected at all costs. This, I think, qualifies as protection."

"Thank you," Sera said. "Where's Mara?"

"She's with the Lady Darika."

He hurried from the room, thrusting his senses outward to pick up the scent of the demon. Now that he'd sensed its true nature, its foul aura was clear, but he didn't want to lose it. Not when they were so close. Kyle drew a deep breath and summoned his special sight. Though the demon was gone, he could see fading wisps of its essence along the hallway. They had to hurry or it would be lost.

"Quick, this way," he said over his shoulder as he raced through the deserted corridor and down a flight of stairs.

"Of course it has to be in the basement," Sera grumbled as they descended yet another staircase, this one dark and narrow, and in an area of the building Kyle had never seen before.

"Don't like dark spaces?" he asked.

"Who does?" she said, her face tight. "It's creepy."

"Why don't you flash some of your immortal glow, then?" Kyle suggested as they paused for a minute in a tunnel that disappeared into two offshoots in either direction. She obligingly flared her deifyre, illuminating the dark space in a soft, reddish-gold glow. He stared at her out of the corner of his eye, watching the flames tumble from her shoulders in a sparking waterfall. Seeing her in goddess form never failed to amaze him.

"Feel better?" he asked.

"No."

"You're a goddess," he said with a snort. "With blazing swords of fire and light. And you're afraid of a puny little demon?"

"Fear and worry are two different things. She scowled at him. "I'm *worried* that that puny little demon is leading us into a trap. And the minute we start underestimating them is the moment we lose. Which way do we go?"

"There," he said pointing to the right.

They both jumped as a rush of air slammed into their backs, announcing the arrival of Ilani. And she wasn't alone; Mara and Darika stood with her. "Ilani said you found one," Darika said by way of explanation.

"Yeah, it scuttled down that tunnel."

Their heads turned in unison, all four goddesses nodding.

"It's strong," Mara murmured.

Kyle exhaled slowly, using his sight to see the spots of dark mist. He didn't need special abilities to smell the faint odor of putrefying flesh. He gulped down a surge of bile. "That kid doesn't have much time. I've seen what happens with upper demons like that and their effect on mortals. Human bodies can't sustain their energy. They decay fast."

Ilani's lips twisted. "Demons love rotted flesh."

"Did you know him?" Sera whispered, pale-faced. "Steven?"

"Not really. He was a nobody."

"The ones demons love the most," Darika said, grim determination flaring in her face. "Come on, let's go. Kyle, lead the way and I'll follow. Sera, you stay in the middle, and the Yoddha will take up the rear. We move as one."

They sprinted down the narrow, cold corridor, following its mazelike twists and turns. The trail was still strong—until it abruptly disappeared. Kyle drew a sharp breath as he took in his surroundings. The demon had vanished into thin air.

Sera poked him in the side. "What's wrong?"

"It's gone," he said in a furious hiss.

"Gone where?"

He shrugged his shoulders. "Portal. That's the only answer."

She looked as confused as he felt. Portals had to be created by gods or goddesses, or by him, and even then, gaps between the realms could not be sustained for prolonged periods. "Maybe, but how?" Sera asked. "This is the basement of a school. Doesn't make any sense."

"Actually, it makes a lot of sense," Mara said slowly, her gaze scanning the space. "This school was constructed on what used to be an old burial ground."

Kyle looked at her then and huffed his surprise. Mara and Ilani were in full battle mode, deifyre flaring and weapons extended. So was Darika. She looked nothing like the composed girl from earlier. Now, eight arms sprouted from her body, holding a plethora of weapons—a trident, a mace, a bow and arrows, a discus, a thunderbolt, and a sword. Her face was fierce, and Kyle blanched at the ferocious look in her eyes.

"Burial grounds?" He couldn't suppress the shudder that ran through him as he looked around, half expecting to see bones protruding from the earth. "But if the demon did go back to Xibalba, where's Steven?"

A mortal body wouldn't be able to survive for long in the Dark Realms. The demon would have abandoned it somewhere.

"Here," Mara said, illuminating a dark corner of the room. Kyle could see the deathly pale, rail-thin body from where he was and shivered. Demon possession took a brutal toll as it fed on the flesh it contaminated.

Kyle couldn't help gagging at the sight of the boy's pustule-ridden body. "Where the hell is the demon?"

"Forget the demon," Sera hissed. "Is he alive?" she asked Mara, nodding to Steven's motionless body and clutching her hands to her nose.

"Barely."

Sera glanced at Mara and made her way to where the Yoddha stood. "He'll die if we leave him here."

"I've got him," Mara said, scooping the limp boy into her arms. Her dark eyes met those of the solemn Yoddha-in-training standing behind her. "Ilani, defend the goddesses until my return."

The younger Yoddha bowed, nodding. Kyle noticed that she was already armed with a blazing sword and a short dagger. Sera's gaze met his as Mara disappeared down the hallway with Steven.

"You were right about this demon being strong and old," Sera said to Kyle, her brow furrowing. "If the traces I sensed are right, I think it could have been here long before Azrath."

Kyle's eyes narrowed. *Before?*

"Some kind of backup plan in case Azrath failed to bring down the wards between the realms."

"The Demon Lords never really trusted him," Kyle said slowly, considering the possibilities. "Ra'al must have had his underlings in place for a reason. So . . . this is Plan B for the apocalypse."

"But how?" Ilani asked. "They can't portal in and out themselves."

"The ancient ones can," Kyle said. "Sera and I faced a churel demon last year that drew its own portal. And if she's right about this one, then it's as old, or older, than the one we fought. They're the right hands of the Demon Lords."

Suddenly, a sharp, sulfurous scent pierced the stale air of the basement as something rippled along the walls, making the hairs on his body rise in warning. Mordas appeared in his hands in the blink of an eye, even as Sera's twin blades of fire extended from each of her palms. "It's back," she said in a low controlled voice.

"Careful," Darika warned. "You know what we are here for."

Kyle nodded. They needed to capture the thing. Not kill it.

Correction. Make that things, he noted, as a dozen pairs of glowing, pale eyes took shape around them, accompanied by a cacophonous noise. The demon had gone to Xibalba and come back with its friends. They were outnumbered and surrounded.

Kyle hefted the black blade in his fist. It wasn't the first time and it wouldn't be the last.

He met Sera's eyes and grinned. "See you on the other side."

The Belly of the Beast

T he demons seemed to be coming from nowhere, dozens at a time. The faster Sera and her friends killed them, the more the creatures spawned. Sera's blades flew with lethal precision as they obliterated demon bodies into puffs of noxious ash. Out of the corner of her eye, she saw Darika making headway with the ones surrounding her. Her arms were a blur as they cleaved through the demons' ranks, but Sera could see the same frustration on her face as more of the little beasts kept attacking.

"Where are they coming from?" she shouted over their shrieks. "Kyle, can you see a portal? See if you can close it."

His answer was little more than a grunt as he fought off his fair share of beasts. "There isn't any."

"Then how are there so many of them? There has to be one. Find it!"

"Look at their feet," Darika panted. "They're backward-facing. These aren't demons—they're vetala. They live here."

"Ve-what?" Sera asked.

"Vampires. Spirits stuck between this realm and the others."

"*Vampires?* Are you freaking kidding me?" Sera balked at the thought—these things looked nothing remotely like the drop dead gorgeous vampires in movies. No Edward Cullens in sight. Couldn't a girl catch a break?

"I wish I were," Darika grunted as she swung through the thin wraith-like creatures that seemed to swarm from the very earth. "They're more like what your generation calls zombies. The vetala haunt corpses, possessing them and wreaking havoc on the world of the living. This unsanctified burial ground must have been a haven. These might have been sleeping here for centuries, so something must have roused them."

Sera fought an eye roll. She knew exactly what had awakened them—the demon that had cleverly lured them here and then skipped off to Xibalba. "How do we get rid of them? Doesn't seem like anything we do is working."

"If we cannot kill them," Ilani said, "we must return them to their rest. Lady Darika, as the consort of Lord Shiva, you alone can do this."

Fending off a handful of wraiths, Sera exchanged a desperate look with Kyle. He shrugged, but Ilani was the one to offer up the explanation. "Lord Shiva is the spiritual master of all animates, including the ganas—ghoulish spirits like these." She waved a hand. "They are meant to cause confusion and chaos, but they serve him."

"Can you summon him?" Kyle asked, slashing through three vetala as they leapt toward him.

Darika shook her head. "Yes, but it is not wise to summon him here. Ilani is right. It's up to me." She spread her eight palms wide and closed her eyes in meditation.

Suddenly, the frantic vetala stilled as if in response to only something they could hear. The abrupt silence in the chamber was unnerving, making a wave of gooseflesh erupt over Sera's skin. The spirits seemed drawn to whatever Darika was doing, their wraith forms swaying as if under some strange, godly compulsion.

"She manipulates material energy and the ganas as Lord Shiva does," Ilani whispered, making Sera jump. "So she can release the vetala from whatever has awoken them and compel them to return to their slumber."

"Is it working?" Sera asked dubiously. She kept her swords in defensive positions, expecting the creatures to leap out of their trance at any moment.

"I believe sh—" The last part of Ilani's sentence was swallowed by a shocked gurgle as a gaping red hole flared wide at her feet and hooked barbs dug into her calves, wrenching her halfway into the smoldering portal.

"Kyle!" Sera screamed, grabbing at Ilani, whose body had sunk to her thighs in the yawning pit below. Horrified, Sera wrapped her arms around the Yoddha's waist, trying to keep her from descending farther. "Something's got her."

Kyle lurched to her side, skidding to the floor and using Mordas to hack into the barbed metal tips burrowing into Ilani's legs. Whatever was pulling her down was strong, and the ugly weapon hooked into her flesh was barbaric. Sera recognized the metal whip—it was similar to the one Jude, the leader of the Preta, had used to pin Daevas in place so he could raze the deifyre from their wings. The last time she'd seen the Ifricaius had been when she and Kyle had fought for their lives against her uncle. Had one of the Demon Lords found it?

"Hurry," she shouted to Kyle. Darika was still in her self-imposed trance, keeping the vetala in thrall. With a pained moan, Ilani flared gold fire around them, her eyes glazing as she held on to Sera. Her body slipped several more inches until the Preta weapon was no longer visible.

"I can't get it," Kyle panted. "Whatever has her is out of reach."

"Help me haul her up, then," Sera cried.

They pulled together, but whatever horrible force on the other end refused to relinquish a single inch.

"I'm . . . sorry," Ilani moaned.

"No, no, you hold on," Sera said. "We'll get you out."

"Too . . . late." Spots of gold froth flecked Ilani's lips even as her cheeks turned ashen. "Already . . . poison . . . Xibalba."

Sera looked down in horror, and sure enough, sickly, inky tendrils curled up the Yoddha's skin at her waist, creeping into her deifyre and transforming the glowing wings into dull cinders. Sera had never stopped to ponder what happened to deities once they were exposed to Xibalba, but now she was seeing it firsthand. The touch of the Dark Realms literally burned them to embers. Ilani bucked in her arms and, suddenly, the bonds ensnaring her slackened and released.

"Pull, Kyle," Sera said urgently, scrambling backward.

But it was a cruel trick. Without warning, the portal cinched shut, severing the Yoddha's dying body in half. Ilani's back snapped and arched before she slumped against Sera, crumbling to white, flaky ash.

"Oh my God," Sera wheezed, her breath ragged at the sight of flakes of the dead deity floating to her lap. Kyle's arms went around her shoulders. "What the hell was that?"

"A message," he said dully.

"Saying what?"

"The gauntlet has been thrown," he said, gagging, his own brown face unnaturally pale. "They wanted us to have a taste of what's coming. The vetala were a distraction, and Ilani was the target."

Sera met his eyes and saw the grim truth there. He looked as sickened as she felt by the revelation. Of the three of them in that basement, Ilani had been the most vulnerable. The Dark Realms would not hurt Sera, Darika would have been harder to kill, and Kyle's ties to Xibalba were still undetermined. Kyle was right. Ilani had been *targeted*.

With a start, Sera looked around and realized that the vetala had disappeared, and Darika was coming out of her trance. She blinked, staring at the two of them, her gaze dropping to the pile of white cinders in Sera's lap. "What happened? Where's Ilani?"

Sera pushed past the lump in her throat. "Gone."

"How?" Darika asked.

"Some kind of portal opened up beneath her, and something dragged her in," Kyle explained, his voice breaking on the last word.

Darika knelt at Sera's feet, pressing two of her palms together and placing the backs of her thumbs to her own forehead. "I am sorry. Our only hope is that she will be delivered swiftly to Illysia for her sacrifice."

"And if not?" Kyle asked in a dead voice, rocking back to his heels. "What if her soul is stuck down there?"

"It won't be."

"How do you *know*?"

Darika stroked his arm in a gentle, calming motion. "That

is the way of karma. Ilani's deeds in this lifetime will determine her next. She is not meant for Xibalba."

The silence in the chamber was underscored by melancholy as Darika whispered her goodbyes for Ilani's departed soul. Sera couldn't help feeling a sense of loss deep within her heart. After the past few months, she was no stranger to death, but this felt different. Maybe Kyle was right—maybe it was some kind of message.

"Did you banish the vetala?" Kyle asked when Darika was finished, pulling Sera from her thoughts.

"Yes," she replied, worry creasing her brow. "They yielded, though with great reluctance. They are bound to the gravestones that lie beneath the school, but it seems they were promised freedom by the ones who led us here."

"Freedom?"

She nodded. "Before they returned to their tombs, they hinted at what was promised to them." Darika sighed and stood, running one of her palms through her hair in an all-too-human gesture of irritation. "The spoils of a war to end all wars. A war that will destroy the barriers between the realms, where the mortal world will be a free-for-all feast."

"But who woke them?" Sera whispered and rose to her feet, avoiding looking at the remains of the departed Yoddha. Though she knew that what Darika had said was true, that Ilani would return to Illysia and be reborn in some other form, it made her heart hurt. "Was it Ra'al?"

"I don't know." Darika drew a frustrated breath. "We need to convene with the Trimurtas. Though the word of the vetala is circumspect, we cannot afford not to take what they have said into consideration." She waved a hand. "Especially after what has happened to Ilani. Come, we must make haste."

"Wait," Kyle said. "We still haven't found out how the demons are getting into the Mortal Realm." He glanced at Sera. "Your dad once told me that some portals leave a residue, a trace of their path. If we can figure out what dimension of Xibalba that was, maybe we can figure out which one of the Demon Lords is behind this."

"How?" Sera asked.

"When you were taken that first time to Xibalba by the churel demon, Micah showed me how to keep the portal open. I needed Micah's strength then, but I can do it now on my own."

Sera sucked in a sharp breath at the mention of Micah, the Sanrak who had helped them defeat Ra'al. She frowned, certain that Kyle had also told her that what he and Micah had done had been excruciatingly painful. "Are you sure?"

"Yes," Kyle replied, though fear crept through his eyes. "I should be able to do it now."

"Kyle—"

"It'll be okay, Sera. This is what I do." With a determined shake of his head, he knelt and pressed his hands to the spot where Ilani had been slashed in two. His lips formed an incantation that Sera didn't understand, though she certainly felt its power. Whatever he was chanting resonated so deeply within her that she could feel the tug of Xibalba in her bones, clawing up her arm from her right palm. The sigil there burned at the invocation.

Feeling Darika's eyes settle on her, Sera quelled the feeling, pressing her hand into her thigh. Even though Darika seemed to be on their side, for all Sera knew, she might have been one of the ones who was afraid to allow Sera into Illysia.

A faint red glow appeared beneath Kyle's fingers, growing brighter as he retraced the Azura markings. He grunted and slammed his fist into the center. A hot red spark burst around his hand and the portal that had taken Ilani winked back into existence.

Kyle looked up at Sera and propped his arms on either side of the hazy gateway. His face looked haggard, but his expression remained determined.

"Here goes nothing," he said.

"Wait! You don't know what's in there," Sera said. "Or if it's the same one."

"It is, trust me. And we won't know who it's loyal to unless I look." He paused after a deep breath. "I'll take one peek and then come right back, I promise."

Darika cleared her throat and shook her head. "And what if whatever killed Ilani is still there? We can't risk losing you, too."

Sera was surprised at the impassioned note in her voice, though she wholeheartedly agreed with the goddess. She placed a hand on Kyle's shoulder. "She's right."

"We won't have another chance like this," he argued. "Either I go after the demon now, we capture it, and we learn which level of Xibalba we're dealing with, or we keep flying blind." His gaze swung between the two goddesses. "You both know who I am and where I come from. Xibalba won't hurt me."

Sera exchanged a glance with Darika, but the other goddess was nodding despite the fretful look on her face. "What he's saying makes sense," Darika said.

Sera's lips thinned. "And what if the same thing happens to you as Ilani, and the portal closes?"

"It won't."

"How do you know?"

He shrugged with a forced grin. "Trust me, if Ra'al wanted to kill me, he wouldn't do it by portal splice. If I know anything about my father, it's that he'd want me to suffer right in front of him, probably for the rest of eternity."

"I guess you have a point."

Darika stooped beside Kyle to press a swift kiss to his cheek. "If you're going to do it, be quick. Ten seconds at the most—anything more and the risk of discovery will be too great. The Demon Lord of whatever level you wind up in will be aware of your presence in seconds. Be careful."

"I will."

Sera blinked at Darika's concern, and Kyle looked as surprised as she felt. Sera didn't know which was worse: facing unknown demons or having to choose between two goddesses, one of whom was notorious for death and brimstone. She stifled a crazed giggle. Maybe she should tell Kyle that he'd be better off being tortured by Ra'al for eternity.

"You heard what Darika told you," she said instead. "Ten seconds. And try not to do anything stupid like die."

He exhaled with a crooked grin. "Can't say I don't keep things interesting."

⚜

The portal felt like day-old dirty fry oil. Slimy, tepid, and scummy. Kyle's heart hammered in his chest, its tempo speeding up with each tight breath he drew. He had no idea what he'd see on the other side, but he'd meant what he said. This was an opportunity they couldn't pass up . . . one *he* couldn't pass up, despite the cold dread sitting heavy in his stomach. He wasn't scared of what he'd find. He was scared of what Xibalba would do to him. What it would awaken.

Stop, you stupid coward.

He wasn't human anymore. He was immortal. It would take a lot more to kill him than a Preta weapon, and he controlled the portals between this world and Xibalba. He looked up one last time. Sera's expression was unreadable, but the pulse leaping at the base of her throat mirrored his. She was as terrified as he was.

Darika, too, seemed rattled. She hadn't seemed remotely concerned about him before. Or maybe he'd been so caught up in Kira that he'd misread the signs. He blinked. *Had* there been signs?

Time and place, moron.

His gaze hitched to the portal that glowed like hot coal below him. He could feel its heat blanketing him. But it wasn't scorching. It was warm and welcoming. Even now, his skin tingled with anticipation at the thought of what he was about to do . . . as if he were going home.

But Xibalba wasn't his home. Nothing about it was home.

With a shuddering exhale, he sank face-first into the portal. The snatch of sulfurous air was immediate, sizzling into his lungs and choking him. He gasped and wheezed, blinking tears from his eyes as he took in the details of where he was. He didn't have much time. Ten seconds was a blink of an eye.

One.

It was deserted. But Kyle knew more intimately than anyone how deceptive the landscape of Xibalba could be. He wasn't in Ra'al's seventh dimension—that much he knew. Thick red dirt the color of rust stretched as far as he could see. It wasn't any kind of plains. The earth was damp and rolling like an undulating carpet. Alive. He flinched as a hand pushed up from the scarlet soil like some kind of macabre growth. It was covered in maggots and ridden with pus-crusted sores.

Two.

The hand was connected to an arm and a shoulder, both littered with oozing lesions as they pushed up from their morbid place of rest. Kyle blinked as a torso appeared, topped with a head and a familiar face. *His* face.

Three.

The mouth of his doppelganger leered, displaying rotted teeth and a lolling, blood-tinged tongue. A foul stench filled his nostrils and he gagged as the distended tongue veered toward him.

"It's not real," he told himself, closing his eyes and fighting the raw hallucination. But it *felt* real, which was just as dangerous. He drew a shallow breath into his lungs, but he couldn't help the feeling that the thing was infecting him somehow. Poisoning him.

Four.

Without warning, his entire body started to convulse, and his doppleganger smirked.

"Why have you come here?" it asked.

"Who are you?" Kyle grunted.

Five.

"The better question is, who are *you*, Prince Kalias?" It cocked its head to one side, a hand rising to scratch at its cheek. A chunk of flesh came away in its fingers. "A false heir, so it would seem."

"That's not my name, and I'm no one's heir."

"You are bound by blood." The creature, some kind of demon Kyle was sure, licked at the putrid section of flesh it held in its grip. "And blood is blood."

Six.

Kyle groaned in frustration, ignoring the phantom pain in his body as his burning eyes scanned the space. He wasn't diseased, he wasn't dying—even though every second felt like it. It was some kind of delusion meant to destabilize him. The demon wasn't going to volunteer information. And he had only four seconds left to work that out on his own. Or demand it.

"Where am I?"

"Why should I tell you?" his doppelganger retorted, clambering from the red dirt until they were nose to nose. Kyle held his ground though the reek of it was near overpowering.

"You said I'm the heir."

"No, I said you were the *false* heir." The demon's long bloody tongue snaked out to lick his cheek and Kyle recoiled from the wet swipe. His skin burned from the acid the creature's saliva left behind. "You taste like deifyre."

Six. No, seven.

He stumbled in his counting as the sting of the demon's fetid touch eclipsed every thought in his brain—in the exact spot where the goddess had kissed him. The flesh of Kyle's cheek flaked, eating through to his jaw and his teeth. He could only imagine what Ilani had felt, considering she was made entirely of deifyre. The pain would have been excruciating.

Eight.

Nearly paralyzed by the demon's poison slashing through him, Kyle released one of his hands from his grip on the side of the portal in the Mortal Realm and grabbed the thing about the throat.

"Where am I?" he hissed, his fingers tightening and sinking into the sludge of the corpse's neck. His anger only made the creature's grin widen in glee.

"There's some of your father left in you yet," it crowed. "Kill me, Prince Kalias. Claim my life and your place."

"That is *not* my name."

"You can never escape who you are, boy. She will die for you. They will all die."

Nine.

The demon's face twisted and reformed until it no longer resembled him . . . until it was no longer remotely human. A snarling, muddy animal snout snapped far too close to his face as his eyes took in the length of a matted, hairy body to crudely taloned feet.

This was no middling demon. It was a Demon Lord.

In that instant, Kyle knew exactly where he was.

"You can run only so far," the Demon Lord mocked. "Your blood, immortal or not, is ours."

Kyle mustered all his strength to club the creature away, and wrenched himself up through the portal, sealing it shut behind him.

Ten.

Falling to his haunches, he exhaled and vomited.

Keep Your Friends Close

❧❧❧

Sera hurried to where Kyle was hunched over, wincing at the stink coming off him. He smelled like rancid meat.

"I'm fine," he mumbled, swiping at the back of his mouth with his sleeve. He turned to face her and Sera blanched at the livid, puckered flesh of his cheek.

"What happened?"

"Got a small taste of what happens to deifyre in Xibalba after that kiss." His eyes flicked to Darika. "I ran into Lamasha."

"Lamasha?" Darika's eyes were round as she looked from Sera to Kyle. "Are you certain it wasn't Ra'al? You know how much he loves to play with other forms. Could you have been mistaken?"

Kyle shook his head weakly while Sera concentrated on healing the welt on his face. "Trust me, I'd know Ra'al in any form. It was Lamasha. I was in the fourth." He winced as the wound pulled tight, knitting together, and the pain lessened to a dull roar.

"Any more hints on what they are planning?" Darika asked.

Kyle shrugged. "I don't know, but it obviously involves the rulers of the other dimensions. We have to assume that it's no longer just Ra'al at the helm."

Darika nodded thoughtfully. "His defeat at your hands would have been seen as weakness. A coup was to be expected."

Sera frowned. The last time she'd confronted the Demon Lords of Xibalba, she'd had the misfortune to meet four of the seven: Ra'al, the most powerful lord, that of the seventh and the worst dimension of hell; Temlucus, lord of the sixth; Belphegar, lord of the fifth; and Dekaias, Kyle's twin brother and lord of the first. They had all been terrifying in their own right, but she'd never met Lamasha, or the Demon Lords of the second and the fifth.

"The fourth," Sera said, trying to recall what she'd read about the different dimensions in Xibalba, thanks to the resourcefulness of her little brother, who had scoured the Internet for information and nearly gotten himself killed in the process. "That's the dimension of disease, right?" she asked.

"Yeah," Kyle said.

Sera fought back a shudder as another waft of putrid air reached her nostrils. "What did she say to you?"

"She called me the false heir and she wanted me to kill her to take my place," Kyle said. He looked like he had more to say, but sealed his mouth shut at the last moment. A flicker of something like resignation passed over his eyes. Sera squeezed his shoulder. She knew all too well of what it must have cost him to venture back into the Dark Realms after everything that had happened. Xibalba's dark claim on him was hard to overcome. And she would know—she fought the pull of it every single day.

"Was that all?" she whispered.

He shook himself and shot her a caustic look. "No more than the usual. 'Blood is blood,'" he intoned sarcastically. "'You can never escape your father. You're a prince of Xibalba. Take your place and reign in hell.' Clearly, they didn't get the memo that that ship has sailed, even if the Ne'feri didn't."

She grinned at his bravado. At least he still had a sense of humor about it. "You're not Ra'al, Kyle," she said. "You know that. They're just trying to get to you. That's what they do—sow seeds of doubt, hoping one will take root."

"Yeah, I know." The humor faded from his face as his fingers clenched the hilt of Mordas lying in his lap. "I hate that place. And knowing that I'm from there."

Sera gripped his shoulders harder, forcing him to face her. "Listen to me. The Trimurtas made you an Azura Lord," she said. "They saw something in you that was worth saving. Hold on to that. It's about who you are now, not who you were or where you come from, do you hear me?"

"I don't want to hurt anyone. You, especially. Lamasha said I would."

She gritted her teeth. "If I thought for one second you were a danger to me, do you think I'd be here with you at my side?" She glanced at the silent goddess standing next to them. "Do you think Darika would be here? Or that Dev would let me be here alone with you? The Demon Lords are going to say anything to weaken you. Don't let them in."

"I know." But his response was quiet. Whatever else that Demon Lord had said, it had shaken him to the core. And it had to do with *her*. She vowed to get to the bottom of it before he allowed it to eat him up inside.

Darika moved quickly back the way they'd come, drawing their attention. Her eyes narrowed down the hallway that had led them here. "Someone's coming."

Sera and Kyle scrambled to their feet. "Demon?"

"No. Human." Darika squinted, confusion flitting across her features. "I think."

Sera made her twin weapons disappear, and Mordas did the same in Kyle's hands, while Darika resumed a more human appearance. They remained wary, but the face that peeped around the entryway was a familiar one . . . and explained Darika's confusion.

The new arrival was *half* human.

"Nate!" Sera exclaimed, her relief turning instantly to aggravation. "What on earth are you *doing* here?" Her eyes flicked past him. "Alone! What were you thinking?"

"Tracked you." Nate grinned. "And I'm not alone. There's a Yoddha around somewhere, though I might have lost her."

"You *tracked* us? What does that even mean? How? Why? Shouldn't you be in school?"

"Which of those do you want me to answer first? Anyway, it's lunch period," he replied nonchalantly and sauntered into the chamber. "Smells like dead butt in here."

"Are you serious, right now?" Sera threw her hands up in exasperation. "You have one minute to explain, or I serve you up on a platter to Mom. And we both know how that's going to end."

"Fine," he said. "Don't give yourself a heart attack. I overheard Mom and Dad talking last night, after your big secret meeting, about what you guys were going to do at the school, and I wanted to help."

"You overheard? You mean eavesdropped."

"Sure," he said with a mischievous wink. "Anyway, I knew Mom would never let me, so I decided to bike over here during lunch and see if you'd found anything." He glanced at Kyle, who wore the same incredulous look Sera knew she must have on her own face. "And it looks like you did. Was it a demon? Did you kill it?" Without waiting for an answer, Nate peered at Darika with interest. "Nice trident. I like your third eye." He stuck out a hand. "You must be Durga."

That eye—which no human should have been able to see—narrowed at him. "Thank you, and yes. Though please call me Darika."

Sera sighed, staring from the goddess to her brother. "Darika, this is my little brother, Nate. He's a know-it-all and is cruising for serious trouble."

A smile crossed the goddess's face as she studied Nate. "Half Sanrak," she said. "Sophia's blood. How old are you?"

"Eleven."

Darika's hand closed around Nate's, and at the contact, Sera sensed a burst of energy so potent that it made her sway. She wasn't the only one to have felt it either. Kyle inhaled sharply, and Darika looked surprised as she stared down at their joined hands.

"Powerful," she murmured.

Nate's green eyes lit up. "Powers? Like can I fly? Like Mom and Sera?"

"Possibly."

He grinned and wiggled his eyebrows at Sera. "See? Told you I'm a demigod. Just like Percy Jackson."

"A demigod who's going to be grounded the minute we get home," Sera muttered under her breath as she grabbed his hand and started down the hallway. She didn't even look back to see if Kyle and Darika were following. She needed to get her meddling little brother out of there. "What if another one of those demons had been lurking down here? You can't go running off like this without protection. It's not safe."

Instead of being chastised, Nate's face lit up. "So you *did* find one! Was it totally gross?"

"Did you hear a word I just said? You could have been killed."

He glared up at her. "You're starting to sound just like Mom." He pulled something out of a pocket inside his jacket. "I told you—I saw a Yoddha. And I can totally take care of myself."

Sera halted in her tracks to stare at what looked like a glowing slingshot in his palm. "Where'd you get that?"

"Micah."

"Micah?"

"Yeah, he's been teaching me stuff. Mom asked him to."

Sera's brows snapped together. She hadn't known about Nate's lessons with a Sanrak deity. "What kind of stuff?"

"That's classified." He smirked, backing out of her reach. "But I'll tell you if you have any valuable information to trade."

She snaked a hand out toward him, but he darted out of the way and skipped behind Kyle, who looked like he was struggling to contain his laughter.

"You are *so* dead when we get home," she warned him as they climbed the stairs and pushed open the heavy metal door to the upper level of the basement.

A row of industrial lights illuminated the space and they all blinked as their eyes adjusted from the gloom of the sub-basement. It was a storage room of some sort, filled with moldy crates and stacked old furniture. When they'd chased the demon through here, it'd been pitch-black.

"Did you turn on the lights?" Kyle asked Nate.

"No."

Sera stared at him. "How'd you find us, anyway?"

"Skills."

"Nate, I'm serious," she said. "Did something draw you down here or tell you to come this way?"

"No, I told you. I tracked you." Nate flushed as if imparting some precious secret. "Turns out I can sense deifyre—yours in particular." Sera's jaw dropped as she stared at her brother. He hesitated. "It's because we're related. Micah's been working with me on identifying the differences between yours and Mom's. They're similar. Anyway, if I focus hard enough, I can pretty much find you wherever you are."

"That's . . . useful," she said after a beat, frowning. "Not sure that I like the idea of being a GPS tracker in human form, though."

"What else has Micah been teaching you?" Darika asked.

"Mostly how to control and gather my energy. It's hard though, like trying to hold a breath inside my chest and then directing it to do things."

"Like what?"

"Healing. Moving things. Using it as protection. Or as

a weapon." He paused, staring up at her. "Micah said my powers come from my mom, and that she used to be a powerful warrior. Is that true?"

Sera felt Darika's glance slide to her. They both had collective memories of their own past incarnations—all goddesses did. Sera felt the memories bubble to the surface. In a past life, Sophia had been Sera's Sanrak guardian when she'd been another avatar. And Micah was right—Sophia had been a formidable warrior. She still was.

"Yes," Darika agreed. "In her time, she was one of the greatest leaders of the Sanrak."

The faintest whiff of sulfur made them all freeze. The smell meant one thing. With a frustrated growl, Sera moved to stand in front of Nate and shoved her brother behind her back as she, Kyle, and Darika took up defensive positions. Weapons appeared in their hands.

"More vetala?" Sera whispered.

"No," Kyle said. "They didn't smell like that."

Her eyes scanned the space. "Where are they?" She didn't have to wait long for the answer—a group of five juniors and seniors slipped out from a row of crates. Sera recognized two of them from geography. They looked just like a bunch of students skipping class, but the subtle odor said otherwise. "Kyle?" she asked.

He nodded, raising Mordas in his hand. "Demons."

"Don't hurt them," she said as Darika shot her an incredulous look. Once more, Darika did not look like her meditative self—she looked ferocious, like her sister. "They're just kids," Sera justified. "They're innocent."

Darika's eyes flared, her trident and sword appearing

in brilliant starbursts. "They are *not* innocent. They knew exactly what they were doing when they agreed to be hosts. It's a reciprocal trade. Don't fool yourself, Serjana."

Déjà vu, Sera thought.

Though Darika seemed more reasonable than Kira, she didn't want a repeat altercation.

"They're *teenagers*."

"Who knew what they were doing," Darika shot back.

Sera's deifyre blazed. "You've been asleep too long if that's what you think. In the teenage world, if someone promises you an inroad to the in-crowd, you take it. Everything in high school is life and death. You think a fleeting deal with a devil to be popular means that a kid is evil? It just means they want to fit in." She turned to Kyle. "Do your thing."

She watched as he sucked in a breath, stripping the demons from their human bodies and banishing them back to Xibalba in one fell swoop. But even as he did so, a new trio of kids appeared from behind the crates. Sera dismissed her weapons, shooting Darika a cautionary glare. Two girls rushed her, compelled by the demons within, but with immortal speed, Sera ducked, dispatching each with rapid blows to the temple. Their bodies slumped to the floor as Kyle exorcized the demons from them with a word.

Out of the corner of her eye, she saw the last student dive toward Darika, who grabbed the boy by the neck. Sera held her breath as the goddess held his body high. The boy's eyes rolled back in his head as the demon within fought futilely against her immortal strength. After a tense moment, Darika released the boy, flinging him to Kyle's feet. He quickly purged the demon from its host.

"Thank you," Sera said.

"Don't thank me yet," Darika said in an emotionless voice. "Your affinity for the mortals has always been your greatest weakness. In the end, they will be the ones who destroy you."

"That may be so," Sera replied coolly. "But their souls are not lost to Xibalba. Who are we to condemn them?" She waved a hand. "I've seen the face of true evil, and this is not it. Trust me, they are pawns, not monsters."

Darika bowed her head slightly. "As you say."

"Sera," Nate called out in a low voice, a thread of fear permeating his tone. She turned to see five of the ugliest demons she'd ever seen lurking a stone's throw from where he stood. Her breath stalled in her throat.

Where did they come from?

These ones did not have hosts. And they weren't small, either. The largest was the shape and size of a massive gorilla. A dark gray hide riddled with bulging veins covered its entire mass, a row of razor-sharp tusks protruding from a gaping lower jaw. Red eyes jutted from its head and its clawed fists were the size of shovels. The other four were smaller but no less hideous. Jagged teeth pushed outward from their mouths.

"Pishachas," Darika whispered from behind them. "Flesh eating rakshasas."

Nate's eyes were like round green orbs as he stared at the demons, his breath coming in spurts and fits. Sera could see that the pishachas reveled in his fear.

"Don't move," Sera warned him. "And try to relax."

"What?" he squeaked. "Why?"

Darika's voice was low. "Pishachas are known for being

vicious. And greedy. They consume anything and everything, and feed off human emotion."

Their eyes converged on Nate.

Despite his earlier bluster, his small body trembled. "Sera . . ."

She signaled to Kyle and Darika. There was no way she could take out all three of them on her own without putting Nate in danger. Even with his fledgling Sanrak gifts, he was still human, which meant he could die if one of them bit him.

The creatures shrieked to each other, and Nate clapped his hands over his ears. They seemed fixated on him. Sera guessed that it had to do with the Sanrak energy mixed with his mortal form.

"Child," the big one articulated after an eternity of chatter, its distended eyes fastening onto Nate. "What you?"

"A boy."

"Not boy." A narrow tongue snaked out to lick one of its own crimson eyeballs. "More."

Sera took advantage of the pishacha's preoccupied fascination to attack. She gestured to Kyle as she surged forward, dispatching one of the smaller pishachas with her swords. The rakshasa shrieked as the celestial flames of her blades cleaved through its bulbous body. Two more turned to ash as Darika took care of them, and Kyle destroyed another.

"Run, Nate!" Sera flew at the big one, but it sneered at her and winked out of sight as Nate scrambled out of its reach. "Where'd it go?"

"It's shaded," Kyle shouted as he swung Mordas in wide arcs. "Still here. Darika, can you see it?"

Her third eye emerged as she scanned the room. "Behind you."

"Where's Nate?" Sera yelled, sudden awareness prickling her skin. Panting, she swung around, trying to see where Nate had run to last. But just as she spied him hiding near one of the crates, the lead pishacha materialized out of thin air and clutched him in its grip. Nate looked so tiny in the shadow of the hulking demon that her heart faltered.

"Don't hurt him," she blurted out.

The pishacha leered at Nate, its eyes rolling backward as if scenting something too delicious for words. Its thick claws caressed her brother's vulnerable neck, and Sera knew that one wrong move could be disastrous. She raised a hand, motioning to Kyle and Darika to remain still.

"What do you want?" she asked in a low voice.

"Want the pure soul," the pishacha said.

"Take me instead," Sera said. "Whoever your lord is will be happy to have me. I am the avatar of the goddess Lakshmi. I am more powerful than this boy."

The pishacha cocked its head to one side, considering her proposal. "The girl offers nothing of value to my lord."

"Who is your lord?" Kyle asked from behind her.

"The true lord of Xibalba." The pishacha smiled and bared row after row of needle-sharp teeth.

"Ra'al?"

"Yes and no." A hissing sound that passed for a laugh gurgled past its lips. "Lord Ra'al is part of the whole."

More sounds came from the pishacha's mouth, ones that made her stomach clench. She recognized the rhythmic chanting. The rakshasa sounded like it was summoning a portal—and it planned to take Nate with it. The only demon she'd ever seen open a portal had been an ancient churel, but that didn't mean this one could not. Sera readied her body for attack—she'd sacrifice herself if she had to for her brother's sake—but just as she was gathering her power to hurl it at the creature, a loud crack rang through the air.

The pishacha howled, stumbling backward with a smoking hole right between its eyes, and released its grip on Nate. Not to lose a second, Sera dashed forward to rip him out of the creature's reach before turning to face their rescuer.

Her mouth fell open in shock.

"Jem!" she gasped as he re-chambered a smoldering shotgun. "What are you doing here?"

He smirked at her and lounged on the doorjamb. "Killing a demon?"

"Wait, *what*?"

He patted the holster as they all gaped at him. "Special Ne'feri tulsi rounds. You know . . . holy basil? Designed to stop any demon in its tracks."

Xibalba Claims Its Own

ᔕᔕᔕ

"**Y**ou're Ne'feri?" Sera's voice was shrill.

Kyle rolled his eyes. Of course he was—he'd pegged Jem for a bit of a control freak. It made sense. In fact, he probably should have guessed.

Jem hesitated. "Well, not on this side of the pond."

"And you didn't tell me?" Sera shrieked.

He shrugged. "My dad thought it would be best for me to keep a low profile."

Darika's expression was inscrutable as she bent to awaken the rest of the unconscious teenage hosts and usher them back toward their classrooms. Kyle stooped to check on Nate for injuries as Sera stalked toward Jem.

"You okay, little man?" he asked Nate.

"Are you kidding? That was freaking *awesome*!" Nate's eyes shone as he turned to stare at the unmoving mass of the pishacha demon. "Is it dead?"

"Looks like it. I don't know about awesome, though," Kyle said, ruffling Nate's curls. "Got pretty hairy there for a minute. You could have been a demon buffet."

"I know, right?" Nate exclaimed with a delighted grin.

"Seriously, did you see that thing? It smelled like an old fart. Do you guys fight rakshasas like that all the time?"

"Slow your roll, dude," Kyle said, unable to suppress his smile as Sera shot them a glare over her shoulder. "And keep it down, or you'll get us both into trouble."

Nate peeked around him. "Guess Jem's in for it, huh?"

"Your sister's not a fan of secrets. Come on, let's get you out of here before you're reported missing from school."

He approached Sera with Nate in tow and cleared his throat. Sera still looked frazzled. Kyle nodded to Jem. "Lucky timing," he said. "And even luckier shot."

"Thanks, man, but no luck about it."

Kyle supposed he should be grateful that Jem had shown up when he did, but he didn't feel anything but unease. Knowing Jem was Ne'feri didn't mean he was ready to let his guard down. It was going to take a lot more than being in the right place at the right time for Kyle to trust him.

Sera shot him an urgent look, her concerned gaze running over her brother for any other injuries. "Kyle, we need to get Nate out of here. More of those things could come back."

"What about the pishacha?" he asked.

Nate huffed aloud. "You mean the demon that *was* there a minute ago?"

They turned to the spot where the demon had been laying. There was nothing there now but a glowing circle with red and black ashy embers marring the floor.

Kyle hissed his frustration through his teeth. "Damn it," he swore under his breath, stalking toward the sizzling sphere. The smell of sulfur scalded his nostrils. Kyle sighed as Sera joined him.

There was only one option. And Sera wasn't going to like it.

He swallowed hard, squaring his shoulders. "I'm going in after it."

To his shock, Sera nodded grimly. "I'm coming with you."

"No, it's too dangerous."

She eyed him, one fingertip rising to brush his previously injured cheek. "That's exactly why you're not going alone. Plus, it's not safe doing it so soon after your last visit. You got this and you threw up, remember? You could be vulnerable."

She was right, of course. He still felt somewhat nauseated. "That was different. Lamasha got a hold of the deifyre that was on my skin. I'm fine now. I can handle it."

Sera nodded. "What about Nate?"

"I can take him—" Jem volunteered.

"I'll see that he gets back," Darika cut him off as she returned from getting the students back to class.

Kyle could have sworn he saw a shadow of annoyance cross Jem's face, but it disappeared as quickly as it had come. Kyle met Darika's stare as she swept past him and stopped her with a touch of his fingers against her wrist. "No more farewell kisses?" he teased in a low voice.

"That didn't go so well the last time," she said, her eyes flicking to his bruised face, where she'd kissed him before. "Come back in one piece and we can talk about it."

He grinned. "Now, that's worth staying alive for."

Sera shot him a half-amused look as Darika and Jem left with Nate. "You're playing with fire."

"How so?" he asked, all innocence.

"They're sisters, Kyle," she said in an exasperated tone.

"*Goddess* sisters with infinite power at their fingertips. And in case you haven't noticed, Kira is a little unhinged."

"I can handle Kira."

"Can you?"

He scowled at her, irritated by her censorious stare and determined to ignore the uneasy feeling her words elicited in the pit of his stomach. "Honestly, how is my love life any of your business? Did I interfere in yours?"

"You kind of did," she said evenly. "And it does become my business if your actions put innocent people in jeopardy."

"I'm not putting anyone in jeopardy," he said incredulously.

"Ever heard the saying 'hell hath no fury like a woman scorned'? That doesn't come close to covering the storm heading your way. I have a feeling that Kira won't be forgiving if she finds out some clueless boy has been leading her on."

"I'm not leading her on." He paused, running a hand through his short, tufted curls. Sera was his best friend, and though her unsolicited honesty annoyed him, she was one of the few people he trusted. "Kira scares me a little, and Darika can be hard to read," he ventured. "But they're both interesting."

She sent him a withering look and rolled her eyes.

"What?" he asked.

"Boys," she scoffed. "It's such a double standard, isn't it? A girl gets caught between two guys, and it's a love triangle. A boy does it, and suddenly, it's options. Where's the fairness in that?"

"Um . . ." His mouth opened and closed. She had a point. He could make a quip that at least it wasn't a quadrangle, but she probably wouldn't appreciate it.

"You need to make a decision, before someone gets hurt." She chucked him in the shoulder. "I'd like to avoid a whole different kind of apocalypse on the heels of this one if I can help it. Demon Lords I can stop, but twin Tridevi goddesses are another matter entirely."

He gulped. "Don't worry, I will."

Sera knelt at the edge of the still smoldering gateway. "Now, what's the plan with this portal?"

Grateful to no longer be discussing relationship shapes, Kyle drew a deep breath. "We find the pishacha and haul it back." He met her eyes, then looked at her right hand, the one marked by the rune of Xibalba. "I have Mordas, but you're going to have to call on your hellfyre down there. You cool with that?"

Her lips tightened, but she nodded. "I'll have to be."

Kyle knew that she didn't like using the dark side of her powers, or the fact that her deifyre didn't work in Xibalba. The last time they'd been there together, it had been eye-opening for both of them. He didn't want to think about what this excursion would bring.

"You ready?"

"Oh, crap," Sera murmured, her face going pale as her gaze hitched on something behind him.

Kyle bristled and turned, wondering what fresh hell they were about to face, but his stomach dropped at the sight that greeted him: Mara had returned, and she wasn't alone. She'd brought Sophia with her.

At the best of times Sera's mother terrified him, and right now, her expression was pure wrath. Her lips were pulled so flat that her mouth was just an angry slash in her face. She surveyed the wrecked basement room.

"Where's Nate?" she demanded.

Sera stiffened like a deer in headlights, so Kyle tried to answer. "Nate . . . um . . . he was here. But he's not anymore."

"When?" she snapped.

"About five minutes. Darika took him home."

"He came here on his own, I sw—" Sera's words were cut short by her mom's glower. "Tracked me somehow. I'm sorry, Mom, I tried to send him back, but then the pishacha appeared and nearly took him—" She broke off abruptly as her mother's scowl went supernova. "He's safe, don't worry. Like Kyle said, he's with Darika."

"Thank the gods," she said in a strangled voice, though Kyle could see the strain start to leave her shoulders. "Were you hurt, Sera?"

"I'm fine, Mom."

To Kyle's shock, Sophia gentled her gaze before turning to him. "Thank you for looking out for Nate, and for her."

Taken aback, he stammered his response. "I didn't do much, but you're welcome."

Sophia nodded to Mara, who was standing watch at the entrance. Kyle met the Yoddha's eyes too, and he felt her sorrow from where she stood. She would have sensed it the instant that Ilani had died. And though death was a heroic end for any celestial warrior, that didn't mean that those left behind wouldn't miss them.

"Are you two coming?" Sophia said over her shoulder.

Sera bit her lip, avoiding her mother's eyes, and Sophia halted mid-step. Kyle watched the wheels in her head turning as she belatedly put two and two together, her eyes falling to the portal glowing faintly beside them. Her lips pressed thin.

"Don't tell me you're planning to—" She broke off, her ferocious glower returning in full force. "No, I forbid it."

"We have to go after the rakshasa, Mom," Sera began. "It's our only chance."

"No."

"This demon was a pishacha," Sera said. "It was old and powerful. It said things about the new lord of Xibalba, and Ra'al's time being over. This is the demon we need—the one that can tell us who's really in charge. What they're planning."

"Sera—"

Sera stood to face her mother. "I'm not letting Kyle go in there alone. And I'm the only one who *can* go with him. We don't have much time. Either we do this now, or we watch everything and everyone we love die. I can't let that happen." Sophia's glare softened, and Sera pulled her mother into a tight embrace. "We'll come back, I swear."

"That's an impossible promise," Sophia whispered, her hands shaking at Sera's back, but Kyle saw the resignation in her expression. She understood that this was the only chance they had.

"Then I promise not to do anything dumb."

Kyle rolled his eyes and Sophia smiled at him through her tears. "I'll make sure she doesn't," he said. "We'll be careful, Mrs. Caelum. And if anything goes bad, I'll portal us out instantly."

"Take care of her," Sophia said in a choked voice.

"I always will."

To his surprise—this day seemed to be full of them—she grabbed him close and hugged him, too. "What's the matter?" she asked him at his startled chuckle.

"I'm not sure that hell isn't freezing over right now," he joked. "Six months ago, you kind of hated me."

"I didn't hate you," she said slowly. "I just questioned your choices." She gave her daughter a long-suffering look. "But now I've come to understand that some of those choices were made by a certain someone else with a very stubborn streak."

"Told you he wasn't all bad, Mom." Sera smirked and looked to Kyle. "You ready for this?"

"Yeah."

As they approached the portal again, Kyle chanted under his breath, waving his hand above it and re-creating the portal through which the pishacha had vanished. It didn't take him long—he was becoming more comfortable with his abilities— and soon the portal glowed an unholy color and shimmered to life. Sera squeezed her mother's fingers one last time and nodded at Kyle.

He reached out his hand to hers and together they stepped into the glowing circle.

The blast of blistering wind was immediate, battering their faces with the force of a tornado. He could feel Sera's fingers slipping from his, and he tightened his hold. Bits of rock and sand cut into his cheeks, leaving stinging welts in their wake as his body was twisted and flung a thousand different ways. The only thing he could feel was the clammy grip of Sera's palm.

"Hold on, Sera," he shouted, but he didn't know if she could hear him above the diabolic howling of the wind. "Don't let go."

But the pull was inescapable. He could feel his fingers losing their grip, could feel hers slackening as a tremendous gust ripped them apart. Her scream came to him like an echo of an echo, and then he was flailing and tumbling into dank, empty space.

Struggling to right himself, Kyle peered through the whirlwind, fighting to see beyond the storm. His eyes teared as grains of sand embedded themselves in the exposed parts of his cornea.

"Sera!" he screamed.

But it was too late. She was gone.

Beneath the Bowels

❧❧

Sera's eyelids cracked open to reveal a scorched, orange-hued sky. Her back ached from laying on a hard, unforgiving surface. Sharp rocks cut into her elbows as she levered herself up. The soft sounds of water reached her ears, and for a second, she wondered whether she'd been dreaming, safe in her world between worlds.

A glittering body of water to her right caught her attention, but she suddenly realized that there were no trees, no birds, no sound at all but her heartbeat rushing in her ears. The silence felt alive.

Sera hauled her body upright, taking in her surroundings. She was on a cliff. The land around her was desolate and dusty despite the lake she'd seen. When she looked back at it, her blood curdled. It wasn't filled with water. No water could look that red or that viscous. She retched, spitting out a mouthful of pink-tinged bile. The hungry earth sucked up the moisture like a sponge, and Sera had the distinct impression that it would consume anything alive. Including her.

She wasn't safe at all.

She was in Xibalba.

Kyle. He had to be here, too, somewhere. She had no idea

which of the Dark Realms' dimensions she had arrived in. Or whether she was as alone as she seemed to be.

She stood, her bones aching with the effort. Whatever storm they had faced upon entering the portal had left her battered and bruised.

Catching sight of the gaping hole at the bottom of her shirt, she tore off the frayed hem. She didn't seem to be hurt in any other way, though she checked herself from top to bottom just in case. In the seventh, she'd once seen souls being devoured by leechlike demons. And she wasn't entirely sure she wasn't in Ra'al's domain. She could be anywhere.

She had to find Kyle. And she had no idea where to start.

"Get off this cliff," she muttered to herself. "That's your start."

Dusting her hands on her jeans, she began the descent from the rocky bluff. After fifteen grueling minutes, she took a break on a ledge. Her breath wheezed from the effort, and her thirst was near unbearable. She had to have made some decent progress, she thought as she shaded her eyes and looked to the rolling landscape below. But the distance to the ground looked exactly the same distance away, and the torn hem of her shirt lay in the dust at her feet. She was right back where she'd started!

She blinked, thirst making her thoughts fuzzy. Had she imagined climbing down?

Eyeballing a ledge about ten feet down, she took a running jump and landed squarely in the middle of it. Her knees screamed from the force of the drop, but she grunted in satisfaction and looked down. The stupid piece of frayed hem was still two feet away. Impossible.

Or maybe it was just Xibalba.

She had one option open to her: hellfyre. But despite what she'd told Kyle, deep down, she was terrified to summon it. Hellfyre was born of Xibalba, after all. However, she'd be stuck here if she didn't. It was the lesser of the two evils . . . in an inherently evil realm. Sera shuddered. She was damned if she did and damned if she didn't.

"Screw it," she said, gasping as she felt the flames envelop her body.

The hellfyre that surrounded her was a deep red, much like the shade of the lake below. The color of blood. She shoved the thought away. Dev had once told her that it was the color of life. Now, it felt like the harbinger of death.

None of that mattered now, though. She had to find Kyle. And a smelly pishacha demon.

Power suffused her limbs as she leapt from the cliff, her fiery wingspan twice the length of her body. She'd been mistaken—the lake she'd seen was more like an endless ocean. She skimmed the surface of the crimson sea, seeing the churning of bodies trapped beneath its waves to suffer an eternity of torment. Even as she flew above it, she could feel the steam coming off the surface, and every now and again, the same whiff of cooking flesh would reach her nostrils.

Sera glanced over her shoulder. The infinity cliffs where she'd been stuck were thin outlines in the distance. Veering across the bloody sea, she continued toward the rise of another landmass. Every so often, an arm would rise from the liquid below her as though begging for release, but there was nothing she could do. Those souls were meant to be here. It was not her place to absolve them of whatever sins had brought them to Xibalba. But she felt the ache of leaving them in her marrow.

Her resolve almost broke when the face of a child thrust above the surface. The boy couldn't have been more than ten or eleven. Nate's age. What could he possibly have done to be condemned to such suffering?

"Please," he cried, his plea pitiful and terrified. "Save me, Serjana Maa."

Mother Serjana.

Maybe the boy was in the wrong place. Surely he wasn't meant to be in Xibalba. Sera felt her flight falter and she halted in midair before descending, the tips of her wings making ripples on the suddenly flat surface of the red sea. The boy held up an arm and Sera reached down at the same moment.

If she had hesitated, the creature rising from the depths would have swallowed her, but she saw the shadow and churn out of the corner of her eye and bolted upward. An enormous beast leapt up, its serrated teeth snapping at her heels. The child smiled and Sera belatedly realized that it wasn't a child at all.

Of course it wasn't.

Barbed tentacles shot toward her, one catching the end of her ankle, and she screamed. It burned like acid. She swerved up, trying to dislodge the thing's hold, but the jellied tentacle only burrowed more deeply into her skin. The rakshasa hauled her down toward the roiling ocean, a thousand greedy maws opening wide with the promise of fresh blood a hairsbreadth away.

Her wings ached from trying to propel her body upward. Each time she gained an inch, the demon dragged her down two more. Its monstrous eyes studied her, cool and calm, and Sera realized that in some way she was being measured. The rakshasa had to be a servant of the Demon Lord of this dimension. She could sense the power of its master behind its gaze.

"Release me," she seethed.

The monster laughed, igniting a cacophony of shrieks across the sea of blood, and making Sera cringe in response. "Why should I?" Its voice was as guttural as its grating laugh.

"You know who I am and what I can do."

"And?"

She addressed the Demon Lord watching behind its servant's vacant eyes. "Face me and I will be happy to demonstrate."

"Spoken like a true warrior," it replied. "But I prefer to see you suffer. Torment, after all, is my greatest pleasure."

Temlucus. It had to be. A shiver wound through her. He was the Demon Lord of torment, which meant she was in the sixth dimension of Xibalba. An image of him—a hooded specter of death—flooded her brain. When she'd seen him last, he'd been scorched and charred, his eyes like burning embers. He was the one who had thrown a dagger into Kyle's shoulder to draw the blood needed to summon the Kali demon.

"I should have known it was you," she ground out, her strength waning. She could feel the poison of the demon's barbs sinking deep into her flesh and weakening her even more. It wouldn't kill her, she knew, but the agony made it difficult to focus. "Ambitious Temlucus."

The demon's puppet laughed again. "Ra'al was weak. Unfit to lead. Too consumed by thoughts of his own legacy to see the future."

Sera dropped three more inches toward the bubbling surface of the sea. "And you're a better choice?"

"The KaliYuga is imminent. What you saw was a taste of what's coming, and no one, not even the venerated Trimurtas, will be able to stop it."

"You think they won't stop you?" This time, it was Sera who laughed. "Trust me, Kali won't hesitate to wipe it all out. And then what will you have? Nothing to feed your depraved souls. You'll wither and die."

The rakshasa yanked at her body, dragging her close enough for a second tentacle to join the first. Her left foot disappeared beneath the surface to the knee for a full second before she wrenched it free.

Sera gulped in a breath of air and summoned her weapons. Blades of scarlet fire extended from each hand and she flipped upside down in midair. In a smooth motion, she sliced at the tentacles holding her prisoner, even as talons rose up from the deep to tangle in her hair.

Bloody droplets splattered her face and dribbled over her lips. She gagged at the fetid taste. Her blades swung through other faces and arms writhing beneath the surface as a dozen more feelers from the rakshasa sprang in her direction. Gasping, Sera soared upward out of reach. Her entire left leg throbbed, but she didn't dare look down at it. She'd felt the demons in the blood, devouring her, sucking on her flesh. She needed to stay calm to face the Demon Lord.

"Why don't you come out from hiding, Temlucus?" She forced a mocking laugh. "Or are you truly that afraid of me?"

The rumble was slow at first, but gathered volume to become a roar. The entire landscape shifted. The sea bubbled

and burst into flames, and thunderous clouds convened over-
head. Acid-colored lightning forked across the sky in angry
bands.

"Afraid? You dare to insult me?" This voice was not the
guttural bark of the demon. No, these words were steeped in
the same sonorous tones she'd remembered . . . the ones that
were at complete odds with the demon's decrepit body.

"I meant no insult," she said mildly. "It was an honest
question. After all, I'm not the one hiding behind the faces of
my minions."

Temlucus did not answer, but a blackened atoll rose from
the sea, tall ebony spires of volcanic glass spearing upward.
Sera descended to its solid surface, where the Demon Lord
sat on a glossy, onyx throne, watching as a massive fortress
formed around them.

Temlucus's true form was not handsome. Unlike Ra'al,
who assumed the form of what people most desired, Temlucus
reminded Sera of a man caught in a burning inferno. Beneath
his sagging cloak, hot bands of ropy, reddened flesh intertwined with darker, charbroiled patches on his muscled chest.
Embers flaked from the molten grooves in his skin. In one
hand, he held a forked spear.

Simmering yellow eyes regarded her in silence before he
spoke. "You look well, Lady Serjana."

"Wish I could say the same. Where's Kyle?" Sera alighted
on the ground, but left her hellfyre to curl around her in a
protective shroud. Temlucus's eyes glittered.

"Ah, Prince Kalias, I assume. Your ever faithful . . . servant."

"He is no longer a prince of Xibalba, nor is he a servant of
mine," she said, her voice hardening. "Where is he?"

"Enjoying the climate?"

Dual flaming swords extended from each of her hands. "I'm not in the mood for your games."

"You forget your place." Steam curled from his mouth as his lips parted in a hiss. "You are in my domain now."

"And you forget who I am," she roared.

Hellfyre burst around her in a raging firestorm as brilliant, red mehndi vines twined up her arms and neck, curling across her cheeks and above her brow to form a crown.

Should she choose, Sera could lay claim to every realm in Xibalba . . . become the real Queen of Hell, so to speak. She could force every Demon Lord to bow at her feet. But doing so would mean giving up any claim to the Mortal Realm or Illysia. She would be bound to Xibalba forever.

Sera shoved away the eminently satisfying image of Temlucus groveling before her, his scorched cheek pressed to the dirt. "Do not make me ask again," she demanded. "Where is the Azura Lord?"

Temlucus scowled at her, then nodded to two wraiths nearby. They disappeared, but returned within moments, dragging Kyle between them. Sera suppressed a sigh of relief.

"Kyle?" His glazed, milky eyes rose to peer in her direction. There was no recognition in them. There was no *life* in them. "What did you do to him?"

Temlucus waved a careless hand. "Let's just say he was hunting a pishacha and he found one. It decided to make itself at home."

In Kyle's body.

Sera balked. Pishachas were old and strong, with the power to take on different forms and become invisible—and like the vetala, they preyed on mortal flesh and energy. Possession by one was said to drive mortal men insane. But she'd never heard of one occupying an immortal host.

"You lie," she said.

"Do I?"

Kyle's eyes rolled back in his head, and for a moment, the sheen of scarlet appeared in them. She could feel the malevolent energy from where she stood. Sera shook her head in confusion. "But he's immortal."

"He is a son of Xibalba," he said.

Sera's brows snapped together. Something wasn't making sense. Even if his blood were still tethered to the Dark Realms, Kyle would never have allowed his body to become invaded by some demon. He was far too strong for that.

Unless . . . he'd done it on purpose. To find out what the pishacha knew.

With a start, she had to admit that Kyle's ploy was brilliant. He'd managed to ensnare the pishacha with his own body. But now it was up to her to get them out of there and not make his strategy be for nothing. She inched toward Kyle, but was stopped by a tut-tutting noise from Temlucus. More shadow wraiths appeared around them.

"Release him," she commanded.

The Demon Lord's lips peeled back from his teeth. "I may be forced to acquiesce to your wishes, Lady Serjana," Temlucus said evenly, "but Prince Kalias entered my domain of his own will and is my guest." He favored her with a conciliatory bow. "Unless, of course, there is something of value you can offer in exchange. Say, a service to be rendered at a later time?"

"Never." She couldn't agree to such a thing. Who knew what he would ask for? And she'd be bound by her word to give it to him.

There was only one alternative—the right of challenge. She'd have to fight Temlucus in hand-to-hand combat to barter for Kyle's freedom.

It was the way of Xibalba. An eye for an eye.

She cleared her throat. "Very well, I'll fight you for him."

"I expected nothing less," he crowed, standing and signaling to one of the shadow wraiths. Sera wondered for a second if she had miscalculated. Did he *want* to fight? His exhilaration was clear as he clapped his skeletal hands. "And the champion of my choosing approaches."

She'd forgotten that he had the right to select a fighter in his stead. Her eyes narrowed at the person being escorted by the wraith, and her stomach fell as she recognized the shoulder-length, dark-brown hair and piercing, golden eyes. He was dressed in a yellow shirt and his smile made her chest constrict. Every cell in her body fired at the sight of him.

Dev.

Only it wasn't Dev. Because Dev could not be in Xibalba.

Sera's breath caught in her throat as she understood the true identity of the newcomer. It was Ra'al, the Demon Lord of the seventh. Sera frowned as he sauntered closer, the scent of marigolds following him. Dev's scent.

"What is this?" she snarled.

"My champion," Temlucus boasted.

Her brows knitted together. Since when had Demon Lords worked together? Fought for each other, even? It didn't make sense that Ra'al would fight any of Temlucus's battles. "He is a Demon Lord."

Temlucus's grin was triumphant. "One who owes me a favor. Lord Ra'al will fight in my stead. If he wins, I will reward him with his son." His grin widened to something horrible. "They have unfinished business, you see."

Of course. Ra'al wanted revenge. She didn't want to think of what he'd do to Kyle as punishment for defeating the apocalypse demon.

Sera gritted her teeth. "And if I win, I take Kalias with me."

"Agreed. But let's cross that bridge when we come to it, shall we?"

Ra'al, with Dev's face, approached her, his hands outstretched as if to embrace instead of fight. Sera blinked.

It's not him. It's not him.

Her weapons flared as she swung them in a low arc, only to crash into a black staff that appeared like magic in her opponent's hands. Her eyes met his and she nearly stumbled. She knew it was her mind playing tricks on her. Ra'al took the form of whomever you trusted the most, down to the last tiny detail.

Dev's expression was entreating.

"Sera, stop," he said. "It's me."

Even the warm tenor of the Demon Lord's voice matched his. She hesitated for a second and the sweep of his staff made her land flat on her back, the wind knocked out of her. Rolling to the side, she narrowly missed the sharpened tip of his weapon, which nearly impaled her.

She jackknifed to her feet, this time keeping her eyes closed—it was the only way she could fight him and win.

Using her other senses, she struck and parried, dancing out of the way of Ra'al's blows. In her mind's eye, she could see him like a mass of dark energy.

The real Dev, she knew, would be this power's opposite. He'd be all light. The thought of him filled her with purpose, renewing her strength and her attack. Her swords felt like pure air as she spun, surprising Ra'al and putting him on the defensive. He was powerful—but then again, so was she.

"Sera." He resorted to pleading, using his voice as a weapon now. Her heart rose into her throat as its familiar tones curled around her. "It's me. Don't you see? They're forcing me to fight you so that you can kill me."

She faltered and felt the staff slam into her spine as her knees buckled, the wind knocked out of her. Before she could rise, the weapon swung into her chin, making her see stars. Blood pooled in her mouth—she'd bitten her own tongue. Gasping, she opened her eyes to see Dev crouching above her, his beautiful face earnest.

"Sera, love, are you okay?"

Bewildered, she glanced around. They were alone on a gorgeous beach. "Where are we?" she asked, her senses spinning.

"You know where we are," he said, smiling. "You're safe."

Her head buzzed. "No, there's something. Someone. I forgot."

Soft fingers grazed her cheek, and Sera fought off a strange feeling of revulsion. Dev's touch felt alien. Reptilian. But his eyes glowed with light and love, his scent surrounding her like sunlight on a warm summer day. "There's no one you need to remember but us."

She nodded as her eyelids flicked closed, but the ache was

insistent, demanding that she remember. She was somewhere else. "Wait. Kyle, he's . . ."

"You never loved me, did you?" he said, eyes glittering. "You chose him. And left me. You are a deceiver."

And then she knew.

She knew it was a lie. The real Dev would have let her go.

With a cry, Sera launched to her feet, and the beach fell away as Temlucus's fiery dimension swam back into view. Her vision was clear now as she faced Ra'al. He still wore Dev's face, but she no longer felt confused. She deflected his strike easily, watching rage flare in his eyes. He howled as one of her blades seared a fiery gash down his chest. Dev's face melted away to reform into that of a young girl, and then a myriad of other faces as she drove him back with relentless attacks.

"You could never be him," she whispered. "You don't know his heart."

Within seconds, she had her swords crossed at Ra'al's throat.

"Yield," she ordered.

His face had settled back into one form. Not Dev, but the aristocratic man with long white hair who she'd met the first time she and Kyle had visited the seventh. That wasn't Ra'al's true form, either. He bared his teeth at her, hatred burning in those colorless eyes.

"Yield," she said, "or I send you back to that hole you call home."

"I'd sooner kill my own son than yield to you."

Sera sensed rather than saw his arm rising, before forcing her hand and scissoring her blades together. The body beneath her crumbled to dust as Ra'al disappeared, expelled back to the seventh.

"Restrain her," she heard Temlucus shout.

That lying snake. She should have known he had no intention of fulfilling his end of the bargain. Sera didn't want to think about where she'd wind up if she did die. Illysia didn't want her in her current form, and with her luck, she'd end up right where she was—in Temlucus's clutches for eternity. She braced, expecting to be rushed by a dozen of the shadow wraiths congregating around them. But the only one coming toward her was Kyle.

Demon-possessed Kyle.

"What are you doing?" she yelled, sidestepping his first clumsy rush. But he took no notice of her words. He rushed forward again, his hands reaching for her neck. She let him get close. "Kyle, you have to fight it." He didn't answer. She grasped his shoulders, shaking him, even as Temlucus's manic laughter filled the air. "Are you with me?"

Something appeared in Kyle's hands then and she felt its malevolence like a tangible force. Mordas. Her breath fizzled in her throat at the sight of the ugly, black blade that had claimed so many lives—mortal and immortal. She didn't want to hurt Kyle, or to leave him, but he was giving her no choice.

His mouth opened, but the only sound he made was a pained wheeze. His hands trembled violently on the hilt of the weapon, as if he were fighting himself. And weakening by the second.

"Kyle," she whispered in one last-ditch effort. "Are you *with* me?"

"Finish her, Kalias," Temlucus cawed. "Finish her and claim your rightful place."

Kyle's lips opened again, his eyes rolling back in a way that made her stomach recoil, but it was his voice that spoke—not the pishacha's. "Use. Mordas. Cut. Demon. Killing. Me."

He turned the blade with shaking hands to his abdomen.

Sera exhaled hard. He couldn't possibly mean what she thought he meant.

Did he?

She had no time to ponder it. Closing her eyes and summoning a portal in the same breath, she grasped his hands over the hilt of the weapon and plunged the blade into Kyle's stomach. The sound of his scream and Temlucus's howl rolled into one.

The last thing Sera saw before being sucked into the void was the body of the exorcised, dead pishacha demon. Relief was swift, but as she clutched Kyle's inert body to her, she could only hope that she hadn't made a horrible mistake.

THE DEVIL YOU KNOW

❧

They landed in a heap on Sera's living room floor, steam pouring off their bodies. Kyle moaned as agony lanced through his torso. He cracked his eyelids just enough to see Nate leaping up from his spot on the sofa, his green eyes going wide and his mouth falling open into a soundless scream. Following his stare, Kyle looked down to where Mordas protruded from his belly.

Holy hell.

His fingers curled into the carpet at his sides as another wave of searing pain nearly made him black out.

When he'd told Sera to use the weapon on him, he hadn't realized just how much it would hurt. It felt like his entrails were being torn from his body and consumed by fire ants. It hurt to move. It hurt to think. It hurt to freaking breathe.

"Kyle. Kyle, can you hear me?"

Sera's voice sounded far away. He blinked and concentrated on her, registering the outline of her head before her features came into sharper focus. He tried to respond, but couldn't even shape the words with his lips. It was taking all his energy to stay conscious. He managed to utter one word: "Yes."

"Hold on, okay?"

"What happened?" Sophia shouted, racing into the room with Sam at her side.

"We found the pishacha," Sera explained to her parents. "Or Kyle found it, and trapped it in his body. It was killing him so he . . . he made me stick that thing in him."

"He trapped a rakshasa with his body," Sam said, his eyes cutting disbelievingly between them. "And then made you stab him with that sword."

Kyle wanted to laugh. Even half out of it, he was aware of how ludicrous it sounded.

"Yes," Sera said. "I think becoming one with the pishacha was the quickest way to find out how they were getting into the Mortal Realm. Kyle took a risk, though I'm not sure it paid off." She paused, flinching as her gaze centered on the festering wound in Kyle's stomach. "We need Dev."

Within seconds, the room exploded into blinding light as Dev, Mara, and Micah appeared. Kyle wanted to joke about Sera's epic summoning talents, but all that escaped his mouth was a wet, bloody warble. In the background, he could hear her explaining what had happened in Xibalba. Oddly, the presence of the deities lent him some clarity. Or maybe he was becoming numb to the pain spreading like molten lava across his middle.

A familiar person loomed close.

"Heard you trapped a rakshasa with your face," Micah said as he stooped to examine the wound.

Vaguely, Kyle registered that the Sanrak looked exactly as he had four months ago, when he'd seen him last—like a young choir boy. Kyle's mouth cracked into a smile as his uncooperative tongue pushed the words from his mouth. "Hardcore . . . Azura . . . Lord."

"If you say so." Micah laughed, his nose wrinkling as a shadow of concern passed over his face. He nodded to Dev and Sera, who joined him on the ground.

"Tough day?" Dev said, passing his hands over Kyle's sides with a crooked grin. "You must be the only immortal who's ever decided to catch a demon using himself as bait."

"Keep . . . interesting."

"I'm going to need help to remove this." Dev pointed at Mordas, careful not to touch it. "The sword will not relinquish its hold so easily."

Dev's gaze shifted to Sera hovering on Kyle's other side. "You're going to have to be the one to remove it," he told her. "None of us can touch it." He drew a breath, his stare sliding to where Sophia and Sam stood, and then flicking to Nate, who was still crouched on the sofa. "It will not be easy to do or to watch."

Sophia followed his eyes and hissed through her teeth at the sight of her son. "Nate! You shouldn't be here. Go to your room right now!"

"Mom, I can help."

"I will ground you for the rest of your life if you don't move this instant," she yelled, throwing her hands up in aggravated frustration.

Nate paled, but stood his ground. "I can help."

"Nathaniel Caelum, so help me—"

"The boy is right." The voice was Micah's. Every head in the room swiveled to him. "I've been teaching him. His gifts are like nothing I've ever seen. His healing abilities, in particular. They may prove useful."

Sophia's eyes narrowed at the deity who had been her

partner through several lifetimes. "He's half mortal. How could his abilities rival those of Lord Devendra?"

"Kyle is an Azura Lord," Micah responded, not even flinching at the look in Sophia's eyes or the scathing tone of her voice. "He may not respond to Lord Devendra's curative powers. But your son is not solely of Illysia."

"Micah may be correct," Dev agreed in a soft voice. Sophia's lips thinned to the point of nearly disappearing, but after a moment she nodded curtly. Dev was one of the Trimurtas, after all, and even if she disagreed, as a Sanrak, she was oath-bound to serve him.

"Nate," Micah said. "Come over here."

Kyle met the boy's eyes as he crouched. An array of emotions was visible on his face—including horror. Kyle grimaced. At least kids couldn't hide their true thoughts. "Hey . . . little man," he wheezed, trying to reassure him. "Should . . . see other guy."

Nate's grin was watery. "Hopefully he's dead. Because you look like you got creamed."

Micah took Nate's hands and put them on either side of the wound. Kyle flinched at the contact. The entire surface of his flesh felt as if it were on fire, and even the slightest touch sent ripples of agony through him.

"Focus on what we've been learning," Micah whispered. "Push your energy out and let it connect with him. Let your energy surround him."

Nate nodded and closed his eyes. Kyle drew a shuddering breath as he felt the boy's consciousness intersect with his own. It felt like the softest fluff. Using his gift, he focused on Nate and bit back a weak gasp. The boy was bathed in an incandescent aura, more like light than flames. It was not a color he'd ever seen before.

A Sanrak's deifyre was silvery white. The Yoddha had golden deifyre. Sera's was the color of the sunset. But Nate's aura was a shimmery silvery hue tinged with the palest pinks and blues. Iridescent, almost. The boy's mortality was a part of the whole, weaving through his Sanrak form, but there was something else there, too. Something indescribable. Its beauty rendered Kyle mute.

Just then, a brutal surge of pain ripped him from his thoughts and he glanced up, focusing once more on the inhabitants of the room. Sera's fingers were wrapped around Mordas's hilt, scarcely touching it, but the barest press still made his back arch like a bow.

"Hold him down."

Kyle registered Dev's voice as Mara and Sam took hold of his feet and Sophia took up a position at his shoulders.

Sophia's eyes bored into his, flooded with compassion. "It will be okay," she whispered, brushing damp curls out of his face. He didn't know if she was saying that for his benefit alone, or for her son, who knelt a foot away, eyes tightly closed. Kyle suspected that it was probably for both of them. He swallowed and fought to control his shallow breaths.

Dev squeezed his wrist. "Okay, this is it. We can't do this without you."

"Wait!" There was another flash of light as a deity appeared. This one, he felt on every level. Kira. His heartbeat spiked in response, making Dev's fingers tighten on his wrist.

"You cannot be here," Dev growled.

Kira's dark eyes flashed to his, a tempest brewing in them. "And who are you to command me?"

"You know very well who I am. And Kyle needs to be as calm as possible." Dev paused as if choosing his words carefully. "Your presence is not conducive to that."

"You do not control me," she hissed. Her back arched like that of a feral tiger about to defend its young. Kyle could feel the vibration of her power buffeting him in waves. There was something else, too, just under the surface. She *wanted* to be here, not for any other reason than to be near him. He blinked and licked cracked lips.

"She . . . stay," Kyle ground out. "Be fine."

They both turned to stare at him, and after a second, Dev nodded. Kira knelt at Kyle's right shoulder, her fingers skimming over the skin at the base of his throat. Her touch didn't make him wince as the others had. He focused on it instead of the pain. Tiny frissons of electricity raced beneath her stroking fingertips, reaching from his collarbone to his toes. *She* had come, not Darika.

Even in his half delirious state, he knew that Sera was right—he had to make a choice before things got out of hand. It wasn't fair to either of them.

If he made it out of this alive, he would.

He nearly passed out as Sera's fingers curled more securely around Mordas's hilt, the black blade clinging to his insides as if reluctant to let him go. His entire body seized and bucked. It took all the strength of the immortals restraining him to hold him down as Sera pulled on the weapon. Pain exploded along his veins like an electric charge. He could feel Micah's and Nate's healing power, but it was nowhere near a match for the excruciating current barreling through his body. It was as if the blade wanted to cleave his very soul from him.

Sera groaned, her head falling back and her hands trembling violently on Mordas's hilt. Her emotions were written on her face, but more than that, he could *feel* them barreling through her. Kyle realized that she, too, would be experiencing every sensation of his. The weapon connected them like a bridge between their souls.

Though it paled in comparison to the pain rocketing through him, he also felt the depth of her caring for him. He also felt her love for her family, and the tense thread of fear that coiled through it all—the fear of loss, and the fear of what she was. What she would become. It was weirdly humbling. Her journey had been so harrowing, and yet she faced it with courage and determination. She may have been terrified, but she didn't let it stop her. Sera never let *anything* stop her.

Not even him.

His back jackknifed upward as she yanked on Mordas's hilt.

Sera cried out and released her hold, her voice breaking on a sob. "I can't do it. The pain is . . . too much."

Kira bared her teeth. "Then think about what he's feeling."

"Don't you think I *know* what he's feeling?" Sera shot back, wheezing. "I *feel* it. Every brutal second. If you think it's so easy, why don't you give it a shot?"

"Fine," Kira snarled. "I will."

Micah lurched forward. "No—"

Kyle opened his mouth to stop her, but he wasn't fast enough. Neither was Micah. The second Kira's fingers touched Mordas all the energy was sucked out of the room.

Lights popped in their sockets and sparks flew. Kira's body was propelled across the room, crashing through the wall into the kitchen.

"What happened?" Nate whispered, his eyes round.

Micah exhaled. "Deifyre and Mordas don't mix."

"What happened to her? Is she okay?"

"She'll be fine," Micah assured him as Sophia moved toward the smoking frame of the goddess. "It was only the hilt. If the blade had touched her . . ."

"Sera," Dev said gently, indicating the mark of Xibalba on her palm. "You will need to summon the power of that rune to control the sword."

"You don't understand. Mordas wants that part of me . . . the darkest parts." Her breath caught in her throat. "I wouldn't know how to do it."

"You need to will the sword to release," Dev added softly. "It feeds on energy. Offer it something more."

"Offer what?" she said.

"Power."

She recoiled, as if struck. "I'm not about to bargain with a sword forged in the bowels of Xibalba."

"You are the only one who can do it, Sera." Kyle focused dully on the voice that had spoken. It came from near his feet—Sera's father. Sam continued. "You're not negotiating with it. You're simply asserting your will as its master. As a goddess of all three realms, it will bend to you."

She balked, her eyes meeting Kyle's and falling away. "I can't," she mumbled, so quietly that no one else could hear her. "I don't want . . . anyone to see me like that."

He knew what she meant. She didn't want her family, Dev,

and the other immortals to see her caught in the throes of the Dark Realms. But it was the only thing that could save him. "They love you, Sera. No matter what. And I trust you," he wheezed, reaching for her hand.

Kyle closed his eyes. He knew what she was terrified of. She didn't want to lose more of herself to Xibalba than she already had after their recent trip. And Kyle could never ask it of her, no matter the cost to him.

It hurt to breathe. Mordas was already draining him. Maybe it would be best to just give in. Another Azura Lord would take his place, and he'd be free. Free of his ties to Ra'al. Free of the memories of the mother who had sought to murder him. Free of all of the self-doubt and wanting to be accepted.

"Sera," he said. "You don't . . . have to."

"He will die if you don't," Micah said to her, sending him a glare that was the opposite of the Sanrak's usual tranquil expression.

"Die?" she choked. "But he's immortal."

Micah's expression was grim. "Mordas doesn't discriminate. Kyle will return to the fabric of the realms."

"Doesn't matter," Kyle rasped, feeling his strength fading with every breath. "She doesn't . . . have to do it."

"Yes, she does," Nate said fiercely, his green eyes flashing as he turned to his sister. "Kyle is your best friend. He went to Xibalba to find me when no one else could. He would have died for us, and you know it. We owe it to him to try."

Sera's face went pale, but she resumed her position at Kyle's side. "Nate's right. We can't let him die. I won't." She nodded at her brother. "You ready to do this?"

"Yeah." Nate pressed his hands to Kyle's sides once more and closed his eyes, summoning his healing abilities. The boy was strong, there was no doubting that. Kyle already felt a blissful numbness settling over his torn flesh.

Kyle braced himself as Sera grasped Mordas, the connection between them yawning open again. Surprisingly, the pain wasn't as terrible. He felt feeble, as if the blade had sapped his strength. Dev raised his hand to place it on Sera's forearm, and Kyle could feel the immediate surge of strength funneled through her body. Not just strength—but also love and devotion, courage and integrity. The bond between the two of them filled Kyle to the brim.

"Do it," he muttered through gritted teeth, clamping his own hands around Sera's. Tears leaked from his eyes as his best friend laced her fingers through his.

"Don't you let go," she whispered.

"Won't ever."

Kyle drew a breath and held it as Sera's hellfyre flared, no longer the color of a blazing sunset but rather a dark garnet red. He could feel the power blasting into the sword and felt it start to give in to her compulsion. She was strong, powerful. No one else could have commanded Mordas to relinquish its victim—no one but Ra'al or one of his progeny.

The scream that tore from his bowels matched hers as Mordas ripped loose from his gut, carrying sticky tendrils of graying flesh with it. Sera flung it to the side, her hellfyre's color waning.

"It's out," Kyle wheezed, and registered Dev's uneasy look. "What's wrong?"

"You're not healing."

Micah glanced down at the raw mess of Kyle's intestines. "It may take a while."

Dev shook his head as if he could see something that Micah could not. "No, his flesh is dying. The wound is a mortal one—the blade was holding the seam of the injury together."

"What does that mean?" Sera gasped. "You have to fix it."

"I cannot."

Nate shoved forward. "I want to try."

Micah grasped the boy's arm, stalling him. "We do not know what it will do to you. His father is—"

"I know who his father is," Nate said. "I also know who *he* is. And who I am."

"What do you mean who you are?" Sam asked.

"I feel it inside, Dad," he said. "Telling me how to help. I can do this."

"Nate—" Sophia stared at her son with round, fearful eyes. Her voice shook. "I can't lose you."

"You won't," he said with a jaunty smile. "I promise to live to give you as many gray hairs as I can manage." Her lips wobbled in an answering smile as she nodded, her face ashen.

Nate grinned at Kyle and winked. "I got your back, bro."

Wrinkling his nose, he pushed past his sister to press his hands directly to the gaping wound. Kyle felt nothing but slight pressure—but he knew it would take a miracle to heal him now. Black dust had already crusted the edges of his wound, though Nate didn't seem to care. That pale, opalescent light burned again beneath his fingers, becoming incandescent as Nate's power filled the room.

In disbelief, Kyle could feel a tingling as the edges of his wound threaded together. Nate was doing something that no god could do—he was healing dead Azura tissue. Even Dev looked astonished.

Nate slumped backward as the light faded, collapsing into Micah's arms.

"Is he okay?" Kyle asked urgently, pushing himself up to a sitting position. To his surprise, he felt no pain at all. He glanced down at his stomach. It was completely healed, the reddish tinge of the flesh there the only indication that he'd ever been injured.

"He's fine," Micah said, earning a collective sigh of relief from Sera's entire family. "Just exhausted." The Sanrak blinked in wonder at the sleeping boy in his arms, his voice an awed whisper as he met Sophia's watering eyes. "I told you he was special."

"I owe him my life," Kyle said.

"We all owe you ours," said Sophia. The sentiment shocked Kyle into silence. His pulse leapt as Kira appeared at Sophia's side.

Kira launched herself across the room and threw herself on top of him. "I'm glad you're alive." She squeezed him so hard he swore he could feel his sore ribs crack.

He didn't care. He hugged her back just as tightly.

When they broke apart, Kyle met everyone's eyes in turn.

"Thanks for not giving up on me." He drew a ragged breath, knowing he had to tell them the truth. "But for now, we have bigger problems. I found out why the demons are infesting the Mortal Plane."

"Why?" Kira asked.

He paused and cleared his throat, ignoring the words that had just made him the focus of the room's attention. He sucked in a deep breath. "This time, it isn't just Ra'al. *All* the Demon Lords are working together. As one."

THE LIGHT
AND THE DARKNESS

❧⚬❧

Sera lay on her bed, trying to focus on her math workbook. It was two in the morning and she couldn't sleep. She'd tossed and turned for hours before finally giving up, hoping that some mundane activity like trig would put her to sleep. But her brain wouldn't cooperate. It was brimming with other things—like the looming end of the world and the fact that all the Demon Lords were plotting its demise.

She sighed and slammed her workbook shut. They'd stopped the KaliYuga once before, but that didn't mean it couldn't happen again.

A soft scratch on her door distracted her from her morbid thoughts and Nate's blond head peeked into her room. She motioned for him to come inside, pressing a finger to her lips. Gray shadows darkened the tops of his cheeks, making him look far older than his years. Sera wasn't surprised that he was awake, too. She pushed back the blankets.

"Couldn't sleep?" she whispered as he climbed into her bed and nodded tiredly. "Me neither."

Nate tucked himself below the sheets and curled into a ball. "Do you think what Kyle said was true?"

"About what?"

"About the Demon Lords working together," he whispered.

"You heard that?" she asked.

Nate nodded sheepishly. "Yeah. Did he say anything else about what was coming?"

She eyed her little brother. He'd been passed out—or at least he'd seemed to be—when Kyle had explained what he'd learned while possessed by the pishacha demon. She debated not telling him more, but then shook her head. He was a part of this now, too. Keeping secrets from him wouldn't do any good. And he'd earned it. Nate had saved Kyle's life. He deserved to know the truth. She of all people knew how much it hurt to have secrets kept from you.

"No, but he's worried they will want to use him somehow, as they did before. So for now, no more portals."

Because while the Trimurtas had been caught up in the mystery of the demon infestation, the Demon Lords had been conspiring. Kyle had learned from the pishacha that the Demon Lords were working *together*. The influx of demons was all part of a ploy to distract the Trimurtas and to misdirect from the real threat.

Nate yawned. "How are you planning to get rid of the rakshasas that are here already?"

She couldn't articulate an answer. It was the one part of the plan that had bothered her. The only option they'd been able to come up with was to kill the hosts *and* the demons, which meant hundreds of innocent people would die. She would do anything to avoid that—which meant that they didn't have much time to figure out what the Demon Lords were planning and find a way to stop them. She sighed. That was where the second part of the plan came in—the part that included a second trip to Xibalba.

Opening herself up to Mordas had changed something inside of her. She couldn't pinpoint what, exactly, but she *felt* it. It was an awakening—some seed of deeply buried knowledge was stirring. It wasn't about wickedness or immorality. It was an inner awareness of what Xibalba represented—not evil, but rather something necessary for human existence. It was free will mired in passion and desire, and that will's relationship with karma. Good could not exist without its counterpart.

The knowledge both confused and frightened her. She wanted nothing to do with the Dark Realms, especially if it could tether her to them forever. But she felt it deep down; there would come a day when there would be a reckoning for her soul, and she would have to choose. A part of her wanted to believe that she would never side with Xibalba, but things weren't always that black and white. If she had to do it to pre-serve the greater good, Sera knew she would.

The seed of consciousness in her belly pulsed as if in response. She was haunted by so many desires—she wanted to rejoin Illysia. She wanted to be with Dev. She wanted to be an ordinary teen, regain some semblance of normalcy. But her wants were selfish, she knew. What was the point of being a goddess if she could have none of those things?

"You okay?" Nate asked.

She nodded. "Why?"

"You looked really upset for a second."

Sera stared at her brother lying beside her and felt the sharp edges of her irritation dissipate. "I feel powerless sometimes," she confessed. "Like I can't control anything. Like we're fighting an enemy we can't see."

"That's life, though, right?" Nate's voice was quiet. "Fighting a bunch of unseen battles? It's kind of like role-playing games, where every choice has a consequence, or takes you somewhere new. We can't predict the outcome, only what we choose to do. But I guess those are games, and this is real life." He pursed his lips as if deep in thought. "Sometimes we make mistakes, and I guess that has consequences too."

She rumpled his curls. "How did you get so wise?"

"A lot of work."

Nate yawned again, his thick eyelashes starting to droop against his cheeks. She poked him, and his bleary eyes focused back on her. "What does Micah say about your gifts?"

"What about them?"

She struggled to find the right words. "Are they going to . . . change you?"

"He says he doesn't know." Nate chewed on his bottom lip. "But I can feel them doing something inside me. And I see things. I know things. Like how I knew I could help Kyle. And other things."

Sera narrowed her eyes. "What kind of things?"

Nate took a long time before answering, and when he did, his voice was so quiet that she could barely hear it. "I see the questions people have. The ones they're afraid to ask."

A rush of goose bumps peppered her arms. "Like what?"

"Like the one you had just before."

Sera bounced upward so suddenly on the bed that it made Nate startle. "What are you talking about?"

"The question you had about the point of being a goddess."

Sera gaped at him. "Do you know the answer?"

"Yes."

"What is it?"

He shook his head. "I can't tell you. It would be cheating. Dev says we all have to find our own answers."

"Dev?" She swallowed. "Have you been talking to him, too?"

"I've been talking to all of them," Nate replied. "The Trimurtas." He closed his eyes and then reopened them. "You don't have to be scared, Sera. It's natural to have those kinds of questions."

"What's your question then?"

"Whether or not I'll die."

His clear eyes met hers, making her skin prickle. It felt like she was carrying on a conversation with a stranger. But this was *Nate*. Her annoying little brother, who got into trouble for his hacker escapades and made her giggle with his snarky wit. This was the boy who built LEGO Brick castles, stalked J.J. Abrams, and saved every penny for film school.

"You're not going to die, Nate."

"The living know that they will die."

Sera frowned at him. "You quoting *Harry Potter* again?"

"Ecclesiastes." Nate sniffed and smiled at her, snuggling more deeply beneath the blankets, his eyes drifting closed.

"Since when are you reading the Bible?" she asked in disbelief.

"It's just a book, you know. And it's interesting. I'm reading other scriptures, too." He yawned sleepily. "Love you, Ser."

"I love you, too, buddy."

Within seconds, she could hear his gentle snoring.

Sera stared at her baby brother for a long time. His mouth twitched restlessly, as if his questions plagued him even in sleep. Sera stroked the blond curls from his temple, soothing him with hushed sounds. A boy his age should be dreaming about mundane things, like Minecraft and Xbox, not existential questions about life and death.

What had he meant? Did he really believe that he was going to die? *Soon?* Even in the next couple of days when hell was unleashed on earth? The thought of losing Nate made her heart pound violently in her chest. *No*, she vowed firmly. Not if she could help it. The question was—*could she?*

There was only one person who would know for sure.

Sera stared at the runes on her palms and slowly pressed them together. Time slowed and stopped as she left the mortal world and entered her sanctuary in the realm between realms. She hadn't been sure what part of her sanctuary her state of mind would conjure, but was pleasantly surprised to find herself on a beach instead of the cliffs. The ocean always made her feel calm.

Dawn was just streaking the sky in pale lilac swatches, and there was a crispness to the air that made more gooseflesh rise over her arms. She wasn't cold, though. She walked along the water's edge, her bare toes digging into the cool sand. The sand was not like the silky sand from previous beaches in her realm. It was heavy, grainier. The roughness felt good against the soles of her feet.

She knew what she had come for, but now that she was in her world, Sera relished a moment of solitude in a place where the two sides of her nature didn't make her feel like she was caught in an eternal tug of war.

She sat, wrestling with her thoughts.

Sera loved what Illysia represented. But there was a reason that she alone could walk all three realms. The truth was, she loved the vibrancy of the mortal world, too. She loved the innate passion of human beings and the fact that each day meant something. Each day was a fresh start, a chance for them to make something of themselves.

And even Xibalba fulfilled a purpose. Because without the darkness, there couldn't be light. Without the Dark Realms, there would be no balance. That was the beauty of the human condition—free will and the ability to choose one's own path, whether that was one of sacrifice or selfishness, virtue or vice.

She didn't love being tied to Xibalba, but that didn't mean that she couldn't understand its significance in the greater scheme of things. That balance represented the crux of samsara.

Sera felt Dev's arrival before she saw him. "Hey," she said, turning to him as he walked toward her. He wore a loose, yellow, cotton shirt and flowing pants knotted at his waist. His expression was somber, but a light glinted in his golden eyes.

"May I?" he asked, indicating the place at her side. Sera nodded for him to sit. "Couldn't sleep?" he asked.

"No," she said and turned her attention back to the swelling sea. "My mind is too restless." She paused, her fingers digging nervously in the sand. "And I'm worried about Nate."

"How so?"

"He thinks he's going to die."

"He's mortal," Dev said softly. "At some point he will die."

Sera stared at him. "But not until he's lived a long life. Right?"

He hesitated, his warm gaze falling to her, offering comfort as if he knew his answer would not. "Perhaps."

That single word made warning bells go off in Sera's brain. "Do you know something you're not telling me? He's my brother, Dev. If there's something going on, I have to know."

Dev's hand crossed the short distance between their bodies to close over hers. Her breath hitched. Whatever he was going to say had to be bad. She met his eyes and saw the indecision in them. "Spit it out. I can handle it, I promise. What are the Trimurtas saying?"

"Nate's future is unclear," he began. "He is meant for great things, that much we know, but his path is mired in tragedy."

"What does that mean?"

He drew a slow breath, his fingers squeezing rhythmically. "Micah believes that either Nate or someone close to him will die in the coming war with Xibalba."

"Someone close to him?" Her voice was a pained whisper. The only people who were truly mortal in her family were her father and her brother. "Like my dad?"

"We do not know."

"Then what *do* you know?" she snapped, even though she knew it was unreasonable to get angry with Dev. He would tell her the truth if he knew any more.

"Micah has also reported that Nate has had visions," Dev said after a beat.

"Of what?" she asked frowning.

He turned her to face him. "Of the war. Of what will come. Of his role in the fate of the Mortal Realm."

"What role? Stop speaking in riddles." She pulled a hand through her hair in frustration. She could sense that he was keeping something from her. "We have to keep him safe. Regardless of these new gifts, or whatever Micah is seeing, he is only a boy. The fate of the Mortal Realm shouldn't rest on his shoulders."

"I fear that neither of us can predict his role in the coming days. From what the Trimurtas can tell, Nate was chosen by Brahman to be his instrument long before he was given life as your brother." He sighed softly and pulled her close. After a moment, she relaxed into him, appreciating his warm strength. She breathed in his soothing scent of marigolds and cloves, and felt her worries dissipate slightly.

"Does my mother know about this? Nate's part in what's to come?"

"Not yet, but she will."

Sera shook her head. "She won't be happy."

"Sophia will understand," Dev said.

His expression softened as he smoothed her hair out of her face. The lighter gold flecks in his beautiful eyes were mesmerizing as his thumb stroked across her chin, leaving a flurry of tingles behind.

"I've missed you," he said.

"I've missed you, too."

His fingers brushed her cheeks in small, feathered touches before tracing her lips. "You belong with me in Illysia."

Flushing, Sera curled her right hand into a fist and stared at the raised, red rune near the cusp of her wrist. "That's not possible, thanks to this."

"We will figure out a way."

As if to quiet her saturnine thoughts, Dev swapped his fingers on her lips for his mouth. The kiss was sweet, clearly meant to make her forget her fears. And it did, to a degree. His mouth tasted of cloves and mint as he nibbled her lower lip. Sera's pulse raced, aligning with his as it did every time he touched her, the connection between them as strong as time itself. Thousands of memories poured into her brain from past incarnations. He had always found her, in every lifetime, no matter what.

Dev wrapped his arms around her as he deepened the embrace, making her entire body feel like it was part of his. He rained kisses across the rise of her cheekbones and on her brow, touching his lips to her eyelids and her nose, before finding her lips once more. By the time he was finished, she couldn't remember what she'd had for breakfast, much less her worries about Illysia.

"Better?" Dev asked, snuggling her closer as they watched the sunrise.

She snorted. "Confident, aren't we?"

"Somewhat."

Sera laughed and rolled her eyes. "I should play harder to get."

"If I hadn't already loved you for a few thousand years, that might work."

"And if we manage to survive the next few days, what about the next thousand years?" she asked, leaning contentedly against him. "Will you still love me then?"

His voice was soft. "I will love you until the end of time, *meri jaan*."

An Eye for an Eye

Kyle looked at the sleeping girl beside him, her dark hair strewn across the pillow in a wild tangle, and groaned under his breath. As if he could have made things worse—being on his immortal deathbed had obviously made him reckless.

And stupid.

Kira was a *goddess*—a volatile, impetuous goddess, unforgiving at the best of times. They'd talked for hours, then made out for hours more. They'd fallen asleep just as dawn was breaking across the sky.

It could have just as easily been Darika lying there. In fact, some deeply hidden part of him wished it had been her, instead of Kira. He'd never felt so torn in his entire life. It was like he was being pulled in two directions. One minute he was into Kira, as he had been last night, and the next he was into her sister.

Sera was right. He was an idiot, playing with fire.

Ruthless, unforgiving, burn-you-to-ash goddess fire.

Kira's passion made her exciting, but it was a destructive, explosive thing. Last night had been everything he'd needed at that moment—but now, watching her sleep, Kyle wasn't so sure. It wasn't regret he was feeling. It was more an uneasy burning in the pit of his stomach. Now he understood what Sera must have felt when she came back from Xibalba last year—and what had prompted the unexpected kiss between them. Last night with Kira had been the same as that moment: instinctive.

Stupid.

Creeping out of bed, he pulled on a T-shirt and decided to go for a run. It would help clear his head. He hoped.

He ran at a punishing pace, and by the time he returned to the house sweating and panting, his legs felt like noodles. As he opened the front door, he heard female voices coming from the kitchen. Bracing himself, he peeked around the doorjamb. Carla—his foster mother—was at the stove flipping pancakes, and Kira sat at the table sipping a mug of coffee.

"Just in time," Carla said, catching sight of him.

His stomach rumbled with hunger as she placed a heaping plate of food on the table and signaled to him to sit. He hesitated in the doorway as Kira let out a low laugh. "Why are you acting like you've never had a girl stay over before?" she teased.

"Because he hasn't," Carla chirped.

"Not even Sera?"

Carla shook her head, avoiding his glare. "Not even her, and he was in love with her for years. I was kind of relieved to see someone else, actually."

"Why is that?" Kira asked, clearly relishing his discomfort.

"Unrequited love is never fun."

"That's enough," he ground out, and this time Carla took heed. "I'm going to take a shower," he mumbled.

"But the food will get cold," she protested. "Eat. It's not like you haven't ever eaten without showering first. In fact, just last week you went three days—"

"Carla," he growled.

She smiled at him, waving a hand. "If I promise to stop talking, will you eat your breakfast?"

"Yeah." Burning with embarrassment, Kyle sat and shoved a forkful of pancake into his mouth, meeting Kira's amused gaze over the rim of her coffee cup. Her dark hair was damp, as if *she'd* had a shower, and she was wearing one of his sweat-shirts over her jeans. She saw the direction of his stare.

"Hope you don't mind," she whispered. "My shirt had blood on it."

"No problem," he muttered, shoveling more food into his mouth.

He didn't know why he felt so tongue-tied around her. He'd opened up a lot the night before, telling her about his life with Carla and his past in the foster home. Though, like Darika, she would have already known most of his sordid history, it had felt good talking. She'd asked him about the Preta and he'd told her everything—about Azrath and Ra'al, and what he'd felt when he'd found out who he really was. He'd never shared any of that with anyone, not even Sera. It'd been liberating—a weight off his chest. But now, he felt vulnerable, as if he'd made some kind of dumb mistake.

"I'm going to get the paper. You two behave yourselves," Carla said in a voice so cheery it made Kyle cringe. Could she be any more obvious about his lame love life? "And eat up."

When they were alone, Kira's hand slid across the table to brush his. The touch was light, but sent a live wire of electricity ricocheting through his veins. The unwelcome weight in his belly didn't mean the attraction between them wasn't alive and well. Clearly. Kira was *Kira*.

"Thanks for letting me crash," she said. "I know it was hard to talk about all that stuff last night."

He blinked at her. "It was good to get it out."

"How's your wound?" she asked.

Kyle sucked in a sharp breath as she reached forward to lift the hem of his sweat-soaked T-shirt. She peered intently at his torso and nodded, her fingers lingering slightly before she leaned back in her seat. He knew that the flesh there was completely healed, with no sign of external injury.

"Immortal genes," he said with a shrug and took another bite.

"I think you have Nate to thank for this one," she said, squinting at him. "That sword would have killed you other-wise."

He stopped chewing at the thought. Kyle wondered how close he'd actually come to Mordas finishing him off. If he had died, the blade would have returned to Ra'al. But he hadn't.

As if summoned by his thoughts, the ugly, black blade materialized in his open palm. Kira hissed at its sudden appearance, scooting her chair back as Kyle hefted the blade.

"It won't hurt you," he murmured.

Its thin red spine burned along its length like a hot ember, as if it'd been fed to bursting. It had been, Kyle realized—with *his* blood. The pulse in his palm leapt against the hilt of solid bone, the black metal of the sword's blade glittering in response.

"You trust that thing, even after what happened?" Kira asked, her mouth curling in distaste.

"It belongs to me."

She glared daggers at him. "It tried to kill you."

"No, you're mistaken," he said slowly, feeling the solid, comforting weight of it in his palm. Even now, it felt like an extension of his own arm. "I allowed it to strike me, to get rid of the pishacha. There is a difference. Mordas's allegiance is to me. And I keep it sated." He pursed his lips grimly. "If that wasn't the case, it never would have reappeared for me now."

"That thing is dangerous," she insisted. "You should get rid of it. It is a threat to you and everyone around you."

Kyle could have sworn he saw fear flicker across her face as she spoke, her eyes darting to the blade in his palm. She was right to be disconcerted. Over time, Mordas had been wielded in terrible ways, razing deifyre from wings and killing gods. But he understood it. He understood what motivated it. Kyle drew a breath and watched as the blade dematerialized.

"Mordas is mine."

"It's born of Xibalba," she shot back.

Kyle met her stare coolly. "As am I." Something hot and angry swelled inside of him at the disapproving look on her face. "Isn't that what you liked about me in the first place? That bad-boy spark that appealed to your destructive nature?" He hesitated for a beat. "Or was it all an act?"

Her eyes narrowed, glittering dangerously at the sardonic tone of his voice. "Tread carefully, Kyle. Do not mock me."

"Or what?"

Her human avatar shimmered hazily for a second, making

his stomach lurch. "Or you will not like the outcome, I promise you."

"I don't do well with threats." Kyle cleared his throat, growing warm with unease as he squared off against the goddess opposite him. He crossed his arms over his chest, then exhaled, watching her. "Why are you even here, Kira?"

Her lips compressed, dark eyes flashing. "You needed a friend."

"I have enough friends."

He knew he was being cruel, but he couldn't stop himself. He felt exposed. Confused. And he didn't like it. The way she looked at him as if she could see all his fears and doubts made his defenses go up. Kira was exciting and fearless. He liked being with her, but the truth was, he was panicking.

"Maybe you should—"

Then a terrified yelp rent the air, cutting his words short as he shot to his feet. It sounded like Carla. Mordas appeared in Kyle's hand as he took off running in the direction of the scream. The smell of sulfur assaulted his nostrils as he neared the door leading into the garage.

"Demon," he muttered to Kira, who had followed him. A heavy, golden staff materialized in her hands. The perturbed look was gone from her face, replaced by grim resolve. She nodded.

"Stay here," he said over his shoulder as he kicked open the door. "In case there're more."

He didn't miss her scowl as she ignored him and followed. The scene that greeted them was gruesome. Kyle gritted his teeth at the sight of the hideous demon with engorged veins near the rear of the garage, hovering over his foster mother.

The garage door was half open. His lip curled. He was getting sick of Temlucus's pishachas. They were like cockroaches— get rid of one and three more showed up.

Kyle's eyes flicked to where Carla's body lay at the thing's feet, the newspaper still clutched in her grasp. Her eyes were closed, but her chest rose and fell with shallow breaths. What appeared to be a tire iron was lodged in the demon's guts. The fiend hadn't killed her, and it looked like she hadn't gone down without a fight. His mouth curled in an approving grin. Pishachas were fast and clever, but Carla had somehow managed to get a solid strike in. She was hardcore.

"Hey, Ugly, how about you pick on someone your own size," he said, waving his sword and drawing the creature's attention.

The pishacha leered at him, its bulbous eyes pitching backward in their sockets. It gripped the end of the tire iron and flung it to the ground, green ichor pooling from the wound. The demon's body went hazy, and for a moment Kyle thought it would vanish. But then a long, red tongue snaked from its mouth to lick Carla's face. And before Kyle could move, the demon flickered once more to an indistinct haze and slithered into her body. Kyle's eyes widened as his foster mother rose on shaky legs, her unseeing eyes glazed as the pishacha claimed possession of her mortal body.

Hell.

"Mine," it hissed through Carla's lips, a wash of foul steam blowing into Kyle's face as it ambled toward him.

"She is not yours to take."

"Eye for an eye."

Kyle blinked. Was the demon referring to the pishacha he

had killed? He hoisted Mordas high. "The rules of Xibalba do not apply here."

"But Master was in Xibalba." A rictus smile pulled Carla's mouth from ear to ear, making Kyle's stomach sour. A muscle ticked in his jaw.

"I'm not your master," he growled.

"You have to kill it, Kyle." The command was from Kira. "You can't help her now."

"No," he said through clenched teeth. "I can banish it and save her." He pointed his empty fist to the floor to create the portal that would send that thing right back to the sixth. The ground shimmered like an oil stain as the portal began to form.

"No, Kyle." Kira stepped to his side, a restraining hand on his arm. The shimmer of the portal winked out as he lost his focus. "No more portals. You know what the Trimurtas decreed."

"I know what they said," he grunted. "But I can't let her die. She's the only mother I've ever known."

He didn't want to think about the Azura female that had been his biological mother, the one that Ra'al had impregnated. No, Carla was more of a mother than that thing had ever been.

Kira bared her teeth in frustration. "Even as you speak, the pishacha is eating away at her brain, stealing her sanity. There may not be anything left of her to save. And we can't risk it."

"I don't care," he snarled. "She deserves more than *this* . . . than that *thing* sucking her soul dry. I'm going to send it back in pieces to Temlucus."

"I can't let you do that," Kira said, putting her body between him and Carla. "I am bound to the laws of the Trimurtas, just as you are."

He turned to stare at her, unmoved by her ruthless expression or her fighting stance. "You just ate in Carla's kitchen, talked with her, laughed with her. She's not disposable. She's a person."

"You're emotionally compromised."

"And you're heartless."

She flinched as if he'd struck her, but Kyle knew that Kira didn't really feel anything. The hardwired emotional response was the human response that could only be expected of her mortal form. The goddess within would not be subject to such trifling feelings.

He'd been a distraction to her, nothing more. And Carla was a blip—a human soul that could be discarded as easily as a piece of trash. His mouth tightened as his eyes flicked from the goddess to the demon. He couldn't tell which one he resented more—the one that was bound to do what it was born for, or the one that was choosing to take the easy route.

"Do what you must," he said, Mordas like lead in his palms.

"Kyle, you have to understand what's at stake. I—"

He cut her off with a scowl. "Save it. If I have to fight you, I will, but I'm not letting the only decent mom I've had die. Not when I was the one to bring that thing here."

They stared at each other in a silent battle of wills. Kyle drew a shattered breath, clutching Mordas in a death grip. He squared his shoulders and lifted the sword. He had no chance, he knew, if she went into full goddess mode. But he couldn't stand there and do nothing.

He *didn't* want to have to fight her. Not now. Not ever, if he could help it. Not because of his feelings for her, not because he thought he would lose (and he definitely would), but because this was what Temlucus wanted. The Demon Lord wanted war among the gods and those who protected the Mortal Realm. If they were fighting among themselves, no one would be paying attention to whatever they were doing.

"You won't reconsider?" she asked.

"No."

After a tense beat, she nodded and lowered her staff. Kyle could feel the relief sweeping through his body. "I hope you know what you are doing," she said, standing aside. "Do what you must, but I can have no part of this. I am bound to the oaths I have taken."

Kyle nodded, but his thanks were lost as Carla lurched toward him in a drunken movement. The fact that she'd been unconscious when the pishacha possessed her made it harder for the demon to control her. And Kyle hoped that it meant the thing would be more focused on commanding her unresponsive body than devouring her mind. He didn't want to consider the possibility that Kira had been right and it was already too late.

He knelt and pressed his fist to the floor, calling forth the portal. Closing his eyes, he compelled the essence of the pishacha, drawing it out of Carla's body as if pulling a worm from her flesh. It fought him, of course, howling as it came, but it could not resist the call of Xibalba. The demon solidified as it tore free from Carla, and Kyle grasped it around its slimy neck.

He lifted Mordas high in his free hand. "Why did Temlucus send you? What does he want?"

"Lord Temlucus did not send me. Lord Ra'al did."

Kyle's teeth snapped together. "Why?"

"Lord Ra'al wants Master's return."

"I will never return," Kyle growled. "And I'm not your goddamned master."

The pishacha cackled, a wild, maniacal laugh, even as the sword descended in a swift arc. *"Master* will have no choice."

It was still laughing when the sword cleaved it in two and Kyle banished both halves to the bowels of Xibalba. He sealed the portal and rocked back on his heels, cradling Carla's body to him. She was safe.

His head spun with what the pishacha had said—that Ra'al was the one who had sent it. Kyle rubbed his arms. He felt dirty, sullied. Once more, it seemed he was some pawn in a game he did not understand. Why would his cursed father want him back? Demon Lords did not easily forgive, and when he became what he was Kyle's ties to Xibalba had been renounced.

Hadn't they?

His eyes drifted to Kira where she stood at the door, watching him gather Carla in his arms. Her face was unreadable, her posture rigid. If anything, the altercation with the pishacha had showed him how different they were. Kira would have killed Carla in a heartbeat, not for any other reason than for the protection of the Mortal Realm. The greater good.

A small voice argued that she hadn't.

But how long would that last? Her threat to purge the Mortal Realm still hung over him. And with the pishacha's threat about his ties to Xibalba, he couldn't take the chance.

This was it—the crossroads of who he wanted to be. The old Kyle would have chosen Kira in a heartbeat. She embodied everything he used to be. But now he was different. And he needed to walk a different path—a less reckless, less damaging kind of path.

Kyle swallowed hard. "Look, Kira," he said slowly, not looking at her, though he could feel her attention. "It's obvious that this was a mistake."

"A mistake?" Her voice was soft, but the air around her fairly crackled, raising the hairs on Kyle's arms. The light in the garage flickered.

"You and me. We're like oil and water."

"What are you saying, Kyle?"

Here it was—his chance to end it before it got any worse. He had to choose.

"I don't want to hurt you," he said, exhaling hard. "But maybe this—whatever *this* is—isn't the best idea right now, with everything going on."

"You're breaking up with me *now*?"

"I . . . think it's the right thing for everyone."

"For everyone? Or just you?"

The silence was interminable, the gulf between them broadening with each heartbeat. With a hollow laugh, Kira turned to go, but paused at the door. "I'm not heartless. I know you think I'm not like Darika. But what you don't realize is that we are one and the same."

Kyle frowned, but couldn't dwell on her cryptic words as Carla moaned, drawing his attention. She stirred in his arms, her eyes opening.

"Hey," he said gently. "You okay?"

"What . . . happened?"

"You fell and hit your head on the edge of the car," he said, watching her closely. Her eyes seemed dilated, but she didn't seem to be confused, or like she was suffering any maladies from the possession. "Can you move? Hear me okay?"

Nodding, she blinked and shuddered. "Horrible . . . dream."

"Let's get you inside," he said.

As he helped her up, he kept his body carefully angled so that she wouldn't see the tire iron coated in green muck lying on the garage floor. If she did, she'd realize that her dream had been no dream at all, and that reality was, in fact, the stuff of nightmares.

Keep Your
Enemies Closer

~⚬~

"So, is Carla okay?" Sera asked Kyle, squinting at him with concern from across the dull peeling plastic of the booth's table. Sal's was the only place he'd felt he could talk freely, so they'd decided to skip the school cafeteria for lunch. Sera hadn't minded. She'd been on edge at school ever since their escapade in the basement, and the knowledge that the vetala were still there only added to her growing unease.

He'd just finished explaining what had happened with the pishacha demon. She quieted as the waitress brought them their food.

"Yeah, I think so," Kyle said. "She took the day off today from work because she said she felt tired, but she seemed like herself. Time will tell, I guess."

"That's good." Sera took a sip of her soda, drumming her fingers nervously on the table. "And the demon said that Ra'al sent it?"

Kyle nodded with a huge bite of his burrito. "Mhmm."

"That's disturbing that he's targeting your foster mom. He must want your attention pretty badly."

Kyle stopped chewing and eyed her. "Well, it worked. I asked Micah to ask one of the Yoddha to stay with her, just in case Ra'al decides to send another."

"Mara?"

"No, someone else. Mara is . . ." he trailed off, closing his eyes for a second. "She's here. With us. She's your guardian, after all."

Sera tried not to roll her eyes as she nibbled the corner of her grilled cheese sandwich. The Yoddha had become her second shadow. "If you're here," she said aloud. "You might as well join us."

The barest rush of wind against her cheek was the only sign that the Yoddha had heard her, but seconds after Sera had issued the invitation, a girl walked out of the bathroom. Tall and fierce in stature, Mara had her dark hair plaited into two face-framing braids, and she was dressed simply in jeans and a T-shirt. Her dark skin glowed as if it couldn't quite conceal her true nature. She looked so much like her sister Maeve that Sera caught her breath.

"You want to order something?" Kyle asked as she sat beside Sera.

"Just water, please."

They signaled the waitress for a glass and waited for her to deliver it before resuming their conversation. Sera eyed the Yoddha, bitterness rising within her. "You know that I can take care of myself, right?"

"Of course," she replied with a deep incline of her head.

"Which one of them told you to follow me?"

Mara bowed her head again. "Lord Devendra."

Sera sighed, swallowing her resentment. There was nothing she could do about Dev's protective streak, especially after recent events. And it wasn't Mara's fault either. She turned her attention back to Kyle. "So what happened with Kira?"

His eyes flicked to Mara before he responded, but it wasn't like she wouldn't already know what had happened. "Nothing. I ended it."

"You *ended* it? When?"

Sera noticed the flush creeping up his neck as he focused his attention on his food. "Yesterday morning," he eventually mumbled.

"Before or after the pishacha?"

"After."

"But you said that it was early." She frowned, but then understanding hit her in a rush. "Oh."

"It's not like that," he said, reading her face. "We just talked."

"Not that it's any of my business, but *please* tell me you at least *kissed* her! Or should we get you some lessons from Nate, the lady-slayer?"

Kyle's flush deepened as her teasing fell flat in the awkward silence between them. Sera stared at her best friend. He wouldn't meet her eyes, which was odd, even for him.

"Hey, Kyle, look at me." He raised his gaze after a moment and she was shocked to see real misery lurking in his eyes. "What's wrong? You know I'm happy for you, regardless of which one of them you choose."

"I know," he said quietly. "It's just that it's been—" He cleared his throat, chugging his water and glancing at Mara, who might have been a statue for all her participation in the conversation. "The thing is, it's been you for so long that I don't want you to feel like I don't . . . care anymore."

She reached across to grab his hand and squeezed. "I would never think that. You're my best friend in the world, and if things had been different, who knows what would have happened. But things are the way they are, and neither of us can change that. Lemons and lemonade, and all that. I just want you to be happy."

"Yeah."

Sera checked the time on her phone and signaled to the waitress to bring their check. They only had an hour for lunch and she didn't want to risk getting into trouble by being late. "I guess that means you chose Darika?"

He shrugged. "I guess."

"What do you mean you guess?" Sera asked. "You just told me that you ended it with Kira. Unless you're not interested in either of them—and if that's the case, you could have fooled me."

Kyle shook his head. "No. It was something Kira said when she left. She said that she and Darika were one and the same."

"Because they're twins?"

"Maybe."

The sisters were both similar on the surface, though in temperament they were quite different. But goddesses could manifest in any form at any time—they had full control over whatever shades they chose to wear in the Mortal Realm. Even Dev's appearance could change on a whim. Or hers for that matter. She fingered the red-gold strands of hair falling over her shoulders and stared at them thoughtfully. A year ago, they'd been black, thanks to her mother. Now that Sera thought about it . . . just because Kira and Darika were sisters didn't mean they had to look identical. It was curious.

She turned to Mara, who had remained quiet during the entire exchange. "What do you know about them? Kira and Darika?"

Mara smiled. "The goddess Parvati has many faces. She exists in fearful and friendly forms; she is an incarnation of shakti, the divine feminine force."

"No riddles," Sera said frowning. "Are they twins?"

"They are both parts of the whole."

Sera thought of the many stories she'd heard of how the gods and goddesses had come into being, and how her mother had told her that in the end, they were all part of Brahman.

"Did Kira say anything else?" Sera asked, her gaze flicking to Kyle, who was staring at Mara with an arrested expression, his burrito forgotten.

"Just that she wasn't heartless."

Sera glared at him, surprised at his cluelessness when it came to matters of the opposite sex. "You told her she was *heartless*?"

"It's not like she cared," he said defensively, his blush returning. "She's a goddess who doesn't feel anything. She thinks we're all pawns, and that humanity is expendable."

"I think you're wrong about her. I think Kira does care—about the Mortal Realm, about me, and about you. She wouldn't have come rushing to your side if she didn't. And if what you told me is true—that she let you banish the demon possessing Carla despite her loyalty to the Trimurtas—that's another sign that she's not as merciless as you've made her out to be." Sera drew a breath, considering her words even as she could feel Kyle's disgruntled look settling on her. "You know, my mom once described Kali as a mother bear defending her cubs. She'll stop at nothing to protect them—even from themselves."

"By killing us all?" he shot back.

Sera shrugged. "That's a last resort, and you know it."

"Whatever. She's gone now. And good riddance."

"You don't mean that," Sera said. But Kyle didn't answer, standing instead with a resolute look on his face. His coolness was a defense mechanism, Sera knew. He tended to clam up whenever he felt cornered, and she guessed that he wasn't as unaffected as he was pretending to be.

His scowl was painted on as he slammed a twenty to the table. "Let's get out of here before we're late."

"You're welcome to come with us," Sera said to Mara, who had stood as well, her beautiful face composed. "Kyle has his car, and it's not like we aren't going to the same place." The Yoddha nodded, much to Sera's surprise. It couldn't be easy sitting there listening to an uncomfortable conversation—about teen angst and crushes, of all things—especially when it involved another goddess. Sera almost grinned, but caught sight of Kyle's face as he stalked past and thought the better of it.

The ride back to Silver Lake High was quiet, the silence fraught with tension. Sera kept sneaking glances at Kyle, but he wouldn't even look at her.

"I'm sure you'll get a chance to apologize," Sera ventured after a while.

"For what?" he snapped.

She grinned at him. "For being a first-class douche pot pie."

"I was not," he said, but the corner of his lip twitched slightly at the ridiculous insult. "And that's kind of harsh. It was more on the douche paddle level."

"Total pie." Sera snorted as her phone buzzed with a few rapidly incoming texts. Two were from Jem, the others from her mom. The smile fled from her lips as she read the messages from her mother, feeling the blood drain from her face. Mara leaned forward as if she could sense her swift mood change.

Kyle pulled the car to the curb. "What is it?"

"Turn around. We need to go to my house."

"What happened?"

"Another possession," she ground out, tucking the phone back into her pocket. "Jem's there."

"He wasn't in calculus today," Kyle said, his brow furrowing.

"It's not Jem," she said. "It's Nate's friend, Stella. The neighbor." She sucked in a sharp breath. "Jem was the one who found her trying to crawl through Nate's window." Sera turned to the Yoddha in the back seat, who had already flared into full battle mode. "Go to Nate's school. Find him."

"But I am tasked with your protection."

"My brother's life is more important than mine." She gritted her teeth. "I'm ordering you to go, Mara."

Nodding unhappily, the Yoddha left, and they made the drive to Sera's house in less than ten minutes, coming to a squealing stop in the driveway. The smell that greeted them was reminiscent of the school basement—a dry, rancid odor, that of a corpse that had long since decayed.

"Vetala," Kyle muttered as they burst into the kitchen.

Sera took in the sight of her mother standing in full deifyre armor with Jem tucked protectively behind her. The little girl was huddled in a corner, rocking back and forth and making keening noises. Her eyes were rolling back in her head as she sobbed, and the rank smell was definitely emanating from her small form. She was definitely possessed by *something*.

Sera glanced at Kyle. "Is it a vetala?"

She watched as he squinted at the hunched figure and nodded after a few moments. A shudder ran through his body as his eyes refocused. "Yeah. Similar to the ones from the school. This one hasn't been asleep though—it's been well-fed, and it's strong."

Sera suppressed a shiver at the thought of one of those things feeding on human beings, sucking their bodies to husks. No wonder they were called vampires in some parts of the world.

"How long has she been like this?" Sera asked, edging closer to the creature. Blackened veins discolored the child's arms, and her flesh was graying and sickly. "What did it come for?"

"Since Jemitra found her," Sophia replied. "And it was trying to get into Nate's bedroom, presumably to find him."

"Is he safe?" Sera blurted out, her eyes rising to her mother's. "I sent Mara to him at school just in case."

"Sam's on his way there, too."

"How did you see it?" Kyle asked Jem. "How did you even know what it was?"

Jem ran a hand through his dark hair, his normally vibrant blue eyes leaden. "I'm Ne'feri, remember? I've seen my share of demon possessions. And I thought it was strange that she was up on the roof, climbing into Nate's room. By the time I got Mrs. Caelum and we went upstairs, I could tell from the smell."

"What were you even doing here?" Kyle asked with a frown. "Skipped school today?"

Sera shot him a look. "Kyle."

"No, it's okay," Jem said with a bland smile. "I'd be wary, too. My mom was sick. She sent me to the convenience store to get some juice and I happened to be walking past."

"Walking past." The simmering tension in the room shot through the roof.

"That's what I said."

A muscle ticked in Kyle's cheek. "I don't believe in coincidence."

Jem's mouth tightened and Sera intervened before things could escalate further. "Look, we're all on edge," she said. "I'm grateful that Jem was in the right place at the right time, and able to spot the vetala before something terrible happened. It's obvious that that thing was here to hurt Nate, and we need to save Stella if we can." She paused, distracted by a piteous moan from the child as a wave of convulsions rocked her slim form. "Kyle, do what you need to do."

His eyes slid to Sera and then to Sophia before flicking briefly to Jem. He lowered his voice. "I don't know that I can after what happened with Carla and Kira. She said it was forbidden, and the Trimurtas may not be so forgiving a second time."

"She's an innocent kid," Sera said. "We have to."

"I can't."

Sophia paled as a wail from the girl echoed in the space.

"We can't leave her like that. The demon's killing her. You have to send it back."

"No, Kyle's right. I think that's what they want you to do anyway," Jem pointed out. "They want you to banish it back to Xibalba so it opens a two-way portal, right?"

Sera froze. "*What* did you say?"

The realization hit her even as it swept across the other people in the room. The blood drained from Kyle's face. Her gaze fell back to Jem, her eyes narrowing.

"What did you mean?"

The silence thickened, holding them all immobile for precious seconds. Jem's eyes flashed with frustration, and a sardonic twist curled the edges of his mouth as he stepped closer to her mother.

"I gave it away, didn't I?" he said, correctly interpreting Sera's horrified expression. "I should have remembered how perceptive you are."

Mordas appeared in Kyle's fingers, but neither of them moved at the sight of the ifricaius whip Jem was wielding, its black tentacles weaving around Sophia's body like headless snakes. It was similar to the barbed crop Jude had used last year to capture Daevas, and the one that had entrapped Ilani.

Sera swallowed the rush of fear in her throat as the tips of the whip grazed her mother's skin. "Jem, what are you doing?"

"What I came here to do," he said evenly.

"But you're Ne'feri."

His mouth broadened into a cold, inhuman smile. "Not exactly. Your father, you see, felt that my dad was unfit to remain a member of the order, and as a result, my family was forced to leave in shame. He made his peace with it when he died, but I never could."

"Your father's dead?" Sera asked, confused. "But you said you moved back. Your family was supposed to come to dinner."

"Why do you think I kept rescheduling?" He laughed, and the sound of it felt like a thousand beetles crawling all over her. His cold eyes met hers. "They're all dead. My father, my mother, my brothers. I had to prove myself worthy."

The fear in her chest expanded. "*You* killed them?"

"'Kill' is such a harsh word," Jem said. "I delivered them home." His cool stare settled on Kyle, who hadn't moved from where he stood. Nor had Mara. The smile returned to his lips as he studied Kyle from head to toe. "Your instincts served you well about me, though clearly not soon enough."

"Why, Jemitra?" The soft question came from Sophia.

Jem's stare flicked to her, the whip's tentacles vibrating as if in tune with his thoughts. "We were banned. Exiled. Shunned." He hurled the last three words like bullets. "And now your dear husband will pay for what he's done. And all of you."

Sophia's eyes went wide as the barbed tips of the whip lodged into the flesh of her upper arm, pulling a scream from her mouth. Sera lurched forward involuntarily.

"Not one more move, my friend," Jem warned her. "We both know how painful this can get, and as much as I've loved your mother, I will not hesitate to rip her to pieces before you get within one inch of us." His smile widened. "I'm sure you saw what this beautiful weapon did to that Yoddha."

"Why are you doing this?"

His eyes caressed Sera, making her flesh prickle. "Payback. You see, at first I was just going to take Nate—the prophesized hand of the gods. Lord Temlucus wanted him so badly. But I saw an opportunity and I took it. And now Samsar will pay when I take all of you."

Sera blinked at him. "What are you?"

"He's human, but as the Ne'feri serve the gods, he serves the Demon Lords," Kyle said quietly from behind her. "His soul is on the brink."

"I'll just leave sweet Stella here as a gift for Nate when he returns." Jem smirked, wrenching his hand backward so that Sophia dropped to her knees, writhing in pain. To her credit, she remained silent, though her deifyre flickered and darkened at the edges where the barbs continued burrowing into her flesh. "And then we'll all get what we want, won't we?"

"I can't let you do that," Sera said. Fiery rapiers extended from her palms, and Jem squealed his delight, his blue eyes widening appreciatively.

"I still can't get over the fact about who *you* are," he said, waving his free hand. "Who knew that little Sera Caelum would turn out to be a goddess of Illysia?"

"Jem, revenge is not going to get you anything."

He nodded solicitously. "I know. But it will make me feel better. Closure, you know. Trust me, I lost any sense of empathy years ago." He drew an amused breath. "And, well, with what's coming, figure I better get satisfaction while I still can." The sound of the front door opening and closing made him grin and pull the whip tighter around Sophia. "Let's not spoil the surprise for dear Samsar, shall we?"

"Dad, don't come in here," Sera yelled, even as the chains

sank deep into her mother's flesh and she slumped into a senseless faint. Sophia's deifyre winked out completely as her father rounded the corner, not heeding her desperate warning, and froze at the tableau greeting him.

"Stella!" Nate's cry as he sped across the living room floor toward his friend jerked them all into action.

"Nate, no," Sera cried, but it was too late. Nate skidded to a stop right at the feet of the whimpering girl. She could only watch in horrified silence as the creature wrapped its arms around her brother, squeezing his vulnerable throat with slow, relentless force.

"Perfect," Jem crowed. "I couldn't have planned this better myself."

Revenge Is
Best Served Cold

❧

Adrenaline surged through Kyle's limbs. Mordas pulsed in his fingers like an extension of his own arm, and he longed to sink its thirsty blade into Jem's body. He'd always had an odd feeling about the boy, but his gifts didn't tell him whether beings were evil, only what they were.

And Jem was human.

Albeit a terrible human.

Kyle squinted now, studying him. The boy was mortal, but that didn't mean his soul wasn't as tainted as the fiend that controlled the girl. Humans had free will, and he had chosen to become what he was—a servant to the Dark Realms. The Demon Lords would have granted him power, Kyle knew, like the ability to use the Preta weapon he wielded now. Ra'al's doing, no doubt.

What Jem had said earlier, about the portals going two ways, had to be a mistake. Kyle banished rakshasas, he didn't release them.

"Take me," Sam said to Jem, his hands going wide. "It's me you want, isn't it?"

Pure rage suffused Jem's face, spit flying from his mouth.

"I want you to suffer for what you've done to my family. What you took from us. What you took from *me*."

"Vik was wrong," Sam said. "He knew the consequences of his choices."

"So you kicked him out of the Order?"

Sam shook his head. "I didn't kick him out. He took the life of his opponent, another Ne'feri. That alone was punishable by death. I counseled him to leave the Order, for the sake of his family."

"The shame followed us."

"That was on your father, son, not you," Sam said gently.

Vitriolic laughter erupted from Jem's mouth. "I'm not your son. And I've done far worse things than he ever did. He was grateful when I finally put him out of his misery. You know the saying better to reign in hell than serve in heaven? Well, it's true."

"You are wrong."

"Dad," Sera whispered. "He killed them all. Uncle Vik, all of them. He's with Temlucus."

Sam paled, his hands falling to his sides. Jem watched him as if he were nothing but a mouse caught in a trap. "Lord Temlucus told me about you—about what you used to be. And now look at you, a shell of your former self. You're pathetic. And there's nothing you or anyone else can do to stop me."

Kyle waited, his body coiled and tense, watching Sera carefully. He was the closest to Nate, who slumped unconscious in the vetala's arms. Once Sera gave him the signal, he would do everything he could to save the boy. Disgust curled in his belly as his eyes flicked to Sophia, whose body was ravaged with the poison from the whip. He'd seen the weapon at its worst when Jude and his Preta minions had used it to bind immortals to the earth so they could steal deifyre from their bodies. As a powerful Sanrak, Sophia wouldn't die. But the pain had to be excruciating.

"Let my brother go," Sera said.

"I'm afraid I can't do that. Promises and all. The three of you are going to have to come with me." Kyle's eyes met his at those words. Jem grinned at him. "Oh, Lord Ra'al has wonderful plans for you, Kalias."

"That's not my name," he ground out. "And I'd do as Sera says."

"Why?"

Sera's lips flattened. "I don't want to have to hurt you."

"You forget that I know you, Sera. You won't do a thing, not while your mother and your brother are in danger," Jem said, eyeing her. "At least that protective instinct hasn't changed. Now, weapons down, or you lose two family members. Your choice."

But before Sera could do anything, a blinding flash detonated at the far end of the room, causing Kyle to shield his eyes. In the same moment, Jem lunged toward Sera's father. The heel of the whip caught Sam squarely in the side of the head, even as the tentacles lanced toward Kyle like the head of a Hydra. He tightened his hand around Mordas and slashed wildly at the serpentine feelers.

Kyle's eyes readjusted and he realized that someone else was in the room—another immortal presence. For a second, he thought it was Kira, and then realized that it was Darika. In her goddess form she was as fierce as Kira, though far less spectacular. Kyle felt an odd twinge in the pit of his stomach and frowned. Disappointment, maybe.

"Stop," Sera shouted to Darika as Jem dove toward where the vetala crouched. "He has my brother. And my mom."

Darika met Kyle's eyes grimly and nodded. "Do it now! The boy must not be harmed."

She'd come for Nate. Gritting his teeth, Kyle knelt and pounded his fist against the floor, chanting swiftly as a portal appeared beneath his palm. It was easy to cleave the vetala from Stella's body before banishing it back to Xibalba, but what he hadn't counted on was the sheer number of demons pouring from the brief opening.

As if they'd been waiting . . .

Jem had been right.

Darika was a blur as she destroyed the ones in her reach, as was Sera, who stood protectively in front of her mother and father, her weapons spinning with fiery accuracy. Nate lay in a motionless heap beside the exorcized body of his friend. And only Jem stood in Kyle's way.

"Close it!" Sera shouted. "How is this possible? Since when do your portals go both ways?"

"I don't know," Kyle panted.

But they had way worse things to worry about.

Kyle dodged one of the barbed tips of the Ifricaius shooting toward him. He sealed the portal and stood to face off against Jem. Only now, a hazy cloud surrounded Jem. Black veins pushed from his skin, a row of spines appearing along his shoulders. His eyes were red and bulbous, indicative of the pishacha that had now taken up residence in his body. This wasn't a simple possession. Jem was a willing host who had offered his mortal body as a vessel to one of the demons that had just come through the portal. It wasn't symbiotic. It was something worse.

"Darika," he shouted, his eyes darting to where the goddess was fending off a dozen vetala. "You need to get Nate out of here." Jem screamed his rage, but could do nothing but stare at Kyle with baleful eyes, his covetous gaze dropping to Mordas in his palms. Kyle noticed the direction of his glare. "I'm sure you've heard about this little blade. Your weapon is no match for it. Nor is the demon you're currently making out with in there."

"You don't deserve it," Jem snarled. "Lord Ra'al said it would be mine."

"My father loves to make promises he can't keep." Kyle hefted the blade in his hand. "But if you want it, come and take it."

Jem rushed him, the demon within giving him extra strength and speed. Kyle brought Mordas up to meet the six-pronged whip flying toward him. Steel smashed steel as his blade severed one of the heads, which quickly regrew. Kyle swung upward and down again, his arms aching from the effort of opposing the six heads of the Ifricaius. He'd forgotten how much he hated the ugly weapon.

Out of the corner of his eye, he saw Darika dash toward Nate and drag him over to where Sera and her parents were. The two goddesses squared off against a burgeoning horde as more demons appeared. They weren't the vetala from before. These were varied in size and savagery. Nor did they have human hosts.

Kyle faltered in surprise. There was no way that so many of them could have come through the last portal in one fell swoop. No, these had to have been among the demons that had come to the Mortal Realm before . . . the ones that had been waiting.

"Kyle!" The warning was Darika's.

He snapped to attention and deflected one of the tips of the whip from burrowing into the side of his head. Ducking low, he kicked Jem's legs from under him, sending the Preta weapon skidding across the floor. The boy scrambled to his feet and staggered toward the whip.

Kyle gripped Mordas, torn. He had a choice—he could end Jem's life then and there, or he could get Sera and Darika to safety. But he couldn't do both. Snarling in frustration, he leaped over the sofa and joined the two goddesses in their battle. Mordas ripped through demon after demon, but the surge was unstoppable.

"There's too many of them," Sera panted, glancing down at her parents. "And Mom's fading fast."

"We need to split up," Kyle said as he speared a freakish demon that looked like a bat-balloon hybrid. Gore splattered over them.

"That's not an option."

He grunted and slashed wildly at two more demons flanking him. "Let Darika take Sophia and Nate back to Illysia. You can get your dad to the Ne'feri. And I'll stay and take care of him." He met Sera's eyes. "They want you, not me. Even if they get me, I'm just payback for Ra'al. You need to get your brother some-where safe, Sera. If Temlucus went so far to get him, he must somehow be the key in all of this. You saw what he can do."

Her eyes narrowed at him as she considered what he was saying. Finally, she nodded. "Fine, but if you die, I'm not coming to find you."

"You said that last time."

She slashed viciously through a slug-looking demon. "Well, now I mean it."

Kyle made a fist and beckoned the portal that would take Darika to Illysia. His eyes met hers, a thousand emotions reflected there. She was covered in filth and blood and gore, but none of that could disguise her inner light. He felt that strange pang again, as if something were missing, but now wasn't the time to dwell on residual emotions.

"Go," he told her. "And be safe."

"You, too." She grabbed Sophia and Nate, and they vanished through the portal. A couple of demons tried to follow, but they were incinerated by the celestial wards that defended the Light Realms. For a moment, Kyle wondered what would happen if he expanded the portal to kill every one of the demons in the room. It would likely wound him as well. He'd already learned what goddess power did when Mordas was in his hands. And there was no telling what it would do to Sera, who was still bound to all three realms.

He bared his teeth at Jem, who stood a few feet away, Ifricaius in hand. "Time to finish this."

"Kyle," Sera cried. "Come with me."

"What are you waiting for? Get Sam out of here," he shouted over his shoulder as he vaulted over the coffee table, disemboweling the last of the demons below him with one well-calculated movement of his blade. He didn't wait to see if she did as he asked, but ran hell-bent toward Jem. He crashed into the boy and they slammed into a nearby bookcase, sending all the books flying.

One of the whip's tentacles wound around his wrist, the

barbs burrowing into his flesh like steel maggots. He screamed at the hot blast of pain rocketing up his arm and Mordas clattered to the floor. Jem lunged for it, but Kyle threw his knee into the other boy's gut and crashed his shoulder into the wall with his free hand.

But either he had miscalculated or he'd misjudged Jem's strength; the boy twisted out of Kyle's grip and heaved his body over his back. The air was smacked out of him as two more tentacles dug into his body, making his spine arch like a reed in the wind. In some dark corner of his mind, Kyle knew that it would be nothing compared to the agony that Sophia had felt. He was an Azura Lord and this was an Azura weapon.

It burned like the fires of hell.

Hissing through his teeth, he wrapped his fingers around the whip and ripped it from Jem's hands. The barbed tips came away with chunks of flesh from his thighs and torso, but Kyle didn't stop. A growl tore from his mouth as he freed himself of the weapon. Power and pain merged into one beast roaring to life within him.

Jem's eyes widened and he scrambled to get Mordas. He reached for the sword and screamed his frustration as the sword disappeared, only to reappear in Kyle's hands. "I thought I told you that Mordas belongs to me."

"Doesn't matter," Jem said, his eyes rolling back as if the demon inside was communicating something to him. "It's already done."

"What's done?" Sera blurted out.

Kyle shot her an exasperated look. She never did anything she was supposed to. "I told you to get somewhere safe. Where's Sam?"

"He's with Mara and Dev," she said quickly. "They're convening the Ne'feri."

"Those pathetic humans can't help you." Jem's tone was jeering. "Not against what's coming."

Sera inched carefully forward, no weapons in sight. Kyle started, but she stalled him with a slight frown. She spread her palms wide. "Jem," she pleaded, "if you're in there, it's not too late to do the right thing."

"If I'm in here?" he mocked. "Who exactly do you think this is, if not me?"

"You've been coerced by Temlucus. He'll betray you."

Jem laughed, the sound an echo of something Kyle had heard before. Warning signals rang in his brain. "You silly girl. Lord Temlucus won't betray me."

"He will."

"No, Serjana, he won't."

The use of her full name had Kyle on alert even as the boy's face shifted. Kyle blinked, using his other sight to see the pishacha lengthening its hulking form into something long and lean and imminently recognizable. Burning ember eyes scorched into his. The indistinct shadow was tethered to Jem's flesh by stringy tendrils.

"Temlucus," he whispered.

"In the flesh, as they say," the boy's lips spat.

"What?" Sera said, raising disbelieving eyes to him. "How?"

Kyle forestalled her. "It's not him," he said. "It's a projection of him inside your friend. The pishacha is his conduit." He paused as brittle understanding flooded him. "That's why he wanted Nate so badly."

"Nate, why?"

"Because Jem's mortal body is failing, and without him, Temlucus cannot exist in this dimension. Remember what Nate did for me after Mordas? Nate's power extends beyond this realm. He can fortify anything that is dying." His eyes met Sera's. *"Anything."*

"Clever boy," Temlucus cheered. "But no matter. This body will last long enough to see us through."

"But why Jem?" Sera blurted out.

"You already know why," Temlucus said, waving a hand across Jem's body. "Tortured soul bent on revenge, a willing vessel, existing ties to this family. That is and will always be your greatest weakness, Serjana—your trust in the nature of humanity." His spectral eyes shifted to Kyle. "You sensed something early on, but you've always followed her like a sheep. No true son of Ra'al would be so pitiable. Or so weak-willed." His lips stretched wide. "You will fail, as you have failed at everything else in your useless life."

Kyle swung Mordas in a swift upward arc before his arm met resistance. He blinked to see Sera's forearm blocking his. She shook her head.

"Stop. You can't kill him. It's still Jem in there," she said, her gaze narrowing on Temlucus, who hadn't so much as flinched at the deadly sword swinging toward him. It was almost as if he'd expected it. Kyle thought he'd be beyond baiting from any of the Demon Lords, but obviously not.

His hand shook as it dropped to his side at that thought, realizing how close he'd come to killing a human. Despicable as Jem might be, he was still mortal and—until his soul crossed—potentially redeemable.

"The Trimurtas will stop whatever it is you're doing," Sera said, her hand resting against Kyle's as if she didn't quite trust him not to cleave Jem's head from his body. "Didn't you learn your lesson the last time?"

Temlucus smiled. "Last time we put our faith in the wrong leader."

The wrenching sensation in Kyle's center was instant. His back jerked ramrod straight, his cells awash with sensation, as if his skin was being separated from the rest of his body. "Do you feel that?" he whispered.

Sera blinked, going still. "I felt *something*."

"Demons," Kyle breathed. "Thousands of them. So many I can feel it from here—a shift in the balance of the realms."

"Where?"

"If I had to guess, I'd say the high school."

Their eyes converged on Temlucus, but Jem's face was inexpressive, resuming its natural coloring as the demon within him relinquished its hold. Jem slumped to the ground.

"Temlucus is gone," Kyle said, making sure that all traces of the demon were no longer there. "What do we do with him?"

"Take him with us," Sera said. "We can't leave him here."

They raced to Kyle's car. He glanced at her as they secured Jem in the back seat and bound both his hands and feet. They weren't taking any chances that he'd wake up and do something stupid. "You need to let Dev and the others know," Kyle said.

Sera frowned as she slid into the passenger seat. "This doesn't feel right," she said. "Like it's a trick or something."

"It probably is. But we can't take the chance that thousands of kids are going to die at those demons' hands," he said, slamming on the accelerator. "They want us to come. And we can't *not* go."

Their eyes met, and Sera nodded. "Why Silver Lake High?"

"Burial grounds," Kyle said. "The ones we saw in the basement. I felt the shift in the fabric between realms when we were there after the vetala appeared. Like something was welling up beneath the surface."

She stared at him. "Why didn't you say anything?"

"I didn't think that the vetala there would be protecting something far worse," he said, raking a hand through his curls.

"Worse like what?"

He drew a breath. "Like a fissure between the realms. I thought it was an old portal or something, but maybe I was wrong."

"A fissure," she echoed, her eyes going wide with alarm.

"Yeah." He nodded more firmly. "Otherwise, what were they doing there?"

"Could you be wrong?"

"Always a chance."

The school building loomed into view. It looked normal from the outside. The parking lot was full of cars but empty of people. Even the air around them was deadly still. There were no birds, no noises, no nothing. The silence was eerie. Unearthly. Gooseflesh puckered the skin of Kyle's arms, and from the look on Sera's face, she was feeling as uneasy as he was.

"Can you sense anything?" she asked. "Are they inside?"

Kyle concentrated, pushing his awareness outward until he felt the thrum of darkness. Once it caught him, it gripped his consciousness hard, sucking it toward the center of the building. It was like a scene out of a horror movie—students lined up in neat rows, their eyes vacant and their faces stricken in terror. His breath deserted him at the thick, eddying mass of dark energy surrounding the comatose occupants like a swarm of angry hornets. One by one, each body was filled until nothing of the mass remained. They turned in unison toward him, their faces holding identical rictus grins.

"They're inside the gym," he whispered, his knees buckling as he slammed back into his numb body. "It's too late. We're too late."

Sera shook his shoulders. "We have to try."

"There's nothing we can do for them."

"We took an oath, Kyle," she cried, tugging on him to follow her into the school. "And I'll do this with or without you."

"You don't understand." He grabbed her arm roughly and dragged her back. "They're all hosts."

The Cost of a Soul

꩜

Sera stared at her best friend, her mouth agape. He couldn't be saying what she thought he was. He couldn't be insisting that they abandon all those kids. But it seemed like he was determined to do exactly that. "We can't leave them," she insisted.

"The rakshasas want us to go in there," he said. "And we can't. I can't put you in that kind of danger. You saw what happened the last time I created a portal. Scores of demons came out." His face tightened. "It's been happening all along. *I've* been the cause of them infiltrating the Mortal Realm. It's *my* fault."

Sera frowned. It was on the tip of her tongue to insist that it wasn't his fault. But it was mindboggling. If she hadn't seen it with her own eyes, she wouldn't have believed it. When Kyle banished a demon from the Mortal Realm to Xibalba, the portal went both ways, allowing other demons to escape.

No one could have predicted such a thing could happen— but then, of course, there had never been an immortal quite like Kyle before.

They both turned at the sound of a car screeching into the lot, tires squealing as it came to a stop inches away from where they stood. Darika leapt out with Sera's father in tow.

Sera stared at them wildly, her face pinched. "I told Mara to get him somewhere safe," she accused the other goddess. "Why would you bring him here? He's mortal."

"I made her bring me," Sam said. "I need to see Jem. He will be marked with some sort of rune that ties him to the Dark Realms. If we can remove it, I think he can be saved."

"You didn't see him, Dad," Sera said. "He doesn't want to be saved. He wants revenge. He's more demon than mortal, and no dissolved demon rune is going to save him. Not now."

Sam shook his head with stalwart tenacity. "I refuse to believe that he's lost to us. Where did you see him last? He won't have gone far."

"He's in the car," Kyle said, avoiding Sera's glower.

They approached the vehicle cautiously, and Sera half expected Jem to have disappeared. It was like that horror movie cliché—you capture the bad guy and he magically escapes from his restraints only to return in the bloody finale. A pent-up breath escaped her lips as her eyes settled on the motionless form lying in the back seat. Okay, maybe this wasn't going to be that type of movie.

Or not.

As soon as Kyle opened the door, Jem lurched upward and sprinted from the car on all fours, like some kind of crazed beast, in the direction of the woods. Her father took off after him.

"Dad, no!" Sera swore aloud and followed them. She stopped halfway and glanced over her shoulder to meet Darika's burning eyes. "Save the kids in the gym if you can," she shouted. "Kyle can release them."

She had no idea if Darika would help or not; the goddess had been more placid than her sister. Sera blinked, correcting herself—she'd been more amenable than her darker side, the avatar of her berserker nature.

Sera sighed. With what they were up against, they could do with some of Kira's untempered ferocity. She understood why Kyle had made the choice he had, though. Kira was volatile. It would be like being in a relationship with electricity: beautiful and exciting but with the underlying risk of being electrocuted to death. Darika, on the other hand, would smile benevolently until the last heartbeat before she destroyed you.

The minute Sera entered the woods, she felt the change in the air. It pulsed with the collective energy of thousands of demons. Her goddess senses tingled. She could feel them plucking at her consciousness with stinging touches.

The balance was shifting enough to put all the realms in chaos. These demons did not belong here. Maybe Kira had been right in the beginning—that it was an infestation that needed to be cleansed.

It seemed that time had been against them from the start. And now they were way beyond saving those they'd tried to help . . . and the Demon Lords were ahead of the game.

Had they made a mistake?

But this wasn't the time to dwell on the wisdom of past decisions.

Drawing a determined breath, Sera plunged into the woods, following her father's trail through the brush. Thank the heavens for Girl Scouts. The daylight was almost blocked out by the canopy above, making her pulse gallop as she quickened her pace, her swords glowing silvery white and glistening red in the darkness. The hairs on the back of her neck prickled as the demon energy swelled with each step farther into the woods.

Faces snapped at her from the trees, looming in and out of her vision. She could feel searing breath on her cheeks and smell the sourness of decaying flesh, but when she turned to look, there was nothing there. She wasn't afraid, though somewhere deep inside, she knew she probably should be. Even with her goddess strength, fighting a few dozen demons would not be the same as taking on a horde of hundreds. Her breath stuttered at the thought, but she pressed forward doggedly.

Sera halted in the center of the copse. A cacophony of screeches filtered down to her, and the darkness undulated like it was a living thing.

Or *things*.

"Dad?" she called, flaring her light so that she could see a few feet ahead of her.

A muffled grunt came back in response, from somewhere to her right. She pushed through the trees in that direction until the sound of a scuffle reached her ears. She hastened her stride, pointy twigs and what felt like sharp claws tearing at her face as she ran by, though she healed as quickly as she was struck. The sounds of the struggle grew louder as Sera burst through the thicket to an open glade.

Her father lay locked in the arms of some kind of beast as a circle of spectators watched. The onlookers weren't human, though some of them were still connected to mortal bodies. Most of them were demons . . . except for the one boy at the far end of the clearing, who looked on with a gratified smirk.

Kyle had said Jem was still human. Rage suffused her entire body as she dove into the center of the ring, her swords at the ready. She would put an end to this right here and now. And then she would deal with her former friend.

"No, Sera," her father panted, stalling her. He held a dagger that was coated in green ichor. He was bleeding from a gushing wound at his cheek and his shirt was soaked in bright red blood, but he seemed lucid.

She froze, her sword inches away from the throat of a scaled demon that looked like a cross between a crocodile and a horse.

"If you intervene, you will break the terms of the agreement."

Her disbelieving gaze spun to her father's, her stomach plummeting. "Agreement?"

"The right of challenge." It was Jem's insouciant voice that offered the explanation. He raised a hand, signaling a halt in the contest. "Your stupid father challenged Lord Temlucus for the rights to this mortal shell. As that of a former Azura Lord, the challenge from Lord Samsar was accepted. And since my lord is not here, he has chosen a combatant in his stead."

"Dad, that's suicide," Sera whispered and then turned her rage in Jem's direction. "You know he's mortal and no longer an Azura Lord. The contest is not well matched. How can you even consider this?"

"We were not the ones to issue the challenge," Jem returned coolly.

She hissed through her teeth. "Then you must renege on the grounds of . . . the grounds of mortal disparity."

"We will not."

"Then I will fight on his behalf," she shouted.

Jem smiled as if he'd been waiting for her to say just that. "The battle has already begun, and I assure you, Lord Samsar's bond, mortal or not, is binding."

"You just started!"

"And blood has already been spilled." Jem's voice deepened to something guttural as Temlucus spoke through the boy's body, making gooseflesh prick her skin. "You know the rules, Lady Serjana. Once a challenge is issued, the battle must be fought."

"You're a liar," she growled. "I learned that lesson the last time you cheated on a right of *challenge*."

"That was a draw," he said. "Lord Ra'al made the killing stroke you failed to deliver. There was no victor."

"So you say. Yet I was the only one standing."

Temlucus ignored her and clapped Jem's hands. "Come, let us not tarry longer. My loyal followers are hungry for fresh blood."

Sera turned back to her father in one last desperate plea. "You don't have to do this. Temlucus will not relinquish his hold over Jem that easily, no matter how much you want to save him. Your life isn't worth the cost. Please, Dad."

"Every life is worth it."

His quiet response made her heart tremble. "But you're human. It's not a fair match."

"I have some tricks up my sleeve," he said, with a crooked grin that nearly made her throw herself into his arms. "And have some faith in your old dad. Though I'm no longer immortal, I still know how to take out a rakshasa."

They both stared at the horse-crocodile demon. It had a row of razor-sharp tusks protruding from its lower jaw. Sera nodded, her jaw clenched, and stepped out of the circle into the onlooking horde. Tongues licked at her exposed flesh and she shuddered. She let her deifyre flare, creating a buffer of space around her. One nearby demon was not quick enough to get out of the way and leapt backward with a shriek as it was singed.

"Play nice," Temlucus warned.

"If you attempt to cheat your way out of this, there will be more than hell to pay, I promise you," Sera returned. "You and all your followers will burn."

"I look forward to it."

Her heart hitched in her chest as her father squared off against the demon in a low crouch. He kept his weight on the balls of his feet, and he remained alert, despite the blood congealing on his cheek. The fiend lumbered forward, and he darted out of its way. Sam was fast and nimble, the daggers in his palms drawing greenish-brown lines across the creature's pelt as he skirted past. It howled loudly and snapped its jaws a hairsbreadth from his face.

Numb with dread for her father, she raised her eyes to Jem's. Even across the glade, his glittered with satisfaction. Temlucus wasn't watching the fight. Instead, he was watching *her*, as if the outcome was guaranteed and the prize would be seeing her crumble when her father lost. Sera kept her face carefully composed, refusing to give him any gratification. She jutted her chin forward and arched an arrogant eyebrow. His response was a slow-breaking smile, as if he could see right through her ploy. Tearing her gaze from his, she focused on the fight at hand.

Sera's fingers curled into fists at her side as her father and the demon circled each other again. He'd gotten in a few more attacks, but he was starting to breathe heavily, and his momentum had slowed. The light cuts from the daggers would do no lasting damage to the beast, and sooner or later, her father would tire. Then the creature would strike.

She sucked in a strained gasp when the demon landed a clubbed punch on her father's side, sending him skidding across the forest floor. She only let out the breath when he stumbled to his feet with a groan, clearly disoriented. The beast scooted toward him, jaws open to deliver the finishing blow, but Sam managed to roll underneath it, swiping at its furred underbelly in the process. The smell of foul guts permeated the air.

Sera blinked, expecting the demon to heal, but the gaping wound remained open. Her eyes flicked to her father's daggers, noting the runes of Illysia etched on their blades. Her left palm tingled as if in recognition of the shield and the wing she saw there—Dev's runes. She heaved a sigh of relief. He must have given her father the knives to protect himself. Her father did have a few tricks up his sleeves, after all.

She stared at Jem, noticing that the smug smile had disappeared. He seemed more agitated now that Sam might actually have a chance. The demon swayed as its life force ebbed from its abdomen.

"Finish it," Temlucus snarled to the wobbling demon. "Or I will finish you."

Obediently, the brute charged toward Sam, howling with rage. Entrails leaked in its wake, but some unnatural, unearthly force was compelling it. Sam was able to move out of the way of its yawning mouth and pointed tucks, but couldn't avoid the punishing swipe of its claws. They raked ruthlessly across his back, ripping through his shirt and the muscles below. Screaming, her father buckled to his knees and crashed to the dirt. Bright blood soaked the shredded material.

"Get up, Dad," Sera said, falling to her own knees and keeping an eye on the demon that was struggling to right itself, having fallen into the crowd of its brethren. "You've nearly won. *Get up.*"

His answer was a moan, and drops of saliva flecked his lips. Blood drenched the earth beside him in rivers of grit-sodden red, and she could feel the rising delight of the demons on either side of them as they wound themselves into a feeding frenzy.

"You have to get up," she whispered. "It's nearly over. Think of Mom and Nate. Dig deep, Dad."

Sam flopped to his back, his body shaking uncontrollably. His hand reach toward hers as a thick stream of blood bubbled from between his lips. She made no move to hide the emotions on her face, though she could see Temlucus's triumph in the gloating expression that eclipsed Jem's face.

Her fear solidified in her chest as she stared at the demon ambling back toward them. "Dad! *Please.*"

Sera's sobbing scream lodged in her throat as the demon's shadow fell over them. It was close, so close . . . in striking distance, but it stood there unmoving and quiet. The noise in the glade dulled to one of deathly, thick silence. Sera's eyes flicked upward—the demon was waiting for Temlucus to order the deathblow. Her gaze met the Demon Lord's. The seconds ticked by as they stared at each other. He would savor the victory . . . relish every moment of her agonizing impotence.

"Any last words?" he drawled. "Do you wish to plead for his life? Offer something else in exchange, perhaps?"

"Don't . . . you dare," her father managed through a mouthful of blood. Tears leaked from the corners of his eyes as he struggled to focus on her. "My . . . death . . . honor."

"No!" Sera cried, her heart breaking as the man who had fathered and raised her lay dying while she did nothing. Screw his honor. She could not—would not—let him die. She stood, facing Jem. "Wait—"

She was on the verge of doing something foolish when she felt a new presence. The demons around them screamed and scattered as Dev emerged, the burning light of his aura making the few that were standing too near go up in flames.

"Dev," she said.

"Lord Devendra," Temlucus greeted him, frustration flashing across Jem's face. "What brings you here?"

Dev smiled, his words as calm as his face. "I'm here to stop my beloved from doing something she will regret."

"It's my choice," Sera shot back.

"Lady Serjana is right," Temlucus said. "It is *her* choice."

"One that violates the terms of the challenge," Dev said. "A victor must emerge. Only one must be left standing, according to the laws of Xibalba."

Temlucus sneered, twisting Jem's features so violently that his face took on a demonic slant. "What do *you* know of our laws?"

"Enough to know that Samsar's bond cannot be broken or traded."

"Unless a new challenge is made," Temlucus shot back. "Or we finish what we started."

Sera swallowed the gulp in her throat as the demon inched closer. The claws of its hind legs scraped against her father's lower half. One more inch and its jaws would be in striking range. A single snap would take her father's head off. Sera started forward, swaying deliriously. Gentle but powerful hands rested on her shoulders and she tensed. She could feel Dev's strength radiating toward her, but she didn't want any of it. Nothing could take away the desolation filling her blood like poison.

"It's what he wants," Dev said into her ear.

"It was a trick," she said, darting a venomous look toward Jem. "He tricked him into an unfair challenge."

Dev pulled her against him as misery filled her in waves, drowning her spirit in despair. "Your father knew the risks when he accepted the terms. In his day, he was challenged many times. You cannot do what you are thinking, my love. Samsar would never forgive himself if you offered yourself in exchange. You are far too important."

"What will happen to him?" she whispered, closing her eyes, the sight of her father lying there too much to bear.

Temlucus's laugh filled the area between them. "Don't you worry your pretty little head about it. I have a special spot reserved for him in the sixth. Just know that his every day will undoubtedly be filled with thoughts of you."

His leer made helpless tears spring to her eyes. Dev's forearm curved around her chest and the scent of him filled her nostrils. Her pain was liquid within her, filling all the hollow spaces in her heart. She loved her father, but Dev was right—she could not save him, not when everyone else hung in the balance.

"Are we going to stall all day?" Temlucus jeered, baring Jem's teeth in a ghoulish chortle. "Kill him," he commanded the waiting demon.

Sam's eyes met hers and held them until the demon eclipsed her view by falling on top of him. It was nearly half dead from the festering wound her father had inflicted with his Illysia-blessed daggers, but still awake enough to widen its fearsome jaws for the final blow. Both her father and the demon went still.

Dev's arms held her close and a keening sound burst from her lips as the creature moved, its huge body quaking. Sera's remaining strength deserted her in that moment, and she slumped against Dev.

Temlucus had won.

It was over. Her father had lost.

Tears trekked down her cheeks as, once more, she looked toward Jem. The gratified look she expected to see was not there. His mouth was turned down in resentment. Confused, she looked back to where the demon was moving at her feet, slow to realize that the movement was coming from *beneath* it. Shaking arms pushed the beast to the side, and finally she saw two daggers embedded in the demon's throat, as her father emerged covered in demon slop. His chest rose and fell in a shallow motion.

Sera broke free from Dev's grasp and fell to her father's side, embracing him and offering him her strength. "You did it," she cried. "How?"

"Told you I knew a few tricks." He drew a fractured breath, his lips quivering into a smile. "Help. Up."

She and Dev held him between them as he faced the defeated Demon Lord. Jem stood there sourly, Temlucus burning like an angry shadow behind his eyes. "You think you have won," he said. "But you have not."

"Release the boy," Sam said.

Temlucus did not respond, but within moments, Jem drooped, his body collapsing at the base of a nearby tree. Dev waved a palm and dispersed the remaining demons in one fell swoop.

"Help me," Sam said, lifting a trembling finger toward where Jem lay. Sera frowned. Her father had risked so much—and for what? For a kid who had tried to murder him and his whole family?

Dev helped to turn Jem over and stripped the shirt from his shoulders. Just as her father had said, a scarlet rune marked the graying skin there, in the shape of a scythe surrounded by flame. Temlucus's rune. Sera didn't know how she knew that. She just did. Just as she knew all the runes of all the Demon Lords. Just as she had known all the levels of Xibalba.

"Sera," her father wheezed. "Erase it."

Her frown deepened. "Me? How?"

"That." He nodded to her right palm.

"No."

"Only way."

Dev took her hands carefully into his. "He's right. Yours is the only rune that will eclipse the one that is there."

"But he will be marked to me," she protested, suddenly remembering the green-and-black raptor demon bearing her rune that she had met in Xibalba months before. *Izei*. It had been bound to her somehow, and had saved both her and Kyle from a gruesome death in one of the pits of hell. "I don't want that. He'll be a slave."

"He'll die otherwise, and his soul will be forever in Temlucus's keeping," Dev said. "Temlucus will have won."

Sera inhaled sharply and tore her palm from Dev's grasp. Without a second thought, she slammed its heel onto the rune etched into Jem's skin. Torment pulsed through her in frantic, scattered beats, and her back arched like a bow as her rune seared away the brand beneath it, erasing and reforming it with her own.

But for an eternal instant before the sigil dissolved, she and Temlucus were connected. And in that moment, Sera saw. She *knew* beyond the shade of a doubt what was on the horizon.

The end of the world wasn't coming.

It was already here.

POWER PLAY

⌘

"I told you it was a lost cause," Kyle muttered with a look over his shoulder at the girl behind him.

Darika, in all her goddess glory, dispatched three demons loitering along the otherwise deserted corridor. Blood speckled her clothing, but her features were composed, impassive with the exception of her customary and secretive smile. She was the consummate warrior striding into battle. Today, a menacing tiger walked at her side. Four pairs of arms held various weapons, including a mace and a bow, but the trident was currently impaled in the torso of a demon the size of a small horse. She grunted as she tore it loose and caught up to him.

"You were the one who wanted to save the mortals," she told him in a low whisper. "And you have been granted your request. Surely you do not wish to give up now?"

"There are hundreds of kids in there," he replied. "All controlled by demons. There's no way we can save all of them."

"We can try."

"You sound like Sera," he said, dodging a flying demon that swooped down from some hidden vent. He swung Mordas in a skillful arc, catching the demon on its second pass. The birdlike creature disappeared in a shower of yellow embers.

Darika eyed him. "Is that a bad thing?"

"Of course not," he said. "But it's not easy when any portal I create only lets more of them enter the Mortal Realm." He darted a circumspect look to her. "Maybe Kira was right—they should all be purged so we can start fresh."

Darika met his stare with a cool one of her own. "That is still an option. Kali is the great liberator, the deliverer of moksha. Death is a certainty in this life."

"And you? What's your role?"

"You already know that," she said mildly, unresponsive to his belligerent tone. "I am the sum of the collective energy of the gods, meant to defend those oppressed by demonic forces." She stopped in front of him to block his way, then dragged him into an empty classroom nearby. "What's really bothering you?"

Kyle swallowed and met her eyes, misery threatening to choke him. "I feel like this is all my fault," he began. "If I hadn't banished all those demons in the first place, I wouldn't have allowed so many to infect this realm. I thought I could . . . save everyone. Instead, I was the one to doom them all. They're here because I opened the stupid portals!"

"You could not have foreseen this," she said. "Not even the Trimurtas knew what your ties to Xibalba would produce. Or that your portals would go both ways, allowing the rakshasas to escape."

"*I* should have known," he insisted. "I am the seed of Ra'al, unworthy of redemption. All of this happened *because of me*. All I've done is cause chaos and death because of this disgusting blood that runs in my veins. I brought this upon them."

She eyed him, that ever-present half-smile tilting the corners of her lips. "Don't you think you're being just a tiny bit dramatic?"

"What?" he sputtered.

"Unworthy of redemption?" She smirked, her eyes rolling skyward, but Kyle failed to see what she found so funny. "That sounds like something Ra'al would say."

He couldn't curb his sour response. "Maybe I'd be better off with him."

"Is that what you want?"

"No."

"Then stop being so stupid." She winked at him and squeezed his arm. "Or do I need to go berserker battle-crazy on you?"

Kyle blinked at her expression, uncertain of her meaning. Did she mean that *she* would go into berserker mode, or that she'd summon Kira? He couldn't quite ignore the increased stammer of his pulse. If Kira were here, she'd probably deliver him straight to Ra'al, no questions asked. She'd never tolerate his pity party. That was one of the things he liked most about her—her unfailing, brutal honesty. He supposed he should be grateful for Darika's compassion, even if he felt that he deserved none of it.

"Do you really think we can save those kids?" he asked after a beat.

"That's more like it." Darika thumped him on the shoulder, making him wince from the force of it. "I think *you* can."

"But what about the dual gateway thing?"

"Let me worry about that," she said. "Ready?"

He hoisted Mordas and nodded. "Yes."

Together they exited the classroom and made their way down the silent hallway. It was deserted and still, like a creepy scene out of some horror flick. Kyle couldn't curb the shivers that raced across his skin in icy bursts. The Demon Lords would know they were coming. They would be ready to unleash whatever atrocities they had planned. He could only hope that he and Darika would have enough time to release the kids trapped in their clutches.

Kyle had no doubt that they were walking into a trap, but they had no other choice and time was short. The tug on his center grew more insistent the closer they got to the gymnasium, and the push of so many energies made him suddenly disoriented. He wondered whether it had anything to do with the burial ground below where they walked, but he shook his head. Delayed paranoia was starting to make an unwelcome appearance.

Then again, he'd never felt this discombobulated by demon energies before. He paused and tried to settle himself, but nothing seemed to assuage the hollowness within him that was growing wider by the minute. Whatever monstrous thing awaited them in that room would not be friendly or forgiving.

"The gym is around the corner," he whispered over his shoulder. "There are a lot of them."

Darika closed her eyes and exhaled. "I know. I can feel the shift in the balance."

"We're going to need help."

"It is coming."

Kyle drew a sharp breath. Hopefully, assistance would arrive long before a throng of demons swarmed them. "Should we wait?" he whispered.

But fate, it seemed, was not on their side as the walkway erupted into dissonant screeching. The noise was not coming from the gym, but from the opposite end of the hall. In moments, they would be trapped. They exchanged a silent look before grasping their weapons and taking up positions on either side of the gymnasium doors.

Darika clasped her hands together and closed her eyes, her lips forming some kind of silent mantra. Her eyes flickered open and the firm resolve Kyle saw there bolstered his own failing nerves. "Let's go."

They pushed open the doors, expecting to be attacked immediately. But they were greeted instead by rows and rows of motionless human bodies, surrounding a glass sculpture that looked chillingly like some kind of altar. The massive structure stood in the middle of the gym's basketball court, ebony crystal shards glistening around its concentric base like a crown. He sucked in a breath at the gleaming circle at its epicenter that shimmered in an erratic motion. It was a portal, though it seemed to be not fully formed, winking in and out of existence.

"Welcome, Lord Kalias." A tall figure appeared from behind the altar. "And of course, Lady Durga."

Every bone in Kyle's body recognized his father's voice. Sera had once said that Ra'al's default form—that of the aristocratic older man—looked like Gandalf from *The Lord of the Rings*. But he wasn't in that form today. Kyle bit his lip until he could feel blood seep into his mouth. The form sauntering forward was Kira's. Darika let out a soft gasp beside him.

"He takes the form of those you lo . . . trust," Kyle explained in a hollow voice. The woman ambled toward them, and with each step, Kyle could feel his strength falter. Ra'al embodied Kira down to the last detail—from the wild tangle of black hair and red lips to her trim, black-clad figure.

"Hello," she said, her dark eyes flicking to Darika. "*Sister.*" Her tone was mocking as she raked them both with a chilling stare. "Guess that old mortal saying about three being a crowd is true. Look at you two, all cozy."

"It's not really her," Kyle said, stifling the swift rise of guilt in his chest. It was what Ra'al did—he preyed on fears and insecurities, and then turned them against you.

Darika's answer was soft. "I know."

At the quiet affirmation, Ra'al's form shifted, morphing into a new shape. This one was also feminine, but with red hair falling in soft waves and glistening silvery eyes. "Or perhaps you desire Lady Serjana instead." Ra'al laughed, the musical tones identical to Sera's. "I never could quite decide whether you would be a better choice than Devendra, especially after that kiss." Her voice lowered to something sweet and hypnotic. "You remember, don't you?"

"Kyle." The short hiss was from the goddess at his side and he swayed unsteadily on his feet, blinking wildly. His treacherous father had moved nearly to within arm's reach. "Use your sight," Darika urged. "That thing in front of you is not who you think it is."

Breathing heavily, Kyle summoned his ability, and the mortal layers that formed Sera fell away. The illusion was shattered as his father's true form burst forth. Blood red and beastlike, with curling black horns crowning his head. His father leered at him.

"Still so easy to bait," he jeered. "Are you sure the Trimurtas made you immortal?"

"What do you want?" Kyle snapped.

"What I've always wanted, my son." Ra'al laughed. "For you—"

"I am no son of yours," he bit out.

"—to claim your legacy," Ra'al continued as if he hadn't spoken. "Claim your place where you belong, as you have always been meant to do. Learn at my side and assume your throne in time. You were born to rule. I know you feel it—that impulse calling you back to where you truly belong. It's in your lifeblood, the meat of who you are."

Kyle frowned at his loquaciousness. Something wasn't right. Ra'al was stalling. Though the Demon Lord had always enjoyed hearing himself speak, it seemed like he was wasting time on purpose. It wasn't like him to wax poetic about Kyle's birthright. Ra'al wanted to punish him, not to exalt him as his successor, which meant that all of this was part of some farce . . . some other illusion meant to disrupt. Or distract.

Kyle's gaze spanned the room. He suppressed an involuntary shiver. He had no doubt that he and Darika had been shepherded here. The human bodies around them hadn't moved, but he sensed a growing restlessness among them, as if the spirits within were preparing for something. He had to throw Ra'al off balance, buy some time. Steeling himself, he shifted Mordas to lie across his front like a shield. The Demon Lord's eyes flashed with something akin to irritation.

"If that's so," he said mildly, tapping Mordas against the fleshy part of his forearm. "Why do you answer to Temlucus?"

His father's burning eyes lanced to his. "I do not answer to him."

"Sure looked like you did last time I was in the sixth," Kyle replied. "He chose *you* to fight for *him*. Who knew that the great Ra'al could be commanded like a servant? Like some common gladiator in his master's ring?"

"I am no servant," he snapped.

"Right."

Kyle's mocking tone made Ra'al's mouth thin to an angry sneer. "Temlucus may think he's the one in charge, but I am the father of the son whose power holds the key. The Kali-Yuga is my legacy, not his."

Kyle tried to not let his surprise show. The demons needed him. Again.

"Any remnant of your demon blood running in my veins has long been exorcized," Kyle said. "And if you think I will help you, then you are about to learn the same lesson as last time."

"We will see who learns the lesson."

The chilling undertone in Ra'al's voice was the only indication that all hell was about to break loose. Pandemonium exploded as demons attacked them from all corners of the gym. Kyle felt Darika shift at his side and as he peered at her over his shoulder, he sucked in an awed gasp. Her four pairs of arms had evolved into ten, each holding a weapon. Though the expression on her face was still contemplative, the look in her eyes was fierce and indomitable.

"Try not to hurt them," he shouted as he ducked a kick from a boy in his calculus class. He shoved the hilt of Mordas upward and the boy crumpled to the ground. He turned his attention to a group of cheerleaders that didn't look in the least friendly as they swarmed him. Their sharp nails scratched at his face and arms, drawing welts of blood. It took every ounce of his skill to not kill them with a careless swipe of Mordas.

Incapacitate was his edict.

He dared a glance at Darika and noticed with relief that she was doing the same. Boys and girls surrounded her in moaning heaps, clutching their injuries. She was a whirlwind as she decimated the rushing horde. Kyle shook his head and turned back to the task at hand. It was worse than a pep rally. *A demon pep rally.*

A girl from English that he'd hooked up with sophomore year ran full throttle toward him to crash into his chest, tumbling both of them to the floor. Not quite finished, she snapped her teeth closed near his ear. He rolled out from underneath her and scrambled away, only to collide with three jocks from the baseball team staring down at him with matching diabolical grins. He curled into a ball to avoid their kicks and braced his hands over his head to protect himself from their metal spiked cleats. Mordas skidded out of reach across the slippery court floor. Kyle watched in horror as a senior he vaguely recognized bent to pick it up.

"No," he managed to shout, but it was too late—hot red embers swallowed the kid's hands and traveled like fire up his arms. The human and the demon within howled in combined agony at the touch of the ruthless Azura weapon. Within seconds, the boy was a human-sized lump of charred ash.

The kicking halted as the demons were mesmerized by the dark fire, and Kyle took the chance to spring to his feet. With a powerful grunt, he vaulted over prone bodies and scooped up

Mordas in the process, knocking kids out left and right as he made his way to where Darika fought at the center of the gym.

"The altar," she shouted to him.

His eyes flew to the menacing, crystalline structure rising atop the sea of human bodies. Darika was right—he had to get to that altar and destroy it. Whatever Ra'al and Temlucus were planning, it would have something to do with that thing. Something bloody and sacrificial, no doubt.

He looked around wildly for any signs of his pernicious father, but it seemed that the Demon Lord had disappeared. His father was as slippery as an eel, and was probably watching him right at that moment. Kyle fought off another wave of kids and climbed his way toward Darika and the altar. "When's your help coming?" he said, moving to stand so that they were back to back against the relentless churn of human bodies.

"Already here," she said as her trident sent three kids scuttling across the gym floor to the half-court line. His gaze swept over the crowd to see Mara and a few other Yoddha battling it out near the entrance of the gym. Gratitude poured through him, but it was short-lived as he was swamped by more flailing bodies. Even with the help, the horde of mortals seemed inexhaustible. The ones that had been disabled were scattered about with broken limbs and unconscious bodies, driven by the unholy forces within them.

"They're killing them," Kyle said, breathing hard.

"We need to get to the altar," she said. "Destroy it."

"Easier said than done," he muttered, fending off a dozen demons that appeared to have vacated their hosts. This time, he didn't hesitate to use Mordas, slicing and dicing like he was the one possessed.

His body went numb as a pack of ugly pishachas appeared, seemingly from nowhere, and started *feeding* on the bodies of the kids that lay exposed and helpless on the ground. Bile rose in his throat. He had to do something!

Kyle pulled all his energy into him so brutally that the lights in the room flickered and popped. Wind rushed in his ears as the force filled him like a storm. That was more like it.

"No, Kyle!"

Darika's warning came like a dull, slow echo from far away. The unexpected rush of power inside of him was heady and intoxicating. He'd never felt so potent before. His body strained with it as if his skin could barely keep it in. He would banish all of these monstrosities.

"I can do it," he growled triumphantly. "I can banish them all."

"That's what they—"

But her voice faded into the background as he knelt, the roar in his brain obliterating everything but his single goal. His fist slammed to the basketball court, cracks fissuring outward from the force of it. The portal burst outward in a shimmering flare so bright that he had to close his eyes. Satisfaction filled him as demon after demon was sucked into the cloudy doorway of the portal.

"KYLE!"

Sera's voice pierced through the haze holding him prisoner. Befuddled, he opened his eyes. He tried to smile, but as her face filled his vision, he registered the horrified look in her eyes. He couldn't recall the last time he'd seen such eviscerating fear there. Why would she be scared? He was getting rid of the threat once and for all.

It was at that precise moment that he felt himself start to tumble forward, as something hooked into his forearms and burrowed deep. He recognized the barbed tips of an Ifricaius immediately. More whiplike stings followed, fastening to his hips, thighs, and his torso as they shot upward from the other side of the gateway.

White-hot streaks of agony lanced up his limbs as his body was yanked downward, hooked by the very demons he'd just banished. With an inhuman roar and a burst of raw strength, he fought and almost tore free of the chains, but a score of lingering demons rushed from the corners of the gym to land directly on top of him. Thrown off balance, he toppled into the opening.

The last thing he saw was Ra'al's triumphant face staring at him from the base of the bleachers. A gratified grin stretched his mouth from ear to ear. His voice was a mocking echo.

"Time to learn that lesson, *boy*."

GODDESS IMMORTAL

❧❧

Sera pounded on the wooden floor through which Kyle had vanished until her nails cracked and her knuckles bled. Gentle but firm hands pulled her back.

"He's gone," Darika said. "They're all gone."

Sera's gaze swept the space. The goddess was right. All the remaining demons had disappeared. Though it was far from over.

"We have to go after Kyle."

Dev cleared his throat. "That may not be the best idea."

"You're wrong. They're going to kill him or do something far worse if we don't—"

But the rest of her words were strangled by the gasp that rose up from the depths of her chest as she followed the direction of his stare. The altar at the center of the gym had started to glow. Huge fissures rocked the floor, cracking through the boards of the basketball court and webbing up the concrete walls. The earth trembled beneath their feet and she clutched at Dev for support. Something was happening beneath them. Something they couldn't see. A sulfuric stench filled the gymnasium, followed by a hot blast that notched the temperature up.

"What *is* that?" she whispered.

Dev inched forward and froze, his palms lifting upward. "The balance is shifting. Can you feel it?"

Sera concentrated, closing her eyes. It was true. She could feel the subtle change that Dev mentioned. It was a sensation that tugged at her whenever Kyle opened a portal, like a summoning. A tethering to other planes of existence. Only this one was far bigger than anything she'd ever sensed. It felt like the wards between the realms were collapsing.

"You can't be here," Darika said to Dev in an urgent voice, as if she'd come to an identical conclusion. "If the Mortal Realm falls, you must protect Illysia. Convene the Trimurtas. We will face whatever comes forth and figure out a way to obliterate it."

"She's right." Sera nodded. "You have to go. Illysia will be the last stand if we fail here."

He stared at her, concern in his honeyed gaze, and Sera struggled to keep her face impassive. "You won't do anything foolish, will you? You have a bad habit of leaping first and thinking later."

"Darika won't let me do anything stupid, don't worry." Sera met the other goddess's eyes and nearly burst out laughing at the dubious expression she wasn't quick enough to hide. Dev's stare moved between them, as if he had his own doubts, and she hurried to reassure him. "I promise I won't do anything rash."

"Sera—"

The altar glowed in a shower of sparks, cutting off what he was going to say and drawing their collective attention as each of the pillars transformed into blood-red crystals. Hot yellow markings scoured their edges and a wave of pungent heat rolled outward in an oily haze. It smelled like Xibalba.

"That's what they needed Kyle for," Sera said slowly. "He's the conduit."

"But how?" Mara asked. Sera's gaze flicked to the Yoddha as she approached them. She was covered in demon gore and what looked like bright streaks of human blood. Sera flinched at what that meant—the loss of innocent human lives. And there would be more before this was over. She could feel it deep in her bones.

She blinked, sorting through her thoughts before answering Mara. "They wanted him to open the portal before. This whole thing was a trap. Just like the smaller portals that allowed demons to escape Xibalba. Only now they're using Kyle to keep it open." She glanced up. "With that altar."

"Why?"

Dread filled her. "Isn't it obvious? They're sending something back."

"Then we must destroy it."

Mara and Dev surged forward. Sera frowned—why wasn't he *leaving*? Mara was a few steps ahead of Dev, and Sera watched, rooted in horror, as the Yoddha's body was sucked into a near invisible fog that extended out like a protective web. A scream tore from Mara's throat as the runes of Xibalba did their worst, sinking into her deifyre in molten streaks. It was like the immortal had entered the Dark Realms and was being reduced to cinders.

Dev reached for the Yoddha, managing to grip her arm, and for a moment it looked as if he could pull her out of the demonic mire.

Darika's shout cut through the gym as she barreled toward them. "Lord Devendra, no!"

"Stay back," he commanded her.

Sera blanched as the goddess stopped dead several feet away, her normally unreadable face agitated. "Dev—" Sera began, unease wicking through her.

"It's okay," he told her. "I see it."

Sera blinked, letting her senses take over as she studied the barrier holding Mara in place. It moved like something alive—like a blanketing undulation of heat. It was some kind of protective veil, she realized. One more step and Dev would be too close. And even as one of the most powerful gods, he would not be immune. Sera thought of the way her own rune had scorched Dev's skin and shuddered.

"Let me help," she said. "It won't hurt me."

"No, we can't risk it," he said. "Stay there."

He grunted and pulled, using all of his immortal strength to try to extricate Mara from the demon shroud. Her shriek had turned into a whine of agony as her deifyre smoldered and flaked to ash. Half of her golden aura was blackened as Dev inched backward, his arms straining. His deifyre flared impossibly bright, so bright that Sera and Darika couldn't keep their own eyes open.

Then, with an inhuman roar, Dev stumbled backward, his light returning to normal, and collapsed on the gym floor. Sera rushed to his side as Darika knelt next to the wounded Yoddha. Mara was gasping for breath, half of her body a charred mass. She was alive, but barely. The scripts of the Dark Realms undulated along her body, eating through the parts of her that remained untouched. Sera could feel the rune of Xibalba on her right palm flaring in response and it sickened her. Balling her hand into a fist, she clenched her jaw.

"Is she—"

Dev shook his head. "She's dying. But at least she will return to Illysia. If she had been taken . . ." He trailed off, but Sera knew what he meant. If her soul had been consumed by the veil, she would have been trapped in Xibalba. The Yoddha moaned as Sera stroked her hair.

Suddenly, Mara's back arched and she clambered to her knees. Ashes fell like a shower of gray dust from her crumbling body. She stood tall, her skin writhing as if something was worming its way beneath its surface. Tremors rocked through her body as Sera, Dev, and Darika scrambled backward.

Mara's eyes rolled back in her head. "You cannot stop what is coming." Sera's swords extended from her palms at the guttural threat, and the Yoddha laughed. "Not even you can stop us, Lady Serjana."

"It's not her," Dev said, a massive blade appearing in his hands.

"Of course it's not her," the thing with Mara's face mocked. "Her spirit was delicious. A taste of the feast to come."

Dev raised his weapon, but Mara's stolen body laughed again, an ugly, cacophonous sound, and flung itself into the undulant veil. The rest of her fizzled in a shower of sparks as Dev swung into empty air. The lack of a target threw him off balance, and he tumbled straight into the path of the barrier.

"No!"

The scream tore from the depths of Sera's body as she dove toward him, shoving him out of the way with her palms at the same time that her back connected with the shield. The breath was knocked out of her as the veil ensnared her. Sparks licked across her skin, making the rune on her right palm awaken.

But, as she'd guessed, the shroud had no adverse effect on her.

"Sera," Dev panted, pushing upward to face her where she stood, half in and half out of the circle. "Are you okay?"

"Yes."

He frowned, as if noticing her hesitation, and beckoned her forward. "Then come."

"Wait." Sera licked her dry lips. The void in the center of the altar was a portal, as Dev had suspected. Strangely, nothing was exiting it, but she could sense something terrible forming at its base. And right now, she was the only one who could find Kyle and break the two-way aperture he'd created between the realms.

"Sera, don't do this." Dev's voice was a plea. He knelt before her.

She could feel the heavy stares from the other Yoddha. Dev was her consort, but he was also one of the most powerful gods in Illysia. Seeing him kneel to anyone was sobering. And soul-destroying. Indecision poured through her as she straddled the two realms.

"Please," he said quietly, as if he could read her hesitation. "We can find another way to help Kyle."

"How?" she whispered. "You know this is the only way."

"I can't lose you."

A sob rose in her throat. "We're together until the end of time, remember? Even if I die, you'll find me again."

He stood then, inches away from her, and reached for her left hand. Sera gave it to him, watching as he bent his head to the spot where his rune lay and pressed his lips to her skin. His touch seared her as he pushed upward to close the distance between them, his lips finding hers. The runes on both hands flared bright as their deifyres flickered and merged—scarlet flames bursting with sparks of hot, silvery-white light. She felt his strength filling her. Awareness bloomed along her veins as her goddess side grappled with the pull of Xibalba.

Dev broke the kiss, his eyes searching hers. His grip on her hand tightened. "You must reconsider."

"I have made my choice," she said. "I'll come back, I promise, once I have Kyle." He held her palm in an unbreakable grip and she stared down at their joined hands. "Let go, Dev."

"I cannot."

"You must." Sera stepped back an inch, the motion taking the rest of her face and most of her body behind the glimmering contour. It hung like a toxic curtain between them. Darika jolted forward, anxiety written all over her face at the Protector's proximity to a barrier that would not be merciful. The veil floated dangerously close to the tips of his fingers, but Dev showed no signs of releasing Sera.

Darika cleared her throat carefully. "Lord Devendra, I must caution you against touching that shield. The fate of Illysia is at stake, should anything happen to you. Please, my lord."

"No," he whispered.

Sera blinked at the catch in his voice. "Why, Dev?"

He swallowed hard, his fingers trembling against hers. "The vision your brother saw. The one I told you about, where someone close to him dies?"

"I remember."

"It's you," he choked out. "*You* die. You will die if you go to Xibalba, Sera. That was what he saw. He saw your death."

At his words, Sera felt the floor pitch beneath her feet. Fear took hold of her.

Nate had foreseen her death. *She* was going to die.

She'd seen so much of death, watched so many of her friends pass, but the thought of her own death was too much to bear. A terrified, selfish, and all-too-human part of her deflated with the knowledge. Normal girls didn't have to worry about dying. Normal girls didn't have to fight the worst kind of evil for the future of humanity.

You're not normal.

So get over it.

Sera gulped in several breaths, steeling herself. She was a goddess, and people needed her. She could condemn Kyle to his fate and save her own life by stepping back outside the boundary. Or she could follow in his footsteps and die in the process. Neither was palatable, but there was only one choice she could live with. She could never let her friend die.

"Visions are not cast in stone," she said, her voice shaking.

"Nor are they always accurate," Darika added, and Sera met her eyes gratefully.

She wondered for a moment whether, if their positions were reversed, the goddess would choose to go after Kyle. Love was a strange thing, but so was duty. Darika was oath-bound to protect Illysia and, by extension, the Mortal Realm. Would she be swayed by her feelings for Kyle?

In that instant, Sera could see into the other goddess's soul and found the answer to her question. Though not a surprise, the raw truth of it shook her.

No, Darika would leave Kyle to his fate.

So should you. The thought was Dev's.

You know I can't.

"Why?" His mouth shaped the word, but no sound emerged.

"Because I am bound to protect you and this world in which we live." She drew a deep breath. "If it is my fate to die, then I die protecting the ones I love. Please, Dev, let me go."

"Never."

"I thought that's what you would say. I love you, remember that." She inched away, moving her hand ever so slowly backward. Darika's gasp was loud as Dev's fingers blistered red in response to the veil creeping closer along Sera's wrist. It wasn't even touching him, and already his skin was becoming singed.

Sera could feel him holding on and fought with every bit of power she possessed. "I don't want to hurt you."

He bent again, his lips grazing her knuckles before sealing themselves to the rune on the fleshy part of her palm—*his* rune, the shield and the wing. The veil pressed dangerously close to the skin of his face, making her breath seize in her chest as the brilliant deifyre there hissed and sizzled. His eyes met hers through the translucent red miasma. Shadowed pain haunted their golden depths. "Find me."

"I will."

Without another thought, she extracted her hand from his and withdrew completely behind the curtain. At the full claim of Xibalba, her blushing deifyre shimmered into crimson hellfyre, eliciting the stunned attention of every other deity in the gym.

No one but Kyle had ever seen her in this form. Not even

Dev had ever seen her fully like this—like some demonic angel spawned from the darkest depths of hell.

Keeping her eyes downcast, she composed herself. She hated the way the hellfyre crept over her skin as if it were something alive. Coupled with the stares, it was too much to take. Sera turned and strode toward the glowing altar.

"Sera," Darika called out. "Be careful."

Sera nodded, risking a glance over her shoulder. The goddess was staring at her with compassion, not judgment. It was as if Darika understood the presence of a darker nature. She would, Sera realized, with an incarnation like Kira who was guided by far more destructive and bloody impulses. Sera refused to look at the boy at Darika's side. The boy holding her heart in his hands.

"Take care of him," she told the other goddess. "And if anything happens, keep my family safe, too."

"Wait!"

The shout was from a male voice as a new form shuffled his way through the Daevas tending to the injured. Sera recognized him with a sinking heart. "Dad."

He stopped at the edge of the veil, his hand rising to chest level. She raised hers to match on the other side. "You don't have to do this," he said.

She smiled through the sudden sheen of tears. "Says the man who wouldn't back down from a fight with a demon if it killed him."

"You're not just going up against one demon, Ser-bear. You're going up against all of them."

"I know. Someone wise once told me that death and honor go hand in hand."

"Where'd you get to be so stubborn?"

"I heard that genetics have a lot to do with it." She smiled, pushing her hand through the curtain to lace her fingers through his. He gasped at the heat of the veil but held firm.

"Be safe, my daughter."

She smiled grimly, staring at them all in turn. "Kill anything that comes through this portal, even if it looks like me. Temlucus and the other Demon Lords will stop at nothing to unleash the KaliYuga."

Squeezing her father's hand one last time before releasing it, she turned on her heel and approached the portal. The bottom of it swelled and retreated like viscous black ink. Her swords flared to life in each of her hands. She had no idea where it would take her, but she knew without a doubt that whatever lay on the other side would not be welcoming. Huffing a breath, she climbed to the edge, bracing herself for the drop, and froze.

The space shifted as another being entered the void with her. Her eyes darted to the base of the portal, but what had arrived hadn't come from there. Sera turned in slow motion.

Jem stood there, his face pale and his mouth set in a grim line. "I'm coming with you."

"No."

He lifted his shirt to reveal the spot where her rune had been seared into his flesh. "This happened because of me. They used me. I . . . I want to help, make up for what I've done. Let me do this, Sera, please."

Frowning, she weighed the value of having Jem there. On the one hand, he could help her, seeing as how Xibalba hadn't killed him yet. On the other, he could be a liability, the need to keep him safe one more distraction she didn't need. And the demons could use him as leverage against her. Though his betrayal was still fresh, she couldn't stand to have his blood on her hands. She started to shake her head.

"I've been there before," he interjected. "To the second. I know my way around."

Her eyes narrowed on him. "The *second*?"

"It's where they're holding Kyle. Temlucus told me."

Sera exhaled—the second dimension was ruled by Nequ'el, the Demon Lord of war and enslavement. His was one of the few dimensions she hadn't visited. She recalled the image of Nequ'el in the online research Nate had given her so many months ago. He looked like a dog with a man's body.

Enslavement. It made sense that they would keep Kyle there for whatever it was they were planning.

"No," she said. "It's too dangerous."

"I can fight. You wouldn't have to worry about me." His voice was quiet. "I owe you. I owe them."

Sera sighed, staring at his resolute face. "Fine. But if you die, that's on you."

"Agreed."

Without a backward glance, she closed her eyes and jumped into the blue-black pool, the sticky fluid sucking her body down like a ravenous beast. Sera's mind emptied of all thought—and of all memory—as she plummeted into the space where love would be nothing but weakness. She stripped away all emotion, all empathy.

It was time to become a monster.

The Champion
of Xibalba

❦❦

Kyle's eyelids cracked. He was in a dark room, lying on some sort of stone altar. Its edges were rough, and they cut into the exposed skin of his back. He was bare-chested, clad only in his jeans, and both his hands and ankles were restrained with the familiar barbs of an Ifricaius. He looked down and winced as the movement pulled his sore skin tight. Fresh runes were carved into his upper chest.

He was not alone, either. Kyle could sense the demons in each corner of the room, keeping silent watch. Rakshasas of some sort, he expected. They remained in the shadows, so he could not determine what manner of demons they were, or whether he had the power to coerce them. Being the son of Ra'al might still have its benefits.

"Welcome back, Lord Kalias."

"That is not—" he began and then broke off, his gaze focusing on the one who had spoken. The voice was nasal and high-pitched. He did not know this Demon Lord, although he knew *of* him: *Nequ'el*. The head of what looked like a black Doberman rested upon the muscular body of a man. Short black fur covered the thing's neck and half of its shoulders.

As far as Demon Lords went, Nequ'el was not as unpleasant to look at as some of the others. "Where is Ra'al?"

"Your father is busy."

"Why have you brought me here?" Kyle asked, watching the Demon Lord carefully.

"To fulfill your destiny, of course."

Kyle bared his teeth in a hiss, straining against the chains tethering him to the stone. "Whatever pitiful attempt Ra'al and Temlucus are making to invoke the KaliYuga, it will not see the light of day. I will not yield."

Nequ'el smiled. "You already have," he said, with a pointed look to Kyle's bare torso.

Kyle craned his neck again. The runes formed a circle with seven points—symbolizing the seven levels of Xibalba, each marking representing one of the Demon Lords. He recognized his father's rune at the topmost point. Each of the spikes led to a strange-looking rune at the center of his belly, right at the bottom of his sternum. He squinted at the thing.

"What is that?"

Nequ'el's grin widened, his beady eyes glittering. "I suppose it won't hurt to tell you. It's the rune of the avatar of Xibalba."

Kyle blinked his surprise. *"Avatar?"*

"We got the idea from that new friend of yours, the incarnation of the goddess Durga."

"What about her?"

Nequ'el cocked his head. "Have you ever heard the story of how she came to be? It's quite fascinating, really. She was created by the Trimurtas to fight the imbalance caused by the reign of the rakshasa Mahishasura. She was the ultimate embodiment of the three gods—wielding all their collective shakti and susceptible to none of their weaknesses."

Kyle tried to follow what the Demon Lord was saying, understanding that he wasn't talking about Darika, but rather the goddess Durga. His breath stalled in his chest as all the pieces came together. "Wait, you made a Demon Lord avatar?"

"Not just any avatar," Nequ'el howled gleefully. "An immortal Azura, born of each of us." The Demon Lord indicated the rune etched on his own wrist—a series of three triangles that resembled the face of a dog. "Here's mine." He then pointed to the matching one to the left of Kyle's ribs, and moved to another. "This, you must know, is Ra'al's." Kyle swallowed at the image of the tri-curling horns. "Your brother Dekaias's," he continued, indicating another that looked like a lock of hair curled around a trident. "Along with each of the others. They all connect to this." His fingernail stroked along the length of Kyle's sternum to stop at the eighth rune at the center. "Aranyasura."

"It won't work," Kyle countered, ignoring the chill the name had spawned across his skin. "Whatever you create will still be bound to Xibalba."

"Not with your blood. Just as you were tethered to the last apocalypse demon, so you will be tethered to this one. While you live, she will be able to pass between the realms through the very portal that brought you here and awaits your return. It won't be long now."

The possibilities assaulted him in a rush. No wonder they had wanted to lure him into opening the portal in the first place. The gateway he'd summoned to banish the demons had been the start of their attack. And Sera had known. Panic spread through him—that thing in the gym was holding the portal between the realms open. Oh, God, what had he done?

"Don't worry, young Kalias," Nequ'el crooned. "Lord Ra'al can be forgiving, at times. And after all, you will have an eternity to beg his forgiveness. Once he has eaten his fill of the mortals, he will be in a more forgiving mood." He nodded to the rakshasas on guard in the room. "Enjoy your new accommodations."

"Wait." His mind raced. He did not know Nequ'el well or understand what motivated him, but Kyle knew one simple rule: all demons were egocentric. Their universes began and ended with themselves, and Nequ'el would be no different. Thinking quickly, Kyle allowed derision to color his tone. "Do you really think that Ra'al and Temlucus will reward you as you deserve?"

The Demon Lord paused at the threshold but did not turn. "Go on."

Kyle suppressed his sense of triumph, keeping his voice even. "If what you've told me is true, you hold the key to the plan's success here, in your dimension. *You*. Not them, you."

Nequ'el turned then, his upper lip curling slightly across the row of teeth. "What is your point?"

"If I'm the key, then neither of them could have made your Aranyasura without me. And yet you are the one who has me—their most valuable asset—in your hands. Tell me, Lord Nequ'el, what have you received for this gift? For this sacrifice?" Kyle paused, letting the charged silence between them swell dramatically. He wanted the moment to be perfect for his next words. He could almost hear the wheels turning in

Nequ'el's head, see the frustration mounting in those beady, black eyes. Kyle lowered his voice. "Such an important role to still be last in the pecking order, do you not agree?"

A low, unearthly whine emanated from the Demon Lord's throat. "What do you mean?"

"You are last, are you not?" Kyle pursed his lips. "My father is first in line, followed by Temlucus, then Wyndigu, then maybe Belphegar." He squinted thoughtfully and made a big show of considering the rest of the lineup. "Lamasha next, and then Dekaias, because everyone knows that the son of Ra'al will have some favor. Which leaves you, dear Nequ'el, dead last."

"You are mistaken," he growled.

"Am I?" Kyle shrugged nonchalantly, then winced as the movement of his shoulders tugged on the bonds around his wounded wrists. "If that is true, then why are you here tending to me while they welcome the KaliYuga without you? To them, you are unimportant. Small. *Insignificant.*"

The rumble that came from Nequ'el's throat was awash with rage as the Demon Lord strode toward Kyle and cracked the back of his hand against his jaw. Though the blow made him see stars, Kyle did not move or allow his contemptuous expression to drop. He arched an eyebrow.

"You are as slick as your father," Nequ'el bellowed. "Don't you think I see what you are doing?"

Kyle's teeth felt loose in his mouth, but he pushed the words out anyway. "What do I have to gain? I'm tied up. I don't expect you to free me. You're not *that* stupid. But you are smart enough to know when you're being played." Kyle's eyes narrowed. "They've always underestimated you, haven't they? You are the master of the dimension of *war*, and yet when your brothers are poised to enter the greatest conquest of their lives, you're stuck behind the battle lines. Says something, doesn't it?"

Nequ'el raised his hand to strike again, but paused to let it hang in midair. Without another word, he marched from the room. A sigh eased from Kyle's throat as his muscles relaxed against the stone table. Every bone in his body ached. His jaw felt dislocated, but it would heal. Eventually.

Though he knew that getting under Nequ'el's skin might not be enough to get him out of this room, he hoped he'd damaged the Demon Lords' fragile hierarchy to buy himself some time, or at the very least derail some of their plans. Dissention in the ranks could cause mistakes. He'd already seen the clash of the egos when Temlucus had stood up to Ra'al the last time they had tried to unleash hell on earth. Demons were special snowflakes like that.

Closing his eyes, Kyle calmed his erratic thoughts. He needed to think—to figure out a way out of this mess that he'd created by acting without thinking in the first place. He couldn't escape the Ifricaius binding him to the table. He'd seen what they'd done to actual Daevas, immortals far more powerful than he. The dark weapons had bound them to the earth.

But he was still the son of Ra'al.

That had to mean something, here in Xibalba. Otherwise why would they have needed him? He was the eighth seed—the blood from which Aranyasura had been spawned.

Kyle suppressed a shudder. Imbued with all the strengths of the seven Demon Lords—just as Durga had been forged from the gods of Illysia—their creation would be fearsome. And powerful. But if she'd been born from his blood, then she would be bound to him, too. Which meant he had to get to her before she was unleashed upon the Mortal Realm.

Kyle concentrated, feeling the heartbeat of Xibalba pulsing all around him. He could summon Mordas, but the sword would do little good if he couldn't wield it. No, there had to be another way. Movement in the shadows caught his attention and he seized upon an idea. It was worth a shot.

"Come forth," he commanded. Nothing happened. If the rakshasas had heard him, they paid no heed. He repeated his command, putting as much force into the words as possible. "As heir to the seventh, I command you to come forth. Now."

A scraping sound ensued, like jagged metal on metal, and if he could have clapped his hands to his ears, he would have. Kyle braced himself, expecting the worst. Four forms materialized from the shadows that had shrouded them. He could feel two near his shoulders, but they remained just beyond his line of sight. The two near his ankles, however, he could see clearly.

Kyle sucked in a sharp breath. He'd expected pishachas, but these rakshasas weren't ugly and deformed. Stunning to look at, with bronzed faces and flashing dark eyes, they were manushya-rakshasis—female demons in human form. Though they were nude, a cascade of dark, curling hair covered most of their bodies—which like their faces, were sculpted perfection.

His father had a perverse sense of humor.

"Release me," Kyle commanded.

They laughed at him, the sound like a rustle of leaves. "Why should we?" they said in unison.

"Because I am your master."

"We have no master." Their laughter erupted again. "But if we did, we would want it to be you." They came closer, running their fingers along his ribs and his limbs. Kyle kept his eyes closed, as if avoiding looking at them would make him less susceptible to their charms. One of them trailed their hands along his wrist, skipping over the ifricaius bond and stroking the inside of his palm.

Kyle didn't hesitate. He closed his fingers, clutching the hand there. Recognition jolted through him like lightning. Recognition and power. So much power—each of them linked to the next by *something*. But it was transient and not yet fully formed. The manushya-rakshasis needed a host. For a moment, he wondered if that host would be him. His spine arched as feminine laughter filled the room in a loud unending rustle, and his skin felt as if it were coming apart at the seams.

No, he was not the vessel the manushya-rakshasis sought.

He was nowhere near strong enough.

But they wanted something from him. Something important.

Gasping, he struggled to draw breath as they surrounded him, the scent of smoky incense permeating the air as the manushya-rakshasis touched each of the runes in succession. His body bucked, compelled by something unseen, the chains bearing down to hold him in place. A point on his chest burned as though a knife was being inserted through his ribs. He felt warm blood trickling down his chest, the sensation of rough tongues scraping along his flesh.

Kalias . . .

He screamed and opened his eyes to see the rune at the center of the seven, glowing red like the fires of hell. The mark on his chest pulsed with awareness. His heart raced with fear. The manushya-rakshasis had used him. They had needed his blood and his rune to become one.

Kyle closed his eyes.

They'd needed both to become Aranyasura.

⁓

"This way," Jem called to her. Sera followed warily. They were in a desert, and she didn't like being this exposed. Xibalba tended to be full of surprises—and not the good kind.

"Are you sure this is right?" she wheezed as they plodded up yet another sandy dune. "And remind me why I can't fly, again?"

"Yes, I'm sure," he replied. "And *we* can't fly because your deifyre will kill me, and you'll only fly in circles. This dimension is built so that there's no way to escape, above or below. Nequ'el likes punishment. He forces his slaves to trudge endlessly through this desert without water or sustenance, letting the sun burn them until they're nothing but husks."

Sera shuddered, recalling the image she'd seen of the Demon Lord with his long line of mendicants.

"This whole plane is an unending maze," Jem said. "You just can't see it. Trust me, we're on the right path, and we're nearly there."

"What do you mean, it's a maze?"

In response, Jem bent to collect a stone that lay on the surface of the sand. He threw it a few feet to the right—and it instantly sank into some kind of hole. "There are traps like that one all over if you don't know where to step. And you'll be sucked into way worse levels of this dimension, or sent back to the start of the desert. Those who step out of line or who try to escape pay for it."

Sera frowned. "How do you know the route?"

"I told you," he said. "I've been here before."

Following his footsteps carefully, she doubled her pace to catch up with Jem, who didn't even seem out of breath. Sera frowned, every instinct within her warning her *not* to trust him. He had murdered his family. He may have been possessed, but it was hard to reconcile where free will had come into play. *He* had been the one to slaughter his loved ones.

Sera exhaled a troubled breath. She stared at the boy who had been her friend. When Jem had returned to Silver Lake, she had wanted so badly for things to go back to the way they had been—but now she realized how unrealistic that was. They couldn't turn back the clock, and neither of them could change who they were.

"There," Jem said at the crest of the dune. He pointed toward what looked like another sea of rippling, golden sand. But unlike the last, this desert was not empty. At its center was a spindly tower. "That's where they're keeping him."

"How do you know?"

"Because it was my idea."

Sera's eyes shot to the boy she'd known for half her life. How had he become this person—so twisted and angry that he'd made a deal with the devil, or *devils*? And now he was bound to her, by force. Either Jem was truly a victim, or he was more cunning than anyone she'd ever met.

"This way," he said, taking eight measured steps to the

right and starting down the other side of the dune toward the tower.

They walked in silence for a long while. Sera's thoughts were chaotic, full of anxiety over Kyle's capture and Jem's murky loyalty. She wished for some way—any way—to speed her journey along, and to finish it herself. But for the moment she had no choice but to trust Jem. And maybe try to make amends.

Sera cleared her throat. "I'm sorry about your parents."

He flinched as if she had struck him, but plodded forward. "Me too."

"Why did you do it?" she asked softly.

"I . . . was lost." His answer floated back to her after a long pause. "Temlucus offered me revenge, and I took it." Jem's voice cracked. "But I killed them for nothing."

"It wasn't you."

His laugh was hollow. "Of course it was. *I* did it. I watched them burn, in a fire that I set." The laughter was replaced by dry hacking sobs. "I had to prove myself, you know? Prove myself capable." Halting mid-step, he spat the last word, his body trembling as he fought for control. "Worthy of their loyalty."

"Whose?"

"The ones who rule Xibalba."

Sera fought a wave of compassion. "Temlucus is a Demon Lord, Jem. They've coerced many men into doing terrible things. That's what they do. They seduce and they lie."

"How would you know?" he whispered, shooting her a tortured look over his shoulder. "You're born of Illysia. How would you know what it's like to feel so powerless that your only way out is to trust the word of a demon? Your life is a cake walk."

"Cake walk?" Sera sputtered. "If you only knew. Finding out you're a supernatural being with ridiculous powers, responsible for everyone? And you can't set foot in Illysia because you're also tied to hell? Yeah, total cake walk."

He turned to face her, his eyes damp and pained. "I did things. Unforgivable things."

"You're human. You can still be redeemed."

"How?"

Sera's smile was gentle. "Atonement. Sacrifice."

"Sacrifice," he murmured.

She wrapped her arms around him in a hug, feeling his close tentatively around her waist. For a moment, the second dimension of Xibalba fell away and it was as if they were kids again, hugging in her backyard before throwing themselves into the pool on a hot summer day. She hoped he was feeling the same wash of memories as he gripped her closer.

"It's going to be okay."

"I know," he whispered.

Maybe it was the note in his voice or the flex of his body against hers, but Sera was warned of movement just as he launched them both to the right. Struggling to hold her footing, she could only clutch at him as they fell toward the gleaming desert. Their entry was soft, much like falling into a pool of quicksand. It swallowed them, sucking them down into its gravelly depths. Sera's hellfyre flared as they sank deep, but Jem's arms only tightened as it seared his skin with angry flames. Dev's parting words echoed like a death toll in her head.

"What are you doing?" she shouted, fighting uselessly to stay on the surface.

Jem's face was sorrowful. "Saving you."

"No." She gasped. "You're *not*."

"I am," he said quietly, sand rising to their chins. He held her close, his eyes full of regret mixed with madness. "You don't know what's coming. What they've put into motion. This is for you, Sera. I'm doing this for you. I'm *saving* you from the hell that this world will become."

"What are you talking about?"

"Don't you see? She'll kill you all. And the realms will fall."

THE GATEWAY
TO HELL

❧⟶⟵❧

Sand scoured her throat, her eyes, her mouth. It coated her tongue and scraped her skin until it was raw. The desert was eating her alive. Sera gathered her power and pushed out, her hellfyre swirling in a golden tornado of grit and dust as she rose from the depths of the pit that had swallowed her.

"Hold on, Jem," she ground out. "I've got us."

She looked down, her hand still gripping his, and bile rose up in her throat. There was nothing left of his arm but withered bone. His mortal form hadn't stood a chance against the demonic desert.

A sob caught in her throat as she hovered there, unwilling to let go and knowing that she had to. She felt an odd ache in her heart as she remembered Jem as a carefree boy, instead of the creature he'd become.

"Find your way home," she whispered after a long beat, and she released her friend's skeletal hand, watching as the sand sucked him into its depths in a matter of seconds.

A soul could climb the ladder to moksha, no matter where it began the journey—even in the Dark Realms. She only hoped Jem had the strength and will to find his way. The Demon Lord of this dimension would not make it easy.

Flying upward, she felt herself being sucked into a vortex. Sera summoned her energy, holding her center still and forcing the tempest swirling around her to die down. To her surprise, it obeyed. Bits of sand slowed in midair as the desert itself responded to her authority. Sera blinked. She was entirely in control.

For the first time, she wasn't afraid. She was the goddess of all three realms. Being marked by Xibalba didn't make her beholden to the Dark Realms. No . . . it gave her *advantages*. Like influence over the dimensions. She'd been so fearful of being corrupted that she hadn't stopped to understand what the power of the rune meant. It was eye-opening. And formidable.

She raised a palm. "Stop."

Her hellfyre flared brighter as she negated the rules of the realm. They did not apply to her. The suspended sand fell back to the desert floor in a shower of golden dust as she crossed the undulating shore toward the tower. Nequ'el's wards pulled at her from every direction, but she ignored them, making her way slowly toward the place where Kyle was being held.

Below her, bodies churned in the sand, begging for her to save them as she drifted past—including one with Jem's face. With a harsh breath, she pushed on toward the entryway of the tower. Her feet touched the cracked stone floor and she waited, her hellfyre weapons bursting forth to light the shadowed space.

She peered into the gloom. A narrow, curling staircase began at the bottom of the column, leading upward into the darkness. The circular space was empty, but Sera did not let down her guard. Adrenaline flowed through her in waves.

Without warning, she felt a tremendous shift in energy coming down the stairs. Its immensity threw her for a second. Whatever it was felt larger than any rakshasa she'd ever felt before. Eminently powerful. Like an amalgamation of energies—intense and unidentifiable.

Sera braced herself, but whatever it was didn't reach her. It dissipated, escaping through an opening a few levels above her. Whatever it was had to have known that she was there, but it hadn't stopped. *Why?*

Frowning, Sera crept up the narrow, crumbling staircase. It didn't take her long to reach the top. Her breath deserted her at the sight of Kyle tethered to a stone altar. Jem had been telling the truth.

Drawing near, she flinched at the raw wounds on Kyle's chest. He hadn't noticed her arrival and was focused instead on sawing away at his bonds. Blood dripped from the stone as the edge of Mordas cut into the chains at his wrist. Given the awkward position of the blade, he couldn't help cutting himself at the same time.

"Kyle?" she whispered.

His head turned in slow motion, his eyes opening and closing dazedly, as if he thought she was some demonic apparition. He drew a shuddering breath and resumed his position, staring at the ceiling and rocking his hand back and forth. "Go away, demon," he muttered.

She took a few more steps, wary of the darkening shadows in the corners. "It's me, Sera."

The motion stopped and he contemplated her again with a squint. "Where were we when we first met?"

She almost laughed. "I was stuck up a tree, inviting you to a fake tea party."

A muscle in his cheek twitched, but the suspicion in his eyes remained. "Easy enough to know. Something harder," he muttered, resuming his sawing with choppy strokes. "They're always watching."

He was right. There was nothing either of them could ask the other that anyone couldn't already know. She approached the table with decisive steps and hovered over him. Her hand closed over his stalled fist and forced the point of Mordas up toward her bare throat. The obsidian tip of it dug into her skin, turning the point of entry blindingly rose-gold. Only a weapon of Xibalba could summon her deifyre in hell. "Believe me now?"

Mordas clattered to the floor. "Sera, what are you doing here?"

"Saving you?"

He blinked wildly, trying to see around her. "Did you see her? Aranyasura?"

"Who?" Sera rested her flaming blades against the barbed edges of the Ifricaius holding Kyle down, grunting in satisfaction as the chains fell away.

"The thing they created."

"You're not making sense. What thing?" But even as she said the words, Sera knew what he was talking about. That massive burst of energy she'd felt. "What thing, Kyle?" she repeated as he sat up, and she grimaced at his oozing wounds. His Azura blood would heal them but his wrists and ankles still looked like tenderized meat.

"The manushya-rakshasi."

The name sent a ripple of dread through her body. She shook her head. "I didn't see it, but I felt it. I felt *something*."

"They've created their own version of Durga," he said and stood on unsteady legs, wobbling as his face contorted with pain. "Just as Durga was an incarnation of the gods' energies, Aranyasura is a demonic version of theirs."

Sera felt her blood turn to ice in her veins. "Is that even possible?"

"If the gods can do it, so can they."

"How can we stop it?"

His eyes dropped to the rune at the center of his chest, and Sera blinked as she spotted the chaotic mark. "She's tethered to me, just like the last one was."

"So you can banish her back here."

Kyle shook his head. "It won't be that easy this time. She wasn't born of Xibalba like the Kali Demon was, Sera. She was made. *Created.* They used my blood to give her the ability to pass between realms." He paused, swallowing hard. "The only way to imprison her here would be to kill me."

"No, not an option."

"It may be our only one," he said. His eyes met hers and he gripped her hands between his. "There's something else, Sera. Aranyasura's body is incomplete. She needs a mortal host, one that is strong enough to withstand her powers. I thought it was me, but it's not."

"What do you mean?" Sera's mind was reeling as she remembered the energy she'd felt. No mortal body would be able to contain something like that. She'd seen what possession by ordinary demons had done to Jem and to others.

Nothing human *could* contain the mass she'd sensed, unless that person was imbued with special abilities. Special, regenerative abilities.

"No," she whispered as understanding struck.

"Temlucus never wanted Nate for himself."

"He's just a kid."

"One with a lot of power. You heard what Darika said about him. Micah, too. He's what they want, I know it." Grabbing Mordas, Kyle knelt on the cold, stone floor. "We need to find her before she gets to your brother. Because if she does, she'll be unbeatable. No immortal will be able to stop her."

Sera stared at her best friend, the weight of Dev's words coming back to her. Sera squared her shoulders. She didn't want to die, but she knew the truth in her bones: she'd give her last breath if it meant saving any one of her family. That was never going to change, not even if she knew her own death was near. She would do whatever it took to protect them.

"Where are we going?"

Kyle looked at her grimly as the portal began to form beneath his fingers. "Remember when I re-created the portal in the basement of the school where the vetalas were?"

"After Ilani died," she said dully.

"Right."

"You said you saw Lamasha." She frowned, putting two and two together. "*Hers* is the dimension lying beneath those burial grounds."

"Yeah," he said. "The Demon Lords are in the fourth."

It made sense. If the burial grounds were an inactive portal lying beneath the school, they would be the perfect spot to rip a hole between the realms. She frowned, recalling the altar in the gym. "Wait, when I came through the portal at the school, it led me to the second."

"It was meant to," he said, matching her expression. "That's where it took me. But if the Demon Lords were all here, we'd feel them." He closed his eyes, flexing his power. "It's empty. Even Nequ'el isn't here. They're somewhere else."

"What if you're wrong? What if they're in a different hell dimension? We only have one shot at guessing where they are, or we'll be too late to save Nate."

"I'm not. You have to trust me."

Trust, it seemed, was a fragile commodity these days. She'd been betrayed in small ways and big ways, by both friends and enemies. But in her heart, she would trust Kyle with her life, and she knew he would never willingly put Nate in danger. He loved him like a brother. Kyle was family. She stared at him for a long moment, then nodded.

"They're going to sense us the minute we get there," he said grimly.

"Wait, I have an idea," she said and flew down the stairs to where she'd seen the replica of Jem rising up from the sand.

Within seconds, his face emerged. The wails coming from his lips were pitiful. *It's not Jem*, she told herself, despite the ache in her stomach at the sight of his face. With just the briefest hesitation, she reached down and cleaved her sword through its skull, demon gore spurting in all directions. Holding the severed head, she retraced her steps back to where Kyle was waiting.

His gaze was horrified. "What the hell, Sera?"

"I'm going to shade us."

"With *Jem*?"

"It's not him," she said in a pained voice, the sound of his name eating through her resolve. "Jem died getting us here. This is Nequ'el's way of trying to show me who calls the shots."

It didn't take long to create a shade using the creature's essence. She'd done it once before, using one of Ra'al's most trusted servants, when she'd first ventured into Xibalba. That shade had been the only reason she had survived.

Casting the rotten essence out like a net, she saw Kyle flinch in disgust as he felt it settle over him. Sera felt the same—like she was swaddled in layers of grimy scum.

"What do you sense?" she asked him, watching carefully as he squinted at her, his brow wrinkling in revulsion.

His gaze shifted into one of surprise. "I sense a rakshasa."

"Good. Let's hope that's what they see, too."

He stared at her, incredulous. "You're amazing."

"Master of the hottest demon trends on the runway," she replied with a wry laugh. "One of my many talents." She sobered as she took his hand. "Ready?"

Kyle nodded, squeezing back. And after a beat, they entered the portal together.

❧

The swell of demonic energy was cloying, sweeping toward them in thick bursts. He was right. The Demon Lords were all here. Kyle could feel their collective power ebbing and flowing, and shifting the balance set by the Demon Lord who reigned in the fourth dimension.

Kyle fought his gag reflex as the sour mix of rot, vomit,

and feces assaulted him. "Fourth floor, dimension of depravity and disease."

As he and Sera exited the portal and gathered their bearings, Kyle looked around warily. The dimension looked almost the same as the last time he'd been here. He could recall the scarlet tilled pastures. The ones he had seen before had been bare, but those surrounding them now were lush with vegetation. He swallowed a rush of bile as he realized why the flora was so rich. The plants were fertilized with flesh and blood.

Sera's whisper at his ear made him jump. "Where do you think it is?"

"What?"

"The other end of the altar?"

He focused on the pull of the demon auras, reaching for where they were the most concentrated. "That way," he said in a low voice, pointing to a rocky path that meandered away from the grotesque meadow. "And Sera, be careful."

The pathway descended into some kind of tunnel leading underground. The earthy walls around them rippled as if they were alive, while yellow crevices with oozing abscesses ran their length. Kyle suppressed a shudder. It felt like they were walking deep inside some festering, dying body.

Several demons passed them, but none seemed to notice the strangers in their midst. It appeared that Sera's shade was working.

After several minutes, the tunnel narrowed and they had to hunch down to move through it. Kyle could feel the wet tunnel walls touching his skin and he recoiled, spitting a mouthful of bile to the side. Though he could hear her shallow pants, he couldn't risk talking to Sera and being overheard. In a place like this, even the walls would have ears.

The passage widened and came to a sudden end. An enormous grotto yawned before them. They were in the mouth of one of many caves lining the immense precipice inside the caverns. Other silhouettes gathered in nearby holes and the demon stink was a thousand times worse. Kyle held up a fist and pressed a finger to his lips as Sera approached their ledge. Her eyes widened when she took in the scene below. It looked exactly like the burial grounds in the basement of Silver Lake High—full of swirling, restless vetala.

But that wasn't what stole Kyle's breath.

An altar, identical to the one in the school's gymnasium, lay at the bottom of the cavern, jagged crystalline shapes spearing upward from it. They glowed red and yellow, and a swirling, dark, vaporous form rippled at its center. He knew without a doubt, even before feeling the colossal mass of energy, that it was Aranyasura. The altar was merely a catapult, meant to transport her to the other end.

The Demon Lords stood in a circle surrounding the structure. Kyle's gaze honed in on his father. Clothed in his true form, Ra'al seemed agitated. So did Temlucus, who stood beside him.

"Where is he?" Dekaias whined. Kyle's attention darted to his brother—Demon Lord of the first—and he drew a swift breath at seeing a familiar face so close to his own. No matter how much he expected the resemblance, it was always a shock. "He will ruin everything."

Kyle blinked at his words and counted the Demon Lords. They weren't all present. He felt a sense of satisfaction as he realized who was absent. Nequ'el. His strategy had worked.

"I will gut him from snout to heel," Belphegar shouted. His slovenly, beastlike form, that of a man and woman wrapped in a lascivious embrace, made Kyle flinch. Sera's sickened expression matched his. "Someone needs to teach that dog a lesson."

"Will that be you, Belphegar?" The lazy response was from Nequ'el himself, who hustled toward the others from a nearby passageway.

"Where have you been?" Ra'al growled.

Nequ'el shot him a measured look. "Making sure your progeny was well cared for."

"You are late."

His head cocked. "So it would seem."

The tension between the two Demon Lords vibrated through the space, but Temlucus lifted a hand. "What is it, Lord Nequ'el? Air your grievance."

"I wish to be the first through the portal once the wards have been destroyed."

Kyle could feel Temlucus's rage even from where he crouched, but the Demon Lord's resonant voice did not reflect it. "The order has already been cast."

"And I am last," Nequ'el seethed.

"What is this about?"

Nequ'el squared his shoulders. "I am the one who has caged the son of Ra'al in my dimension, the one who holds the key to our plot. And yet, my place—my *importance*—is not recognized." His scathing glare flew to Dekaias. "I am the Lord of War, and though we are on the eve of battle, that pissworthy insect strides into the fight before me."

"You fool," Ra'al bellowed, lurching toward Nequ'el. "You do this now?" Nequ'el growled, two razor-sharp discs appearing in his hands as Ra'al lowered his horns and prepared to charge.

"Enough!" Temlucus roared, making the walls of the grotto shake. Silence descended. "The order has been decided."

"Then see how you fare without me."

Sera stiffened beside him as Temlucus grabbed Nequ'el by the scruff of his neck, a patchwork of embers extending out from beneath his hand. The Demon Lord struggled in his grip, but he was no match for Temlucus's superior strength.

"You have already given your pledge," Temlucus thundered. "You will fulfill your oath, dead or alive."

The net of embers extended in a glowing web over Nequ'el's skin, and it wasn't long before a pained, submissive whine escaped his lips. Ra'al's face lit up with glee as Temlucus drained the weaker Demon Lord to within an inch of his life. Temlucus wasted no time, flinging Nequ'el's moaning form like a dead weight toward the base of the altar, and the rest of the Demon Lords took up their respective places.

Kyle exchanged a fraught look with Sera.

"What do we do?" she asked.

"I have to destroy the portal before that thing gets out," he whispered. "It's the only way."

Sera nodded grimly and they leaped from the ledge together toward the altar, drawing the stares of thousands of demons.

"Finally, Lord Kalias." Temlucus turned his eyes to Kyle and flashed a rictus grin. "And Lady Serjana. Always interesting to see you."

Stunned, Kyle faltered for a moment at the welcome. Had Temlucus known he would come? But his thoughts scattered as a burning sensation took over his chest, the central rune there searing his skin. Without warning, the portal flared into existence, shining a hot red. It had been dormant before, but now it was awake. Kyle felt himself sway.

He was the eighth rune. The key to the gateway.

"Predictable to a fault," Ra'al hissed, his face triumphant.

The roar was deafening as thousands of demons swarmed them. Sera's fiery weapons were a blur, but she cleaved a path toward the black stones of the altar, her hellfyre flaring in vicious bursts and incinerating demons left and right. Kyle followed her path, Mordas appearing in his hand. They had one goal: destroy that doorway.

Ra'al blocked Kyle's way. "You can never escape your legacy."

"Watch me," he shot back.

His father laughed. "Ever the optimist. But once more, my useless son, you are too late."

Kyle's gaze shot to Sera, who had reached the stones and the vapor. The four manushya-rakshasis from the tower appeared, now joined together in the form of a creature with four heads and a tangle of arms and legs, like a grotesque but beautiful arachnid. A warning rang low in Kyle's gut.

Those eight arms reached for Sera at the same instant the shout left his lips. His chest felt as if it were on fire as the altar ignited, shielding Sera from view and swallowing her whole. Kyle veered backward, out of his father's reach, while the glare intensified. He gritted his teeth and gathered his strength.

He wasn't useless.

He was the defender of the wards between the realms.

Kyle stared his father in the face, then head-butted Ra'al with all the force he could muster. "And once more, you underestimate me."

With a frenzied roar, he leapt over the enraged Demon Lord, launching himself into the shimmering doorway, and sealed it shut behind him.

To the Death

❧

The gym was a shambles, bits of exploded wood and concrete everywhere, as if a bomb had been detonated at its center. Bits of graying crystal littered the floor, the stench of sulfur hung thick in the air. No one seemed to have been hurt by the blast; from what Sera could tell, the gym was mostly empty, though she could detect movement at its edges.

Dazed, Sera rolled to her feet, her twin blades kindling. She blinked, her gaze recognizing a few Yoddha emerging from the periphery—it was as if she'd never left. Then again, time flowed differently in the Dark Realms than it did in the Mortal Realm. Hours there were mere minutes here.

She looked around wildly for the four women from the portal. They were nowhere to be seen. Sera shuddered at the phantom remnant of their touch—the demon avatar was powerful, imbued with the strengths of all the Demon Lords.

Her stare fell to Kyle, who lay in a motionless heap a few feet away. She hurried toward him, skidding as she reached his side. His eyes were closed and a nasty bruise was flowering on his forehead, but his chest rose and fell with shallow breaths.

"Kyle?" His eyelids fluttered open. "What happened back there? Did you do that to the portal?"

"Yes." He blinked, trying to sit up but crashing backward with a groan. "Did you see Aranyasura? Where is she?"

"She disappeared when the portal fissured." Sera eyed him, frowning as he fingered his brow. "What happened to you?"

"Decided to take my father on . . . with my face. Help me up," he said and reached out a hand. Grabbing his wrist, Sera pulled her friend up against her, bracing as he fought to keep his balance. "Did Aranyasura say anything to you?"

Sera shook her head. "She didn't have to. When she touched me, it was like I could feel all her thoughts, see all she planned to do. She is driven by one thing—her hunger—and she means to satisfy it. Once she is strong enough . . ." Sera trailed off, dread filling her as she realized exactly where the demon would go. "Is Nate safe?"

"Yes," Dev announced, appearing beside them. "He's in Illysia, with Sophia and Micah."

Even covered in blood and gore, Dev was a sight for sore eyes. With a wild half-sob, Sera flung herself into his arms. Struggling to keep it together as she absorbed some of his strength, she drew several gulps of air into her lungs and composed herself.

When Darika joined them a moment later, Kyle cleared his throat, and she turned back. The expression on his face made Sera's blood run cold.

"What is it?" she asked.

"Aranyasura's blood is still linked to mine," Kyle said quietly. "Which means that once she's strong enough, she can create a portal to Illysia."

"That is not possible," Darika interjected. "No demon can breach Illysia."

"She's not exactly a demon," Kyle explained. "She's a constructed Azura being. We don't exactly know what she's capable of." He stared at Darika. "They made her in your image."

"My image?" she choked out.

"Just as you were once created as the ultimate weapon of the gods," he said, "they created her as *their* weapon to fight us."

"She's strong," Sera added, remembering the colossal energy she'd felt. "And the more she consumes, the stronger and more corporeal she'll become. Who knows how powerful she'll become."

"Let's not wait to find out," Darika said, her face darkening. "She'll head toward the town, and the shortest path is through—"

"—the woods," Kyle finished. He nodded to Dev. "Call the Yoddha and the Sanrak. We're going to need all the help we can get, including the Ne'feri."

"I'm going with you," Dev said.

"No," Darika said. "Your place is in Illysia."

Dev's glance slid to Sera. "My place is at her side."

"My lord Deven—" Darika began, but her words were cut off by the obstinate look on Dev's face.

For once, Sera agreed with the other goddess. If anything happened to Dev, the Trimurtas—and Illysia—would be at risk. But she recognized that pigheaded look when she saw it. She said nothing as his giant sword materialized in his palms. His brown eyes met hers in a ferocious, possessive stare that made her knees feel like jelly.

"You know the rules," Sera said.

He smiled. "Don't die."

Together, they ran from the gym toward the woodlands surrounding the school. Once outside, Dev summoned the remaining Yoddha and Daevas who had gotten most of the surviving students to safety. Her father was waiting with the students for the paramedics, and for that Sera was grateful. Fifty-odd Ne'feri warriors joined them, their faces grim. Sera noticed that Beth and her family were among them, and she met her friend's eyes with a nod. Whatever Beth's stance on Kyle had been, they needed all the help they could get.

A blinding light appeared as Micah and a dozen other Sanraks materialized at the edge of the woods.

"Where's my mom?" Sera asked him.

"With the other Trimurtas."

"And Nate?"

A smile curled Micah's lips. "Upset he's missing out, but also safe."

"He needs to be under lock and key," Sera said in a panicky whisper. "You don't know him like I do. He'll find a way to run away and do something stupid."

Micah squeezed her shoulder. "He's protected, trust me. He's with Lord Taran."

She chewed her lip doubtfully. But she couldn't have asked for better protection for Nate. Taran was as powerful as Dev.

"This way," Kyle said, taking off at a run with Dev close on his heels. Some of the others followed them, but Sera let her deifyre flare and flew instead, floating high above the tree line. She was joined by Darika and two of her warrior Sanraks. Sera swallowed hard, wondering whether her own guardians, Mara and Ilani, would be replaced—and what the fate of those Yoddha would be. It seemed that everyone who came close to her ended up dying.

Shaking off the sudden feeling of dread, Sera pushed on, keeping connected to Dev as he kept pace with her below.

I'm worried about Nate, she thought to him.

Nate is in good hands.

You know my brother, Dev, she said, *and if he wants to do something, he's going to do it. I'm worried that he'll put himself in danger. Kyle is the host that Aranyasura needs to survive. If anything happens to him, I won't be able to forgive myself.* She expelled a harsh breath. *I don't trust anyone else, Dev. Please, you're the only one he'll listen to.*

Lord Taran is with him.

She didn't hesitate. *It's* Nate *we're talking about.*

Dev didn't respond for a minute, but the answer came back as she knew it would. *I'll make sure he's safe.*

He soared up to meet her mid-flight and caught her in an unbreakable grip. They hovered in midair, his silvery-white deifyre flaring around her until their mingled auras shifted into a pale, blushing pink. Sera almost melted from the look in those golden-brown eyes, and she nearly forgot how to think as he leaned in to kiss her fiercely.

"If I do this, promise me you won't do anything reckless," he muttered against her lips.

She widened her eyes innocently. "I'm never reckless."

"Of course you aren't."

With an unconvinced smile, he shook his head.

Looping her arms around his neck, Sera slid her fingers through the dark waves hanging over his shoulders. The blue tattoos on his throat shimmered in the light and she stroked his skin, watching a cerulean ribbon undulate beneath her touch as if it were alive. Aranyasura was strong, but she was one Azura, while they numbered in the dozens. With any luck, this would all be over quickly.

"I'll be careful, I promise," she said. "Just look after Nate."

After a long moment, he nodded and kissed her hard. Sera was flooded with relief as she felt Dev's energy dissolve from the mortal plane. There had been a moment when she thought that he'd see straight through her ploy. As powerful as Aranyasura was, they could handle her without him. But his safety, and Nate's, were vital.

She caught up to Darika and the others, feeling the goddess's eyes settle on her with something akin to admiration. "Well done," she said.

"Men," Sera said with a shrug. "They think the world will end without them."

"Thank you for getting him back to Illysia."

"Thank me later," Sera said, meeting Darika's gaze as they crested a heavily forested hill. Though they were both shaded from the view of any mortals below, Sera still felt vulnerable in the air. "When we get rid of this Azura abomination."

"Kyle blames himself for her existence."

"It's not his fault."

Darika was quick to reassure her. "I'm on your side. *His* side. Trust me, I know it wasn't his fault." She huffed a breath. "*He* feels responsible though."

"Do you like him?" Sera asked suddenly, studying the placid goddess.

To her surprise, Darika flushed. "Yes."

"He likes you, too."

Several moments passed before Darika spoke again. "My sister spoke well of him when she was here."

"Why did she go away?"

"She didn't. Not completely, anyway," Darika said, somewhat cryptically. "Kira appears when she wants. And right now, she prefers to not be here. We have always had a . . . tumultuous relationship."

"For what it's worth, I think she has a good heart."

"She does."

They shared a smile before an explosion beneath them sent a plume of fire up into the sky and shook the earth so hard that cracks appeared on the ground between the trees. They were nearly to the town, Sera realized in horror. The goddesses dove down to join the fray, with the other Sanraks hot on their heels, but neither of them was prepared for what awaited them on the edge of the decimated forest.

Sera's hand flew to her mouth at the sea of human bodies littering the fringe of the small town. Mostly visitors to the Kensico Dam Plaza County Park, they were nothing but empty husks, drained of their life essence. Her eyes widened as she saw Kyle hurtling through the air to crash into the side of the stone dam. Three more Yoddha followed him.

Sera's breath stalled in her throat as she beheld the creature that was Aranyasura standing on a smoking pyre of dead humans and deities alike. Her assorted faces kept shifting as she fought, from pensive to amused to vicious.

As Sera had seen in the portal, Aranyasura was a monstrous, spectacularly beautiful, four-faced creature. But now, she was several times the size of any normal human. Her translucent skin was the color of glowing embers, marked by deep yellow, runic script. Four enormous, red wings sprouted from her back. They, too, were etched with rippling, vine-like inscriptions.

In her true form, she was terrifying. And in battle, she was mesmerizing.

Six of her eight arms moved with blinding speed, wielding wickedly forged weapons. Two awaited the return of curved discs just thrown to slay incoming Yoddha. Sera guessed that, like Durga's, all of the weapons were gifts from Aranyasura's makers—a sword that looked suspiciously like Mordas, a burning staff, a pike, the pair of three-pronged discs. Aranyasura was strong and fast, and if the growing pile of bodies at her feet was any signal, she was skilled.

Sera gritted her teeth and dove down to where Darika was helping a bloody Kyle to his feet. His arm hung limply at his side and he was covered in fluid and gore, some of it black and some red.

"She's too quick," he panted. "The more she kills, the stronger she gets. And the more powerful the deity, the more invincible she becomes. You have to hold back the Sanraks." His expression was bleak. "And you, especially, need to stay out of reach. You and Darika." He looked around. "Where's Dev? He can't be here either."

"He's with Nate," Sera replied, distracted. "Wait, how is this even possible? She can't absorb immortals' power."

Kyle shook his head. "I'm guessing that because she is the embodiment of Xibalba and all the Demon Lords, she's a living extension of the Dark Realms. Any immortal that touches her will be consumed by her . . . by it."

"Good guess," Sera said scowling. "Could you be wrong?"

Kyle's smirk was forced. "Put it this way—if I'm right, we're screwed."

"Use your abilities," Darika suggested. "What do you see? She has to have a weakness somewhere."

"I've already looked." His voice was thin, already weary. "She has none. She looks the same with my powers as she must to your eyes. There's no other hidden form."

"Try again, damn it," Sera swore. Kyle grimaced as she grabbed him by his bruised shoulder. "Look beyond the physical. It has to be there. What about the runes?"

His stare fastened to hers. "That's it! You're freaking brilliant."

Sera watched as he calmed himself with a gulp of air and summoned his sight. Concentration deepened the notch in his brow, and a myriad of other emotions flicked across his face before he made a noise that sounded like relief and nearly collapsed against Darika.

"You were right," he whispered. "We *can* weaken her."

She stared at him. "How?"

"Each of the seven runes are associated with a chakra. It's her prana, her life force—the intersection of energy and physical matter."

"So if we destroy these chakras, we can hurt her?"

He nodded. "It's our best shot."

"Then we attack the chakras," Darika said decisively.

Sera cleared her throat, her gaze cutting between them. "Okay, so . . . where are they?"

Kyle's and Darika's stares converged on her, making her feel foolish. "You have to focus. Use your third eye," Darika said.

Sera shot her a dry look. "I hate to break it to you, but I don't have one of those. Unlike you and Kira."

"You do," Darika said. "Just because it's not on your face doesn't mean you can't use it. Where do you think Kyle's gifts come from? It's the power of his invisible eye—his spiritual connection with the universe." She leaned in, smoothing the spot between Sera's brows with her thumb. "Close your eyes and focus. Clear your head. Let your mind's eye do the seeing. Focus on this point, beneath my finger, and push your consciousness outward."

Sera followed her directions, clearing her mind of all noise. It was dark at first—red, then dark, then light—but eventually a form started to take shape. The silhouette of Aranyasura appeared. Seven faintly glowing orbs ran the length of her spine, each marked by a rune. The first was above her head, and the last gleamed at the tops of her legs. A thin line connected each of them—a line, she realized with a gasp, leading back to the boy at her side.

"I see her tether," she whispered. "To you."

Sera trembled in her meditative state as her mind's eye focused on Kyle. She'd never seen him like this before. He was almost all bristling energy, held together by the boundaries of his immortal body. The light of Illysia and the darkness of Xibalba bent at his command. Awed, she gasped for breath. If she'd ever thought, somewhere deep down, that Kyle was still linked to Ra'al, she stood firmly corrected. He was an Azura Lord through and through.

Darika took her arm, pulling her out of the trance. "Ready?"

"Remember what I said," Kyle warned them both. "If you

fall at her hands, she will take you into her." He turned to Sera. "I don't know what will happen to you, given your ties to Xibalba, but I'd rather not find out. So try not to be that thing's dinner."

Sera nodded grimly, her weapons flaring. Aranyasura was already bigger than she had been ten minutes before. Only a few Yoddha and Sanrak remained standing out of the dozens of immortal and human warriors that had led the charge, and their offense was feeble. The humans had retreated to safety. Sera paled at the smoldering heap of bodies amassed while they planned their attack.

Aranyasura's translucent form had already started to become opaque. Sera focused with her inner eye, and sure enough, the chakras lining her spine had become brighter. At full strength, she would be unstoppable.

"Serjana Maa," Aranyasura's faces thundered mockingly in unison as they approached. "I was hoping you'd be here. Come to join the cremation? We met so briefly before that I didn't get a chance to introduce myself. I am Aranyasura."

Sera's lips flattened. "You will pay for what you have done."

Aranyasura laughed. "And you will be the one to issue the punishment?" Her eyes flicked to the goddess at her side. "How sweet, I see you brought friends, including the one who inspired my creation." Her arms swung with keen precision. "I'm going to enjoy this . . . and the taste of both of you."

Sera followed Kyle's lead as he dove in, dodging Aranyasura's deadly arms as Mordas cleaved toward one of her lower chakras. He missed by an inch as Aranyasura's flaming staff connected squarely with his belly. The blow sent him skidding across the ground.

But Sera noticed that the demonic avatar left it there. Frantically, she wondered if it was because of the tether linking her to Kyle. If he died, did that mean she would as well? Sera's stomach sank at the thought—but she knew that if things worsened, sacrificing Kyle to defeat Aranyasura would be something she'd have to consider.

Darika attacked from the right, but was also unsuccessful. In her true goddess form, she had as many arms as Aranyasura did and they were evenly matched. Sera took advantage of the distraction to sneak in, her swords cleaving into the rakshasa's back. She was so intent on spearing the chakra dead center that she didn't see the pike swinging toward her. It lodged in her thigh with the force of a battering ram.

Sera screamed, stumbling backward. But the pain of the blow was nothing compared to the blinding burn of her deifyre at the dark weapon's touch. One of Aranyasura's faces settled on her, triumph written all over it. "You taste good, little goddess. A few more strikes and the only bit of you left will be of Xibalba."

Sera's eyes narrowed as her Illysian power healed her and she rushed in again. She was still disoriented from the first blow, and one of those flying discs nearly took off her head as she made a desperate duck to avoid it. She lost her balance, and the sword that resembled Mordas hissed up the side of her arm. The sting was identical to the earlier blow, but this time it was accompanied by a spreading, hollow sensation in her chest. Struggling to draw breath, Sera staggered as the weapon in her left hand flickered, the light of Illysia dimming slightly. Conversely, the sword in her right flared brighter.

What the hell?

"Isn't this what you've always wanted?" Aranyasura crowed, seeing her confusion. "To find your true place? I can show it to you." One of her many faces smiled, exposing multiple rows of tiny sharp teeth. "*Queen* of Xibalba. We have seen your darkest thoughts, sensed your secrets. We know how badly you want to leave all this behind." Her four faces spun, all displaying the same conciliatory grin. "Be *normal*. But you are *more* than normal. Join us and we will give you the life you crave."

Sera faltered, recalling when she'd had those feelings—her moments of weakness. She shook her head. "No, you're wrong."

"Are we?" the rakshasi mocked.

Kyle joined Sera, gasping for breath, and Darika renewed her attack beside them. But even Sera could see that both her friend and the goddess beside him were fading as Aranyasura grew stronger.

"She's too powerful," Kyle said on a pained gasp. His eyes narrowed on Sera's face before sliding to the gaping wound on her arm. "What's wrong?"

"It feels like I'm fading," she choked out. Kyle squinted at her for a moment before his eyes went blank with shock. "What do you see?"

"Xibalba is draining you," he whispered, making her heart shudder. "You need to stay here, Sera, and recover if you can. I have to help Darika and the others."

"I'll fight with every bit of light left in me if I have to."

"I know you will, but you can't," he said. "Once this is over, people here will need you, and I made a promise to your mother and to Dev."

Oh, God, Dev.

"He can't know—" she began desperately.

They both shielded their eyes as a blindingly white light cracked the sky like lightning. Aranyasura clapped a pair of her hands in glee at the newcomer's arrival.

"Welcome, Lord Devendra. I was wondering when I'd be seeing you. Come to save the day?" She lurched toward him, but was thwarted by Dev's Sanrak guardians—a veritable army of them.

"Dev," Sera cried as cold dread punched her in the gut. Her beloved flew to her side, carrying a groaning Darika in his arms. He set her down gently and turned to face Sera. "What are you doing here?" she asked. "It's exactly what she wants. You need to protect Illysia."

He stroked her cheek. "How do you expect me to stand by and watch you die? Watch any of you die?"

"I'm not important," she said, beating his hands away and fighting the urge to throw herself against him in the same breath. "Illysia is important. The innocent people who will die on this plane are important. Nate is important. You have to go, please. *Please.* And take Darika with you before things get any worse."

"Sera's right," Kyle said. "You need to leave."

Dev frowned. "You can't do this alone."

"I know," he agreed. "I have an idea. It's kind of crazy, but crazy may be all we've got right now." He stared at the bleeding goddess lying beside them and drew a long breath before finishing. "Darika, it's time to summon your sister."

"You're right," Sera said with a gasp. "That *is* insane."

Kyle nodded. "Kira is the only one who can stop this."

The End
of the World

❧❧

It seemed like a genius idea . . . at least, for the few breath-less seconds it took Darika to communicate telepathically and get an answer. Unfortunately, Kira wanted nothing to do with any of them. And more obviously, she didn't want anything to do with *him*. Not even with the fate of the world hanging in the balance.

"What do you mean she won't do it?" Kyle asked. "We're on the brink of the KaliYuga."

"She says we brought this on ourselves," Darika replied dully, a faint flush coloring her skin. "Said you had to live with the choice you made."

Kyle stared at her, at a complete loss. "You're saying she's going to punish the entire Mortal Realm because I didn't want to *date* her?"

"Hell hath no fury," Dev muttered, earning a glare. "I learned from experience."

"My sister tends to take things personally." Darika cleared her throat and smiled weakly. "Plus, if we're being honest, you and I both know that she's the one who you really miss."

Kyle opened his mouth to protest and she raised a hand to

silence him. "It's true, and you know it. Tell me your heart doesn't scatter when she enters a room. Tell me you haven't been looking for her whenever you see me. You don't see me like you see her. We both know that the only reason you chose me was because you were afraid of losing yourself with her."

"No, you're wrong."

"I'm right, Kyle." Darika took his hand, squeezing gently. "It's okay, I'm not hurt. I get it. I was the safer bet, but sometimes you have to go with the choice that scares the hell out of you."

His eyes widened, but he nodded. "She scares me a lot."

"Tell me about it," Darika said wryly, her lips quirking into a crooked grin. "I have to live with her."

Kyle wanted to speak, but something was expanding inside of him, something like awareness. It spread across his torso and his chest, warming him like fire. He leaned in to kiss Darika on the cheek, feeling heavy and light all at the same time. He didn't want to hurt her, but deep down, he knew she was right. "How did you know?"

"I was born with the gift of foresight," she said with a low laugh, clutching her ribs and grimacing slightly. "Also known as women's intuition." She paused, watching him. "It's not going to be simple. Kira doesn't forgive easily, and she's angry. She feels rejected."

"If we're going to do this, you're going to have to talk to her, Kyle," Sera said.

"How? You heard Darika. She's pissed."

Sera threw her hands into the air, sparing a glance to Aranyasura, who still had her many hands full with Dev's guardian warriors. "Since when are you afraid of a challenge? Figure it out. Fast."

"But she's not here."

"She is," Darika said quietly, tapping her breast. "In here."

Both Sera's eyes and his swiveled to Darika as the realization sunk in. Mara had said as much in Sal's diner—that the two goddesses were both parts of the whole. And Kira herself had told him that they were one and the same. He just hadn't understood what that meant. Until now.

Darika and Kira were one, as Durga and Kali had been.

"You're the same," he said slowly.

"We are." Darika smiled. "Now, it's up to you to convince her before it's too late."

Time was running out, and as skilled as the Sanrak were, they wouldn't be able to hold the beast off for long. A third of their number had already fallen and, as before, Aranyasura seemed to have gathered strength from each death.

Kyle drew a strangled breath and sat with his knees crossed in prayer form in front of Darika. He closed his eyes and pushed his abilities out, seeing past the frame and the consciousness of the goddess. He was looking for the part of her that identified as Kira. He just had to find her in there, and hope that she'd listen to him. He sank deeper into the trance binding him to the goddess.

Kyle didn't know what he was looking for until he recognized the intimate brush against his senses. "There you are," he said.

A shape took form in the midst of the goddess's swirling essence, one he recognized. It coalesced into a face and then a body. The reaction in the pit of his stomach at the sight of her was swift and gutting. He'd hurt her because he'd been a coward. How could he have been so stupid? He'd chosen the easy way because he was too afraid to fight for himself. To fight for what he wanted.

"What do you want?" Her voice was like thunder, reverberating around him like a warning of storms to come.

Though he was also formless, he found himself outstretching his palms in a placating gesture. "I'm sorry."

"You need my help," she said flatly.

"Yes, but that's not the only reason I'm here." His voice broke at the fury that shimmered across her face. "I made a mistake, Kira. I was stupid and afraid. I didn't know what I wanted until . . . until . . ."

"Until you realized that the world was going to end and you were going to die?"

"Yes. No." He swallowed hard, searching for the words. He was losing her; he could feel it in the withdrawal of her essence. "I don't know, Kira. Maybe you're right. When I was fighting Aranyasura, I had some kind of epiphany that this would be it. And the only thing I could think about was you. Seeing *you*."

Her voice was cold. "Looks like you got your wish."

"Please, Kira. I want to make this right." Tentatively, Kyle pushed forward, his consciousness bracing toward hers. She bristled, but allowed him to approach. When they finally connected, his entire body went slack, as if he had reached the deepest point of meditation. Of nirvana. Everything inside of him settled into complete harmony.

That was before she surrounded him with fire and brimstone and death.

"You can't make it right," she rumbled, every touch of her furious goddess awareness stinging like the tendrils of a jellyfish. Deadly. Beautiful. He endured it, though each fiery lash made his connection with his physical body stutter. Kyle knew what would happen if he separated from his own cognizance—he would fall into a void of nothingness and be forever lost.

"I made a mistake," he managed, struggling to stay aware. "And I'm sorry."

She tightened her grip. "So am I."

"Kira, please," he said weakly as he felt his physical body fading with each heartbeat. "Don't punish Sera and Nate, and all the humans we're supposed to protect for my mistakes. Help them. Give them a chance. You know what the KaliYuga means."

"It's the end," she said. "And then I will destroy them, as I should have done from the beginning, instead of listening to you. Wiping the slate clean is what was best for them."

"No, you did the right thing. You gave them a chance. And you can do the right thing now. Save them. Fight Aranyasura. There are people worth fighting for. Like your sister. And, even if you never forgive me, I *am* sorry for hurting you." He swallowed hard, the words difficult to get out. "If I could take it back, I would. The truth is . . . I was afraid to trust myself. I was afraid that the darkness inside of me would return. But I understand now. I know that's something only I can control. Not you."

Kyle blinked against the spots of darkness clouding his vision. Gaping holes appeared in his mind, stalling him, disorienting him.

Who was he? Why was he here?

He swayed, memory coming back in short bursts that

faded from his grasp as soon as they appeared. A succession of faces filled his vision.

Sera. Nate. Dev. Darika. Kira.

Kira.

The one he'd hurt. The one who would never forgive him.

"I was wrong," he whispered. "About all of it. But mostly about you."

Everything felt cloudy, hazy, as if his very essence was disappearing. As if he were vanishing from existence. *Who was he?*

"Kyle." The word was whisper soft, a caress against his mind.

The shift in energy was so subtle he almost didn't recognize it, but it went from punishing to something gentler. Dazed, Kyle opened his eyes, awed by the brilliance of the stars and the universe surrounding him. A giant black hole yawned at his feet, beckoning, but something held him back. Something held *him.* He glanced down to see an arm spread over his torso, keeping him from falling. It was connected to a shimmering body. And she was light as she was dark, her blue-black face glistening, those red lips grazing his cheeks, and her eyes like teeming starlight.

"It is not your time," the goddess whispered. "Come, let us finish what we started."

⚜

It was the last stand.

They surrounded Aranyasura in a circle—two dozen Ne'feri, seven Sanraks, three Yoddha, one unsmiling god, one Azura Lord, and two goddesses of Illysia. Sera looked like she meant business, despite her unsteady light. Aranyasura had not killed off everything that was born of Illysia in Sera yet. Kyle's gaze flicked to Kira and he sucked in a sharp breath.

Unlike the myths, Kira did not appear from Darika's brow; she simply emerged from within the other goddess. Now, in human form, she looked as she had when they first met. Black leather pants. Black T-shirt. Nose ring. Kohl-lined eyes. Blood-red lips.

Fierce and fearless. How could he ever have thought that anyone could take her place? Though her mortal avatar made his pulse leap, it was her true self that made his heart stutter.

He narrowed his gaze, venturing beyond the veil and past her mortal shade. In goddess form, her fierceness had no equal. The embodiment of shakti—of pure female divine power—the stories didn't do her justice. Thick, wild, black hair curled down her back. Her three eyes shone with fiery intensity, her midnight blue skin gleaming like polished stone. Clad in nothing but a tiger's skin and a skirt made of severed human arms, she held a scimitar and a spear in one pair of hands and a detached demon's head atop a staff in another. Kyle was not deterred by the garland of skulls hanging from her neck, nor the long red tongue that snaked out to wet her lips. He knew he was biased, but she was nothing short of formidable.

Her scarlet eyes fell to him and she nodded, her lips baring in a smile of pure berserker rage. Though her counterpart Durga was a master tactician in battle and an impressive goddess warrior in her own right, Kali was passion and rage personified. She was unpredictable—just what they needed against Aranyasura.

"Target the chakras," he roared.

With shouts and battle cries, they attacked the beast from all sides. Kira was an obscure shadow as she ducked and weaved, avoiding the demon's many armed strikes. Her spear was the first to strike true, right into the center chakra. Aranyasura's scream was terrible, but it gave Kyle hope. Lifting Mordas, he deflected a strike swinging toward him, and dared to sneak closer. He knew she would not deal him a fatal blow. Gritting his teeth, he dodged one of her flying discs and stabbed low, gouging the lowest chakra right in its center.

Two down, five to go.

But instead of pain, Aranyasura shrieked with pleasure, her neck arching from the sudden burst of power she'd stolen from two dead Sanraks, their throats carved open from the flight of her pronged discs.

"Get your Sanraks back," Kyle yelled to Dev. "We need to keep her as weak as possible."

The immortal warriors pulled back and circled the creature warily. Dev and Sera had made a dent in the throng of smaller demons, but that was not the case with Aranyasura. She had doubled in size and, though clearly wounded, she was far from weakened.

As if reading his thoughts, she leered at him. "It does not matter how many warriors you throw at me, I will consume them all. You have lost. Accept it."

Kira moved so fast she was a blur, her spear cleaving through the air and lodging into the demon's midsection. Gore exploded everywhere as the chakra at her stomach disintegrated. "We accept nothing," Kira shouted, her eyes flashing. "Demon."

Aranyasura's violent bellow shook the earth, causing huge fissures to open beneath them and a score of vetalas to burst forth. They were joined by several of their pishacha brothers, and for a harrowing moment, Kyle expected the Demon Lords to follow. But they remained bound to Xibalba.

"You take care of those," he screamed to Dev and Sera. "We've got her now."

But he spoke too soon. Kira screeched as Aranyasura's blade tore a vicious path up the length of her spine, and the goddess stumbled back, her attack floundering.

"Kira!"

Kyle dove to her side, but she had already recovered, her eyes like burning coals and her mouth flattened into a thin, angry line. Her tongue lolled, and for a terrifying minute, she looked more demon than goddess. Kyle recoiled as her rage took over and a bloodcurdling battle cry escaped her lips.

She was Kali, incarnate.

The goddess fought with her scimitar and her staff, but she also used her mouth, biting with her teeth and lashing with her razor-sharp tongue. Everywhere she touched the demon, she left gaping, bloody wounds, and one by one, she struck at the creature's chakras.

Kyle felt triumph, but he felt fear, too. Kira was both magnificent and nauseating to watch. It seemed that the more of Aranyasura she devoured, the more demented she became. The Ne'feri and the other Sanrak started cheering as Kira stood on Aranyasura's chest, one chakra remaining, her scimitar bearing down on the beast's head.

Covered in blood, Kira bared her teeth. "What say you, demon?" she thundered.

Barely conscious, froth flecking her mouth, Aranyasura rolled her head back. "You cannot stop the KaliYuga. Man will fall. It is written."

"That day is not today."

With an inhuman cry, Kira struck the final chakra on the demon's brow dead at its center, and Aranyasura gave up her last breath. The goddess raised her arms to the heavens and spun in a triumphant circle, her feet stomping on the remains in glee as Kyle and the others watched in mute horror.

But she didn't stop there. Kira gobbled the remaining vetalas in her path, consuming them with gusto, lost as she was to her ruthless appetites.

Kyle had heard stories of how intoxicated Kali became with bloodlust—but nothing had prepared him for this. Kira danced on the entrails of the dead demons, covering herself in their gore, drunk on the slaughter and her passion. He exchanged a panicked look with Sera, who wore the same shocked expression as he. Kyle's mind raced. According to the myths, the last time Kali had lost control like this, Shiva had had to throw himself at her feet to get her to stop.

But Taran, Shiva's latest avatar, was in Illysia.

Sera, however, showed no such compunction. She hurled herself onto the bloody battlefield before anyone could stop her, her twin swords flaring.

"What are you doing?" Kyle and Dev shouted in unison.

"Someone has to stop her."

"Sera—"

She flung a hand out, stalling Dev in his tracks, her face

fierce. "Don't even think about it. Get the rest of the vetalas, and make sure my brother is safe. Even though Aranyasura is dead, Temlucus won't give up on him."

The two goddesses squared off. Kyle knew that Kira did not recognize Sera—in her current frame of mind, she would see her as a threat. She would only sense the part of Xibalba that had come to the forefront of Sera's aura, thanks to Aranyasura's earlier blows. It was like the first time they had fought, only a million times worse.

Kira had been in control then.

Now she was a berserker goddess with only one thing on her mind: destruction.

Grabbing Mordas, Kyle mirrored Sera's movements as she circled Kira. There was no way he was going to let his friend take Kira on alone, not after what he'd just seen. Sera was strong, but Kira was *Kali*. He wouldn't kill either of the people he loved, but if he saw an opportunity to disarm Kira, he would take it. Their weapons clashed, sparks flying from where fire met fire. Despite Sera's injuries at Aranyasura's hands, they remained evenly matched, but one misstep and Kyle knew it would be over.

Deflecting Kira's artful strikes, Sera danced and weaved. She was attacking to maim, not to kill, but Kira wasn't holding back. Her strikes were meant to destroy.

Kira struck out with her spear and stumbled on a slick piece of earth. It was the opening Sera was looking for. Without hesitation, she spun and swung with her swords, forcing Kira to bend unnaturally to avoid being carved in the face. At the last moment, Sera threw out her elbow, using her momentum to catch the other goddess square in the chin.

Their bodies collided and they tumbled to the blood-slicked ground together.

Blinking fiercely, as if trying to get her bearings, Kira stood and pitched backward toward Kyle. Without hesitation, he brought the hilt of Mordas up—but even disoriented, she was able to sidestep his strike. She turned her blazing, scarlet eyes on him, and for a moment Kyle felt eviscerating fear. She would end him without a qualm.

Hauling a ragged breath into his lungs, Kyle dropped his sword and reached for her shoulders. He'd faced her before and she hadn't killed him. Perhaps he could do the same now.

She was saner then, his inner voice warned.

Her deifyre blistered his skin even as he drew closer. The pain was worse than anything he'd ever felt, but he held strong, closing the gap between them. Each inch felt like torture, his mortal skin flaking off in sheets.

"Kira," he said. "Stop. You have to stop this."

Her response was an angry flick of her whiplike tongue on his cheek that nearly made him pass out. She savored his blood, her eyes rolling back. He kissed her, and she bit him on his lip, her eyes boring into his. Without a second thought, Kyle shoved his consciousness into hers, pushing past all the layers of savagery.

Stop this now. Her spear pressed into his stomach, the tip of it piercing the vulnerable flesh there, and Kyle winced against the mouth that still held him prisoner. He held her temples between his palms, and fought her cruelty with aching gentleness. *If you have to kill me, then kill me. But you need to stop this madness.*

It seemed like time came to a halt as the world around

them fell away, and it was only the two of them suspended in each other. After an interminable beat, the scarlet insanity in her eyes shifted to something like reason, and she slumped in his arms.

"Wh—what happened?"

"You kind of lost it," he said with a grin, wincing at the sting of his sore lip. "And took out pretty much everyone."

"Aranyasura?"

"You danced on her bones."

An embarrassed, wry smile curved Kira's lips. "Yikes."

"It was something, that's for sure."

"Did I hurt anyone else?" He shook his head as she reached out to stroke his scorched skin and bloody lip with a finger. "I'm sorry. Thank you for doing what you did."

"Don't thank me. Thank Sera." Kyle raised a celebratory gaze to find his friend, then felt all sensation whoosh out of him.

Sera lay crumpled on her side from where she had rammed into Kira.

His blood ran cold. Why wasn't she moving? The gut-wrenching cry from Dev confirmed his worst fears as the god descended to where his beloved lay.

"No, no, no," Dev cried, turning her over gently.

Kyle's entire body went numb at the sight of Kira's sword impaling Sera straight through her chest. Blinded by anguish, he focused on her body, narrowing his gaze and pushing his awareness out—but there was nothing there but a cold mortal shell.

No sunset deifyre. No breath. No life.

THE GLADE

❧❧

The last thing Sera felt was the silky slide of the immortal weapon between her ribs. The pain was expected. What she did not expect was the peace that swiftly followed. Everything winked out of sight—the battle, the people, the world. It all fell away, until there was nothing left. The entire realm was washed clean, and she became its only occupant.

Blinking, Sera shifted outside herself and studied the scene. Her body was floating upon a lake of delicate white petals, her hands clasped together over her torso. Despite a faint red glow that hovered above her skin, her doppelganger looked tranquil, as if she could be sleeping. But Sera knew better—that stroke had been a killing one.

Someone had died.

Someone with her face.

She looked around again. Though this place seemed familiar, she had never seen it before. Perhaps it was Illysia. Was this what heaven looked like? Or perhaps it was simply her realm between realms. But this place did not feel this same. It didn't *smell* the same. No, she had never set foot here.

Sera wondered what would happen if she took a walk. Her body seemed safe enough in its picturesque, if watery, bed, and she wanted to explore. She would walk, she decided.

Solid ground connected with the soles of her feet and she looked down at the soft carpet of grass. The pale blades of the meadow tickled her skin, as if to reassure her that she hadn't quite left the world yet.

She meandered for a while, admiring the landscape that rolled like a Monet painting in muted pastel colors. The air was balmy and smelled faintly of jasmine. She breathed it in deeply, although somewhere in her subconscious she knew that she wasn't actually breathing. After some time, she came upon a river where two young girls were playing. They splashed each other and giggled. But when they saw her, they turned and ran, disappearing into the nearby forest.

"Hey," she called out, but they took no notice.

Sera decided to follow them. The trees here weren't green, she saw. They were white, with white branches and white leaves. The lack of color struck her as odd, but she did not dwell on it, focused instead on finding the two little girls. Laughter drifted through the slim, snowy tree trunks, beckoning her forward. She thought she caught a glimpse of the girls again, but it was only a trick of the light.

Her legs were starting to tire when she saw a clearing up ahead. Perhaps she would have a rest there. Sure enough, the forest thinned and gave way to another meadow—only this one was covered in vibrant, red grass. Unlike the softness of the first meadow, their blades were sharp and prickly like thorns. And she'd scarcely taken a dozen steps when her feet started to bleed. Odd that she could still feel pain in such a place. Sighing, she sat and blew onto the tender grazes.

"Why are you following us?" a tinkling voice said, and Sera looked up.

It was one of the girls from before. She had hair the color of flame, hair that looked strange around such a cherubic face. Sera noticed the other girl, who was hiding behind one of the white-barked trees. This child had silvery-white hair, but shared the same angelic face as her sister.

"Who are you?" Sera asked.

"We are the daughters of the glade," they replied in unison.

"Is this Illysia?"

Their laughter sounded like shattering crystal bells, and Sera fought the urge to clap her hands over her ears. "No."

"What do you want with me?" Sera asked, a feeling of unease starting to bloom in the pit of her belly. "Why am I here?"

The red-haired child responded. "You are here because you choose to be."

"Am I dead?"

"Your questions are silly." The silver-haired child giggled. "Of course you're not dead. If you were, you wouldn't see *us*, would you?"

They ran off, scampering through the razor-sharp meadow.

"Come back!" She blinked, and they were gone. Were they ghosts? Apparitions? *Demons?* Sera balked as she stared at the thorny carpet beneath her. Wait, was she in Xibalba? But this place didn't feel like Xibalba. It didn't feel like anything.

Her heart tripped over itself as she stood warily, looking around. This place looked nothing like the Dark Realms, and somewhere deep down, Sera knew that she would recognize it if she were there. She gingerly made her way to the edge of the grasslands, back toward the eerie, colorless trees. Her feet left bloody footprints as she retraced her steps until she found another clearing.

"Hello, Sera," a resonant voice said.

Recognition burned in her brain at the sound of the voice before she saw its owner. Her dead uncle.

Now she knew she had to be in Xibalba, or some other realm of torture. Her uncle had been the worst kind of evil before she and Kyle had killed him. Or perhaps she was stuck in some nightmare. She blinked and counted to ten in her head before opening her eyes, but he was still standing there, watching her with a hooded stare. He made no move to approach.

"Azrath," she said carefully, also keeping her distance. Upon further scrutiny, he seemed different than she'd remembered. His close-cropped, pale-gold hair was the same style, but weariness lined his features. She didn't think ghosts could age. If indeed he was a ghost. Or a demon.

"It's good to see you."

"I wish I could say the same." She waved a dismissive hand, then relented somewhat. Perhaps he would be able to shed more light on where she was than the girls had. "What is this place?"

"The glade?"

She eyed him. "Yes, what is it?"

"It's a crossroads of sorts," Azrath replied.

"A crossroads for what? And why are *you* here?"

He smiled, but the expression held nothing but a bitter-sweet kind of sadness. "I am banished from all the realms, and as such, I am doomed to wander this plane."

Sera's stomach dipped. Did that mean that she had been banished as well? The thought of being stuck here, with Azrath of all people, left her cold. This had been his punishment for trying to unleash hell on earth, she realized. An eternity in a realm that was neither here nor there. A realm of infinite emptiness.

Suddenly, Sera wanted to be back where she'd left her body. She wanted to wake up from whatever this was. She did not like being out of control, unable to process what seeing Azrath meant. "There has to have been a mistake."

"He never makes mistakes."

Sera frowned. "He?"

"Brahman," he said, his tone reverent. "The Supreme Being, and source of all creation. He is the creator of all things and is in all things. He is the air and the earth, and the breath in your lungs. He is the beating heart of all the realms."

"Then why doesn't he show himself?"

"Because he is formless."

Suddenly, Sera felt a warning prickle along her skin and her uncle started to morph into someone else. His thin face shortened and widened, and his cropped head of hair burst into a full-on mop of golden curls. He shrank to the height of an eleven-year-old boy.

"Nate!"

She ran forward but stopped short of the boy, frowning. This Nate was dressed in his favorite worn pair of cargo shorts and a black Grateful Dead T-shirt he'd likely purloined from her closet. But *her* Nate was safe in Illysia. Confused, she stepped backward.

Was this some kind of trick?

The person with her brother's face smiled at her, and it was so much like Nate that she had to pinch herself. "Hey, sis. You look like someone peed in your Cheerios." Even the voice was his. And the humor.

Her smile felt wobbly. "Is it you?"

"Of course it is. Who else would it be?"

"Why was Azrath here before?"

Nate's green eyes widened. "No way! Uncle Az? As in Dad's psychopath brother?"

Sera almost laughed at his incredulous tone, and she nodded. "One and the same. Trust me, I'm as surprised as you are." Her eyes narrowed. "It *is* really you, isn't it, Nate?"

He shrugged. "A version of me, I guess."

"Who were the girls from before?"

"Versions of you, maybe?"

She sucked in a gasp and frowned, recalling their odd coloring. It made sense, she supposed, one for each side of her—the light and the dark. Nate plopped to the ground and Sera followed him, sitting cross-legged and facing him.

"You really got worked, didn't you?" he commented.

"What do you mean?" she asked, and he nodded to her torso. Her eyes fell on the gaping wound in the center of her ribcage that discolored her clothing with crusted blood. She hadn't even realized it was there. She touched the ragged edges gingerly and winced at the soreness. "Still hurts."

"Not surprised," he said with an empathetic shrug. "That Kira, wow, she's like those girls from MMA. I'm surprised you lasted as long as you did."

Sera shot him a dark look. "Hey! I can hold my own."

"Yeah, but she's *Kali*. As in the totally renegade warrior goddess who'll bring the rain on all the baddies."

Sera snorted beneath her breath. "She's not all that. And I stopped her, didn't I?"

"You kind of died," he said with a pointed stare to the hole in her chest.

"But I'm not really dead, am I?"

Nate pursed his lips. "That depends."

"On what?" she asked.

"On whether you want to return to me, or to the realms. The choice is in your hands. You are, after all, at the crossroads. You can return as you are, or you can be reborn anew."

Something occurred to her after a moment, as she stared at her brother's eyes. It felt like Nate, but she knew it wasn't really him. Too much age-old wisdom swirled in those bright-green, all-seeing eyes. No, this wasn't Nate. It was something far bigger—something that could only take shape within her own meager capacity for understanding.

It made a bizarre sort of sense. She had seen her uncle because he had died at her hands, and a part of her thought she deserved death for that. But now she was seeing Nate because she wanted to live. And Nate's was a form that made her feel safe.

"What will happen if I choose to go back?" she asked.

"A part of you has died, and you will have to live with that."

She frowned at his cryptic words. "A part of me," she echoed, fear curdling in her chest. Had the good part of her died? Would she be forced to remain in Xibalba for the rest of her days? Away from her family and everyone she loved? She'd rather be dead. Or wander the glade forever, like Azrath.

"Which part?" she asked hoarsely.

"The part that was destroyed by a weapon of Illysia."

He reached for her right hand, and Sera gasped at the rawness of the connection between them. Sudden awareness flooded her mind as her consciousness jolted awake. Her life appeared in a series of flashes—her loved ones, her actions, her hopes and dreams—and she felt herself intertwined with the very fabric of the universe. Nate's thumb stroked over the fleshy part beneath her thumb and the skin there tingled. She glanced down, her mouth parting in surprise.

The rune that had always been there—the rune of Xibalba—had disappeared.

"So I'm no longer tied to the Dark Realms?" she asked slowly, blessed relief flooding her.

"No."

She couldn't contain her delight. "That's good, right?"

"It is how you want to see it," he replied, waving a hand. "You will no longer be able to go there, or to control the demands of Xibalba, or to see into the hearts of those that rule in the Dark Realms. You will become a true goddess of Illysia."

"Is it selfish to want that?" she asked in a small voice.

"No," he said, taking her other hand and stroking the rune that lay there. Dev's rune. Her heart trembled at the thought of him, and Nate smiled. "You are so young, with so much ahead of you. I couldn't ask you to give that up. Not when you have already sacrificed so much."

He rose, and she stood with him. "What about the Demon Lords and the KaliYuga?"

"Darkness will always plot to defeat the light, my child. As a goddess of Illysia, you will only have to become more vigilant."

Sera squeezed his hand. "You're Brahman, aren't you?"

"I am your brother," he replied with a crooked smile that made her long to see her family. "And your mother. I am your father, your friends, your love, your life. I am *you*." He bowed and pressed the tips of his palms together at his brow. "Let us see you home, Serjana."

⁓

After all the silence of the glade, the noise seemed thunderous. Voices buzzed around her. Motion caught her eyes behind her closed eyelids. Her heart thumped painfully in her chest and wheezing breaths filled her lungs.

She was alive.

It hurt like hell.

Even with her eyes shut, everything was so bright that Sera could hardly focus. Her body felt warm, and she could feel small, gentle hands pressing against her chest. The heat she felt was coming from those hands. Soothing the broken parts of her. *Healing* her.

"Stand back," her mother's voice said. "Something's happening."

Sera's eyelids flipped open. She was no longer floating in a lake filled with petals. Dully, she took in the rose-colored walls and the familiar smell of lavender that made her old, tired heart take comfort. She was lying on a bed in a room, one that looked like the bedroom in a house she remembered somewhere deep in her memories. It was *her* bedroom, she realized, as the furnishings took shape.

Sera felt like a newborn, seeing things with fresh eyes and

feeling things for the first time. Blinking away her bewilderment, she focused on the faces swimming in her vision. Faces of those she knew and *loved*, watching her—her mother, her brother leaning over her, her father. Kyle, standing off to the side, hand in hand with Kira, unabashed tears leaking down his face.

And Dev. Her love. Her heart.

His golden eyes held hers, so much wisdom and love eddying in them. His fingers grazed the backs of hers, the touch igniting a slew of memories to burst like fireworks in her brain.

"Hey," he said, his hand rising to caress her cheek.

She leaned into it, her eyes feathering shut for a moment. "Hi."

"How are you feeling?"

A rueful smile shaped her lips. "Like I died."

Laughter filtered through the room as Dev's hand resumed its possessive grip on hers, caressing it gently. "You almost did. Nate saved you."

Sera's stare fell to her brother, Nate, whose palms still rested on her chest. A faint glow surrounded them where they touched her skin. His bright, tearful, green eyes met hers. "Hey, buddy. Thanks for not letting me go."

He threw himself down over her with a sob. "Don't ever do that again, okay?"

"You got it." She laughed through her own tears. "After all, who else is going to keep your head from getting swollen when you hit it big in Hollywood?"

Nate giggled, his eyes meeting hers as he straightened. She smiled, seeing the one who had sent her back in their brilliant, childlike depths.

Brahman.

The one imbued in all things.

She drew a slow breath, feeling her chest rise as the air filled her lungs. Mesmerized, she did it again. It was amazing how one single thing could make her feel so achingly alive when she had been so near death before. When she'd been impaled by a weapon not of this earth.

Her gaze slid to where Nate's fingers had been. There was no gaping wound, but that wasn't what shocked the breath out of her. It was her deifyre, flaring to life and flickering like a glittering shroud. It was no longer red, but an iridescent, silvery gold. Like her mother's. Like Dev's. She had thought it had been a dream. Or wishful thinking.

"Mom," she croaked.

"I'm here, honey," Sophia said, her damp eyes crinkling at the corners. "You had us worried for a while. Are you okay?"

Sera nodded, her consciousness starting to resettle into itself. "I went for a walk. Spoke to Brahman."

Her mother's eyes went wide as she gasped. *"Brahman?"*

"At least, I think it was him. But he looked a lot like Nate." She paused, a sigh escaping her lips. "And Uncle Azrath."

"Azrath?" This time the gasp was from her father.

"It wasn't bad," Sera said, throwing him a reassuring look. "It was brief. I don't even know that it was really him. I think it was my subconscious dealing with my part in his death, and understanding my own, and the part karma plays in our evolution. He was my greatest sin. I took a life, even if it was for the greater good. But then I saw Nate." Her gaze flicked to her brother who still stood at her side. "And he told me that I had a choice."

"I did?" Nate asked, wide-eyed.

"Well, not you, but the you in my head," she said with a smile. "You told me I could return or be reborn." She took in each of the faces she loved in turn. "And I wasn't ready to leave any of you just yet."

"Oh, honey." Her mother leaned down to kiss her forehead. "I was so worried you'd been taken somewhere else. And after what Nate had seen, I was terrified that it would come true." Fear flicked across her face, and Sera understood exactly where it was Sophia had thought she had gone.

"Turns out Nate was right," she said. "A part of me *did* die. Kira's weapon killed the part of me that was linked to the Dark Realms."

"Sorry about that," Kira interjected with a wry grin. "I was kind of out of it."

"No apology needed. It was because of you that we were able to defeat Aranyasura," Sera said gently before turning back to her mother. "And I wasn't sent to Xibalba. I was at some kind of crossroads." She inhaled deeply, recalling the surreal feel of the realm. "They called it the glade."

"I have heard of such a place," a male voice said. "It is the space between the bones of creation and destruction. A realm beyond realms."

A boy with dark hair piled on his head and a blue-inked neck stood at the far end of the room near the doorway. Taran. Or Shiva. Sera frowned as she recalled Kyle and Kira's linked hands, but Taran didn't look concerned. Amusement filled her as she wondered whether he'd been secretly relieved that he hadn't had to stop her rampage a second time. His eyes met hers, as if he knew exactly what she was thinking, and he winked.

Sera felt relieved. She wouldn't want Kyle to be hurt, especially now that he had declared himself. Finally.

Dev squeezed her fingers. "Go on. What happened in this realm beyond realms?"

"I saw myself there," Sera explained, lifting her right hand to display the unblemished skin. "The two halves of me. I could have kept them together, but I chose to let one go."

Sophia frowned. "So you're not tied to Xibalba?"

"Not anymore."

Sophia gasped. "What does that mean? For you? For everyone?"

"It means I can no longer go to Xibalba." She met her best friend's eyes and she grinned. "As much as I'll miss our adventures, I'm definitely not going to miss the smell. Or the demons."

"Hate to be the bearer of bad news, but don't think you're getting away so easily," Kyle said. "Demons are still running rampant in the Mortal Realm."

"I think I can handle that."

"But what does this mean for you as the conduit?" Sophia pushed.

Sera knew what her mother was getting at. She wanted to know whether her changed status as a goddess of all three realms would mean that the Demon Lords would run unchallenged. "I don't know," she answered honestly. "Brahman said we would have to be extra vigilant."

"And we will," her father said with a determined smile. "Together."

Nate's palm slipped into her free hand, his right hand joining their mother's, who reached for Sera's father's. The linking of their palms went on, joining Kyle's, Kira's, Taran's, and back to Dev, who hadn't let go of hers since she had awakened. Sera's heart was so full she could barely breathe.

"Together," she agreed.

Epilogue

"I swear, my arteries are bursting just looking at these hash browns," Kira muttered, her fork sifting through the pile of food on her plate.

"You know, you're immortal. You probably don't have to worry about cholesterol," Kyle commented drily, reaching over to shove a forkful of her greasy potatoes into his mouth.

"You're such a glutton."

"Azura Lord," he said, beating his chest and smacking his lips before stealing another heaping portion.

She arched an eyebrow. "A little glutton lord."

"Good thing you like me," he said, leaning in to kiss her with a mouthful of potato as she fought him off with a disgusted laugh.

Sera stared at her two friends, in their usual booth at Sal's diner, trying to suppress her own grin. "The grease is what makes it so good," she affirmed. "Don't knock it till you try it."

"Years and years of stuck-on grease," Kyle said and drummed his fingers on the tabletop. "I don't think Big Jim ever cleans that grill."

Kira grimaced. "Ew, gross."

"You know, for such a bad-to-the-bone berserker goddess, you're kind of squeamish." Kyle leaned back, patting his stomach contentedly.

"Darika has a far stronger constitution than me." She eyed him with an arch look. "Maybe you picked the wrong sister."

"Not a chance." He reached for her again, and this time Sera had to avert her eyes at the overt PDA. She cleared her throat.

"Sorry," Kira said, though she was clearly unrepentant. "So what are your plans later? You want to come hang out with us? A little demon hunting in the woods? Kyle said the Ne'feri found some kind of nest. Might be Temlucus back to his old tricks."

Sera shook her head. "I have plans."

"If you say studying," Kyle said with a groan, "I'm going to puke."

Sera grinned. "We have finals next week, in case you forgot."

"Yeah, in a busted-up school."

"It's fine. Knightsbrook Academy is lending us their auditorium," she reminded him.

The destruction at Silver Lake High had been blamed on a senior prank—something involving fireworks—gone horribly wrong. As far as excuses went, it wasn't the worst. Repairs to the gymnasium were still ongoing, but that didn't mean that school would stop. That saying about death and taxes being the only certain things in life needed to be amended to include school. If high school didn't grind to a halt in the wake of a cosmic war between gods and demons, Sera didn't know what would ever stop it.

He rolled his eyes. "Let me guess. Dev had something to

do with offering up his old alma mater? Not that *he* has to go back to school," Kyle grumbled, banging on his chest. "Seriously. *Azura* Lord. Why do I need high school?"

"Because you promised Carla."

He sunk down into the booth, dejected. "Right."

"Stop being such a baby," Kira teased him, earning herself a disgruntled look. "And there's a silver lining. I can help you study. With incentives."

Kyle's eyes brightened at the offer. "Have I told you lately how into you I am?"

Laughing, she fended off his advances and stood, tossing several bills on the table. Shrugging into her coat, she turned back to Sera. "So, you were saying something about plans? And seriously, Kyle's right. If it's studying, I'm nixing that right now. You need to come with and let some steam out."

"Yeah," Kyle agreed. "What she said."

Sera drew a breath as they exited the diner, waving to Big Jim, who scowled at her. Some things, like Big Jim's humor, would never change—even though so much else had—and she was grateful for that. It made her feel grounded.

Normal.

She smiled. As normal as her world could ever be.

Kira nodded to the surly owner as she walked past and, surprise of surprises, his lips stretched into something that almost looked like a smile. Sera and Kyle gaped.

"What?" Kira asked, her brow vaulting at their twin expressions of astonishment. "Big Jim? He's Sanrak."

"He's *what*?" Kyle spluttered.

"How do you think we kept track of you two for so long?" Kira said with a grin. "We had an inside man. And don't mind him. He's all teeth and no bite. A big softie, really—kind of like my boyfriend here," she teased.

Kyle gave a playful growl. "I'll show you some bite."

Laughing, Sera shook her head in disbelief. She never would have pegged Big Jim as a warrior deity, but well, guardians came in all forms and sizes. She glanced at him over her shoulder and met his eyes, the hint of a smile still lurking in them. He bowed his head in the barest of acknowledgments, and Sera nodded back.

Wonders would never cease.

Outside, the sun was warm and she lifted her eyes upward, watching the clouds drift across a perfect blue sky.

"Dev's meeting me in a minute," she said. "He's taking me to Illysia."

The residual humor disappeared from Kyle's face as he met her eyes. He nodded, as if he could read every emotion in her heart.

"So, are you okay with that?" he asked quietly.

"I think so."

It had been weeks, and even though Dev had offered to take her before, she'd been resistant. Nervous. Afraid, even. But now, it was time.

"Well, see you on the flip side," Kyle said before pulling her into a bear hug.

Kira shot them a dry look as she climbed into Kyle's car. "Trust me, Illysia is not all it's cracked up to be. They take sin really seriously. Like one time, I used Darika's boots, and they called it stealing." She rolled her eyes, a wicked glint in them. "I *did* put them back a year later. So technically it was only borrowing." She threw her hands into the air, warming to her subject. "And if we're really getting technical, we're the same person, so I was stealing from myself."

Disengaging himself from Sera, Kyle laughed. "You're adorable."

Her eyes flashed. "Call me adorable one more time."

Kyle smirked and turned back to Sera. "It's going to be okay," he told her. "Trust me. You know how I know?"

"How?"

"Because I,"—he smacked his chest—"am an Azura Lord."

"You keep saying that," Sera said drily.

"Seriously, though, you're Serjana Caelum, goddess divine and the best friend anyone could ever ask for. Illysia is lucky to have you. Don't forget that."

"He's right, you know," a voice said.

Dev strode toward them, and Sera felt her heart scatter as it always did at the sight of him in mortal form. He was dressed in his customary yellow with a pair of dark jeans. His shirt cuffs were rolled up to his elbows, exposing intricate blue tattoos that glinted in the sunlight on his muscular forearms.

"Hello, *meri jaan*," he said, kissing her temple and making butterflies go wild in her belly.

They both watched as Kyle got into his car, and Sera couldn't help laughing at Kira's complaint. "We seriously need to get you some new wheels. This is an embarrassment."

"This is *vintage*," Kyle shot back.

Dev grinned at Sera. "They're taking bets in Illysia, you know."

"On what?"

"Who'll murder the other first."

Sera giggled, looping her arms around his neck. She'd say

the odds were pretty even. Then again, maybe it would be a match made in heaven.

Like hers.

The boy who held her heart stared down at her, his eyes shining with a love that had weathered the test of time and would endure whatever was to come. Dev held her close as the world around them started to spin and disappear in a haze of blinding light. "Are you ready?" he whispered.

She pressed her lips to his. "Yes."

Pavamana Mantra

❧~❧

asato mā sad gamaya,
tamaso mā jyotir gamaya,
mṛtyor mā amṛtaṃ gamaya

Lead me from the unreal to the real.
Lead me from the darkness to the light.
Lead me from death to immortality.

Author's Note

Although *Dark Goddess* is a work of fiction, my inspiration for the characters and the world-building this novel is based on Hindu mythology. My father is a second generation Brahmin (priest class in traditional Hindu society), so Indian mythology was an integral part of my childhood. Fascinated by stories and legends of various Hindu gods who incarnated as avatars to avert human tragedy, I wanted to write a story that encompassed some of the Hindu mythology elements that I enjoyed as a child. This series started out with *Alpha Goddess* and continues here. Here are a few interesting tidbits about some of the themes/characters appearing in this novel.

HINDU PHILOSOPHY: Hinduism is one of the world's oldest religions and is also one of the most diverse. It is based on an incredibly large variety of different traditions. The core of Hinduism is the belief in Brahman, the underlying universal life force that embodies existence. Hindus recognize Brahman as the single Supreme Being, and all other gods and goddesses are lower manifestations of that one Supreme Being. Hinduism is the world's third largest religion and is known as one of the most tolerant religious faiths because of the diverse nature of its teachings.

REINCARNATION: The notions of reincarnation and karma are integral to Hindu philosophy. Hindu mythology defines fourteen worlds with seven higher worlds (heavens) and seven lower ones (hells). The earth is considered the lowest of the seven higher worlds. According to Hindu scriptures, man is trapped in a karmic cycle of death and reincarnation (*samsara*) until final unification with Brahman, so the ultimate goal of living is liberation (*moksha*) from this cycle of death and rebirth, and reuniting with the one Supreme Being. Reincarnation is rooted in karma, where a person's actions in one life will determine their fate in future lives.

DEVA & ASURA: Hindu texts and scriptures reference celestial creatures called Devas, which literally means the "shining ones" and loosely translates to "heavenly beings." In the scriptures, the opposite of the Devas are the Asura, power-seeking deities who are considered to be demonic or sinful in nature. They are both an important part of Hindu culture and appear in mythological scriptures, art, and poetry. I use Daevas and Azura in my fictional world, but their functions are essentially similar.

AVATARA: Hindu scriptures talk about the manifestation of a god or goddess into mortal form to avert human tragedy or to guide humanity. This incarnation is called an avatar. You'll see many of them in *Alpha Goddess* and *Dark Goddess*.

TRIMURTI: There are hundreds of gods and goddesses in Hinduism. However, at the top are the Trimurti, which is comprised of Shiva, the destroyer, Vishnu, the protector, and Brahma, the creator, as well as their consorts (the Tridevi), Parvati, the goddess of power and courage, Lakshmi, the goddess of wealth and prosperity, and Saraswati, the goddess of knowledge and learning. In *Dark Goddess*, Sera is a mortal incarnation of Lakshmi while Kira and Darika are human avatars of Durga and Kali, who are goddess incarnations of Parvati.

DURGA: Beautiful and meditative, Durga is the warrior goddess who is a form of the goddess Parvati and consort to the Hindu god Shiva. Her three eyes represent the moon, the sun, and eternal knowledge. Durga was created by the gods as an embodiment of their collective energy to fight a terrible buffalo demon. Representing the demon-fighting side of Parvati, Durga is mostly seen in her eight- or ten-armed form, dressed in red and riding a tiger or a lion, with weapons bestowed upon her by each of the gods.

KALI: Kali is the three-eyed goddess of death, time, and destruction, although she is worshipped for her creative and nurturing aspects in many parts of India, and is seen as an embodiment of *shakti* or divine feminine power. In some stories, it is said that Kali manifested out of Durga's third eye in a burst of anger in the heat of battle. Kali is most represented as being black in color, wearing a garland of skulls as a necklace and a skirt of human arms, with a protruding red tongue and a tangle of wild black hair. The black color of her skin represents her transcendental nature.

KALIYUGA: The KaliYuga in Hinduism is known as the "age of vice" and is the last of the four eras that the world goes through based on Indian scriptures. The KaliYuga is referred to as the darkest age of man, because according to the scriptures, sin is rampant and man is uninterested in spiritual pursuits or closeness to god. The KaliYuga is also associated with the apocalypse Kali demon (unrelated to the goddess Kali).

Acknowledgments

Returning to the world of *Alpha Goddess* to write this sequel has been wonderful, challenging, and illuminating. Writing an #OwnVoices story is not only an exercise in stepping outside your comfort zone, it can also be a lesson in humility—that you may not know everything or that your experience may be singular. After the release of *Alpha Goddess*, I learned tremendous amounts about the Indian diaspora and my own tiny place within it. I'm so happy to share this story with you, dear reader. Thank *you* for reading!

As with the publication of any book, I am grateful to many people.

First of all, thank you to Julie Matysik, who bought the series, including *Alpha Goddess* and *Dark Goddess*, and allowed me to share both of these stories with the world. To my outstanding Sky Pony editors, Alison Weiss and Rachel Stark, whose comments and insights during revisions made this manuscript really come alive—thank you so much, you ladies nailed it! Thank you, thank you, thank you! To the wonderful agent who sold this book, Liza Fleissig of the Liza Royce Agency, thank you for all you've done for me professionally and for your continued friendship. To my writing partner and friend, Angie Frazier, who keeps me off the ledge daily and who makes me laugh, being an author would suck without you. Thanks for being such a superstar. To all the readers, bloggers, reviewers, booksellers, librarians, and educators who spread the word about my books and humble me with your unwavering support, a massive thank you. I'd like to sincerely thank those who make the extra effort to support #OwnVoices stories and narratives that are different. Our stories would not make it to publication without you. Thank you to my father, Pundit Gyanendra Gosine, for his guidance and patient teachings on Hindu mythology for earlier drafts, and to my mother, Nazroon Ramsey, for her love and support. Most importantly, to my family—Cameron, my husband, who never lets me give up and stands by me every step of the way cheering me on to the finish line, and to my beautiful children, Connor, Noah, and Olivia—you are everything in this life and beyond. Thank you.